BUZZ ALDRIN,

WHAT HAPPENED TO YOU IN ALL THE CONFUSION?

BUZZ ALDRIN, WHAT HAPPENED TO YOU IN ALL THE CONFUSION?

JOHAN HARSTAD

Translated by Deborah Dawkin

UWA PUBLISHING

First published in Australia in 2011 by
UWA Publishing
Crawley, Western Australia 6009
www.uwap.uwa.edu.au

UWAP is an imprint of UWA Publishing,
a division of The University of Western Australia

THE UNIVERSITY OF
WESTERN AUSTRALIA
Achieve International Excellence

Originally published in Norway by Gyldendal, 2005

This translation has been published with the financial support of NORLA

Book design by Jon Gilbert
Cover art by LACKTER
Printed by Griffin Press

National Library of Australia Cataloguing-in-Publication data:

Harstad, Johan, 1979-
Buzz Aldrin, what happened to you in all the confusion? / Johan Harstad
9781742582634 (pbk.)
839.8238

CONTENTS

FOOTPRINTS ON THE MOON

FIRST BAND ON THE MOON

I

The person you love is 72.8 percent water and there's been no rain for weeks. I'm standing out here, in the middle of the garden, my feet firmly planted on the ground. I bend over the tulips, gloves on my hands, boots on my feet, small pruning shears between my fingers, it's extremely early, one April morning in 1999 and it's beginning to grow warmer, I've noticed it recently, a certain something has begun to stir, I noticed it as I got out of the car this morning, in the gray light, as I opened the gates into the nursery, the air had grown softer, more rounded at the edges, I'd even considered changing out of my winter boots and putting my sneakers on. I stand here in the nursery garden, by the flowers so laboriously planted and grown side by side in their beds, in their boxes, the entire earth seeming to lift, billowing green, and I tilt my head upward, there's been sunshine in the last few days, a high sun pouring down, but clouds have moved in from the North Sea somewhere now, Sellafield radiation clouds, and in short intervals the sun vanishes, for seconds at first, until eventually more and more time passes before the sunlight is allowed through the cumulus clouds again. I lean my head back, face turned up, eyes squinting, with the sun being so strong as it forces its way through the layers of cloud. I wait. Stand and wait. And then I see it, somewhere up there, a thousand, perhaps three thousand feet above, the first drop takes shape and falls, releases hold, hurtles toward me, and I stand there, face turned up, it's about to start raining, in a few seconds it will pour, and

9

never stop, at least that's how it will seem, as though a balloon had finally burst, and I stare up, a single drop on its way down toward me, heading straight, its pace increases and the water is forced to change shape with the speed, the first drop falls and there I stand motionless, until I feel it hit me in the center of my forehead, exploding outward and splitting into fragments that land on my jacket, on the flowers beneath me, my boots, my gardening gloves. I bow my head. And it begins to rain.

It is a Tuesday. There can be no doubt about that. I see it in the light, the traffic outside the windows will continue to stream all day, slowly, disinterestedly, people driving back and forth out of habit rather than necessity. Tuesday. The week's most superfluous day. A day that almost nobody notices among all the other days. I read somewhere, I don't remember where, that statistics showed there were 34 perccent fewer appointments made on an average Tuesday than on any other day. On a worldwide basis. That's how it is. On the other hand a much greater number of funerals are held on Tuesdays than during the rest of the week. They sort of bunch up, you never get on top of it.

- - - ■ - - -

I had a friend.

And had this not been so, I would never have ended up with a large sum of money in my inside pocket, and been almost run over, I would never have rescued a person from the sea nor been thrown out of various bars. I would not have come inches from jumping three thousand feet down from a mountain, I would never have tried building a boat, and last, but not least, I might never have disappeared.

But I had a friend.

Jørn.

Jørn played in a band.

And I'd said yes. It was some weeks ago now. He'd asked me one evening, as we sat in his apartment in Storhaug. Jørn and Roar were going over with his band, Perkleiva, at the end of July, together with another Norwegian band, the Kulta Beats from Trondheim, they were going to play at some festival over there, on the Faroe Isles, a gig they'd been offered through the Stavanger Council, as far as I understood. Stavanger and Tórshavn were twinned towns, and Stavanger wanted to do its bit for the Faroese National Day, Olsok. Some Danish band, whose name I can never remember, were invited too, as well as all the Faroese artists. That was what I'd been told. More or less. And that I was going with them in the guise of being their soundman. Although that was probably just Jørn's way of trying to drag me along, to get me out, to show me that it could be good doing concerts, playing in a band, he'd never totally abandoned the idea of the two of us playing together, of me singing. He really wanted me to sing. But I kept my mouth sealed. Officially, for the organizers, the reason for my coming was Claus. Claus was Perkleiva's producer, but he and his girlfriend were expecting a baby, it might arrive any minute, so he'd canceled, understandably, more preoccupied with ultrasound than the sound of guitars. And I was, well yes, I needed a vacation, and sure, I'd always enjoyed traveling, and no, I had no other plans.

And I knew a bit about sound.

Not that I had any training as a sound technician, or that I'd ever worked with a band. But I'd always been good at sound. At isolating sounds. I can sit on my sofa with a CD on the stereo and hear all the instruments individually. I don't quite know how, but I can. The guitar, drums, bass, voice, they all take on different colors in my head; I can hear if there should have been more blue, if there's too much brown, or that if a hint of pink somewhere in the background had been turned up, it would have been better. I can hear if anybody sings the least bit out of tune. I've seen every episode of *Counterpoint*. You can't fool me.

I gave up working in the garden the instant it began raining, but before I'd even managed to grab my bucket of flowers and the somewhat overfilled watering can I'd brought out, I was drenched by the torrent of water that the clouds had emptied over me, I dripped my way over the floor, over the flagstones of the nursery shop, set the tulips aside in a vase on one of the two huge, old, wooden tables in the middle of the room and went into the locker room to hang up my wet jacket. I took off my pants and pulled on one of the nursery's overalls, a navy blue boilersuit with a glossy print of a magnolia flower on the back, from the time our boss decided all his staff should dress alike, so as to project a streamlined image, as he called it. And, not least, to promote greater togetherness. To give us a sense of being colleagues. Of being part of a team pulling together. Unity, cooperation. But nothing had come of it, nobody wanted to wear the overalls, it felt unnecessary, we were only a small firm after all, and few staff. And the boilersuits still hung along one of the walls of the locker room, four of them, almost unused, four years on, creases in the arms and legs still sharp. We wore our own clothes now. The boss included. He always had on flowery shirts. Hawaiian. And he was a good chap, even if he never turned up before late into the day, liked sleeping in.

I'd put on the magnolia overalls, they were tight in the crotch and smelled like new as I walked back into the shop, sat behind the counter, turned on the radio, took out the schedule to see what needed doing, one Tuesday in April.

The radio.
The news.
Bombs were falling over Kosovo and Vojvovdina and NATO hadn't hit their intended targets as I marked off the day's first job, which was to drive over to the nursing home with flowers for one of their residents. I looked at the clock. Still half an hour before the others arrived, three quarters before we opened. But they wanted the flowers delivered

as soon as possible, and I had no plans, so I started making up a couple of the bouquets they'd asked for, laid them in a fruit basket, and the Cardigans were on the radio, I didn't know the song, but I tried to hum along as I locked the door to the office, found the harmony, lost the melody, then went over to the radio, turned it off, cast a final glance around, yes, it all looked fine, great plants, nice smell, lovely being here, opened the front door, went out, locked the door, opened the car door, got in, shut the car door, started the car, drove to the nursing home, four blocks away.

It was the same up here practically every day, somebody would get a plant, flowers. And it was always a bad sign. I came up here often, virtually every week, it was where granddad had been at the end, and there had never been many flowers, unless you were about to die. Then there was an excuse. Then a nurse would come snooping around your room, noting the decay that hung in the walls, suggesting things be brightened up, *perhaps we should have some flowers in here, Fru So and So, wouldn't that be nice, and it's so dark in here, shall I pull the curtains open a little?* and as they did, as they flung their arms wide and pushed the curtains to the sides and as the light burst into your bedroom, it would not be long before the flowers arrived, it had already been decided, and soon, in hours or days, young people would cluster in semicircles at your bedside alongside angels or demons, gazing down upon you with mild or damning eyes, hands folded, waiting for you to vanish forever, never to return.

I had two bunches with me, tulips and white lilies, many people liked those, they reminded them of something, I don't know what, but the patients often said it as I came into their rooms with the flowers, as I helped them put them in a vase, *what lovely flowers*, they'd say, and then the memories, always the memories, the mental photo album it took years to go through.

Fru Helgesen was to have flowers in her last days.

Fru Helgesen's days were numbered.

Somebody had done the accounts and decided that enough was enough.

But nobody had said anything to her. She lay in her bed and stared into the white ceiling.

"Am I going to have flowers?" she asked when I knocked, opened the door and came in after a squeaky voice had pronounced *come in* from the other side.

"Of course you're going to have some flowers," I answered.

"Am I going to die now?" She didn't seem troubled, just mildly surprised.

"No, of course not," I said. "You're just going to have a bit of greenery in here."

I was on everybody's team, I changed colors mid-game and played goalie for both sides. I took everybody's red cards and sat on the bench. I found a vase under her sink, began putting the flowers in water.

"Come over here," she said.

I came to her. She beckoned me to bring my ear close.

"You only ever come with flowers when somebody's going to die," she said.

"No, I don't think so," I answered. "Lots of people get flowers."

"But nobody survives them."

"The flowers?"

"Yes."

"Right."

"But they're lovely flowers."

"Yes."

"Yes, they really are, they remind me of something, I don't know what, we had flowers like that in our garden, I think. Oh, I don't know. But they're lovely. Truly lovely."

"Tulips and trumpet lilies," I say. "That's what they're called."

"Lovely. And white, too. Are you a gardener perhaps?"

"Yes, I'm a gardener. I work right across the way."

I made a gesture and pointed in the direction of the nursery.

As though she could see through the walls, the privileged X-ray vision of the elderly.

She looked at the flowers, stuffed in the vase on her table, they were messy, and she noticed it, they were cheap flowers, among the cheapest we had, they wouldn't last long, they'd do themselves in within a few days, at best.

"Do they last long, these ones?" She pointed at the flowers, tried to catch hold of one of the leaves, but couldn't reach, I lifted the vase, held it out to her so she could touch them, feel the leaves, she breathed their aromas in, whistling through her nostrils and sniffing everything in that had once been.

"Yes, they do," I said, "they last a long while."

"Good." She gestured toward the vase as I put it back and got up to leave, and as I shut the door, she was still lying with her arm stretched toward the table. "Good."

I walked into the reception room with the bill, handing it to one of the older women who worked there, she signed it and thanked me, handed me my receipt, asked if I wanted some coffee, but I refused, wanting to leave, and not stay.

"It's always been nice having you come," she said. Then she peered nervously around the room, as though the words she had to say had tumbled to the floor and found themselves in the trash by mistake. "But, ehm, well, this all gets terribly expensive in the long run. Yes, not that, well, I mean, it's certainly not that we think you charge more than you have to, but . . ." I waited, I knew where she was going, and I could have left, but I stood there.

"Well, of course old people do die, and, as things stand, well, it's, we've had to, well we've decided to go over to cheaper flowers, yes, from, from, from a supermarket chain. So . . ."

"RIMI?" I asked.

"No, REMA," she corrected, embarrassed, looking deep into the table. "Yes, one can't get around the fact that they're cheaper in the long run, and they've made us an offer, so, yes." And then, as though the thought had occurred to her there and then, she added: "We just want to make it nice for them in their last days, I'm sure you can understand . . . yes." Her face had practically fallen into the table.

"Of course," I said. "Hardly anyone buys from the nurseries any more."

She looked uneasy. "Really?"

Looked as though she was searching for something more to say.

"Forget it," I said, turned and walked out, drove back to the nursery, let myself in and sat in the chair behind the counter, radio on, and no news, nobody dying, only music.

But I was doing all right, wasn't I?
Yes, I was all right.
I was totally all right.
Had everything I needed.
I was Mattias. 29 years old.
I was a gardener.
And I loved my job.

I really loved it. I'd often come into work early, before the others, maybe an hour before, I'd let myself out into the garden at the back sometimes, icy mornings, breath hanging frozen on the air, I'd sit on the bench out there, sit and listen to the cars as they drove past, wearied engines, unhappy people on their way to jobs they loathed, meetings with people they'd never agree with, to prices they couldn't beat, offers they couldn't match, business that had be put on hold, ideas that had to be scrapped for lack of funds, plans that would never be realized but that remained like little scabs in their palms, that itched every time they met new people with new ideas, shook their hands and greeted them, promising new, unviable projects.

If I could have had just one wish, I often thought it might have been for nothing to change. To have everything fixed for eternity. I wanted predictable days.

I sat in the garden, I was still early. Later, an hour later, the others came strolling in. There were four of us, amongst them a girl of my own age, rather well-built, she'd been to Ås agricultural college, that was virtually all I knew about her, we didn't talk about these things much, we didn't talk much at all, I don't know why, that was just the way things were. If we talked, it was about flowers, about what we had to do, that we mustn't forget to water the new plants in the corner of the nursery, that I needed to prune some bushes. *Had she remembered to prepare the wreaths for the funeral? Remembered to make up the bouquet that had been ordered, and to attach the card; Get Well, Come Back Soon, Happy Birthday, Birthday Greetings, Congratulations, Congratulations, Hearty Congratulations.* Yes she'd remembered, *and didn't I think the chrysanthemums were lovely at this time of year? They're always lovely,* I said, and I cared about these things, this was where I was at, right here, this was my world, my job, the garden at the back of the nursery, that stretched as far as the roundabout separating Hinnasvingene and the A44, on the way to the center of Stavanger. I was a cog in the world; I was not in the way. I did what I was supposed to do. Was a nice boy.

But what did I want?

This was what I wanted.

To be a smooth running cog in the world.

To do the right thing.

Nothing more.

Was that cowardly?

Was it really?

Not everybody wants to be head of a corporation. Not everybody wants to be among the top sports personalities of their country, to sit on various committees, not everybody wants the best lawyers on their team, not everybody wants to wake up in the morning to jubilation or catastrophe in the headlines.

Some people like being the secretary who's left outside when the doors close on the meeting room, some people want to drive the garbage truck, even during Easter, some people want to perform the autopsy on the fifteen-year-old who committed suicide early one January morning, and who's found a week later in the lake, some people don't want to be on TV, or the radio, or in the newspapers. Some people want to watch movies, not perform in them.

Some people want to be in the audience.

Some people want to be cogs. Not because they have to, but because they want to be.

Simple mathematics.

So here I was. Here. Here in the garden, and I wanted to be nowhere else in the world.

It might seem strange then, that Jørn and I were the ones to find each other, to hang out with each other through secondary school and college. We found each other by chance, we were suddenly standing next to each other on the playground, one break when nothing was happening. For some time that had been my spot, stood there almost every break, in my own thoughts and content that way. And on such a day, Jørn came over, asking me about something or other, I've forgotten what. I realized later that he only came over because Roar, his mate who I eventually got to know more or less too, was ill that day. Jørn was probably bored, and I probably looked friendly enough as I stood there. Anyway, we got talking, and I figured he said a lot of good things. Talked about the moon that day, about the universe and all the junk that was orbiting the earth, thousands of satellites, all carrying out totally specific tasks; we just stood talking, not so much about ourselves, but about other stuff. And that was how things went, we'd talk on our breaks, we didn't hang out much at other times, at least not until we started college. Jørn's agenda was different from mine; forward and upward. He wanted as much of the world as he could get. And I didn't blame him. Just never understood why. What he wanted with it. So we never quite agreed. Just as we never agreed over Buzz Aldrin. I'd been interested in astronauts since I was a kid, I'd read tons about them, read everything I could find, read myself through space, moon expeditions from the sixties and seventies. I knew all there was to know about the Apollo program, and I can still reel off every detail of every stage of a launch, the re-entry into earth's orbit, the angles and coordinates, how you come into orbit around the moon and back, why you lose radio contact with Earth every time you disappear around the back of the cheese in the sky. I can tell you everything about Aldrin, the second man on the moon, what his wife Joan Archer thought as she watched her husband on TV walking around up there on the surface. Buzz Aldrin's story had to be read between the lines about Neil Armstrong, and other illustrious men, his was the great story of the parentheses. But Aldrin's father himself had been friends with the great pioneers of aviation history, Orville Wright, the first man to fly, and Charles Lindbergh who flew solo across the Atlantic in 1927, New York to Paris in under a day and a half. Aldrin, for his part, attended West Point, became a major in the Air Force, flew sixty-six sorties over Korea and shot down two MiG planes, before deciding to fly even higher. In 1963 he joined NASA as an astronaut and when the twelfth and final capsule of the Gemini program went up, he was in it, blasted out of the atmosphere and into the black nothingness, and he dared to get out of the capsule up there, floated for five and a half hours in space and proved that a human being could function successfully in a vacuum.

After that he was taken onto the Apollo program.

Buzz Aldrin waited, as the first ten rockets were sent up.

Buzz Aldrin practiced.

Buzz Aldrin prepared.

Buzz Aldrin went through all the details again.

Buzz Aldrin was appointed as the pilot on the Lunar Module. The LM that was to be launched from the Command Module which

Michael Collins was to control and orbit the moon in, while Aldrin and Mission Commander Neil Armstrong would descend to the moon's surface in the LM, come out from its hatch, plant a flag, and call home.

And three astronauts waited in suspense as the *Apollo 10* descended to 15,000 meters above the moon, almost landing, before it became clear that the eleventh launch would be the one to put a man on the moon. Articles were written. Interviews given. Further preparations made. The day awaited.

July 16, 1969. Takings for ice cream that year were greater than the funds allocated to NASA.

Where were you that day, exactly ninety-seven years after the birth of Roald Amundsen, fifty-one years after the last Tsar was executed by the Bolsheviks? Where were you at 1432 hours Norwegian time when the Saturn V rocket ignited and lifted *Apollo 11* with Aldrin on board, where were you at 1433 hours when the rocket shot up, accelerating to seven miles per second, and Aldrin had a pulse of only eighty-eight?

They were even carrying Soviet luggage with them.

The medals of the deceased cosmonauts, Yuri Gagarin and Vladimir Komarov. Armstrong took a tape of the theremin music his wife loved. Aldrin had pictures of his children, gold pins in the shape of olive branches he planned to give away when he got back.

Where were you on July 20, 1969, at 21:17:42 hours Norwegian time, when man landed on the moon? Five hundred million people sat in front of their television sets. Even more sat in front of their radios.

I was between my mother's legs.

Where were you when the second person ventured out of the Eagle in the Sea of Tranquility at 0415 hours?

Had you switched off the TV? Gone to bed?

Then you missed Buzz Aldrin walking on the moon. His boots sank three millimeters into the powdery surface, I lay on a table, and knew nothing. Of the billions of people that have ever lived, Buzz Aldrin was the second man to set foot on the moon, July 21, 1969, while two hundred thirty-eight thousand miles away his family watched daddy on TV, in his spacesuit, watched as he tried to put words to what he saw.

Magnificent. Magnificent desolation. Said Aldrin. Perhaps the world's finest description of a landscape.

He started to walk across the grainy surface.
Explained how it felt to move.
Photographed the landscape, photographed Armstrong.
Collected rock samples.
The Antarctic of outer space.
Buzz Aldrin.

And a flag was planted. President Nixon phoned from the Oval Office and said that the heavens had become part of man's world, and that it served as inspiration for us to redouble our efforts to bring peace and harmony to our planet, and that all the people on the Earth were one, for just one moment. Then he hung up, and intensified his bombing of North Vietnam again. Michael Collins vanished and reappeared from behind the moon at even intervals, Aldrin's wife modestly requested, and was permitted to send up a few fireworks at home, Armstrong and Aldrin were told that Thor Heyerdahl had had to abandon his attempt to cross the Atlantic in a papyrus ship, and Aldrin had said "OK, adios, amigo," and climbed back into the Lunar Module after Armstrong. They took off their spacesuits and the moon dust smelled of wet ash and gunpowder. They covered the windows and lay down to sleep for a few hours, before starting the engines, anxious they might not work, they'd only have one go, one single chance, and if something went wrong they'd be stranded forever; but the rocket's engine started perfectly and they lifted off the surface and ascended, coupled themselves to Collins mid-orbit, crawled over into the command module, disconnected the lunar module and watched it disappear from them for ever and ever, and spirits were high, they might have whistled a tune, but you can't whistle in that atmosphere, so I imagine it being quiet, even though I know it wasn't, because there was still so much to do, so much that still needed to go according to plan, and down on earth they had wives who waited, children who gazed up, waiting for fathers from heaven, and finally they came, landing with a belly flop in the Pacific Ocean, on July 24, 1969, picked up by frogmen, and Aldrin was the last to be winched up into the helicopter, helping the other two first, sitting alone for some minutes in the half burned out spacecraft, completely alone, in the middle of the Pacific, before he was picked up too and taken to the aircraft carrier where the President and weeks of quarantine awaited, before the celebrations could be detonated upon the world, and they could travel around the globe, on instructions from NASA, the astronauts and their wives, hailed by everybody, receiving keys to cities, and even coming to Norway, lunching with King Olav, I've got a picture of it, everything looks very agreeable, but then, if you look carefully, if you put a magnifying glass against the grainy newspaper photograph, aren't there traces of worry in Aldrin's eyes? The seeds of anxiety?

Jørn saw things differently than me. *If you'd been one of the crew on* Apollo 11, *who would you have liked to be?* I asked him one evening; in fact I'd often asked him that exact same question, and then he'd arch his eyebrows and look at me as if it was a ridiculous question, and answer *Neil Armstrong.*

"But Aldrin was the commander of the Lunar Module," I objected, "he was captain of the ship."

"But Armstrong was first on the moon, wasn't he?"

"Yes . . ."

"Armstrong's the one we remember, isn't he? One small step and everything."

"But Aldrin was a more experienced pilot in just about every way."

"And so what? He wasn't the first. It was Armstrong who got to be Columbus, wasn't it, he was the one that pushed on, refused to stop, determined to land on the moon, come what may."

"But it never would have happened without Aldrin. He even designed some of the equipment on board."

"Yes, but still. Anyway, how come you're so certain they even went to the moon? Why were all the recordings so bad? To be totally honest, I figure the whole thing was recorded in some studio in California. They were probably all safely on the Warner Bros. payroll, the whole bunch of them. Which would also explain why Aldrin had problems later on. Because he knew he'd conned a whole world."

"You're totally outrageous!"

"Are you so sure?"

"Jeez, of course. It's obvious they went to the moon, why on earth shouldn't they have been there?"

"Maybe they just pretended, in order to trick the Russians, or to get a bigger defense budget, how should I know?"

"Come off it!"

"Imagine if the money involved was the only really astronomical thing in all this. There's tons to be earned on space exploration, right?"

And so we went on, an endless conversation in orbit.

We never agreed.

Should I perhaps have done something else?

Didn't I have ambitions?

Of course I did.

I dreamed of the same things as you. I wanted to go places too, to have a job I burned for, I wanted to see Prague, spend a year in Guatemala, help the farmers with their crops, soothe my own bad conscience, save the rainforest, wash beaches clean of oil, I wanted *this* party elected into Parliament instead of *that*, too. I went and voted. I wanted to work for the good of all. I wanted to be useful too.

But I didn't want to stand in the way. In the way of people who wanted to be in the front row, visible to all, not that there's anything wrong in it, all credit to those who dare, the people who make a noticeable difference, rescuing airline companies from bankruptcy, laying off thousands and then receiving hate phone calls in the night, taking on the cases that nobody else will touch.

They're cogs too. No less important, just more visible. I just didn't have a need to be seen, to have you tell me when I was being clever. I knew when I was.

I was the kid in your class in elementary school, in high school, at college, whose name you can't remember when you take out the class photo ten years later, to show your boyfriend or girlfriend how you looked back then. I was the boy that sat almost at the center of the class, one desk from the wall, the guy who never forgot his gym clothes, who was always ready for the test, who was never rowdy in class, but answered when he was asked, who never insisted on performing long skits in the school show, who never put himself forward as Student or Class Rep. I was the one you'd been in class with for almost six months before you knew his name. I was the one you didn't miss when I left your class and started at another school, or when I didn't come to your party, the one who stood in the middle of the concert hall and clapped the band back on stage, but whom nobody heard, the one you thought had the most boring life ever, the one you thought didn't have a life. I was the guy you and your friends didn't believe could have a girlfriend, when you heard about it from somebody else years later. *Him? Oh yes . . . him. What? Has he . . . ? Oh well. If he can, anybody can.*

Do you remember me?

Can you picture me?

I was the worst thing of all. I was ordinary.

I was practically invisible, wasn't I?

And I was perhaps the happiest person you could have known.

Then they turned up, one after the other, the rest of the staff, we said a brief hello, didn't talk much, too early in the morning, they were tired, had only just gotten up, their facial expressions were still back at home and wouldn't show up until lunch, we spread ourselves around the room, started to make wreaths and decorations, kept the garden at the back alive.

Later that afternoon I loaded the van, drove into town, worked my way down my list of deliveries, the majority were wreaths for funerals taking place at the end of the day, all around town the flags were raised at half mast, dust was brushed from black suits, and crumpled notes of fumbling words were clutched in the fists of those who would say something after the priest, they gathered at kitchen tables, on squeaky chairs, looked at clocks, waited for it to be late enough to leave, to get it over with, the final salute, and there were bouquets in my van too, with their accompanying ballpoint greetings, *Good Luck with the New Job, Happy Sixtieth, Get Well, Love You,* it was rarely necessary to read the messages before ringing the doorbell, you'd know the instant the door opened what kind of bouquet it was, dark rings under the eyes of people in worn-out dressing gowns, or cheery girls on the way out to their second day at the company they'd finally gotten that job with, hurrah for them all, and I was invited in for coffee once, and even though I *had* read the card and it said *Condolences*, I went in and there, sitting in the living room was an entire extended family, a semicircle of bowed heads, and I slipped off my shoes, and followed after the lady who'd taken the flowers, and who was probably the mother, she sniffed, wiping her nose with her fingers, as she walked mechanically over to the semicircle, I held back a little, peered over them, and a small coffin placed on the table in front of them, crib death in the walls, and I was offered coffee, said nothing, just drank my coffee, parasites had glutted on my words leaving none, I stood in my socks in the middle of a family who had just lost their daughter, and the father rose, younger than me, by some years, so it seemed, he came toward me and hugged me limply, and was followed by the entire clan who rose as if on cue, padded over to me and I was a very hugged flower boy, as one by one, more than twenty unknown family members clutched at my jacket, clung to the fabric, and when I left moments later, not one of them turned around, I simply closed the door gently and went and sat in the van, damp lapels, not quite knowing what to think. From that day on I always refused invitations to come in, stayed on the doorstep, even said no when the twenty-one year old girl in just her underwear got flowers from her dad, she'd just moved into a new flat in Våland and really wanted company, she was so happy, everything was working, but I stayed on the doorstep, had nothing to do in there, *he who enters here leaves all hope behind.*

Two or three hours after having left I was back at the nursery, out at Hinna, it was still raining heavily, and I shuddered as I rushed into the shop, found a chair and sat down. Karsten, the boss, was sitting behind the counter, leather apron on, cutting roses, and without looking up, he said: "Nice that we're getting some rain at last."

"I guess so."

"Let's hope it lasts."

"The rain?"

"Yes, it's so dry in the garden now, we need every drop we can get. Water and warmth always go best together."

Hawaii. That's what he would have liked. A tropical climate. *Club Tropicana.* He'd have preferred it if we'd needed mosquito nets to go in the garden.

And before I managed to reply, he asked: "Were there many deliveries today?" I told him where I'd been, what I'd delivered, and that the local nursing home had decided to find an alternative to us. His chair creaked, he put the flowers down, looked down into the table top.

"Right."

"Right."

It was quiet. News on the radio. Serbia was burning.

"Hmm . . . things aren't going too well."

"Kosovo?"

"The nursery."

"It's only Tuesday," I said.

"What?"

"It's Tuesday, almost nothing happens on Tuesdays."

"Oh, I don't know, Mattias."

He was wearing the blue palm shirt. The leaves hung limp, heavy with coconuts. "Things aren't going too well." Then he picked the flowers up again, and went on working and I walked into the office, the staff room, put the coffee on, sat and listened to the gurgling of the water filtering through the paper, until all the water had passed through and the machine gasped for more, the sound died out and the coffee was ready. I turned off the coffee machine, emptied the thermos, still nearly full from before, poured the fresh coffee in. Sat in the chair, waited for the phone to ring, for Helle to ring. She usually did at about this time. Perhaps it was still a bit too early. I glanced at the clock. Quarter past two. Yes, it was still a bit early.

1986. Helle. Fall 1986, I have to tell you about it, the coldest fall I remember, I'm seventeen, it's the year nobody forgets, although I've forgotten the sequence of events, but it's the year Olof Palme was shot and killed, in the middle of the street, Sveavägen, Stockholm, and by the next morning, the pavement is strewn with bouquets, a sea of flowers billowing across the streets, and the murderer ran up the steps, the steep stairway, and we know everything there is to know about that stairway, the number of steps, and Palme was shot with a .45, possibly, but no one knows for sure, and Christer Pettersson is the murderer or perhaps he isn't, but he can't save the seven astronauts on the *Challenger* that explodes after seventy-three seconds, live on every TV channel, on all those Memorex tapes, and not until a year later will we know that the crew didn't die in the explosion, that the module they sat in shielded them, that they lived the three minutes and forty seconds that it took for the capsule to hit the ocean outside Florida at 160 miles per hour, or that perhaps they died from lack of oxygen on their way down, doubtless they opened one of the oxygen canisters on board, but all seven were found strapped to their seats, eyes wide open, so the space program dies and in Sweden they bury their Prime Minister, and Reactor 4 explodes in Chernobyl, and the Soviet Union has heard nothing, seen nothing, but Swedish surveillance stations hunt for murderers and find vast quantities of radioactive waste drifting closer, evacuations take place at the drop of a hat, cows are slaughtered, forests are burned, but the world doesn't go under because Oliver Stone is putting the finishing touches to *Platoon*, and soon all the world will see how the Vietnam War really happened, and simultaneously Tom Cruise will sit in the airport bar at the end of *Top Gun* in cinemas across the world, after his navigator has died, and Kelly McGillis will come in, sit at his side, say we all make mistakes, that we learn from them and move on, and Tom Cruise will be told that his navigator's dead, that somebody has killed the Swedish Prime Minister and run up the steps from Sveavägen, and that the *Challenger* and Chernobyl have exploded in the end and that it's nearly impossible to go into space, and Kelly McGillis will say *Am I too late? Have you already left?* And there'll be lumps in throats everywhere in the world, because it's 1986 and nothing goes right this year, even though Maradona wins the World Championship and is adored by all, the world is falling apart at the seams and there are still thirty people from the Alexander Kielland platform who have not been found, six years after they scuttled and buried it in Nedstrand Fjord, and it feels like drinking tea in the Sahara, the cups are full of sand.

But in one place, in Stavanger, in the mid-eighties, 1986, some things went right. Amid the confusion.
Helle.

I went to Hetland College in Stavanger, it was the first day of the second year and still almost nobody knew me, almost nobody in the class knew who I was, they'd forgotten me over the summer, and that suited me fine, all I wanted was to sit in the middle of the classroom, with everybody around me, encircled. Anyway, I had Jørn, and Jørn had Roar. And though I wasn't best friends with either of them, they were the ones I'd be around that year. Jørn and Roar.

And Helle.

She started in our class, that second year, one cold, wet morning in August, the third day after the holidays, I'd come into the classroom and put my backpack just inside the door, it was still early and I only intended to leave my bag and go out again, under the shed with the others, enjoy my last minutes before class began, Norwegian, the first Norwegian class in the second year, Fall 1986. We knew some new-comers would be starting, and that some of the class had left, some that nobody had talked to, a few who'd always been alone and couldn't cope, that didn't fit in, that nobody ever asked to stay, there were always some people who left, who walked out of college on the last day before summer vacation in the knowledge that *I will never return,* and nobody turned to look at them, nobody noticed them, as they walked through the gates with an extra heavy backpack or perhaps the lightest shoulders in the world, who knows.

Some had left, and others had come to fill their vacant chairs.

Helle.

Helle had come to fill a vacant chair, to fill the room, to fill the world.

But I didn't know. As I dropped my backpack off in the classroom, I straightened up and turned, saw her there, saw she was pretty, at least in my eyes, knew I'd always remember her, assumed she'd been in here for her previous lesson and left something behind, or that she was in the first year, and that that was why I'd never seen her before. I made myself small, made space for her in the doorway, so she could slip past, and she snuck forward, flung her bag to the floor, slap, turned and went, and was back outside, her boots clack-clack-clacking across the asphalt before I'd quite managed to think the thought to its conclusion:

She's in my class.
Fuck.

Because you've been there too, haven't you, you've been there in that class, when you've fallen in love with one of the others, on the first or third day, and the room seems to grow infinitely small, cramped and it's hard to sit at your desk, and there's nowhere to fix your gaze, because if you look at her, or him, everybody will notice, and if you look the other way, look up, look at the wall, look beyond them and at the blackboard, as if that one particular person doesn't exist, they'll notice that too, and they'll think you really overrate yourself, sitting like that pretending you don't care. Because it can't be hidden. You're totally transparent. Cellophane. And as breakable.

I waited for a few seconds, looked around the room, where was she likely to sit? Should I take the plunge, try to get as close as possible to her, or lie low for a while? She'd sit way in the back. Guaranteed. I put my backpack next to the desk in one of the front rows, saw Jørn's bag near the door too, fetched it and put it next to my desk. There.

Then I ambled out, went quickly down the steps, jumping the last two and went past nearly my whole class, but nobody said hello, nobody said anything, they were busy talking about this and that, I passed by them unseen and found Jørn and Roar sitting on a bench, first years spread across the entire grounds, sitting on the asphalt in groups of two, three, four, clinging onto each other's company, trying to look cool. Some of the new girls were taking a sneak look at Roar, he was considered one of the best lookers in the school, rumors about him traveled all the way from neighboring schools, he had so many friends, was friends with everyone and seemed totally unaffected by it, there seemed to be no division between important and unimportant people for Roar, as long as they were decent and reliable he was content no matter where he was.

"Damn rain," said Jørn, trying to roll a cigarette, the paper sticking to his fingers and lips, tobacco around his shoes, this was not his first attempt.

"May I?" I said, pointing to his rollie, and he handed me the packet, peeled the Rizla paper off his fingers, scrunched the little pieces up and flicked them into the bushes, one, two.

"Have you got any idea who's left our class?" asked Jørn.

"Nope," answered Roar. I was busy rolling cigarettes. I had the knack, had the fingers for it, even though I didn't smoke, swiftly made, they were perfect, two cigarettes of just the right thickness and there we sat, on a wet bench, in the second year, before Norwegian class, killing time.

"I think Bertine's left. Not sure, but I think somebody said it," said Jørn.

"Christ," said Roar, "oh well, didn't expect anything else. You know where she's gone?"

"No idea."

"So who was it that told you, then?"

"It was Anniken that said it. Don't know where she got it from, didn't ask," said Jørn.

"But wasn't Anniken going to leave? I thought she was going to Kongsgård."

"Yeah, that's true," said Jørn. "You're right. Oh well, she's still here anyway."

"Christ," said Roar.

It had almost stopped raining, just a fine drizzle now, but it was still wet in the air, our jackets clung to our arms, swamp-like.

"So is there anyone new, then?" asked Roar.

"In our class?"

"Yeah?"

"Not that I know of. Mattias?"

"Don't know," I said, and added: "I think there's a new girl. Bumped into one when I took my backpack in."

"Pretty?" asked Roar.

I stared into the ground, it was boiling hot under my jacket, I felt huge, clumsy.

"Kind of. All right, I guess."

Then they looked at me. For some moments. Jørn picking tobacco strands off his lips. You've got to be careful what you say. I'd only seen her once, for an instant. I might have been wrong. Or I might have been right. And if I'd said she was pretty, I'd have given them something to think about. Now they had to make up their own minds, and at worst I'd have the advantage. They'd have to take my verdict into account, judge whether their eyes were deceiving them, was she really that pretty? It was complicated, a Rommelian strategy. It was Norwegian next, and the bell went off.

But we waited. We waited and didn't go in, and Jørn slowly finished smoking his cigarette, while we watched the first years get to their feet determinedly, grab their backpacks and dash off clasping their schedules and classroom maps. We knew where to go, we'd been here before, we knew our teacher, that he was always late. We'd been in this country for a while now, I thought, gone through some decisive battles, we'd crawled around in this jungle for a whole year, hence our dark glances. The first graders had just been flown in, squeaky clean. *Xin Loi.* The noise of helicopter blades whirring up gold-brown dust and chewing gum wrappers in palm trees as Jørn stubbed his cigarette out and we began walking towards the classroom.

I made sure to lag behind Jørn and Roar by a few feet, so as to be able to sneak in after them when they entered the classroom, and take a look around the room, see who was new, and in particular to see if She was there. I looked round. And there she was. Sitting, of course, at the very back of the classroom, as I'd assumed she would, alone, it seemed, but then Annette came and sat next to her, they began to chat, to get their books out, and I should have realized she'd end up being

Annette's friend. Nothing wrong with that. Annette was definitely one of the nicer girls, it seemed, even if I'd never talked to her. I went over to Jørn who'd sat down where I'd placed his bag, sat down next to him, began rummaging for my Norwegian textbook, I've no idea why, I knew exactly where it was, the third book in. It had been like that for years, frightened of forgetting my books I always took them all with me, gave myself a bent back.

Jørn had forgotten his pencil case, needed to borrow a pencil from me, no, he wanted a pen, I had one of those too, then the teacher came in, and he looked like a mimeograph copy of how he'd looked on the last day before the summer, just as pale, but with sharper contours, the same nine-day-stubble, the same glance, and if I wasn't mistaken, and I wasn't, he was wearing the same clothes. There was silence as he put his briefcase on the table, and we all expected him to let out a sigh, to sink into his chair, burned out. But Herr Holgersen, middle-aged Holgersen, smiled, smiled at us all. And he welcomed us back.

Then he started talking, and we learned all there was to learn about Dag Solstad's writing, his books about high-school teachers who'd had a tough time down the years, about the war, about betrayal, about all those hard-working folk, and I sat in one of the front rows, tried to take notes as usual, but I felt a burning somewhere in my neck, a stinging, I couldn't concentrate properly, it was so hot, had to put a hand at the back of my head, and Jørn looked at me, half turned toward me to see if someone had thrown something or other at me, but nobody had, and I stared into the desktop, aware that sitting behind me in that room was a person about whom I still knew nothing, a person who had started in my class, for some reason, and who threatened to sweep me out of my anonymous existence and the classroom had become so much smaller, so cramped, since she'd arrived.

During break times throughout the rest of the day I wandered aimlessly as usual, or sat with Jørn and Roar on the bench under the rain shelter, Jørn said something or other about his brother, and Roar answered, I didn't catch what he said, I sat sniper-like waiting for her to come out, and she did, she came out every break, always a bit late, stood in the middle of the playground with a gang of girls from Class C, under the basketball net, obviously knew some of them from before, and that was about the only reason I could imagine for her being here at all, it was a well-known fact that kids that applied for Hetland College did so for one reason only. Hetland, and perhaps St. Svitun's too, was the school you applied to if you weren't prepared to work your arse off for the next three years, if you were already getting fed up. Rumors were rife, and the rumors said that Hetland was the school your average students disappeared to, the ones who cheated on tests, the ones that overslept for exams, the ones who didn't turn up until third period, the ones that left early, turned homework in late, the ones that didn't really know what to write on their university application forms two years later. I'd always imagined I'd go to Kongsgård, that was the Cathedral school in Stavanger, or perhaps St. Olav, I was a good student, did my homework, reviewed for tests, took notes in class, came prepared, tried to glide through it all without any glitches, didn't get in anybody's way, didn't want to, aimed to be easy going, easy to get along with, which was probably why I ended up at Hetland, because Jørn wanted to go to Hetland, Hetland was, according to him, the happening place, it had a theatre society, The Munin Theatre Society, more underground than Kongsgård's hundred year old Idun Society and thus more exciting. Progressive. Jørn liked drama, going on stage, standing up front, Jørn wanted to be seen, loved or hated, didn't matter much which, and of course he got involved with the theatre, later Roar came into the picture too and built stage sets, Jørn got a part, not the one he'd wanted, the lead, he never got that, but one of the others, four lines in the second act of the show *Wanna a Review?* February 1986. I didn't get tickets for the premiere, they were grabbed that year by the more excitable kids, elbowing their way to the front of the line by the door of the theatre club. Instead I waited until the performances were well underway, and one Wednesday evening in mid-February I took the bus out to Hetland, ticket in hand, hand in bobble-jacket pocket, tracked footprints in the snow up to the gym, that was where it all happened, there inside the gym and behind the big curtain, was the stage. Took my seat, had asked for a seat in the center of the hall, sat there, jacket on, hot under the oversized lighting rig that hung from the ceiling, and waited for *Wanna a Review?* to start. It wasn't that great, Jørn recited his lines with precision, though they were rather quiet, rather shaky, and the thin flat Roar had built was rickety, it trembled every time somebody crossed the floor. But they did it, their review, and I was there, sitting in the middle of an enthusiastic, laughing crowd that I didn't know, but that I'd become a part of somehow, in the dark, and we laughed, poked each other's sides at the crudest jokes, the most mocking songs, and then, when the performance was over, we went our separate ways, me in mine and the others in theirs, and the next day I discovered Jørn had become massively popular, that was all it had taken. Four good lines. More people started coming over to where we stood during the break, people who wanted to talk to Jørn, or to Roar, when Jørn was busy. And then I'd move aside, take a step back, open the circle for new people, searched my brain to see if I had something to say, but never did, don't know why, I just liked to stand there listening, an observer, pretending not to exist, as though I couldn't be seen, which was why nobody ever talked to me apart from Jørn and Roar, or even looked in my direction. Which suited me fine. I had my place. I had control.

But somewhere inside, deep inside me, I, the great cog, craved all the attention the world could offer. Just once.

I'd take the bus into town after school, pick up my bicycle that was locked to the rack outside Romsøe Farm and trudge up toward Storhaug. That was my routine. In the morning I'd ride down from Kampen and into town, lock up my bike and take the bus to Hetland High, and then the reverse back home. Apart from on Wednesdays when I had a lesson with Fru Haug. Fru Haug was a singing teacher, I took private classes at her apartment in Nymannsveien, she hated anyone who arrived late or early, but loved boys who had pure singing voices and were neatly dressed, and to her eyes, modern.

Actually it was none other than Alexander L. Kielland that got me singing in the first place. Not the author, I've never had much of a relationship with him, never got the point of *Poison*, never quite understood our teacher's fascination for *Garman and Worse* with its bitter Pietists hiding behind their curtains. No, it was the oil rig. You remember? It happened in 1980, on March 27 of that year, out in the North Sea on the Ekofisk oil field, at 6:30 P.M.. You remember? One of the legs of the *Alexander L. Kielland platform* gave way in hurricane gales and giant waves, metal fatigue or an explosion in several of the stays caused one of its five legs to be torn loose, the *Alexander L. Kielland* keeled over and less than thirty seconds later the platform lay in the sea at a forty degree angle, less than twelve minutes more and the world was turned on its head, the derrick was scraping the bottom and the worst catastrophe in the offshore oil industry was a reality. On the mainland, Stavanger stopped for a moment, Stavanger held its breath, to no avail, only 88 out of the 211 men came back, came home, 123 people disappeared into the water, trapped, shut in the theater where they'd been spending the evening watching movies, unable to find their way out in the chaos and pitch dark, just twelve brief minutes divided an ordinary day from the worst, and a monumental hush settled over the town that day, almost everybody knew somebody who'd been on board or their families, but nobody knew what to say, and time passed, the rig was righted again, but not all the men were found, even after three years, some of them were gone forever and it was summer again, 1983. Jørn gave me a birthday present, his first, he was visibly proud as he handed me a flat package, stood grinning into my living room floor as I ripped the wrapping off and seconds later held an album in my hand, *Mods—America*. I was thirteen and the Mods were the best thing ever, for us and the rest of town, we were crazy about them, and on that album, their second, was a track called "Alexander," a comparatively gloomy affair, with lyrics I found pathetic to put it mildly, thought they were about some teenage kid running away from home and tear-jerky family stuff, I didn't make the connection until Jørn pointed it out, we were over at his house listening to the record for the third time that afternoon, and I was ranting about how this was the weakest song on an otherwise perfect album.

"Just listen to it," I said, singing in exaggerated tones, "*Oh, Alexander, why did you fail us?* Or how about this: *A lost brother is a wound that never heals.* I mean, seriously!"

"They're singing about the oil platform," said Jørn.

"What?"

"The *Alexander*, of course. The Alexander Kielland disaster, right? It failed them. When he sings *Alexander, why did you fail us*, he's talking about the leg. It was the leg that broke and toppled the platform."

"I thought he was singing about his brother or something."

"No, that's just an image. A kind of metaphor-thing. The rig was like a kind of brother to Stavanger, right? A fucking hot comparison if you think about it. If you ever sing in a band or write lyrics or stuff, you've got to talk in images."

"What makes you think I'm planning on that?"

"What, singing in a band?"

"Yeah."

"Nothing, I'm just telling you how it is, that *if* you ever sing in a band you have to be able to do stuff like that."

"I haven't thought about singing in a band."

"No, but if."

That was how I started singing. *Alexander.* I sang that song over and over, ad infinitum, all the while imagining myself rescuing unfortunate oil workers from the sea. But I didn't write songs, and I didn't sing in public. I sang my way through the Mods' records when I was alone, which I nearly always was, knew the lyrics by heart, the way Morten

Abel sang them, wore the vinyl out, until one day Mother got the idea I should learn to sing properly, or perhaps she'd simply had enough of the same songs. Neither she nor Father demanded I use my singing for anything, they were just pleased I had something to do. I'd been ill, I seemed to be improving, and Mother sat me down one day, she had an old friend who had a friend who was a singing teacher, and that was how the decision was made that I'd have weekly classes with her, apparently she was very good, had taught lots of youngsters, and her husband had contacts in the recording industry, he got hold of master recordings of the instrumentals of Duran Duran, and later a-ha, and then I sang to them, again and again, while Fru Haug held forth on singing from the stomach, taught me to sing like them, to reach the high notes, the ones that sat on the top shelf, as she described it. I didn't have anything against this, had enough spare time, so I visited Fru Haug every week for four years, until the Mods were long passé, until Duran Duran had more or less vanished and a-ha were falling apart at the seams. But I never sang for other people. In fact I even stopped singing at home, sang just once a week, behind the thick walls and closed doors of an apartment in Storhaug, and the only concerts I gave were for Herr and Fru Haug, and they would smile and clap and then the coffee and biscuits were brought in and Herr Haug would dive into his briefcase some days and surface with something for me, an autograph from a band he was involved with, signed drumsticks, albums or sweatbands. I'd thank him, go off with them, and when I got home I'd throw them in a box, far in the back of my closet, and forget them. Without a word to Jørn about what I was doing.

- - - ■ - - -

After my lesson that day I biked down to Pedersgata, freewheeled through town and pedaled hard up the hill to Kampen, Seehusensgate. There were no cars in the garage, nobody else was at home, a note on the kitchen table said my dinner was in the fridge, it was microwavable,

Mother was going swimming straight from work, and Father always worked late anyway, had done so for as long as I could remember, a conscientious man, my parents were careful, conscientious people.

Mother worked in child welfare. Looked after youngsters. She had some childhood friends she went swimming with twice weekly, in Hetland's Baths. Synchronized swimming. She'd been doing it for as long as I remembered, I'd go with her sometimes when I was younger, sit at the edge of the pool and watch, the legs of my pants folded up, feet in the water. I remember how great I thought it looked when they made circles in the pool, like flowers in the water, their identical swimming caps. I thought mother looked great, when she got it right, and I liked the way they relied on everyone doing their part. A sense of things hanging together. Mother and her friends didn't make a big deal out of it, there were no great goals, just enjoyed swimming together. Although occasionally, as I grew older, they participated in local competitions, mainly with women's teams from companies or the like, and then Father and I would go and watch her, we'd sit on the benches and watch Mother as she followed the rules, remembered the combinations and made pretty shapes in the water. Father was no sportsman himself, in his opinion he'd jogged enough during his military service, he preferred to watch than to take part. He worked for an insurance company in town, looked after money and was terrified of the word "compensation," it was as though it was contagious, an illness that could strike arbitrarily, that no chemical could eliminate, Agent Orange. Apart from that, he'd had thinning hair since his youth, enjoyed reading *Out in Nature* and subscribed to scientific journals, could never get enough, kept himself informed of the latest technology and explained the workings of the world to Mother, told her about the treasures of the Incas in South America and drift ice in the Arctic. For her part, as far back as the seventies, Mother had forbidden Father to buy clothes himself. He'd tried a few times before then, a valiant attempt, and each time, according to Mother, he'd bought such boring and neutral clothes that he melted into his surroundings, it was almost impossible to know if he was home or not. That was how things were, fine parents to grow up with, they were polite to one another, there were never big rows in our house, not even when there should have been.

I microwaved my food, sat in front of the TV, ate my dinner, obedient boy, ate it up, put my plate away and felt restless, unable to sit still for long, couldn't concentrate. Tried to follow some of the shows, *Film Magazine* on NRK, *Charlie's Angels* and *The Tales of Wells Fargo* on Sky, whatever was playing, but I couldn't, and outside the rain was falling again, a driving rain. Eventually I got up, went out into the hall and called Jørn, but he wasn't home. It seemed he'd gone out, despite the weather, he was out there somewhere, like she was, and for a second I was morbidly jealous, got it in my head that she was out there with him, that they were sitting somewhere, friends together, they were having fun, and they didn't need anybody else. Had that thought for an instant, but pushed it away, went up to my room, didn't do my homework, didn't listen to any records, went to bed early that night, nine o'clock, since I had nothing to do, and nothing would happen that night. And I dreamed that the sea rose, that it came gushing through the window and swept me away with it.

I turned spy that fall. Peeping Tom. I kept watch over Helle, was the first one out at break, last one in. That was the fall I almost froze to death, trench foot and frostbite. And for once, I wanted to be noticed. To be seen.

But I said nothing.

I never talked to her, not because I didn't dare to, but more likely because I was frightened she wouldn't talk to me, and then my whole enterprise, my whole hobby, would be spoiled.

No.

It *was* because I didn't dare. It meant too much.

Cowardly?

Yes, of course. Like everybody else.

Flat-on-my-face cowardly.

And then I did something I would come to regret bitterly.

For years.

I stuck my head out.

It was the committee for the theater society that came up with the idea.

A bad idea.

An amazingly bad idea. They decided to start a new annual event, a fancy dress ball for Christmas. On the last day of term before Christmas. It cost twenty-five kroner a ticket and I hadn't really intended to go, but everybody else was, and no stone was left unturned when it came to distributing invitations, and one October day an invite was shoved under the stone I was sitting on.

Was Jørn going? Was Roar going?

Of course they were.

"I'm not sure," I said.

"Oh, come on," said Roar as if he thought I was just being awkward. We stood under the shelter and I stared at the invitation, I didn't want to go, but that was so stupid, she'd be there, and I'd practically given myself pneumonia standing outside waiting to be noticed by her, I was fed up with going about in my long johns every day to cope with the cold.

But a fancy dress ball? No fucking way!

Nofuckingwaynofuckingway.

And so I let myself be persuaded, without further ado.

The costume was easy to choose. I'd be an astronaut. Of course. With a gold colored sun visor and everything, so it wouldn't be possible to see in, to see my face, only to look out. A bubbly white space suit with the NASA logo on it and white snow boots on my feet.

I spent almost a month figuring it out, a space suit wasn't the easiest costume to make, but there were solutions, and bit by bit the pieces fell into place. I made drawings and Mother did most of the work, the white sail from the old surfboard Father had bought one summer and nobody used became the suit itself, it was stiff enough and made of white nylon, it made a superb whistling noise as I moved. The sail fabric was tacked loosely to the corresponding wetsuit, and then stuffed with cotton wool and sponge, I made the helmet out of father's old scooter helmet, it was spherical enough, I painted it white, put a thin layer of yellow film over the visor, it looked pretty smart when I opened and closed it. Mother sewed a collar made of the sail fabric to the inside rim of the helmet, so it could be tucked down into the rest of the suit and looked as though all the joins were airtight. With Father's help we stuck huge magnets under my snowboots with Karlsson's superglue, they made a great metallic clanking noise as I crossed the floor, because if it's gotta be done, it's gotta be done.

Turned out Jørn's big brother had white ice hockey gloves too, and since he lived at Dale Psychiatric Unit, way out of town, Jørn reckoned nobody would notice if I borrowed them. Besides, his brother hadn't ever played ice hockey.

"What, never?" I asked, as we sat up in my room. I'd just tried the finished suit on for the first time, it fit well, fit as it should, and it was Thursday, the evening before the ball.

"Never," answered Jørn. "I don't think he's even ever touched a puck."

"So why does he have ice hockey gloves?"

"We'll never know."

I thought about Jørn's brother, who'd lived at the home for years and who might never return to planet Earth, imagined some kind of David Bowie figure. Ziggy Stardust. Major Tom. Lost in Space. Without his ice hockey gloves.

That evening, when Jørn had gone, I sewed the name label Mother had embroidered in big blue letters carefully onto the breast of the suit, it said *Buzz Aldrin*. Had to, of course. And it looked fantastic.

Friday came. The weather had turned fair. One of those really beautiful December days. I hadn't talked to her that day either, I don't know why, never seemed to find the occasion, I was probably terrified. I thought about where this would all lead. How I'd cause a disturbance in her life, disorder in my world. How things would go off track, the water would be too deep. I thought of ways to avoid her. To stop thinking about her, concentrated on the stuff I knew, how planets followed paths, how planes took off and landed all the time, the world over, without hitch. I hunted for good reasons to get out of it, and found none.

Friday.

TV in the interim hours.

Pernille and Mister Nelson.

Sky Trax.

The Pat Sharp Show.

Wham's goodbye concert on NRK.

Like the sand in the hourglass, these are the days of our lives.

I called Jørn, yes, he was ready, another half hour, and he'd leave, Roar was already on his way to school, Roar was always early, that was just how it was, and I liked it. Roar came from a family whom time always seemed to work against, there was always so much to do, maybe that was why he always tried to beat everyone to it, to sneak ahead unseen.

Friday.

One should beware of Fridays.

They promise so much.

Like movie trailers.

Only rarely do they live up to expectations.

Most Fridays are lousy sequels.

Back to the Future Part III.

I left home early, took the bus over, had my costume in a big bag, didn't want to go marching through town in that costume, and there wouldn't be a problem changing at school the moment I got there, I could just go down into the locker rooms.

It was snowing heavily, had to plough my way through the snowdrift, looking down at the ground so as not to get my eyes covered in snow. It crunched under my snow boots and I was on my way to a party I'd never normally have gone to. But then, these weren't normal times; nothing was normal in the autumn of '86.

As I walked into the playground, I saw the ground was already covered in footprints, which meant lots of people had arrived already, and I decided to change my plans of walking through the gym to get to the locker rooms, I'd go around the back instead and hope the door wasn't locked.

I jogged around the building, bag in hand, and came to the outer door leading into the locker rooms, tugged at the handle. Locked. Shit . . . Looked around. No other doors. I walked back and forth for a while, wondered if I ought to risk being seen in the gym without my costume, but decided I didn't want that. Started to check the windows into the locker room. They wouldn't budge. Tried teasing my keys in, sticks, anything to get leverage with, but they were firmly stuck. Moved along the row of windows, test, locked, test. Locked. And then at last I found one that wasn't quite shut properly. Only one catch was on, and I managed to open the window an inch on one side, place a stone in the gap to hold it open, and with a branch broken from a tree I managed to lift the other catch, opened the window, and then wriggled my way through the small opening, so that I was suddenly standing in the middle of a darkened girls' locker room.

It was weird standing in here. I don't know what I'd expected. That it should be very different. Different colors, different fittings, maybe.

I'd never lain on my back in the boys' locker room with a mirror underneath the partition, or stood on the taps in the shower, or twisted my head at unnatural angles to get a glimpse of naked girls bodies through the ventilation system in junior school. The line was always so long, and I always stood so far back in it, letting everybody go ahead of me.

But there wasn't much to see. Looked much like any other locker room. Neither did it smell particularly like girls. It smelled like green soap. Floor wax. Gymnasium.

I put my bag down, began to take my clothes off, folded them neatly and lay them beside my costume, hauled on the extended wetsuit, checked everything was in place, put my helmet on, visor up, zipped it up, and then the door into the locker room opened, a hand fumbled for the light switch and there she was, standing in the room, a bag in her hand. Me in my space suit.

Houston, we have a problem.

Engine off.

She leaped back when she saw me. "Oh, I'm sorry, I didn't know anyone was in here," she said, and I raised an ice-hockey-gloved hand, not knowing what to say.

"Hi," I said.

She turned in the doorway.

"H . . . hi."

I took my helmet off, and she walked farther into the room.

"I was . . . I was just changing," I said.

"Your name's Mattias, isn't it?"

"Yes."

"So what are you?" She came even closer. "An astronaut?"

I stood there in front of her, in the middle of the room, my helmet under my arm.

"Buzz Aldrin," I answered.

"Who's that?"

"The second man on the moon. *Apollo 11*. 1969. The *Eagle* has landed."

"But why aren't you Armstrong? Wasn't he the first man?"

"I didn't have his suit," I said.

"Oh." She looked at me skeptically, then smiled, something in her face opened up, the room lit up, I almost had to pull my visor down.

"I'm Helle," she said, stretching out a hand, I took it, gave it a little shake, and pretended I didn't know, all too well, what she was called. It was a nice hand.

"Nice name."

"So is that," she said pointing at my chest. "Aldrin."

"What are you going to be?" I asked, pointing at her bag.

She looked at my hand. "Aren't those ice hockey gloves?"

"It can be pretty cold out in space."

She laughed again, and it really hadn't gone that badly, I thought to myself.

"I'm going to be Joan of Arc," she said, pulling a suit of armor out of her bag. "My mum suggested it, I couldn't think of anything, but it'll be fine I'm sure."

"Of course it will."

She began unbuttoning her blouse, it was getting hot in my suit. She looked up at me again.

"Hmm . . . I think you'd better go, I'm going to change now."

"Yeah, sure. May God be with you!"

"You what?"

"Joan of Arc. She believed that she was acting on divine inspiration. She led the French army to a great victory, the turning point in the Hundred Years' War. Then later they burned her at the stake. Must have gotten her beliefs all wrong."

"Oh."

I stood there scuffing my shoes into the floor.

"Anyway . . . I . . . well, I'll be off. Bye."

"Yeah. See you later."

So I went out of the locker room, up the stairs and into the big hall.

My first real party. This is what I remember. The class parties in elementary school, the home-alone-parties during high school, the late nights out, down by the sea, the making out and the lager, and all those mouths, and smart-looking pants taken off behind the bushes, the drunken girls, I was sitting at home then, that was more my thing, so it was just as well nobody ever asked me. But this was no teenage birthday party. This was a ball. And it's this I remember.

I stomped into the gymnasium. All done up and balloon-infested to be a ballroom, standing on the stage a percussion outfit, guitars, synthesizers, there'd be a concert later, at the other end of the room a disk jockey, Norwegian Pat Sharp dressed like Prince Valiant, table laid with bowls of punch and plastic cups. And in the middle, waves of dancing kids. Pulled down my visor, moved towards the punch, the magnets clicked on the floor as I walked, but nobody noticed. Took a plastic cup of punch, held it clumsily in big hockey gloves, took a slurp, the taste of summer, Hawaii, even though it was December, turned to face the dancing hordes, the landscape. *Magnificent. Magnificent desolation.*

Then somebody thumped me on the back. I turned. It was Jørn, dressed as Luke Skywalker, a good likeness.

"Luke," I said, in my deepest Darth Vader voice. "I am your father, Luke."

"Ha-ha. Hi there, spaceboy." Jørn was in full swing. "Have you seen Roar anywhere?"

"No, I don't think so. Who is he?

"Who do you think? Solo, of course."

"Of course. I spotted Obi-Wan Kenobi in here too," I said. "And Princess Leia. I think."

"Jesus. Leia. Things have got to happen there!"

"But Leia's Luke's sister, isn't she?"

"Yeah, yeah, fuck that, we don't have to go that deep into it, do we? Do you know who she is? Who's Leia?"

"I think she's in Class C. I'm not sure."

Jørn looked at my plastic cup. Punch.

"Have you been down yet?"

"Down?"

"Come on."

I followed Luke out and around to the back of the school, down the staircase to the props room, through the door and into the warmth. There were about ten or twelve people sitting down here, boys and girls, and whiskey on the table. I glanced around quickly to see whether Helle was here, hadn't seen her up in the gym, but she wasn't down here either. Jørn put me in a chair next to the table, pointed toward me.

"This is Mattias."

Only a few heads moved to nod in my direction, most of the people down here were actors, set makers, stagehands, and theatre folk in general. I was handed some whiskey in a glass and Roar came out from the toilets. As Solo.

"Where's Chewbacca, then?" somebody asked in our direction, a tall guy dressed as Conan.

"In his kennel," answered Jørn.

"Yeah, right. And you?" he continued, looking in my direction: "Where's Armstrong?"

I didn't want to answer.

"Armstrong's looking after Chewbacca," said Jørn.

"Smart. Fucking smart. You're a smart guy, Jørn."

More whiskey. Or beer. Or wine. I'd lost track. But there a storm raged in my glass. When we finally resurfaced, several hours had gone, the teachers' generally graceless skits and the principal's speech were long over, a band with the flashy name of Hetland Heroes were up on stage playing "Tainted Love" and out on the dance floor the poor students tried to keep up, but it was hard, almost impossible, I didn't blame them, you needed your sea legs out there, I staggered out into the crowd, the floor heaved under me, Mare Undarum, the gravitational force was slowly, but surely being sucked out of the huge room, it was steaming up behind my visor, big drops started running slowly down the transparent plastic, but I kept the visor down, shoved my way through the crowd as the band started to play "Space Oddity," Bowie strutting his stuff at the ball, and the vocalist is singing off key, not great, standing so cocksure on the edge of the stage, trying his best to reach the notes, and it wasn't an improvement when they tried some a-ha. Luke was fighting a laser battle with Obi-Wan over by the climbing bars and committed patricide, Leia was getting bored, and Helle was nowhere to be seen, so I fought my way to the exit, through the crowded room, the doorway swayed, I tried aiming straight, had to make a couple of attempts and somebody grabbed hold of me, talked to me, but the sound didn't get through the plastic and the wetsuit stuck to my skin, I needed the toilet, needed air, had to find Helle, and I trundled out through the corridor, up the stairs and into the classroom, fell over a couple of chairs and tables in my gigantic suit, and the sound of the band flung itself out of the gymnasium, wound its way up through the floors and into my head, I turned and started back down the hall, Oceanus Procellarum, my hair drenched in condensation and I walked back in, twice as many people here now, I began to feel ill, my heart was beating at twice the tempo at which the band attempted to make "Sweet Dreams" swing and Annie Lennox materialize, and I spun on my own axis several times in the search for something firm to hold, but I didn't know anybody in here, headed toward the punch bowls and found Roar in Solo's shadow, I grabbed him and lurched toward him, he held me steady and suddenly the room went quiet.

"You all right?" he asked, trying to lift my visor, but I shoved his hand away, held the visor down.

"I'm just a bit . . . technical problems," I said.

"Huh?"

"Huh?" I answered, I could see his mouth moving, but couldn't catch his words, too much talking, shouting in the hall, words pouring from the loudspeakers.

"I think I've lost contact with Mission Control," I said. "But we'll have it fixed in no time. Stand by."

And then a voice came over the loudspeakers from the stage, anybody could join the band now, a generous offer, if there was anybody who wanted to try to be a singer, this was their chance, was there anybody who wanted to come up? The vocalist left the stage, arms crossed. Nobody volunteered. Mumbling out on that soft gymnasium floor, and there in the middle, amongst all the Zorros, the superheroes, cowboys and Czech's Majka from space, I caught sight of Joan of Arc. Helle had suddenly turned up from nowhere, and so I put one magnetic snowboot in front of the other, in speedy succession, and did what I should never have done.

I lifted my hand.

Walked toward the stage.

Walked up the small staircase.

Turned to the band.

Gave them a title. They nodded.

Turned to the public. Mumbled.

Opened my visor.

Thought about Fru Haug.

And sang.

I sang loud, as loud as I could, and I sang well. I sang fantastically well. Sang my way through the walls, out through all the people on the floor, and I sang their hats, their scarves, their false mustaches and wigs off, I saw Roar and Jørn standing together in a corner, mouths open, eyes staring, and I saw the people from my class, shaking their heads all around the room, and I sang loud, lifted the roof, because it was something I could do, I had a powerful voice, I don't know why, but I'd always been good at singing, it was just I'd never liked it, didn't like standing at the front of a stage like this, singing for a hungry audience, but right now, in this moment I sing, as I have since childhood, for myself, and the song shoots through the air-conditioning system in the ceiling, out into the snow, through the streets, and I imagine cars stopping at traffic lights, motorists turning down their car stereos, rolling down their windows and letting the snow into their cars as they wonder where the sound is coming from, and couples quarreling in their apartments, holding their tongues, opening their windows and taking each other in their arms, kissing, and children waking up in their beds and hugging their teddies, because somewhere out there someone is singing, and in the end it stops snowing, the clouds clear, and I sing as hard as I can, fill my lungs with air and the band can barely keep up, the vocalist pulls even further to the back of the stage, until he ends up going all the way off into the back room and I stare out into the public, wide open eyes, don't know what to do, I find Helle, and Helle smiles, a big smile, and I can't lower the visor this time either, because I'm singing, and it's so beautiful, a song beautifully sung, and I think how I should have been a singer, because it's the only thing I can do, my voice carries and the song moves to its decisive climax, one of the most popular songs of the year, the year that otherwise went so wrong, and I stretch out my arms, and the song nears its end, I turn to the band, make a rotating motion with my right arm for them to take the last section one more time, the drummer brings down the final beat, and I'm alone, holding the note, and the final vowel sneaks out into the venue, and then it's over.

And I pull down my visor.

And the applause explodes.

And I turn and go.

I staggered backstage, down the stairs and into the girls' locker room, sat on the bench by my clothes, lifted my visor, leaned forward and threw up onto the floor, it ran out of me, in big, belching thrusts, I went down on my knees, emptied myself over the tiles, and it ran toward the showers, sticky streams of beer, wine and whiskey, everything I'd held back all autumn long.

And that's what I remember. Or rather, that's the last thing I remember clearly, I think. At some point everything started to speed up, or my brain started to slow. But I do know I finally tore off my space suit, stuck my head in the shower and turned it on, ice cold water over my head, put my own clothes back on, threw the space suit in the bag, crept out the window, crept home in the snowdrift, four miles with wet hair, made myself ill, lay in bed for a week, before I got up a few days before Christmas, went to Jørn's, but he didn't know what to say.

"Jesus," he said. "Christ Almighty!"

I said nothing.

"Why haven't you ever said anything about it, Mattias?"

"Why should I?"

"But Christ, we could be a band, yeah, me on guitar, Roar on drums and . . ."

"No."

"No?"

"It was just a one off. A rescue attempt."

"And who was in need of rescue, may I ask?"

"Me."

"But my God, Mattias, you *have* to sing. It's criminal not to. You must be the best vocalist since, yeah, I don't know, but for ages."

"No," I answered.

"No?"

"No."

"Really no? Or just no?"

"Really no."

"But what are you intending to do if you're so dead set on not using your potential?"

"I'm going to be a gardener."

"A gardener?"

"Yup."

We sat there staring into the ceiling, Jørn played some records, Roar came by later into the evening, said more or less the same thing, and I answered that I'd never do it again, tried to explain my thinking, and they understood, slowly, but surely, it took time, and I told them about my plans to be a gardener and how they'd begun to take form in my head over the last few weeks, though in truth I'd been thinking it over for the last three years, explained about Helle, dropped cluster bombs of information and revealed more than I had for the last ten years.

I'd spent December 23, Little Christmas Eve, at Jørn's house, we'd hung out in the TV room in the basement of his parents' house, shared a couple of beers, watched *The Countess and the Butler*, and I wondered where they were now; was the countess a big actress or just a one-trick pony-artist, and the butler, what was the butler doing now? Was he decorating his Christmas tree, reminiscing about his past success, did he know this comedy skit was played every Little Christmas Eve in Norway like some ritual incantation. I tramped through the snow back home, up to Ølbøen that sold beer even after one o'clock on Saturday afternoons, up to Kampen School, and it was dark, the snow lay thick in the schoolyard and the streetlamps struggled to light up between the white flakes that landed soundlessly on the ground, I scooped up a fistful of snow, packed it tightly into a ball between my mittens, hurled it in a high arc onto the roof of the junior school so it landed with an explosion, and then continued on my way until a voice called after me.

"Hey, wait."

Somebody came running.

Helle came running.

Of course Helle came running.

What else would she do?

I turned and waited for her to catch up, scooped up another fistful of snow, made another snowball.

"Where did you go? After the party?" she asked when she'd reached me. "You just disappeared."

"Got called back to earth."

"But, you're a good singer."

"Thanks. And you?"

"I stayed." She laughed. "It went pretty quiet after you'd finished. The band didn't play anything else all evening. The disc jockey took over. Where did you learn to sing like that, anyway?"

"In Storhaug."

"That was the most beautiful singing I've ever heard."

"Really?"

"Yeah. Can you throw a snowball up onto the roof?"

"I think so."

"You'll get a reward, if you do."

"Okay."

Snowflakes might have settled on her eyelashes, she might have brushed them away with her red mittens, but she didn't. She tugged one of her mittens off, wiped the snow from her nose, put her mitten back on and shivered with the cold. I patted the ball one last time and threw it up onto the roof. Splat.

Then she put her arms around me and kissed me.

And I put my mittens around her.

Which was how we got together, Helle and I, on Little Christmas Eve.

Sat in the living room with Mother and Father and watched the Christmas Disney Cavalcade, before Christmas Eve dinner.

When you wish upon a star.

A gift from all of us to all of you.

It was a nice Christmas and I got what I wanted.

I spent New Year's Eve with Helle, at a party in Madla, stayed the night at her place and awoke to fresh rolls the next day, her father had been baking, was in good humor, and I stayed a few days into January.

Helle. From Augland. Helle, whose father was in the police, and whose mother was a geography professor. Helle, who lived in the loft at home, who liked the Police and always wanted to go to Café Sting to drink red wine. Helle, who would become my entire world, everything that was good, until one day she would inevitably sink the ship so neither man nor mouse could be saved.

Term started again on a Tuesday, and I remember how it fell completely silent as I walked into the classroom that morning. And still nobody talked to me, apart from Jørn, Roar, and Helle, but I noticed how everybody's eyes licked my whole head smooth and sore as I moved around the playground. If the corridor was crowded outside the classroom where I had my next lesson, they'd step aside so I could go in. As the weeks and months passed it only got worse, suddenly I was horribly interesting, everybody wanted to get me talking in every damned break about my singing, I stood on the playground and froze, trying to keep a low profile, unsuccessfully, of course. The world had discovered Mattias, and there was nothing to be done. It was too late for regrets, even the teachers were out to get me more, posing questions, there was no end to it, and it felt like the walls were creeping in on me, pressing me into corners no matter how big a room I went into. And perhaps that was why, as I stood outside one day engaged in one of an endless stream of meaningless conversations with somebody who had no real interest in me at all, I decided that I'd never poke my head out again. I missed my own world, I'd had control there, just me and space, outer space, Buzz, and me, I still didn't say a lot, didn't make any more of myself during class time, less if possible, but of course that had the reverse effect, they wanted me to join the theatre group, it would be crazy of me not to, they thought, and newly formed bands suddenly needed new vocalists, but I declined, a tall tree in the desert. But Helle was kind, tried her best to understand why I didn't want all this attention, even if she didn't really understand why, and I'd stay at home or at her place, didn't go out much, even less than before, and then towards the end of the third year, important discussions were held about what we should all study, I lied, said I was going to Oslo, to university there, to take some subject, I don't remember what. And quietly I filled in the necessary forms for horticultural college, for the courses and whatever was needed. Only Helle, Jørn, and Roar knew. And they said nothing.

Some people wouldn't want the whole world even if they could have it.

Some people don't want a land of their own.

And some people don't even need a school in Stavanger.

Some people just want to be a part of a whole.

Useful, if inconsequential.

Not everybody needs the whole world.

I just wanted to be in peace.

I sat in my chair, looking at the plants that stood waiting at the door to the shop, they had to be delivered next morning, mustn't forget, it was half past two, and she'd ring soon, as always, soon Helle would call, I'd arrange a time with her, switch out the lights and lock the doors, drive home to Storhaug, to our apartment.

Digital figures on the clock above the door: 14:31.

I sat in my chair, drank coffee.

14:32.

Shifted in my chair.

14:33.

Screwed the lid of my Thermos on tightly, put it in my plastic bag.

14:34.

Helle called.

"Hi," she said, her voice soft as usual through the receiver, through the wires, miles of cable and electrical impulses through town.

"Hi," I answered, still an expectant child, even after all these years. Voices in the background, her room was filled with voices.

"Are you watching TV?"

"Yes," she answered.

"What?"

"Just something that was on. Oprah, I think."

"Right."

Pause.

"So," I began, "do you want to do something this evening?" I fiddled with the flowers on the table, brushed the dust off the tabletop. "Maybe we could go to the movies or something?"

"I've got to go to the gym soon," she said, "and then I'm going to meet Karianne later today. This evening."

"Oh, right."

"Yes, it's . . ."

"No, that's . . . yes, no, I mean, that's fine."

"Are you sure?"

"Yes. Of course. We can do something tomorrow. Or over the weekend. Or?"

"Maybe," was all she said.

The flowers on the table needed water. They'd die in this heat. I swapped the receiver to the other hand.

"Right . . . we'll talk soon then," I said.

"Okay."

"Okay. Love you."

"Me too."

"Bye."

"Bye."

I put the receiver down, left the flowers to die in peace on the table, puttered around for half an hour before locking up and going home.

I sat on the sofa in the living room. Watching the news. Telephone. News flash about a boat catastrophe outside the Philippines. Somebody was calling, I turned the sound off, got up and lifted the receiver, watched the muted news. Mother at the other end. Usual voice. I had an eye on the TV.

"Hello," she said.

Aerial view of a boat being smashed to pieces in the waves, Asian people clinging desperately to the bow.

"How are things?"

"Everything's fine," I say.

Close up of mother and child in a lifeboat, eyes wide open.

"And work?"

"Things just keep growing."

Pause.

"That's good. And Helle?"

"She's well, as always."

"Yes, she always seems to manage so well."

Helicopter nears the water, lowers the rescue cable, people are dragged under in the whirling currents, arms sticking out of the water.

"Yes."

Cut to the reporter who is standing ashore, wet raincoat, wind in his hair.

"Have you had any supper?"

"Hmm," I answered, "nothing much. A bit."

"I see,"

The cameraman zooms in on life jackets floating on the water. The sea rises.

"Do you want to come by the house, maybe?"

"Now?"

"Yes. I . . . I've baked some sweet buns."

"Buns?"

"Yes."

Survivors wrapped in wool blankets, eyes shining, on the oil tanker's deck. Then the boat sinks.

"Okay," I said. "I'll just take a shower, then I'll drive over."

She waited.

"Great, we'll see you then. Bye."

"Bye."

She waited a couple of seconds more before replacing the receiver, she always did, in case I might say something more. Generally, I didn't, I knew she didn't really like talking on the phone, she wanted a face in front of her, a mouth, Father was the telephone operator, he could have sat for hours, talking and talking, discussing anything and everything, so long as he'd found somebody at the other end equally happy to sit talking.

An hour later I was in the car, made a little detour, drove down toward town, a light evening, there were café tables out on the sidewalks and people were drunk, in just T-shirts and wearing sunglasses, despite it being early in the year, the treacherous month, *never trust a girl's winks and smiles, they are as unreliable as the April weather* was Mother's refrain, but the rain had dried and forest fires would soon rage in the countryside again, this was Stavanger, desperate to get summer ahead of time, good weather on credit and covered by VISA for loss in July.

I drove up toward the Atlantic Hotel, up toward the Buchardt Hotel that was under construction, past the SAS Hotel and up toward Kampen, past the Mission High School in Misjonsveien and a little bit further to Seehusensgate.

Finger on the doorbell.

Hesitated.

No.

Didn't wait, walked straight in.

I'd drop by once in a while, once a month perhaps, usually, perhaps twice, sometimes just a flying visit, at other times I'd stay all evening, sit and watch TV with them, depending on what Helle was doing, or not doing, if we'd made plans, or if I was left to myself. We lived separately for a long time, Helle and I. I'd had an apartment in Storhaug, she lived in shared accommodations at Eiganes, together with three girls, who were younger than her, at college, future teachers, all of them. I used to imagine them practicing writing each others' report cards, inventing sicknesses and bad excuses, giving each other grades for their cleaning skills, C+ when one of them had forgotten to put the tea towels through the mangle after washing them or forgot to boil the silverware. We'd been in the apartment we now shared for the past four or five years, we'd gotten it after I'd been forced to move out of another house that was being demolished, an apartment I'd found in an old house in Våland, low rent, moved there in 1989, the summer that Helle went to Bergen to study law and I started working. I'd sort of melted into that flat, over the walls, over the massive floor space, I had the entire third floor, hundreds of fabulous square feet and space for everyone. The rooms had begun to mold themselves around me, I knew every unevenness in the floors, where it creaked, the way the kitchen lights failed to come on until ten to twelve seconds after you'd flicked the switch. I commuted between Stavanger and Bergen during those years, stayed overnight in the little room she had in Bergen, in Nygårdsgaten, near the Grieg Hall. I went with her to some of her lectures, to the parties, sat among the students, their jokes, anecdotes from Hulen, from Kvarteret, secret handshakes and obscure film posters on the walls, I went with her up on Dragefjellet, sat with her in lecture hall, like a rare plant, and when I finally got her back to Stavanger again, she insisted on continuing to live with friends, her old girlfriends, *I need more time before I share a toothbrush with someone,* she said, and I said *yes, okay,* and I wanted her with me all the time, in my rooms, but it wasn't until my house was being demolished and I had to move, that she was ready. She'd already given up her law career by then, had begun in advertising, got herself a good job where she stayed for a while, before finding something better, starting somewhere new. Advertising and law. Two sides of the same coin, to her.

I was at home a lot when Helle was out. Once in a while I would go to Jørn's too, but more often I'd go over to my parents', they didn't have any other children, I was the only living example, the authentic son, and Father always lit up when I came through the door, he'd emerge from the living room smiling, clutching his newspaper and the glasses he'd taken off, and the way he'd look at me, advertisement-like.

Lano soap family.

The homecoming son.

Every time.

And this time too.

I didn't ring the doorbell, generally didn't, it was still home after all, even if it was a long time since I'd lived there. Proper home-home. Didn't ring, walked into the hallway, *hi there,* and I heard father get up from his chair in the living room and then he came into view in the doorway, newspaper in hand, glasses, *hello.* "Great to see you," said Father. I kicked off my shoes and followed him into the living room, just as I'd done so many times, there were practically tracks in the carpet. From the door to the sofa, I'd taken that path so many times, crossed that floor for over twenty years, different feet, different versions of myself, all heights, all ages, and in all moods I'd walked about on these floors, worn the parquet floor in the living room, and now we would sit together again. Father went over to the chair beneath the window, he always sat in that chair, Father's chair, this was a house of routines, rituals. Mother was in the kitchen, as usual, she always had to come *out* of the kitchen as though by chance, *ah, but how lovely!* As though she hadn't known anybody was coming to visit. Mother would always disappear into the kitchen as the front door opened, and then come out as I settled in the living room, rubbing her hands together as though brushing off flour, or something that could dirty the guest, although she'd only been standing out there waiting, it was the custom.

This is Mother.

This is Father.

This is us.
Family.

I asked how things were going, at work, mother worked with kids with behavioral problems, in town, a job she'd begun when I'd finished elementary school, I often wondered whether she'd started it because of me, but I never asked. Did I have behavioral problems? No more than anybody else, I assumed. But still. Mother. And the children. The kid who's incapable of sitting still in class, who wanders restlessly about the classroom until being sent into the hallway, an unruly youngster, and ten minutes later the teacher goes out to fetch him, it's almost always a boy, he's run off, of course, he's run off to the forest, or back home or into town. Eight years old and impossible to do a thing with, and rather resignedly the teacher (although she'd hoped for this—that he'd go off) re-enters the classroom, and the pupils ask where he is, and she: *Quiet now, let's concentrate shall we, all right?* And I thought how he'd be on his way up to the forest behind the school, the big forest that lies just behind the school, the one the other kids never go into, because they've been warned so often about all the dreadful things in there, the drug addicts, rapists, ghosts, heaven above knows, but this is where they gather, the kids who've been thrown out into the hallway, the problem cases from all the city's schools, they meet here in this big forest like Robin Hood and his merry men, and they draw plans up on the forest floor, plan their tactics, make raids on the extra studious, and plan their actions in detail, water bombs and rotten tomatoes, school bags to be filled with water, or perhaps nothing of the kind, they plan how to survive a school that isn't designed for them, for their capacity, for minds that are never at rest.

"And work? Is it going well?" I asked mother.

"Busy. Very busy."

And sooner or later these kids are found in the forest, smoked out of their holes, junior school's Vietcong, and by the time they're handed over to the school, they've more or less given up, and they're placed behind a dividing screen in the classroom, so as not to be seen, so other kids won't be disturbed by their existence, and sooner or later the screen topples again, in the middle of a class, in the middle of a test, and they're thrown out all over again, out into the hallway, to roam again before anybody asks them to come back in. And this time they don't return.

"So many kids have a difficult time, Mattias. So awfully many."

"Yes," I say.

"They've got almost nothing. And their parents, yes, they, well, they're practically absent. They, well, most of them care, it's not that, most of them do care about their children, they just can't make things work. Things just seem to go wrong for them. Their children slip between their fingers. You've been lucky, haven't you? To have parents that took good care, don't you think?" Mother wanted reassurance. It was all part and parcel of my visit.

"Yes," I said. "I was very lucky." And I was.

I never wandered restlessly around the classroom, tugged girls' hair or suddenly issued guttural noises in the middle of class, I was where I should be, I didn't hang around on the ropes in the gym on a Tuesday and Friday, and I was never put behind the dividing screen.

I didn't need that.

Nobody noticed me anyway.

Mother rattled the cups and saucers: "More coffee?"

"Yes, please. It's great coffee."

Father looked out of the window. It was almost summer.

"You know," said mother, trying to get the conversation going again, back onto her job so that we'd have something to talk about. "We should have had people like you on the job."

"Oh?"

"You've always been so conscientious, from your first day at school. I remember the first day you came back with homework, I think you'd been given the task of making knots, can that be right? A cardboard bunny, with holes in its shoes, and thread pulled through the holes. You sat right there at the dining table," she said, pointing, "all afternoon you sat there and knotted and knotted. Until in the end the thread was so worn out it snapped. I had to give you a new one." Mother laughed, looked at me. "And then you thought you were a super hero, do you remember that?"

"No," I said. "Did I?"

"Yes, and you had piles of those magazines. What were they called?" she asked into the air, toward father, but finding the words herself: "*Superman Comics*. What happened to them, by the way? All those comics? You had so many."

I drank my coffee, let her talk, thought about why I'd liked them so much as a kid, the comics that I'd collected for so long. Batman. Superman. Spider-Man—THEY all did good deeds, incognito. Turned up when they were needed. Held the world together. The city's caretakers. Who didn't leave so much as a calling card. They never asked for anything in return, no reward, no public recognition. They just had a job to do.

"They're probably up in the loft, with all the others. I could get them out one day if you want to look at them, I don't know."

"You really don't need to," I answered.

"No, it's probably not important."

Pause.

"Yes, you should have worked at our place, Mattias. The children up there could do with a super hero."

"We probably all could," I said.

"Yes, I suppose we could."

Father turned toward us in his chair.

"Yes, they were good comics," he says.

"Hmm?"

"The Superman comics."

"Yes, they were," I answered.

"And then, he—Superman—yes, he was allergic to that stuff, that robbed him of his strength. What was it? Some crystal?"

"Kryptonite."

"Oh yes, of course. Kryptonite. That was it."

Crossword. Coffee. Conversation. Home. But I no longer belonged. Like revisiting an old elementary school, you sit at an empty desk in a classroom, knees banging into the low tabletop, and you can't quite take part in what's going on around you, the posters you once pinned on the corkboard have long since been taken down, your homework is already complete.

We talked about the nursery, we talked about Helle, and we talked about what we'd do in the summer, Mother and Father were going to France, Father had a brother out there, in Saint-Lô, he'd lived down there for six or seven years now, and father had finally decided that he should pay him a visit.

Father didn't like traveling, he was the only one in our little family who'd rather stay in one place, and Mother frequently went off with friends instead. There were still two months before they'd go, D-Day, but I knew Father was already regretting it. He counted the days, trying to convince himself that things would be fine, they'd be down there for almost three weeks. Father's tactic would be to calculate the days that were left, 18 days, he'd subtract as the days passed, waiting to be discharged, 16 days left, 10 days, 10 more nights in a strange bed and he'd be home again, and he'd think like that for the first week, no matter how pleasant it was, it didn't depend on that, it was the longing for everything at home that held him back. He would sit by the Normandy coast and automatically give everything back home a value he didn't know it had. He would miss his house, his car, the garden fence, the grass, he would miss the fifteen-inch hole in the asphalt of Rogalandsgaten on the way to work. But after a week, or thereabouts, these things would lose their hold on him and he'd forget that he missed his home, phase two, Father slips into French society and practically clings to the concrete of Charles de Gaulle Airport outside Paris, because he doesn't want to go home. Father. My father.

And me?

Where was I going?

"I'm going to the Faroe Islands," I said.

"The Faroe Islands?" says Father.

"The Faroe Islands?" says Mother. "Well, we've never been there."

Father: "What are you going to do there?"

I told them who, what, where, and that Helle was coming too, of course Helle was coming too, if she could get the time off, it was hard to get everything to fit into her work schedule, but she'd probably manage, I said, hard to get the pieces of the puzzle to fit, everybody in the office always wanted to go at the same time.

"No, that's right, it's not easy," said Father.

"There's always got to be somebody home," I said. "Or it just doesn't work."

"Quite," he answered, turning in his chair.

"More coffee?" Mother was already half way up from the sofa.

"No thanks," I said.

She sat down again. Hands in lap.

"And Helle?" asked Mother.

"What about her?"

"Well, where is she today?"

"She was going out with a friend."

"Oh, I see. She's always had so many friends," said Mother, she looked at me, then down.

"Yes."

"One can have many friends, but few good friends. Best friends. That's what I've always said."

"Very true," said Father. He didn't have any friends anymore. Just colleagues. And I reflected on all the people that missed out on him.

And so we sat there fumbling after each other, none of us knowing quite how to grasp the conversation, Father straightened his glasses and

Mother brushed some nonexistent crumbs from a corner of the table-cloth. I rubbed my fingers against my temples.

"Have a bun," said mother lifting the plate for me and I took a sweet bun, dug a little hole in it with my teaspoon, filled the hole with strawberry jam and tried to close the opening by pressing the bun together between my index finger and thumb, that's how buns were best, if you hid the jam and forgot it, imagined that the strawberry jam was just a natural part of the bun. But my mouth was parched.

"Maybe I could have a drop of coffee after all?" I asked Mother.

"Yes, of course," she answered, getting up and padding out to the kitchen to set the process in action.

Father and me in the living room. Searching for something to say. As always. We had so much to tell each other, we just never knew where to start.

Father gestured toward the floor. "Yes, we've just had the parquet polished, but you knew that already."

"Looks good," I said.

"Yes, we're very pleased." He leaned out of his chair, stroked the smooth floor. "Yes."

"And are things okay at work? Nobody's sunk their car to the bottom of a deserted lake and demanded insurance money?"

"Yes . . . well no, there's not much of that sort of thing really." Pause. "What did you really do with those Superman comics?"

"I sold them at the second-hand store. Bought that moon globe with the money. The one with the light inside."

He gave me a knowing glance.

"Thought so."

"Nothing lasts forever," I said.

"You'd have been a good super hero."

"I did the best I could. But I was scared of flying."

Then mother returned with the coffee and sat down, filled the cups. Coffee steaming on the table.

So the cups rattled and the teaspoons scraped against the dessert plates, and the buns were filled with jam again, were closed and lifted to our mouths that were finally talking together as they should, a proper family, and I was lucky, I had such lovely parents, good folk, and we sat in our sofa and chairs, and I knew this house, I'd grown up here, it smelled of us, of me, the scratches on the arm of one of the chairs had been made by me, ten years ago, minimum, perhaps twenty, couldn't remember how it had happened, but I knew it was me that had done it, and that it was all right, I knew that the little dent in the parquet near the fireplace was from the Christmas when one of the logs had fallen out of the fire, we'd been sitting at the other end of the room eating our dinner, our backs to it, nobody noticed it before it started burning quietly on the floor behind us, the smoke rose and met the ceiling, crept toward us and our dinner, and even though the parquet had been recently sanded, there was still a dent there, the traces of us, and up on the second floor was my room, as I'd left it ten or twelve years ago, more or less, they'd barely done anything, put a drying rack in there perhaps, a computer they never used anyway, but it was still my room, and I didn't need to go up there to know how it looked, little had changed, the same ugly curtains at both windows, I'd whined my way into getting them as a fourteen-year-old, a desperate attempt to show Mother I'd begun to understand such things, they were totally useless, of course, nightmare inducing. And the old red down comforter, narrow and thin that used to fall out of its cover, before I got the big warm light blue bedspread one Christmas, the one that was still on the bed with its two used bedside tables at the foot, the creaky steps on the staircase down to the kitchen, Father who always coughed twice in the morning as he came downstairs, he probably still did, Mother outside hanging the washing out, all through the summer, the forest behind the house, Byhaugen a great place in late summer to drink beer, in the winter it looked like Bastogne and as kids we'd dig ourselves in and play soldiers. I lost one of my favorite guns somewhere or other in the forest there, an almost perfect replica of an M1 rifle, bought in Majorca at the end of the seventies. It disappeared as war spoils after one of the greatest battles in Byhaugs Forest in the winter of 1979, I went out with Father several days in a row to look for it, but found nothing, it was snowed under and disappeared, and by the time the Spring came it was forgotten, or I felt too old to go and look for it. I wish I could say I'd found it years later, that I'd tripped over it one day on a walk through the trees and dense undergrowth, but I never did, it was gone forever in the chaos of that afternoon, lost in battle, like so many of the things we don't need, but that we mourn when they disappear, because everything that's ever been, will be mourned, default-mode, more or less.

When Spring arrived and peace finally came to the forest, my gaze had already turned upward, I'd been given a book for Christmas about the moon landing, I'd never thought about it before, it was then I realized that I'd been born on the same night as the *Eagle*, *Apollo 11*'s landing module, had landed in the Sea of Tranquility, on the front side of the moon. Father was still glum sometimes over the fact he'd missed the TV coverage that night, sitting in the hospital with Mother, he'd managed to argue his way into being present for the entire birth, I don't know how, but he wasn't sent out, stayed with Mother throughout, while one of the nurses ran in and out of the birthing room, there was a TV set out in the corridor, she kept them updated about what was going on up above, out in space, for hour after hour there was scarcely anything to be seen, just blackness almost, until eventually this was replaced by a gray mass. Bad noise quality, pictures, crackling. Father bit his nails to the knuckles, pale faced when the nurse came in one last time, she stopped just inside the door, without closing it behind her, Mother and Father could hear the TV outside in the corridor.
Contact light.
Shutdown.
Okay, engine stop.
The midwife looked at mother, straight at her.
ACA—out of detent.

Mother looked back.

Pushed.

Mode control both auto. Descent engine command override—OFF.

Father is about to faint, has to grip the stainless steel table beside him, doesn't know where to look, should he stay, help Mother through the final lap. Should he go out into the hallway, watch the moment he's waited for, for years? This is before the age of rewind, it will happen now, then it will be gone.

Engine arm—OFF.

Father stands there in the middle of the room.

Mother screams.

We copy you down Eagle.

And Mother sends the astronauts to Hell. She has enough to think about.

Father can't decide whether to stay or go, he's in a whirl, looks at Mother, looks out into the corridor.

Houston, uh . . . Tranquility Base here, the Eagle has landed.

His face grows paler and paler, sweat runs, his eyes sting. Noise from the TV out in the hallway, patients and nurses drawing breath, exchanging hugs.

Roger Twank . . . Tranquility, we copy you on the ground, you got a bunch of guys about to turn blue, we're breathing again, thanks a lot.

And then Father drops to the floor. Father faints in the middle of the room, lands with a quiet thump.

Thank you.

Soon Father opens his eyes, sees two nurses far above him.

You're looking good here.

He pulls himself together, sits up, and the two nurses take him under the arm, help him up and sit him in a chair, push him over to Mother, he takes her hand, and Mother screams, Mother gives birth, Father squeezes her hand and the midwife gets ready to catch.

Okay, we're going to be busy for a moment.

It was Christmas 1978 when I got my very first book about the moon, sat absorbed from Christmas to New Year, studying the pictures, the maps. It was then I began collecting the books, hunting for them in bookstores, junk stores, I had to read everything, wanted to know everything. And it was in the spring of 1979 that I decided to vanish into the commotion out there, to be number two, a person who made himself useful instead of trying to stand out, who did the job he was asked to do. But, of course, it's only in retrospect I think that, that it started then, an attempt to pinpoint the exact beginning of a life. Only in fiction, in films and novels can we fix a precise moment of change. In reality choices sneak up, thoughts develop bit by bit, and it was perhaps at some time during this first year at middle school that I made an active decision not to be seen. Eventually some people began to see me as crazy, looking down on me as I went past, or ignoring me completely. Not that it bothered me. At least I got left in peace.

The more friends you collect, the more funerals you'll probably have to attend.

The more people there'll be to miss when they go.

The more you put yourself forward, the more stones people can throw at you.

But the person who is alone disappoints only himself.

Those were my thoughts.

Our coffee cups were empty, just a couple of sweet buns left on the plate, and I was full, had been for ages, Mother and Father were starting to look tired, maybe it was time to go home, lots to do at work next morning, plants to be potted, deliveries to be made, *I love you, Happy Birthday, Sorry for yesterday. Thank you for all your support in this difficult time, It can't rain every day,* so much to organize, and there were still almost three months before the summer replacement staff would come and take over the whole nursery.

I said *well, I suppose I ought to be getting home now,* and Mother said, *yes, it was lovely to see you,* and *it's always nice having you around,* said Father as we went out into the hallway, and hugged, looked like a picture from an IKEA catalogue, got the urge to buy new furniture, in light colors.

I went out to the car, drove home through downtown Stavanger, it had started raining again and the last of the Mohicans still sat on Hansen Corner, soaked to the skin despite being under umbrellas, because in Stavanger it rains sideways, and they held their hands protectively over their beer glasses, sooner or later they'd have to realize that summer wasn't on its way this time either, not yet, despite it seeming so perfect earlier today, and it would be as miserable as snow in April, you just had to accept it, that's how it was, but one day, in a few months, one can always hope for good weather.

I sat up late into the night, watched *Friends* on TV2, one of their increasingly worn attempts at rescuing Tuesdays from obscurity, ate porridge, drank water, waited for Helle to get home. But as usual she had more staying power than me, was more capable of holding out, and I was already asleep by the time she got home, in the morning I got up before her, didn't want to wake her, got dressed and went to work, and when I got back she'd nearly always have dropped by the apartment, left a note, before going out again, I wondered if I should book an appointment, but I never got myself on the list, so we met sporadically and by chance in the bedroom, at the kitchen table, and she'd say *it's busy at work,* she'd complain, *there's so much to do,* and I'd hug her tightly, say it was okay, *it'll be fine, we'll come through this,* I'd say, it felt like pushing an elephant upstairs, and I loved her, wanted her to be home more, oftener, all the time even, the way it had been in the beginning, so long ago, so many years, and she'd say *yes, I know, it's not easy,* she'd say, *there's always so much to do,* and I'd say it was fine, *I'm glad you've found something to do,* I'd say, *that's how it is in my industry,* she'd say, and she'd talk about the advertising industry, one day advertising new chocolates, chips, bigger bags, more for your money, the fat of the land, and the next day advertising slimming products, good conscience in a carton for 44,90 krone at REMA 1000, or trashy music, promoted on TV, saucepan sets nobody needed, pans with cancer-causing Teflon made for next to nothing in Indonesia, and when the cancer is discovered three years later, the pan's been scrapped long ago and replaced with something new, and nobody knows about the little bits of Teflon that flaked off it each time it was used, that crept into the food, that spread around the organism, through the lymphatic system, cell seizures, but nobody blames the cheap saucepan sets, because this week Nicorette is on special offer, the campaign is ready, and next week the big order for a double-page advertisement for Prince cigarettes will bring massive profits, as long as it's finished on time, but it's not easy, usually isn't, there's so much to attend to and the Teflon pans say nothing.

And that was how the days leaped over the cliff edge in flocks, turning into weeks that nobody could stop, until the months vanished into a sunset over wistful calendar horses, and I arrived at the nursery early almost every day, these were the best months, April, May, June, when it grew warmer and warmer with each day, I could feel it, the air warmed, grew drier, despite it raining almost every day, nonstop, and the soil was no longer so cold against my fingers when I put my hands down into it, making space for what I planted.

And I was doing just that, with one index finger poked into the only potted plant we had in our apartment, when the phone rang, one afternoon in June, and I lifted the receiver with one hand while I continued to stir the compost with the other.

"Hello."

"Hi, how's things?" It was Jørn, talking on his cell, bad line.

"Yeah, things are fine," I answered.

"Any plans for tonight, eh?"

"No ... well ... no, I don't think so," I said, wondering whether Helle would be home this evening or not.

"Want to go to Cement?"

"Hmm, I don't know ..."

"Well? It is pretty good at Cement, isn't it?"

"Yeah, yeah ... sure ... it's just ..."

"What?"

We usually went to Cement, Jørn and I. Actually, I liked it, there'd even been a band there one night three years ago with the striking name The Buzz Aldrin Band. But I didn't want to go tonight. This really wasn't the day to meet anybody I recognized, so I suggested a more divey place, somewhere I thought there wouldn't be many people.

"How about Alexander tonight?" I said.

"Alexander, are you serious?"

"Yeah?"

Jørn hemmed and hawed, wasn't really keen, but then changed his mind, without questioning why I wanted to go there, of all places, probably hadn't been there for twelve years.

"Okay. In an hour?"

"Okay."

I tried to call Helle, but her cell was switched off, so I left a note on the kitchen table saying where I was, and that I'd be really happy if she dropped by. *Love you. Mattias.*

But Helle didn't come, and Jørn came twenty minutes late. I was on my second beer, sitting at a table, seating for five, but the bar was half-full at best, a mammoth could have marched through the room without knocking anything over, and for a minute I sat staring at the door in anticipation of something big tumbling in, but the only thing that came in was one of the old alkies, looking as though he'd been steam-cleaned, and then been put through the tumble drier a couple of times, too small for himself, he carried his beer in both hands from the bar, looked around for a place to sit before he shuffled over to my table, sat opposite me and put his beer on the table in front of him, his head scarcely came over the tabletop.

"I'm a sailor," his voice peeped from under the table.

I really didn't want this. Not one bit, so I looked the other way, looked at the clock, tried to give the impression I was waiting for someone.

"I'm a sailor," he repeated.

I said nothing. Looked at the clock.

"I'm a sailor," he said, like a broken record.

"Ship ahoy!" I answered.

"SHIP AHOY! SHIP AHOY!" he yelled back, getting no response, perhaps he was too far out at sea, or perhaps he just didn't have coverage yet.

"Sure thing," I said.

"I'm a sailor," he said, his repertoire looking pretty limited.

"Are you a sailor? Wow, I'd never have thought it."

"I've been a sailor for ... forty years. And fifty years," he snuffled.

"That's a long time, weren't you ever seasick?"

"Seasick ... Hah! No ... No. Sailor. America ... Afir ... Africa, Asia ... America." Then he launched into some shanty or other about Singapore and the girls down there, I'd heard it all before, every alcoholic in this town had been to sea, they'd all been to Singapore and they were all hell bent on singing that song the minute they got your attention, that was just how it was, and he was halfway through the third verse, thumping the beat with his beer on the table so it went splashing all over the place, when the barman walked over to us, he lifted the mini-man up by his collar, pried his fingers from his glass and dragged him outside, it took awhile, despite the barman clearly having done this before, and the sailor managed a whole verse more before disappearing out the door. The barman came back, wiped the beer up from the other side of the table and looked at me.

"A sailor," I said. "Obviously been through some rough times in Singapore."

"They always have," answered the barman.

Jørn arrived, bought a beer at the bar, came and sat with me, and I told him I didn't know where Helle was.

"The Faroe Islands are officially in the bag now," said Jørn. "Got the final phone calls today from Tórshavn. Perkleiva's top of the bill at the Ólavsøkan Festival."

"Great," I answered. "Fantastic."

"I've booked the tickets now too, we'll take the boat on Tuesday, July 27, Smyril Line, from Bergen via Shetland."

I didn't like boats. I didn't like this. I didn't like the Atlantic Ocean. I liked solid ground.

"How long will it take? The boat?"

"Er . . . lets see." Jørn rummaged in his bag and pulled out a little notebook.

"Twenty-four or twenty-five hours. Around ten hours to Shetland."

"Wouldn't the plane be better?"

"It's damn expensive to fly over, costs almost as much as to New York. Besides we've got so much equipment to take. But chill, Mattias, you'll get a compartment and stuff, there's no stress, really. They wouldn't have boats going over if the weather was totally impossible out there. Remember, things have changed a bit since the America Boat. It'll be fucking great. Just imagine, a booze cruise to the Faroes, with a Bulgarian-Faroese band and some old seadog at the bar."

I wasn't sure whether to believe him.

So I said: "Hmm, perhaps."

"And it'll all be free, okay? The organizers are covering our travel and everything. We just have to sit in the car, and hey presto we're in Bergen, hey presto we're on the boat, hey presto we're off to the Faroes. Have you talked to Helle? Is she coming, or what?"

"I don't really know, she hasn't said anything, I don't think she's managed to get things sorted out yet," I said, thinking I ought to talk to her as soon as possible.

"It would be great if you could ask her and get back to me tomorrow.

For bookings and everything. And I've got to find out if the organizers are willing to cover travel expenses for another person."

"Yeah," I said. "But that's not a problem, Helle and I can easily split the cost of her ticket."

"I'll see what I can do, but it's fine. I'm really looking forward to it."

"Me too," I lied, thinking of the boat and already dreading it.

Then we discussed how early we needed to leave Stavanger to catch the ferry from Bergen at three, about who had a car and who'd drive, we bought another beer, laid plans, talked about what the Faroe Islands were like, why we hadn't ever been there before, and we didn't really know why, had no idea, but we'd never thought of going, drank beer and talked about how fantastic Perkleiva was, up there with the very best recent bands, it was going to be great, a great concert, the Faroe Islands, we bought another beer, me and Jørn in Alexander, June 1999, and I strolled back to Storhaug that same night, and this time it was Helle who was asleep when I came in the bedroom, lay noiselessly at her side, didn't sleep, tried to be all heart, to convince myself we were okay.

I'd been together with Helle for twelve and a half years. Four thousand and fifty-nine days. 109,416 hours. Six and a half million minutes. 6,564,960 in figures. A long time. A very long time. In half a year we would enter the third decade in which I'd loved her. But she still didn't want to get married. Didn't believe it would work. I remember the first time I plucked up the courage, we were twenty-five, midsummer's eve up at Våland's Tower, Våland Forest all around us, a view all the way to the center of the city and the surrounding areas, we stood with our arms around each other, it was cold and we were wearing warm clothes, saw the bonfires burning here and there outside town, I turned, had a slight cold, stood there sniffing, not very romantic maybe, but I remember I stood behind Helle, held around her and looked at her, looked at that short, blond hair of hers, the ugly little jacket she always used during cold snaps in the summer, the jacket I was nonetheless fond of, and she stood in front of me, little Helle, letting me hold her as she tossed her head this way and that, humming a song in her head, and suddenly I thought that I felt so good it was hard to bear. There were no more compliments left to give her, it was now or never, my hands went clammy at the thought, I went weak at the knees, but I let go of her, stood in front of her, readied myself, but couldn't do it, the words lodged in the middle of my mouth, a traffic jam, Helle wondered what the problem was: "Nothing," I said, "I just need the bathroom." I stood and pissed against a tree in Våland Forest, looked up at the plateau where everybody was standing, saw Helle among them, looking much as she had at the fancy dress ball, once in a galaxy far, far away, and I had a piece of paper in my pocket, a pen, everything I needed, and I wrote: *Will you marry me?* Then, when I came back up, I slipped the note into her jacket pocket, didn't mention it, but it felt good, even though she didn't find it until the following day, I think, at least she didn't say anything about it, we went out for a few beers, I waited and waited, but she behaved as though nothing had happened, I sweated, had bags under my eyes, problems concentrating, but didn't want to ask, found a note from her in my pocket when I got back to my apartment that night, felt the paper through the padding of my jacket, unfolded it carefully, read it slowly, not that that was possible: *Ask me again another time,* it said. And I did, every other year maybe, it went almost without a hitch in the end, but she wasn't quite convinced, it would make her old, she thought, and I said *that's fine, we can come back to it,* I said, but at least I got her to move in with me, which was when we got the apartment in Storhaug, the rooms we lived in now, I wanted children, but she didn't have time, advertising wasn't the profession for maternity leave, so I waited, grew a beard, shaved it off and waited some more.

We walked a lot in those first years, nearly every day. It was just about all we did. We walked through the entire city, wore out our sneakers in summer and covered the city step by step in the snow in winter, walked and talked, I got to know her, and she was the most beautiful person I'd ever seen, to my eyes at least, she peeled oranges with one hand, could cycle without holding the handlebars, couldn't blow Hubba Bubba bubbles, never achieved it, couldn't curl her tongue in her mouth, but could bend her fingers almost all the way back, played the piano, wasn't brilliant, danced ballet and had more success with that, I was dragged to performances, sat watching as she danced across stage, back and forth, didn't quite get her fascination for it, but she looked sweet enough, up on her toes, and I put plasters on her toenails and dried her tears after performances, went around to her place on Sundays, where her father, the policeman, made Sunday lunch, a good man, a single arm-of-the-law dad, after he separated from her mother, she moved to the Netherlands later, found another policeman over there, and more or less disappeared from the picture, apart from the Christmas cards she sent to Helle every year, a picture of herself wearing a Father Christmas hat, equally tragic every Advent.

And the summers spent at her father's cabin in Sørland, me sitting on the jetty, feet in the water, and Helle swimming around out there, diving to the bottom, brown legs sticking up for an instant before they disappeared beneath the surface and her face came up again, an old bicycle wheel or something else in her hands that she'd snatched up from the bottom, old junk she wanted to bring back ashore, to clean and fix, to hang on the cottage wall, in the end a fine collection of bicycle wheels that nobody knew what to do with lay in the shed at the back of the cabin.

And I remember the presents she gave me, she was always so clever with presents, always got it right, even when I didn't know what I wanted. She liked Jørn and Roar from the first moment, and she had her own girlfriends, so many of them, I always had problems remembering who was who, and they adored her. Helle, who I loved for the thirteenth year and who was almost never home, who was asleep when

I came, who was slowly but surely letting me go, she was being dragged away by gravity and I didn't know what to do.

I'd just come in the door, Helle walked toward me, gave me a hug, seemed happier than usual, smiled, said she'd talked with Nina, she'd just rung, wanted us to go on a trip with them. On Saturday. *This Saturday?* I asked. And she said *yes, this Saturday*.

Which was why I sat by the quay in Stavanger that Saturday, waiting to take the boat out to Lysefjorden, out to Flørli Powerstation, we'd walk up to Kjeragbolten from that side, it was Jørn's idea in fact, an unusual choice, but still, that was what we were going to do, and I stood waiting for the boat to come into the fjord, to moor at the express boat terminal, and Helle stood some way behind me, trying to ring one of the others, Claus, perhaps, he'd still not arrived, and we began to get worried, he was always late, and the boat was coming into view way out in the fjord. I bent down automatically, lifted my backpack, put it on, got ready, I liked to be out there early, I didn't like boats, I didn't like being on water. I like to be prepared. I just wanted it to stand still. Helle got through to Claus, he wasn't far and he came around the corner at that instant and they both came off the telephone.

There were six of us. *Friends.* Going on an outing. It was a Saturday in early July, and I wasn't altogether keen on it, but Helle wanted to go, and I came along. And here I was. A wind was blowing. There would be waves. I didn't want to go, but I'd said yes. Service with a smile.

There weren't so many waves after all, and it was good to be out, noticed it, as we stood on deck, in the light rain, anoraks done up tightly, Helle in my arms, Claus beside us. Claus had taken the day off, was beginning to get nervous at home, circling his pregnant girlfriend, waiting to fling himself in the car at any moment, to drive to the hospital, even though there were three weeks still before the birth. He stood fumbling now with an old Nagra, recording vacation sound effects, the boat noises and humming of the motor, that he intended to mix and use as backing to one of Perkleiva's tracks. And Jørn and Nina were there. Nina was pregnant too, due in January, and they looked good together, I thought. Real Kodak people. Things weren't good between Helle and me. We thought things were fine, but it wasn't true. Didn't know what it was, but there was something there, between us, a lump that didn't melt away when one squeezed it, but just grew bigger, like a muscle infection. I thought of Steve Martin. I thought of my favorite film, *L.A. Story: Let us just say I was deeply unhappy, but I didn't know it, because I was so happy all the time.* That was how it was.

But right now we pretended we loved each other, and I put my arms around Helle on the deck, gripped her around the waist mechanically, my mind elsewhere. Let the games commence. All you need is love.

Actually I'd always loved traveling, taking trips. Unlike father who gripped the chair arm tight, and clung to the sofa cushions and *didn't, didn't want to*, going out into the world was something I'd generally loved. Jørn and I had traveled around Europe a lot at the end of the eighties, early nineties, interrail, we'd gone by train from Denmark, across Poland, West Germany, France, Benelux, and Italy, we'd taken six months off, stood on the platform in Bari, Southern Italy, in the spring of 1992, looked out toward Yugoslavia, debated at length over whether to take the ferry over to Dubrovnik and go into Mostar, Sarajevo, we'd both been to Dubrovnik when we were small, seaside holidays in the seventies, but now? Now, it wasn't sure that we'd get ever out again, if we went in, Bosnia-Herzegovina had declared independence, it might explode at any moment, but Jørn was convinced nothing would happen in Sarajevo, he'd read up about it, the town's inhabitants were from all camps, Bosnian Muslims and Serbs, Croatians, no, he was convinced Sarajevo would be a refuge, but I wasn't so sure, I got him to wait a couple of days and we hung around in Bari, sat on the beach, waiting to see how things turned out, and then the country was blocked from all directions, so we decided to go through Spain instead, Gibraltar, the boat over to Tangiers, Morocco, Jørn wanted to see Casablanca to look for his Ilsa Lund, I wanted to go into the desert, we did both, milled around in Morocco with neither maps nor plans, with youthful arrogance and taking an almost continuous train journey back through the whole of Europe, the night train, only waking up in our bunks when we arrived in cities and light flooded through the curtains of our compartment, caught enough trains for a whole lifetime in those six months, so in the years that followed we flew, went to Asia, Vietnam, Japan, Tokyo, USA, New York, Los Angeles, disagreed regularly, met people on their home turf, was Uncle Traveling Mac, the globetrotter, I just wanted to blend in, I wanted to walk down Fifth Avenue without arousing interest, dash through Shinjuku in Tokyo on a Friday as one of the millions, not as a tourist, but somebody who knew the city, who had grown up there, I wanted to slip into the picture, much easier in New York than Tokyo, of course, but the attempt was always there, to become at one with the surroundings, without disturbing the lives that we trampled right into. Mine was a simple plan: I came, I saw, I disappeared. And I erased my traces as I went back up to the hotel from the beach.

The journey to Flørli was easier, the ferry came in alongside the dock at Flørli Powerstation, now closed down, a new and more modern station having been built inside the mountain and we were the only people to get off here, all the other tourists remained on the ferry as it pulled out again, photographing—click, click, click—their way in towards Lysebotn, making their necks stiff from staring thousands of feet up the mountain wall in the hope of catching a glimpse of the Pulpit, which they had already passed over an hour ago, the landmark announced over crackly loudspeakers in a thick, cooped-in local dialect.

We made our way up the path, up the mountain, a tough walk but manageable, and everyone kept going, Helle, Jørn, and Nina up at the front, me and Claus coming up behind, panting, I felt heavy and the sweat ran down my back, the rain had let up now and the sun blazed high above us and further behind Roar followed, forming the rear guard.

But it was fabulous when we finally reached the vast plateau, found a suitable spot and sat ourselves on the rocks, ate the packed lunches we'd brought, bread with cheese and salami, whatever we'd had on hand, fruit sodas in bottles and it was good to be here, amazingly good, not a soul for miles around and the plateau stretching thousands of feet in all directions, and we looked out over Lysefjorden, farther down the fjord, on the other side was the Pulpit, crammed full of people now probably, standing packed together to the edge, sardines on a mountaintop, about to tumble over the edge in the jostling, saw them in my mind's eye sailing down the side of the mountain, cameras in their hands.

Helle was talking to me more than she had for weeks, she seemed lighter, happier, even if she still seemed distant, and I thought maybe things had at last begun to lighten up for her at work, maybe she was getting some breathing space at last, so we might do things together again, go places, make love on the dining room table, if that's what it took, I was ready for anything, incredibly ready—and I had a really positive feeling about things, I felt it in my own mood, things were going well, I was in good form, truly, my step was lighter, I felt more athletic, talked more than usual, to Nina, to Claus, despite not knowing them that well, I was good company and I began to think things might not be so bad between Helle and I after all, all that was needed was a little time perhaps, and right now the whole summer lay before us.

It was no more than a ten or twenty minute walk from the plateau to Kjeragbolten, the great boulder that lies wedged fast between mountain walls, the perfect postcard view, blue writing on the back of a card; *Hi down there, today we were up on Kjeragbolten in Lysefjorden. The rock is wedged in between mountain walls, and when you stand on it, there's a nearly three-thousand-foot drop. And the rock's only two or three yards in diameter. Some day the rock will work its way loose, but today isn't the day! Everything's great. Say hi to everyone.* Claus was out on the rock right away, Nina took pictures of him, and then I had to take pictures of Jørn and Nina, as they stood there clinging to each other and swaying in the wind. I didn't want to go, it looked slippery, it was a long way down and I was sure my shoes were wet from the path leading down here, from the patches of snow that still lay on the ground here. But Helle wanted to, of course Helle wanted to go out onto the rock, *that's why we came all the way up here, wasn't it,* she said, *of course we're going out on the rock, come on,* she said, taking my arm and pulling me after her, I followed obediently, she led the way, lowered herself onto the block of rock, stretched her hand out to help me over. I clasped her firmly, holding on as hard as I could, and Jørn shouted out that he was going to take a picture of us, we had to face him, and we looked around at the camera, Helle turned slightly away, I kissed her on the neck, but she waved my hand away, laughing tensely, and I thought how much I loved her, twelve and a half years on and I was still in love, and this was a perfect moment for such things, so I whispered in her ear, I felt so assured, even my voice was firm, so while Jørn took pictures, while Nina and Claus stood watching us, I said, *I was wondering if you'd marry me?* And Helle's head jerks away, she looks at me, straight at me, and her face is tired, I can see that now, and tears begin to flow from her eyes and she says *No, Mattias,* and then, quietly and calmly, *I'm leaving you.* Then she looks down, looks away, and I know she means it.

Emergency liftoff.

Game over.

Before you get a chance to blink.

It takes approximately ten seconds before my pulse rate rises. Before I find it difficult to breathe. Before the nausea settles heavily in my stomach. I can't think what to say. Not a thing. Binary codes rush through my brain, tallying up all the reasons in the world for her leaving me, the prognosis for rescuing us from this. It doesn't look great. There's a burning behind my eyes. I feel so hot. I want to take my pullover off, but there's not the space to do it out here on the rock, there's hardly space for two people. I turn to go back. To the mountain. I bump into Helle, and automatically we both step back, and suddenly she loses her foothold, slips, and I have to grab hold of her arm to stop her falling, and there we are standing together once more, balancing on a rock. "None of the others know," she says and I look up, smiling falsely at Jørn who keeps on taking picture after picture, film I'll never develop.

My first impulse is just to step forward. To walk gently out over the edge. Fall nearly three thousand feet down, dragging her with me perhaps. That would be something, just to let myself lean out. The sensation of air rushing past my ears as I accelerate toward the maximum speed for falling bodies, to be mangled by the rocks on the beach below. It would take a week to clear me away. If they could find everything. Perhaps my head would come loose, roll into the fjord and be lost forever.

We were back on safe ground and Jørn passed the camera back to me, I took it, hung it around my neck. Helle told everyone that she had to find somewhere to pee and *Mattias, can you come and help me find somewhere?* I followed her up the path, listless, walking several feet behind her. I knew she didn't need to go to the toilet, I didn't have a thought in my head.

"Mattias," she said.

"Yes," I said, frustrated. "Yes?"

She drew a breath. She had big lungs. I had stopped breathing.

We had been together for nearly thirteen years. Six and a half million minutes. This was the last day. Day zero. She was scraping her boot in the gravel, an unpleasant sound, but I didn't ask her to stop, for fear she might come to a halt altogether, her entire machinery.

'I wanted . . ." she began, drew another breath, looked out across the landscape. I couldn't begin to comprehend what she found to look at out there. As far as I was concerned the whole landscape could just go to the devil, by express delivery. "I'd planned to tell you, this evening—tomorrow or this evening . . . after we'd gotten back home, because . . ."

"Because?"

More gravel scraping. Breathing. Tears. I had no idea what to say. Not a cloud in the sky.

Steve Martin.

"Because I wanted us to have one last good memory together," she said. "Things haven't been so good lately." She had a small nose, slightly turned up, a broad mouth, and thin lips.

Kodak moment. Or perhaps not.

"No," I say. Nothing more.

"I've fallen in love, Mattias."

"Oh?"

I fumbled with the camera in my hand. For a moment I pondered the idea of taking a picture right now, so as never to forget. Desertion at a height of three thousand feet.

"He . . ." She cleared her throat. "He's a bicycle courier, comes into work almost every day." I don't know why she's coming up with that piece of information precisely. I might have started to laugh, but didn't have it in me, my throat was filled with gravel, boulders.

"Okay," I said. "Have you . . . have you known him . . . long, or . . . ? I mean . . ."

Then she began to cry. A torrent streamed down her cheeks, down into the gravel, across the path, over the mountainside and down into the fjord. In truth it was me who ought to have cried. But I was unable, not with everyone watching. And the situation was absurd, I didn't know whether I should hold her or just go. Or whether I should make a TV series out of it and sell the rights, daytime soap for stay at home mums with flowery aprons.

I refused to acknowledge I was dead.

I was Donald Duck. I had run beyond the cliff edge. But I wasn't falling. Because I still hadn't looked down.

"One and a half years," she sniffed. She looked at me. "One and a half years, Mattias . . . I can't do anything about it." And then her voice filled with tears. It was hard to catch what she said, but it was something about how she'd dreaded telling me, how she'd waited, putting it off, that it felt like a huge relief when she'd finally decided to do it, to say it. She'd planned to tell me after we'd been on this trip, our last nice trip together. That was why she'd been more cheerful these last few days. She'd decided, she said, and she talked about the courier, about this person she'd had a relationship with for over a year, and I puzzled over who could play her on the TV series, but only made myself sad thinking about it. She had been sleeping with him for over a year, he'd been allowed to be with her, inside her, in our home, in our room perhaps, and I had no idea who he was. A courier. Don't shoot the messenger, I thought. He was called Mats, that was what she said, she talked about Mats, a devil on the bicycle, for sure, and Mats was more open, Mats went out more, Mats wasn't frightened of the world, Mats wanted to be seen in the world, and she was so sorry, and she was so little as she stood up there on the mountain, snot under her nose and that windbreaker that was far too big that her father had bought, those little hands and I loved her more than I should. I tried to mobilize some feeling or other against Mats out there, but couldn't, because I didn't know who he was, and he might be the nicest person, impossible to tell. Helle cried. I wanted to hold her, wanted to hug her, but it was no longer allowed, because she'd said the reverse password, the doors were closing and there were no more stations on that line. I had to get off here, now, at the top of Norway, among the most beautiful mountains ever, worn down and polished into rounded molars by the ice that was now bottled and sold back to us as mineral water for the people with the world's cleanest tap water. And I'd just found equilibrium, but now the balance was melting away under the sun in June on that mountain and I thought about a show I'd seen the week before, on Swedish TV:

An optimistic attitude to life is more important today than ever.

Yes, I thought.

Objectively speaking the contents of the bottle do not change whether it is half full or half empty, but subjectively the two views are worlds apart.

Sure.

Tell yourself:

Today I feel good.

Today there is nothing that can irritate me or get me out of "balance."

I thought: No.

I thought: No.

I thought: What do I do now?

I thought: what the fucking fuck . . .

And Helle wanted to tell me more. And I didn't want to hear. Incapable of telling her to shut up. So she said all she had to say. Told me about Mats, that she'd missed me so badly, that I'd disappeared for her in the last few years, and I said: "Do you see me now?"

"Yes," she said.

"I'm not invisible anymore," I said.

"No."

I gathered my courage. I took a chance, A new ice age might come at any moment.

"Are you sure? You don't want to wait, maybe?" I asked. "Think it over. I can wait."

"This isn't going to pass," she said quietly. "This isn't some kind of illness I've caught."

Yes it is an illness you've caught. And you can't see it yourself, I thought.

"I'm terribly in love with you."

More than I ought to be, more than you'll ever know.

"I know. Thank you."

"*All I know is, on the day your plane was to leave, if I had the power, I would turn the winds around. I would roll in the fog. I would bring in storms. I would change the polarity of the earth so compasses couldn't work. So your plane couldn't take off.'* Like in *L.A. Story.*"

"But you can't do any of those things."

"No."

I asked if she remembered it, us watching *L.A. Story*, but she didn't answer. She looked away, looked out into the Norwegian landscape and I might have wished I could sing now, that I could have sung her back. I wished I was somewhere different. Anywhere. With the Foreign Legion. On the Faroe Islands. Florida. Because who the fuck will want to comfort Toffle. Nobody.

"We shared some beautiful times," I said, looking at her.

Then I turned. I left her on the plateau, went down to the others, fetched my backpack, put it back on. Helle followed after me down the path, her eyes were red, she said she didn't feel very well, and there was barely a sound between us on the way back, in the three hours it took to walk down to the energy station at Flørli where we waited for the boat. The boat that would take another three hours to Stavanger. We took a taxi home. Helle and I. She put her backpack down in the hall. Changed clothes. Packed. A little suitcase. Stood outside in the hall, put her shoes back on. Suitcase in hand. My little Paddington. Then she left. Drove to one of her girlfriends. And I hoped that Mats was a beautiful person, that he didn't know the sea is rising a centimeter each year, that the poles are melting all the time. That the earth could be wiped out by a single meteor if it crossed our path. If it was big enough. If nobody was looking after us.

And somewhere else, in South California, in a house built in the fifties, Buzz Aldrin hugged his second wife, Lois Driggs Cannon, the girl from Phoenix, Arizona, who he found in the end, got married to on Valentine's Day in 1988. Around them stood all six children from two marriages, together with the only grandchild so far, and the days are spent driving into the Pacific, skiing down the mountain slopes of Sun Valley, Idaho.

I stayed out in the afternoons after that. I made tracks between Jørn and Nina in Våland, Mother and Father in Kampen, home again to Storhaug in the evenings when I was sure Helle wasn't there anymore. Didn't come home before she'd been and gone. She wanted it that way. And every time I went upstairs and let myself into the apartment, it was a little emptier. She moved her things out, her furniture, making the world shrink and the rooms bigger.

I said nothing to Mother and Father. Just told them I was tired. Lay on the sofa. Father sat in the chair next to me, watching the news, drinking coffee, putting his cup solemnly back on the table between each gulp. Mother was worried I wasn't eating enough, stood in the kitchen and made food. She baked sweet buns and put the jam out, asked me now and then what the problem was, but I didn't want to talk, she made meals and put out the best tablecloths. I had no appetite. I tried, but wasn't hungry. I was nauseous and had to excuse myself, dashing into the bathroom, crouched in front of the toilet bowl, threw up those motherly dinners, until my throat was raw, threw up five or six times a day and thought about Helle. She emptied the flat. *I wanna be your dog*, but not like this, I was Laika shut in a capsule, traveling at 6,000 kilometers an hour around the earth, dying from lack of oxygen minute by minute, gasping for air on the bathroom floor, I found a towel in the cupboard, washed my face and went back into the living room. I lay on the sofa and Father said it would pass, *it always passes,* he said, and I stayed until they were going to bed, they followed me to the door.

"And Helle? We haven't seen her for a while?" asked Mother, and I said: "No."

"She'll turn up some time," said Father, and it could happen, you could never tell.

I went around to Jørn's some evenings after my parents had gone to bed. Jørn stayed up late, sat fiddling with his guitar and four-track recorder until the early hours. We sat in his living room. Watched TV. Didn't talk much. Watched all those late night shows. *M*A*S*H. Jake and the Fatman. Walker, Texas Ranger.* I'd told Jørn about the situation, he knew about Helle, how she'd begun to empty out the rooms. He'd asked me if I still wanted to come to the Faroe Islands. Yes, I'll come, I'd said, I was frightened of the boat trip over, but I said nothing about that. I said almost nothing at all. Jørn and Perkleiva had almost finished their first album, *Transatlantika*, he'd made a provisional mix and had played it for me several times, not bad, they made a great sound, it rattled along, I thought they might even make it, this could be big, and I caught myself smiling, happy that I wasn't a vocalist, that I wouldn't have to spend years crisscrossing over Norway, lugging gear in and out of vans, and then later on a larger scale, in and out of airports, through security control, baggage X-rays, delays, hotel rooms, sound checks, a traveling circus of sound. Almost everybody wants to become a star. But hardly anybody wants to be one. And did I? No way. Fever in the night. I dreamed things you don't want to know about.

Mother and Father left for Saint-Lô at the beginning of July, got off all right in the end. In fact I'd already started my vacation too, had the summer staff at the nursery, I'd shown them around, told them everything they needed to know about running the place, but since I had no idea what to fill my own time with, I'd ended up going into work as usual. Got up. Drove down at about six. Sat in the garden and waited. Waited for the others to come. Went through everything again with the temps, who were going in circles not knowing what they were doing, tying bouquets too tightly, cutting roses too high up the stem and wrapping flowers in crumpled paper.

The workload had reduced significantly in the last months. There was less and less to do. This was the year before the future began, and most people wanted to be on the safe side in what time was left. Didn't want expensive flowers that died when it mattered most. And shopping malls sold plastic and silk flowers for 49,90 kroner, half price, maximum five bouquets per household, or cheaper real flowers, roses, tulips in big quantities. The funeral market was more or less all we had left. I'd noticed a change in Karsten over the last weeks. There was something wrong with him. The bags under his eyes were getting bigger and bigger, the nursery was going badly, but there was nothing I could do. I continued packing flowers, made wreaths, but it was summer and hardly anybody died, they waited for the winter. The wreaths piled up in the staff room, dried and rotted away. Karsten came into work later and later. And I was there earlier and earlier. But it didn't help. And the auxiliary staff didn't know anything, they took long lunch breaks without anyone protesting. They'd finish here in three weeks anyway. Then they'd go off back to their studies. Student loans. Small bedsits in Stavanger, Bergen, Oslo and Trondhiem. Tromsø perhaps. Or perhaps they'd go abroad, because they had big plans, there was so much they had to do, studies were long, and jobs were few. There was only room at the top of the pyramid for one or two people. They needed credits, as many credits as possible. Time was short, they already were twenty years old, or twenty-five, and had just begun their studies, had messed around, tried everything. It was getting urgent now, they said, time was running out because one reached one's peak at twenty-seven. From then on everything would go in slow spirals downwards. One didn't get a new job after hitting forty, and on that last Monday, the day before I left, Karsten and I were the only ones left in the nursery. We stayed behind after the others had gone, Karsten had asked me to wait and I didn't have anywhere to rush to. I was packed already. Had been for days. It wasn't difficult to find my things in the apartment these days, it was almost empty, just a chair left, some boxes and a TV. Karsten poured coffee into two cups, squeezed the last drops evenly out into our cups and switched off the percolator. The red light went out, radio on in the background, more rain was forecast.

"Mattias," he said.

"Yes?"

"Things aren't working out."

"I know," I said, looking out of the window, there were almost no cars out there.

"I'm so sorry."

"It's not your fault."

"No. I ..."

"Don't think about it."

"I'll fill out the papers this evening, and then I'll be filing for bankruptcy. It can't go on."

"No," I said simply. I was tired. I wanted to go home, to bed, to sleep. Things were finally falling apart for real, and it was almost a relief to see it.

"Yes, I, well, yes, it's been good working with you, Mattias. You've been the best ... absolutely."

"Thanks."

"And ... well, I've spoken to Jan up at Augland. I've recommended you, if he needs more people at his nursery. But, it's not easy for Jan either, he'll probably go down the pan too, but things might turn around. Next year, maybe."

"Maybe. But it was nice of you, Karsten."

"Wish I could do more."

"And you?" I said, extra positive. "What are you thinking of doing?"

"Me? No, I ... I'm just about old enough to stop now, so ... yes, Torvil and I have got a cottage on Kvitsøy, we've talked about it, perhaps we'll move out there, it's nice there. She loves it."

"Yes, it's nice there," I say quietly, "Very nice. But a difficult location for flowers, with all that wind."

"That's for sure. I'll probably have to give fishing a go instead."

"Yes."

Pause.

"Haven't you made any plans for the summer, then?"

"Oh yes," I said, "I'm going tomorrow ... to the Faroe Islands."

"The Faroe Islands?"

"Almost nothing grows there," I said. "Not a tree."

"Not one?"

"Not one. That's where you should start up, you know. Flowers and trees on the Faroe Islands."

"I don't think so, Mattias . . . So, how long will you be there?"

"Just a week. We're taking the boat over tomorrow. From Bergen."

"I didn't think you liked boats."

"I don't."

"Take care of yourself, then."

"You too."

Karsten got up, disappeared for a moment. I heard him rummaging in a box, noise of wrapping paper, tape. Then he reappeared in the doorway, and I got up and took my jacket.

"Here," he said giving me the parcel. A soft parcel. "This is about all I can give you. A memento. You never know what might come in handy."

"Thanks," I said, taking his hand. I rummaged in my pockets, found the keys, gave them to him, went out the door and closed it behind me. And as I opened my car door I saw him standing there tying a bouquet, he'd put his leather apron on, hadn't given up. Was working until the last minute.

I sat in the car for a long time before starting the motor. The sea rose. A centimeter per year. The icebergs on the coast of Svalbard shrank with each year. The polar bear suffered from pollution and there were only fifteen arctic foxes left in Nordland. The population of Nordland rose, the Mayor of Sevland bit his nails and was terrified that Statoil's offices in Forus would be blacked out on January 1, 2000, and Stavanger would go under as a city, that the lighthouses would go out, the computers fail and ships run aground on Sola Beach, oil spills in every single nook. And hadn't Helle said I'd begun to vanish for her, wasn't that what she'd said up on the mountain? Yes. And now I thought about it, hadn't I begun to fall apart even before she said it was over, that it was finished? Hadn't the joins begun to glide from each other long ago, the continental plates begun to slip out of position to form new countries so the maps no longer matched the terrain?

It's the dead man's handle in my brain that decides it in the end, it swings back and closes the entire system down, and I remember only fragments of the final twenty-four hours. Our apartment. My apartment which was now quite empty. Only one chair remaining. I sat down on it. I sat and did nothing. Watched the TV that stood on the floor flickering, a show about the Serengeti, I think. I don't know. I had the parcel from Karsten on my lap. Hadn't opened it yet. Opened it now, tore the paper, it was a pair of overalls. Karsten had given me one of the magnolia boilersuits we'd never used. Completely unused. Didn't have a single thought. Looked at the TV. Serengeti. Shit. Carried the TV to the window, and threw the set out, sending it onto the asphalt two floors below. It exploded all over the pavement. It was a superb noise. It was an awful TV. Right. Now there was nothing else to tidy away. I think I sat up for a long time. With the boilersuit in my lap. Staring into the wall. My bag packed and ready at the front door. Sat there until the doorbell rang next morning. Jørn and Roar stood outside, the rest of the band were in the car. And we all drove off to Bergen, me dozing off in the backseat, endless roads, on and off the ferry, on to Bergen, a massive boat. The Smyril Line.

We drive on board and the language changes, I no longer understand what's being said. Already in the first hour some people recognize Jørn, kids, they want our autographs, and I pull back, say I'm not in the band, *I'm not one of them* but it's no use, and Jørn says *Look what you're missing out on*, and the boat lies heavy in the rough sea threatening to go under at any moment, and he asks if I won't reconsider, for just one second, joining the band, for his sake. I'm freezing. I sit in the bar in my wool hat. Body shaking. Nose running. I throw up in the toilets as the boat rolls through the night, side to side through the Atlantic, and the Shetland gang with beards and big wool sweaters laugh and shout as they drink. I'm sitting in a bar with the others, a disco below, blue liqueur in a blue room, and I feel so angry, so tired, so excruciatingly tired. Jørn looks at me with wide eyes, yells something or other at me, and then we're up on deck, there's a strong wind and we have to use both hands to keep hold of the rails. We stand on the quarterdeck, I shout to the others, but nobody can hear. Jørn shouts something back, but all I can hear is the sound of water, wind, propellers, I'm handed something and drink it without tasting it. My arms are aching, my knuckles are burning. All I want is to sleep. I lean over the rails, squint toward the wake. The boat plunges down into the waves, rising again on the other side. It is dark, the middle of the night. Somewhere far away to the left there seems to be land, for the first time in ten hours. Might be the Shetlands. Or Greenland. Might be New York. Singapore, for all I know. I know nothing. I sit myself down, sit down on the wet deck, turn my head slowly, see Jørn and Roar and the rest of the band, and a band from Trondheim standing in a semi-circle around me, I lie down, on my back. Let my head bump gently onto the deck. *It's the end of the world as we know it (and I feel fine).*

2

I was in the way, I had been for a long time. I lay there in the middle of the wet roadway with my face squashed against the asphalt, it was raining, it was night, and there wasn't a single tree for miles, just hills and steep mountains, covered in short, green grass, almost gray in the darkness, which vibrated in the wind. I was hungry, I couldn't remember when I'd last eaten, but it must have been close to twenty-four hours. We'd come ashore, we'd arrived in Tórshavn, but I couldn't remember what we'd done, how I'd ended up here, everything lay hidden in a hazy stew deep inside my brain somewhere. I felt nauseous, my head ached as I sat up, in the middle of the road still. My left hand throbbed with pain, dirty fingers, bloodied knuckles, unexplained. Had I punched somebody? Had something happened on the boat? I remembered that I'd been angry, but why? Rain. The droplets that zoomed in on me from four thousand feet above and landed onto the back of my neck, into my hair, dripped down onto the asphalt and made small puddles that trickled slowly away from me. I got up, my back hurt, but I got up, standing on two feet. I remembered wine, glasses, massive mouths that had laughed so much their tonsils showed, I remembered the boat trip across. I remembered that I hadn't actually had that much to drink, but that I'd been ill nonetheless, that the sea had been rough, that the Bulgarian band had played "I Will Always Love You" and something that could only have been "Ten Thousand Red Roses," despite its being sung in Swedish with a Cyrillic alphabet.

I leaned on a traffic sign at the roadside nearby, it said *8okm/t í mesta lagi,* and I reckoned that was way too fast for me.

I stood there for a few minutes not really knowing what to do next. Looked around. Above me the clouds lay heavy, low and dark, they merged with the mist that crept down from the mountains, moistening everything it touched as the wind blew in from the sea just downhill from the road, and the sea spray sprinkled the crash barrier, corroding metal and asphalt.

I looked down at my feet. At my soaking wet shoes. There was a carrier bag at my feet, from a shop in Stavanger I barely recognized. I picked it up, opened it and looked inside, found my magnolia boilersuit from the nursery, still unused, lying there neatly folded and shiny. Why did I have it with me? I began to go through my pockets for signs of what I'd been doing in the last few hours, but didn't find much. A scrunched up receipt from City Burger and a folded Visa receipt from a bar we must have been to, it was a relatively large amount I'd been charged. A flattened pack of cigarettes in my back pocket, also soaked, that weren't mine. I could feel my wallet through the material of my inside pocket, took it out, looked through it. There was nothing missing. Put it back, and it was then I noticed something else in there, something thick. I felt the paper against my fingers, pulled out a small brown envelope, opened it carefully to investigate its contents, and saw the money, a wad of notes. 15,000 kroner. Was it mine? I had no idea. I placed the money back in the envelope and put it back in my pocket.

I stood beside the road sign, it was raining. I had 15,000 kroner in my pocket and no umbrella. Just a plastic carrier bag. And I had no idea what had happened, or where the others were. The road looked equally long in both directions, so I turned left and began walking. I don't know why, I had no plans of going anywhere in particular, it didn't matter where I went. I might even have been heading for town, impossible to say. I just turned left and walked against the wind, one hand holding the carrier bag and the other at my jacket collar as I followed the road, close to the crash barrier. I couldn't remember heading in any particular direction and one road was as good as the other. My shoes squelched at every step, and I felt my toes getting colder and colder in my thin shoes, my skin, swollen from the damp, was starting to chaff and tear against the coarse material.

My notion of time from these days is confused, so I can't actually say how long I followed the road, it might have been for as little as half an hour, but then it might have been hours. It felt that way. The landscape was almost uniform in every direction, naked mountains and plains covered in nothing but short grass, wind blowing across it from all directions. But I think I walked long enough for it to grow dark around me, before the light eventually began to return, or perhaps a narrow crack opened up in the clouds allowing the moon to slip through the layers. Gradually the lorries, that passed me at infrequent intervals, became visible from afar. I could have hitchhiked. I could have stood at the roadside, thumb out, stopped a truck and hitched a ride, in the hope it was going to town. I didn't. I'm not sure why. Instead I just went on walking, making myself small and leaning into the wind, feeling my forehead grow cold from the rain that lashed my face, screwing my eyes tight to be able to see anything at all through the wind and rain.

I think I thought about Buzz Aldrin, the first steps he'd taken in the Sea of Tranquility thirty years ago, he hadn't had bad weather, hadn't had any weather at all, everything had been absolutely still, no atmosphere, not a drop of water, and the footprints he left in the moon dust, in the basalt, would remain there for millions of years, longer perhaps than all of us. My footprints were washed away for each step I took, and not all the world's Red Indians could ever track me down in this chaos.

I walked for half an hour, or hours like this, leaning into the wind, with aching fingers, a pounding headache and nausea, I walked along the road without purpose or direction, I saw the odd sheep that had wandered off from one of the small stone sheds built by farmers to shelter their animals when there were dreadful storms, like now, when all sensible animals or humans stayed barricaded indoors, and the sheep stopped in their tracks when they saw me, cocked their heads, followed me with their gaze until something more interesting distracted them, or until they vanished into the mists ahead, going back to rest. That was when I got the idea. I should have let it pass, but there it was. I was cold, and when the next sheep appeared on the slope, a black, longhaired creature, I crossed over the road toward it, began walking up the slopes, moving closer and closer in, and it began to draw back, slowly but surely, as I came closer. Eventually it suddenly turned, and began running up the mountainside, and I think I ran as hard as I could. Hurtled through the rain, giving it my all, running up the steep slope of slippery grass, thinking that if only I could find the place where the rest of the flock were resting, I could squeeze myself among them, down into their wool, and dry off. But the sheep was quicker than me, it knew where it was going and I'd run out of strength, I lumbered on, I dropped my bag, stumbled on a rock and landed with my whole weight on my hand, a burning explosion of pain surged through my fingers, everything went black for an instant, before I came to again, lying in the wet grass with blood all over my jacket, blood all over my arm, not a single trace of the sheep to be seen. Not so much as a fly.

I brought myself painstakingly to my feet again and picked up my carrier bag, padded quietly and indignantly back to the roadside and continued walking along it, stopped thinking about what I was doing, switched to autopilot and tramped my way on through the landscape, and I could doubtless have walked like this for days, without regard for where I was going, chin pressed into my chest, hands hanging at my sides, one foot in front of the other, mile after mile, following the white road markings, while the rain could make me no wetter than I already was.

I remember walking through a tunnel at some point, it was either early or late, I walked through the tunnel, balancing on a narrow footpath like a dancer on a slack-rope, breathed in the remains of old exhaust fumes, as I came out on the other side a view across an enormous valley opened up to my right, and in front of me, on the other side, was a bus shelter. I dragged myself toward it, sat on the bench. Looked at my watch. It had stopped. Completely frozen at seven-thirty exactly, difficult to say how close that was to the truth. Calmly, I laid my carrier bag underneath me and lay down on the bench. Adjusted myself. It was a big bench, a warning sign in itself; the bigger the benches in bus shelters, the longer the waiting times. This bench was big, and hanging on a wall inside the shelter was a small frame with a sheet of paper giving an overview of bus times. Most of the writing was illegible, the letters washed away by so much water, but it looked as though the bus came to Eysturoy twice a day, except Sundays, when it didn't run at all. I didn't know where Eysturoy was, and I was worried it might be Sunday today, but pushed the thought away. Impossible that I'd been in the country that long, the boat had left Bergen on Tuesday, so it had to be a Wednesday or Thursday, at worst. Or a Saturday, one could never be sure. But probably a Wednesday. I lay down on the wet bench, I tried to curl up, tried to sleep, but it was impossible, it was cold, and it was raining and I felt increasingly awake, it must have been over twenty-four hours since I'd last eaten, I could feel that now, as my stomach began to contract in a desperate attempt to find something to digest. The last thing I could remember, was some half-cold pizza I'd bought at the cafeteria on the boat and which hadn't tasted like much. Later we'd gone up, gone out onto deck. I remember we all stood on deck drinking beer, Jørn, Roar, and me, and the band from Trondheim. We stood there looking down into the wake of the ship in the night, stood watching the stripes stretch back toward Norway, and I think we discussed how deep it might be and the chances of being rescued if one of us fell overboard there and then, and I think we concluded it was deep enough and that the chances of being rescued were infinitesimally small, and we wondered what it would be like, to perish like that, on the surface of an ocean hundreds of fathoms deep, caught in the waves, as the ferry moved off, drowning in the ship's wake at night, hearing the others on deck as they called desperately to you in the water, how long it would take to stop the boat, to turn it, to find the way back in the dark, the chances would be miniscule, and anyone jumping in after you would vanish too, into the waves, into the sea, in minutes, and it's cold at this time of year too, saltwater can be at below-zero temperatures without freezing, and you'd go under, come up a couple of times, go under again, sink, and settle to the bottom, quite still, and you'd never be found. And if somebody jumped after you, on a heroic rescue mission, they'd sink too, and we'd lie in stacks at the bottom, an invisible monument. I think we chatted on like that, drinking our beer, throwing our cans over the ship's railings and counting how many seconds they took to hit the surface, and we debated what we'd do if the boat was sinking and there were no lifeboats, whether we'd stay in our cabins and lock the doors, or go up on deck, and I think I said I'd stay in my cabin, I'd watch the water rise over the porthole, knowing the top deck was still dry, and I'd lie on my bunk, fully dressed, in my suit, perhaps, absolutely still, waiting until the boat was under water and the atmospheric pressure rose and my porthole imploded into my cabin and the sea gushed in and the door hinges gave way and the noises from the corridor and the feet on the metal steps melted away, and the water forced my door open, and for a brief moment, before I drowned, I would float, in my suit, I and all my things would float aimlessly around my cabin, as if we were in outer space.

How long did I lie on that bench? I don't know. Maybe hours. From somewhere far off I heard the sound of a car come closer, slow down and stop, a car door opening and shutting.

Somebody was yelling at me. I didn't understand what was said. Somebody yelled again, wanted my attention, wanted me to talk, but I had nothing to say, turned and lay with my face to the wall. But the blaze of the headlights wouldn't go away, it shone in the Plexiglas of the bus shelter, it burned into my eyes before vanishing for a moment as somebody grabbed me from behind, talked at me, but I understood nothing, nothing made sense.

Words were repeated.

I was no longer listening. Somebody tugged at my shoulder again. Reluctantly I turned around on the wooden bench and stared straight into the face of a hefty guy in his forties with blond hair and a thick wool jumper.

He talked in words only he could understand.

"Eh?"

He switched programs, began talking in Danish.

"Everything all right here?"

"Eh?"

"Are things all right with you?"

I knew how things were with me. And they weren't all right.

"Do you want to get up?"

I got up, sat on the bench in front of him, my plastic carrier in my lap, like a child who's missed the last bus home from school and has to accept whatever help he's offered. The man before me stood looking at me, not too sure perhaps about what he should do.

"Where are you going?" he asked.

"I don't know," I answered.

"So where have you been?"

"I don't know."

He sighed heavily, as though he already regretted stopping, or as though this happened to him every time he was out for a drive, like having to move sheep off the road.

"Are you a tourist?"

"Yes."

"Are you staying at one of the hotels in Tórshavn, perhaps?"

"No . . . I've no idea."

Was he starting to get impatient? Perhaps. He was standing in the rain. Was getting wet hair.

"Are you on your own, then?"

I thought for a moment. Pulled myself together. My hand was hurting.

"No," I said. "I've got friends. I . . . they . . . I don't know where they are."

"I can drive you down to the harbor, if you want."

"No thanks."

"Are you just going to lie here?"

"Yes."

"But you can't."

"No."

Then I lay down on the bench again, shut my eyes, turned away from him. But I wasn't lying there for long. Somebody tugged at me, and it was him again, he lifted me up into a seated position again. I had blood on my trousers. Saliva ran from my mouth. No great beauty.

"I think you'd better come with me," he said.

I didn't want to.

"It'll be fine," I mumbled. "I'll be all right here. On my own."

"That's not the way it looks," he answered, pointing at my bloodied hand. "Come on, you'd better come with me, let's get you inside before you drown." He reached a hand out and grabbed me by my healthy arm, hauled me to my feet, and dragged me over to the car, put me in the passenger seat, put the carrier in my lap. I had my hand in my inside pocket. For a moment I contemplated giving all the money to him, asking him to take me to a hotel, to drive me away, back home. But my hand refused, and settled in my lap.

"I'm Havstein," he said, taking my hand in his own and shaking them both.

"So ... rry?"

"Havstein Garðalíð."

I think I said Mattias.

Then he started the car, drove down into the valley and swung right, taking us along the coast, through the villages and the monotonous landscape, with the radio playing in the background, soft, incomprehensible voices talking, and between them I heard songs I'd once connected with something, with things, with events.

I slept for most of the time, interrupted by the brief moments when I gazed through the window, at roads that snaked gently over hills. The occasional car drove past in the opposite direction, high speed, noise as it passed us, an intense light streaming into the car, music on the car stereo, soft, whispering country and western songs, and this Havstein guy humming along with it, out of sync. Tammy Wynette.

─ ─ ─ ■ ─ ─ ─

We'd stopped when I woke up. Light streamed through the car windows, the water ran in stripes down the glass, I pushed myself up in my seat and this was day one. It didn't come with rain, but the remains of water from yesterday, I was still cold and wet, hair plastered to my forehead, a stale taste in my mouth. I looked at the clock on the dashboard, ten past nine, and didn't know where I was. And the air was fresh as I rolled the window down, poked my head out, tried to catch the oxygen as it streamed past the car in a steady current, loosened my seat belt, pulled my whole body out through the open window, arms on the roof, and it was so wet, the world dripped and I was breathing fresh air again, here, wherever that might be. I felt a little better, better than yesterday, better than the last time I'd given it thought. I slipped back in again, opened the car door, took a first tentative step out onto the asphalt. And

I stood there. Just about. I didn't fall through. I stood outside a Statoil gas station, sun in my eyes, and watched as this man who went by the name of Havstein came walking out of the shop, walked toward me, lifted a hand, waved, I waved back, my hand more feeble than his.

"Hi."

"Hi."

He'd bought bread, a soft drink, milk, he'd got the essentials and I stood there, leaning on the body of the car while he showed me his groceries, put the bags in the trunk, slammed the lid, walked around to my side of the car.

"Good morning," said Havstein.

"Hi."

"Look around," he said.

I looked around, turned three hundred and sixty degrees. An advanced picture postcard.

"Eysturoy," said Havstein.

"Okay," I said.

"Do you want something? Coffee perhaps? I feel like a coffee."

I didn't feel like anything.

"Okay."

"Come on then."

"Okay."

I followed after him into the gas station, through the shop, and in through a door at the very back, where we came to a rundown truck stop café, brown plastic chairs, Formica tables, curtains from the seventies, dirty from cigarette smoke and road dust. We were the only ones in the room, apart from a middle-aged woman in a red apron, who stood waiting behind the counter as we came in, she and Havstein nodded and I was put in a chair, a cup of coffee put in my hands.

"There you go."

"Thanks."

We sat there quietly for a long time, saying nothing. Havstein leaned back in his chair.

"Does it help?" he said finally. "The coffee?"

"Yes." I answered. "A bit."

Silence again. The coffee machine puttered in the background. Sun in at the window.

"Well?"

"Yes," I said.

"Well, here you are."

"Yes. Here I am. It's very nice here."

I was polite. I played along. Felt like an idiot.

"We're fond of this place."

"I can believe it."

"So?"

"So?"

Havstein dug a packet of cigarettes out, lit one.

"So, why did I pick you up last night?"

The room went quiet. We looked at each other, we looked past each other, we looked out of the windows, there were birds everywhere, apart from in the room, the fullness of summer was about to explode out there. In here, time had come to a halt, had taken a seat.

"I don't know," I answered quietly.

Havstein said nothing, drank his coffee, I heard the liquid trickle down his throat, down his neck, heard him swallow.

"On holiday, are you?" asked Havstein.

"Kind of," I answered.

"We were supposed to give a concert here on Friday."

"Today's Thursday."

"I see."

"So, you're a musician?"

"No, I . . . I'm a gardener."

"A gardener? That's good."

Somebody should have taken a Polaroid of this moment, should have caught it on tape, as we sat here, Havstein, whom I didn't know, whose name I hardly remembered, and myself, sitting on a plastic chair opposite him, and I wanted to start talking, to tell him everything, to let it foam out over the table, to chance it. But I didn't. I was silent. Drank my coffee. Watched the birds. They'd built a nest just outside one of the windows, beneath the eaves.

"And the others?" asked Havstein. "Your friends?"

"I don't know, some place or other in Tórshavn, I think."

"Maybe you should call them. There's a phone in the hallway," he pointed toward the door.

"I don't know what I'd say."

"The truth."

"Which is?"

"I don't know."

"I see."

"But you don't want to call."

"No."

"Why not?"

"I don't know."

"There isn't a lot you do know, is there?"

"No."

The woman behind the counter disappeared out into the petrol station, closing the door gently after her. Havstein leaned closer into the table.

"I'm happy to drive you somewhere if you like. If you know where you're going, or where you want to go. I could still drive you into Tórshavn. How about it? It's no problem, you know." Then he hesitated for a moment, before adding: "If not, I really should be heading back home. I'm actually on my way home, I'm going north. To Gjógv. So, what do you say? Shall I drive you to the harbor?"

I looked down. Rubbed the fingers of my right hand across the surface of the table. For every second I sat here, the sea rose, nanometer upon nanometer. I didn't answer. I stared into the table.

"What's the matter?"

"I'm not sure I want to go back."

Then I started to talk. I started telling him everything that had happened over the last weeks, what I remembered of it. I told him how Helle had left me on Kjeragbolten, and how the boulder still hadn't come loose, about the job that disappeared because of the shopping malls, I talked about Mother and Father, about the Christmas ball that year, I talked about not wanting to be seen, about wanting to be one of the many, and I think I talked a bit about space. Havstein sat quietly and listened, drank coffee, nodded once in a while, but mostly sat quietly. I'd opened all the valves, and gave him the long version, I don't know why, perhaps I didn't want to be alone anymore, perhaps the pressure had grown too great and I did it to stop my head from exploding over the Formica and curtains. I just talked, a stream of words, a maelstrom. And then I sat quietly back.

Havstein lit another cigarette. A couple of truck drivers walked into the café, rowdy, they laughed and called out for the waitress, who puttered in through the door at the back and poured them coffee without asking if that was what they wanted. They sat down with her at a table at the other end of the room and talked excitedly at each other, I understood only fragments of their conversation, but it was about trivial things, who'd done this or that, or said that or the other, what they had to deliver and what they had to pick up, and the waitress smoked like a chimney, enveloping them in smoke and told them most of what had happened since they'd been there last, who'd gotten married, who'd split up and gone away, who'd had children and who hadn't, there'd been some births and some deaths, jobs had changed hands, and it was only a week since they had been there last.

"Okay," said Havstein. I looked across the table, I could see he was thinking, and he said: "You can come with me, if you want."

I didn't know what to say. Waited for the continuation. It came.

"I . . . we, live up in Gjógv, a little settlement to the North, myself and three other people, Palli, Anna, and Ennen. Lovely people, all of them. We live in an old filleting factory up there, converted, more or less. You're welcome to stay a few days, get yourself together. If you want."

"A collective?"

"Not quite," said Havstein, and smiled. "I run an institution. Kind of a halfway house."

"An institution?"

"Yes."

Pause. I have been demoted to a psychiatric case. Suddenly I am Jørn's brother, the eternal patient.

"It's not a hospital," he continued. "I'm not taking you in because I think you need treatment. For now. I'd already have driven you to the airport if I did. Sent you home."

"I don't want to go to the airport," I said, looking down into my coffee.

"Exactly." Havstein started to explain: "But you're right to think the people who live up there have spent time in that sort of place before. It's somewhere for people who no longer need to be locked in an institution either here or in Denmark, but who don't feel quite ready to live alone. For various reasons. Let's just say when you've lived in an institution for a long time, over several years, you get a little too used to it. And then it can be good to live in a similar environment. Or put it this way; everybody wants somebody to look after them. So that's what I do. I try to make sure they're okay. Of course anybody who lives up there, or has lived up there, is free to leave. And once in a while they've done just that, they've gone off again. That's really not an issue."

The other table had grown quiet, their ears grew bigger, sliding down to the floor and scuttling over to our table.

"But in theory," continued Havstein, "they can equally well stay as long as they want, given that they have a right to a place. If they're not with me, they can demand a place in a normal institution, until it's proved they no longer need one. Which is more or less impossible. Besides, lots of people who have been in and out of these places don't have proper qualifications, they've missed out on so much schooling, so it's almost impossible for them to get themselves a job. But if I call a fish farm, or the port authorities in Tórshavn for example, and promise that the state will pay half the salary, it smooths the way. You understand? So this is the situation. I live together with three ex-patients, rather than them living with me. Two of them have jobs outside town, and the last works in the Factory. We run a workshop producing knickknacks, tourist items, that's what the state demands, naturally they require some form of input from our side for being allowed to run things like this. Palli's lived there for almost ten years and has been there longest. Ennen came five years ago and Anna closer to six. Right now they're the only ones living there, though there's space for four more. There's another, similar place outside Klaksvík, so we represent an alternative, as long as we last. They're lovely people. And I think they'd be happy for a visit. At the moment there aren't more than fifty-four people living in all of Gjógv, so a new face is generally very welcome."

"Generally?"

"It'll be fine."

Dr. Havstein. I felt institutionalized. Tablets at fixed times. Slit arteries on the bathroom tiles. Eyes that spy along miles of white corridors. I didn't know how to answer. I wanted somebody to look after me. I wanted somebody to take my hand, to lead me home. I wanted somebody to tell me they were happy they'd found me at last.

"It'll work out," he said.

"Will it?"

"Yes," he said. "It always does."

I never said yes. Neither did I say no. We simply drank up our coffee in silence, got up almost simultaneously, and walked out through the gas station. Statoil. Norwegian oil. Full tank. I had nothing better to do. Couldn't be bothered to ring Jørn, search Tórshavn and find him, go out with him again in the evening, sit together with them after the concert and meet all the ghosts from the last month, talk about Helle. I couldn't face setting up the sound equipment.

The sound! Shit! Shit! Shit!

I'd promised to be their sound technician, and now what was I doing? I'd disappeared on them, flown the coop, and maybe they were looking for me. Had they called home? Had they called Mother and Father? I hoped not. Couldn't bear to think of it, I was so tired, so much had gone wrong, practically nothing had worked out.

We stood outside the gas station and Havstein looked at the price of a disposable grill. He caught sight of my hand.

"Have you hurt yourself?" he asked.

I looked down at my hand. It didn't look great. As though I'd dragged it through a nightmare. It had swollen up along the knuckles, dark blue skin and congealed blood.

"I don't remember," I said, and Havstein nodded toward a tap mounted on the wall near by, I went over and turned it on, let the ice-cold water run over my wounded hand, it stung and I had to clench my teeth as I pulled out a bit of paper from the dispenser and wiped away most of the blood, whatever wasn't stuck to the wound. Pulled out more paper, wrapped it round my hand. Then I went obediently and sat in the car, I just wanted to sleep, I just wanted to float away, hover over the town, without worries, like a child in the backseat at night, on the way home from a Christmas outing or a trip to the mountains, fist closed on bags of cookies and orange soda sloshing in a bottle, teeth coated with fur that would have to be brushed off when we got home, before somebody put me to bed, tucked the covers under my feet so they wouldn't get cold, stroked my hair and said there was so much time, how lucky I was to be just a child, there were oceans of time, it was important to take the time you needed.

And that's all I remember of that first drive to Gjógv. I remember how calm I felt and the silence we shared as we drove along, as though the sound had been turned off, and Havstein drove so carefully along the road. We sailed up the steep hairpin curves from Funningur and the view opened up over the fjords and mountains below, up toward Slættaratindur, and I was a miniscule person being dragged across summer-green meadows, farther and farther upward, the windshield of the car was dirty, making the view hazy, before Havstein switched the cleaning fluid on, probably at about the time we passed the top of the last hill, and the windows cleared, an early afternoon sun sliced through scratches in the glass and I had to screw up my eyes, and I saw the little village that spread out below along the shoreline, hundreds of feet down the dry, worn asphalt road, squeezed between two mountains, and if I'd seen a lot of green so far, that was nothing compared to this, the fields spread imperceptibly out into the landscape and rose to become massive hills you could almost stroll over, a completely rounded landscape with no irregularities or jutting knolls, opening itself up in all directions, this, I thought, was like the moon, dressed in grass, this was what it must have been like to walk on the moon for the first time, an untouched wasteland. And I was an explorer of virgin territories, I knew nothing, was nobody, and I think I was grateful. Grateful that somebody had found me, and that the atmosphere wasn't a vacuum, was filled with oxygen, as I opened the car door minutes later and stood before the huge two-story, concrete Factory, on Gjógv's village square, with its view straight into masses of nothing at all.

I was put next to a big, oblong table of solid wood, in the middle of an enormous kitchen, nearly thirty feet long, and Havstein stood with his back to me, rummaging in the fridge, a droning noise filled the room, dust in the air, sun through the windows, and I began to dry out, my skin contracted, as though I'd been gently tumble-dried and had come to rest, the sound of birds outside, chirrup, chirrup. Havstein made the coffee, Havstein poured orange juice into a glass, Havstein came over and sat opposite me, my hands rested on the table, quite still, in a bundle before me.

Havstein got up, went through the room, opened a cupboard, took out a piece of paper, a pencil, came back and sat down. He put the paper on the table in front of me, laid the pencil carefully on the paper, pushed both over to me.

"I need a telephone number," he said.

"For who?"

"Anyone."

I didn't know what to write, the situation was absurd, I ought to get out of here, get away, I should pull myself together, put on my shoes, my jacket, I should get a taxi back into town, back to the band, I should do what I'd promised, what was expected of me. I had no business being here, I didn't belong, had no purpose here, I didn't know who Havstein was, who the others were, I had to get away, get down to town. I had to get back home to Norway. Now.

I wrote the number for Jørn's cell phone on the piece of paper. And under it, his name. Pushed the piece of paper back to Havstein. He got up, took the paper with him and left the room, went up the stairs, they creaked and I heard his footsteps on the floor above, a door being opened, his voice, but not everything he said. He talked quietly, slowly, but firmly. I heard him say Jørn a couple of times and my name. I heard him say something or other about Tórshavn, then it went quiet again. Shortly afterward he came back down the stairs, into the kitchen.

"I'm taking a trip into Tórshavn," he said. "I'm going to meet this Jørn fellow for you. There's nothing to worry about."

Flat batteries. No coverage. The far side of the moon.

All I said was: "Oh well."

Havstein showed me into the next room, which was when it first became clear this was no ordinary house, everything was too big here, concrete walls, and I was in a factory, converted, an old factory, made habitable, homey. I stood in the living room, a gigantic room, almost a warehouse, covered with carpets, with paintings on the wall, those old lamps Mother would have thrown out at the beginning of the eighties, a TV at one end. Big windows, a view over the sea, sofas of a kind I hadn't seen for twenty years. I was told how the TV channels were set up, and Havstein put out some pastries, orange juice, and a Danish newspaper. He was going to Tórshavn, and would return this evening.

"Don't go anywhere," he said.
"Where would I go?"
"Exactly."

He disappears. I sit stock still on the sofa, staring out the window, looking out over the water, the sea, waiting for it to crash through the windowpanes at any moment, for glass to rain over me, for the room to fill, the seas to lift me out of the house. But nothing happens, everything is calm outside, a blue blanket lies over the world and my face warms in the light.

Even anxiety has its boredom threshold, and after an hour I couldn't keep watch over the view any longer; I gave the sea a break, turned my gaze inward to the room, a big room, about a thousand square feet, with feet upon feet under the roof, and somewhere far above a person had succeeded in securing some lamps, great, blue lamps, that would light the room in yellow when it got dark. The furniture and the walls were all brown and light blue, seventies colors, and there were carpets, the whole factory was furnished like a house, a HOME. There were three sofas in here, in a vague semi-circle, they looked tiny in relation to the room's size, almost laughable, and against a wall, the west wall, were three hefty chairs, wingbacks of the good, old-fashioned sort Grandfather had kept at home, toward the end he'd sat in his red wingback chair all day, reading or staring into space, only the latter in his last days, and I remember we visited one Tuesday in May, it was raining and Grandfather was sitting in his chair, sitting with the binoculars in his hand, staring out into thin air. We sat on his bed, Mother and I, but he didn't notice us, not even when Mother said his name several times, or when she put out a bowl of Twist chocolates on the table in front of him, he liked Twist a lot, he used to collect the gold wrappings, collect them in a box under his bed. He didn't see us, and suddenly he lifted the binoculars he'd put next to his chair, pointed them toward the wall on the other side of the room, adjusted the lenses and looked at the picture of Grandmother through them. Then he laid them back in his lap, only to pick them up again moments later to look through them at Grandmother again, bringing her right up close, as though she was standing right before him, as though she was the only one in the room. We sat there for an hour. And Grandfather spent the entire time focusing his binoculars, looking, adjusting, looking. The entire time. I went back a month later. Grandfather was sitting as impassively as before in his chair, looking at Grandmother. In exactly the same position. The next time I went back, it was to help Father carry the chair out to the moving van, and to drive it to the nursing home where Grandfather would be staying. But it wasn't as good there, the walls were too close to each other, Grandfather couldn't focus, Grandmother grew blurred at the edges, as did Grandfather, in just a few weeks, before finally erasing himself completely and vanishing. Once more, we carried the chair out to the moving van, put it in our hallway at home, and there it stayed. And now, the same chairs were here in this living room, in this factory. Chairs made at a time when furniture had to last. I considered sitting in one of them for a moment, but didn't. Instead I got up, stood in the center of the room and looked out the windows, the sound of the birds and the wind outside quieted, merged into the humming of the refrigerator out in the kitchen.

How long did I stand like that? Minutes, probably, before I eventually lifted my feet to walk toward the big kitchen, walked through the room, past the windows, out to the left, into the entrance hall. I hadn't noticed it when I came in earlier, I'd been so tired, but now I saw how enormous the hallway was too, it was nice here, clean, as though there was caring in the walls, and somebody had put their spirit into concealing the Factory under a layer of paint, behind the plants in their big pots, and under the rag rugs on the floor. I walked through the hallway, toward the door at the other end, and reached another steel door, I turned the handle, expected the door to squeak, but it made no noise, I opened the door, went into the room, into a narrow hallway, and my sneakers left an echo as they met the light blue linoleum. Then two more doors, less solid this time, ordinary wooden doors, labeled simply Cloakroom A and Cloakroom B. I chose to start at the wrong end, opened door B. It was dark in here, I fumbled for the light switch, found some plastic device high up on the wall, turned it and the room lit up. I was standing in a locker room. It looked like any other locker room. Metal lockers, worn-out stickers stuck there by the workers who'd stood here once, who'd pasted their opinions to their lockers: *No to NATO, No to the Atom Bomb, No to everything! Yes to nothing!*, and the like, and stickers from cars, models that weren't even sold anymore, and some of the stickers were torn, somebody had tried to scrape them off, given up half way, ripped off the parts that didn't grip the metal and left the rest. In the middle of the room was the obligatory divided bench with its furrows and marks, it triggered thoughts, I imagined entire lives, I saw those cold February mornings long ago, the workers as they walk in, wearing thick clothes that they hang in their lockers, putting new stickers over old, digging their working clothes out, stiffened with old dirt, sweat, and the atmosphere's sleepy, little is said, another day among many, and somebody has to keep the wheels turning, there are fish to be filleted, cleaned, sorted, salted and packed, I don't know, sent out to vans to be driven to town, in the afternoon, and the vans will stop beside the big ships, the doors will open and the cases will be put on pallets, lifted onto the ships, and the ships will sail off, toward Shetland, toward the Orkneys, toward Norway, who knows, England, France, Italy? To whoever wants it, to whatever people don't have enough fish for themselves, and these ships will meet other ships halfway on their way from England, from Iceland, taking fish the other way, and somebody will give a signal out there on the sea, a blast on the horn, a flash of a ship's lantern, and the fish will be unloaded on the quay of some other harbor, and more vans will fetch cases, drive them to the stores, and the cases will be opened, their contents displayed, and the mothers, the fathers will stream into the stores, place the fish in their shopping carts, in their baskets, in their bags, and the fish will be prepared in countless kitchens, the children will turn their noses up, demand more salt and pepper, Father will talk about his day, Mother will talk about her day, and fish will be eaten over the entire land and the ships will have turned back long ago, started their return journey, and back at the factory people will have been in the locker room again, will have sat on the wooden bench at the center of the room, leaving their traces in the wood, pulled on their trousers, boots, sweaters over sweaters and jackets over the top, gone out to their cars, set off for home, a whiff of cod already at the back of their mouths, walked into the house, to the dinner table where Mother has just served the fish she got at the shop, freshly delivered from Glasgow or somewhere, and it is the fabulous fifties and the children are still obedient, sitting around the table, greased hair, neat shirts and pullovers, clean hands folded, and they say grace, give each other Pepsodent smiles and the fish is eaten, and they talk about their day and the daughter sits with her uncreased skirt under the table, white stockings, very thick, plaits in her hair, and Father talks, something or other he's read in the paper, and the rest listen, Father knows so much, Mother's so clever at making food, at sewing, she washes the dishes and helps little sister with her crocheting, knitting, she talks about the future, about finding a good husband, she talks about Father who's upstairs with the son of the house, doing geography, reading about China, and China's full of Communists, but it somehow still gets by, and the evening will come, the night will come, and in the morning Father will get into his car again, drive to the fish factory up north, thoughts filled with the world, and ten years later he'll come home one afternoon, tired eyes, but tonight it'll happen, tonight *Discovery*'s crew will land on the moon, the *Eagle* will come down in the Sea of Tranquility tonight, and nobody has a television set yet, TV won't come to the Faroe Islands until well into the eighties, at least not Faroese TV, and nobody even has a satellite dish yet, so everyone will sit in front of their radios instead, and they'll stay up all night, in the living room, in front of the fireplace, Mother on the sofa, big brother on the sofa next to kid sister who is already thinking of abandoning the Faroes, of venturing out into the world, one foot in another revolution, she eyes the patriarch in his chair, and nobody says anything, nobody talks, they sit listening to the radio, waiting, and the first man gets out, the first man speaks from the moon and nothing will ever be the same again, not now, and it's hard to get up the next morning, more wearisome than usual to make the drive northward to the factory, but minutes before he arrives, the cloud cover breaks and the sky turns blue, it's the middle of summer and most people are free, on vacation, but the fish won't wait, the fish go on swimming, and somebody has to be at work, to keep the wheels rolling, the world turning, he leans over the steering wheel, looks up at the sky, tries to see the moon, even though it's the middle of the day, and he stares up, pulls the car over, stops, stretches right over the wheel, looks up, up, up, and somewhere up there are men who have walked on another planet, and when he looks down again, looks out at the road, he catches sight of the other cars, a dozen cars, that have also stopped, the other workers, and they're all staring upward, and they all start their engines again, drive in a column for the final stretch, mumble among themselves in the locker rooms, and nobody puts any new protest stickers up today, nobody has anything to say for now, and although men are walking on other planets, there are fewer fish in the sea, and early in the seventies the lockers are shut, the stickers are removed, the lights turned off, and the factory is closed, kid sister goes to Scotland, and then to England. Big brother goes into sheep farming with his father, and together they wait, in front of the radio in the evenings, for news of better times, of other journeys to space, or for the announcement that the islands are to get their own television channel, and the announcement is finally made in 1984, and they go out together to the shop in Tórshavn that sells TV sets, they buy the cheapest model and Father and Son install it in the living room, Mother redecorates the room to match it, there are shows each day, and in the winter of 1984 they sit glued to the Olympics in Sarajevo, Yugoslavia, and one evening several years later, on the news, they show pictures from the old factory up there, the production hall, the locker rooms, and Father sees his old locker, gets the whiff of cod somewhere at the back of his mouth, it's been mutton mainly in the last few years, and kid sister rings every month, she's fine, has gone up in the world, talks in broken English, is expecting her second, and they must come over, when the new baby arrives, *of course*, they say, *of course we'll come*, and then it's evening again. But then one day they go. To England. They look her up, show the piece of paper with her address on it to the cab driver, he knows where it is, and they drive to one of the worst areas of the city, in the East End, she lives in a third floor apartment in what they call a council flat, it's drafty, she's pregnant, her new husband isn't bad, no, he really isn't, but things aren't easy, and this job of hers, the one she's told them about for so long, it doesn't exist, she is short of money, they are short of money, it's expensive to have children, it costs to live in this city, and Father, Father is obliged to open his wallet, to pull out the pound notes, and he treats them to dinner, everyone, this extended family, they sit in a restaurant in Soho, a good restaurant, they drink wine, and it's quiet around the table, what can one say? The eighties that hold so much promise. The nineties which will be so mundane.

I turned the light out, closed the door carefully after me, tried the other door, while I was at it, *Cloakroom A*, and that door could be opened too. It was another locker room, not quite so tatty, barely used. It seemed it was being used for storage, cases piled high, right to the ceiling, old mattresses, fishing equipment, food, beer, and the like. A storeroom.

I looked at the clock. Ten past five. I didn't know when Havstein would be back. Some time this evening. He was in Tórshavn. Talking to Jørn, and to Roar too perhaps, and the guitarist, Tomas. Or perhaps just to Jørn. Hopefully just to him. The others didn't have to know everything. They'd hear it anyway, of course, but they could get the summary from Jørn, he'd know what to say, what to do, and I knew he'd call my parents. He'd call Mother in the afternoon, or talk to Father if Mother wasn't the first to pick up the phone, and I knew more or less what Jørn would say, almost down to the words he'd use. Mother would want to phone here, but she wouldn't have the number, of course, and Father would want to come, fly up here, to talk to me. But I couldn't talk to them now, I didn't know what to say, and Jørn would tell her she had to wait, that they'd all have to wait, because I'd come back, of course I would, I'd come back to them all, but I had to sort myself out first, I just needed some time to think, because things had happened so fast in the last months, the last year, things had wound fast forward on the video player and the tape had gotten completely stuck. A tangle of tape. There was no use pulling it out, taking hold and just pulling. The entire machine needed to be opened up, carefully, and the tape needed to be wound out with a pen or pencil, and then wound back into the cassette, put back in the machine and run again. I needed a cassette cleaning kit, a complete overhaul.

Jørn was my man now, and I pictured him and Havstein, whom I didn't know, sitting in a café down in Tórshavn, Jørn resting his head on his hand, beating out a rhythm nobody heard on the bridge of his nose with his little finger, and Havstein talking away, saying things, I didn't know what, but I hoped he'd say that things had got tangled inside me, but that the movie could still be shown in full at a later date, no sense demanding a refund. You just needed patience in this theater, projec- tionists who didn't take a break as soon as the film had started to roll, but who stayed there, sitting in the control room, just in case.

Then the impulse took me: I had to get down to town, had to talk to him myself. Or he could come up here. Jørn. I closed the door of Cloakroom A, ran into the kitchen, fetched my jacket, went out in the hallway, on with my shoes, opened the big, heavy, steel front door and went out, the weather had turned, it had begun to rain, mild drizzle that soaked me through in seconds, I crossed the field, heading for the road, and then it hit me, I didn't know which way to go, there was nobody around, but I walked farther and farther from the Factory, searching for a bus stop, some sign of public transportation, anything. I had to talk to Jørn, tell him things would turn out all right, and hear him say it too, that things would turn out all right, things were just a little tiring now, weren't they, I was just worn out, but it would pass, Jørn was down in Tórshavn, and I missed him, and I walked along the road, my hair wet, a wind was beginning to blow, the rain stopped and suddenly I saw what an idiot I was. Surely it would take hours to get to Tórshavn from here. Even if I was walking in the right direction. Even if I wasn't just way off track. And I found no bus stop. Saw no buses. Havstein might be coming back by now, and there wasn't any point in going down there. So I stopped, in the middle of the road, up on a hill, complete engine stop. I was here, here in this place. Gjógv. On the Faroe Islands. And this was where I was going to stay. Until the tempo slowed. Until things stood still. I turned, began to walk back, back down to the Factory, I wound my way back to the start, moving mechanically down the road, the wind at my back. Heavy clouds had begun to make it dark, the green around me was turning to brown, to gray, and the lights were coming on in some of the houses, curious Faroe Islanders hid behind their curtains and watched me as I passed their wooden houses, running the gauntlet, and neither side was invisible to the other.

He stood farther up the hill. I'd come almost all the way back to the Factory. He stood at the little crossroads where the path leading to the Factory met the paths down to the sea and a little cluster of houses to the left. A small boy stood next to the Factory's mailbox, he looked at me as though confronted with a dinner he didn't want , but which he might manage to eat if he had to.

Then it started raining. Again.

The same kind of rain as earlier. Not a heavy rain, a barely audible drizzle, but a rain that went through your clothes within seconds, I pulled the zipper up on my thin jacket, right up to the chin, my trousers clung against my thighs. I walked toward the boy by the mailbox, and he simply looked up at me as I walked past, I tried to give him a smile, a child-friendly smile, but didn't quite manage it, he waited until I'd gone a few meters past.

He said something in a strange, high voice.

I stopped, turned, didn't understand a jot. "Sorry, I don't speak Faroese," I answered and walked on, but he chirped up again in a language I did understand. Danish.

"I asked if you lived there, at the Factory."

I stopped, turned, didn't really know where I lived, so I told him I'd arrived that day, that morning. He was nine or ten, eleven perhaps, and small, smaller than most youngsters of that age I could think of, he had glasses, almost invisible wire frames, and he might grow into a handsome young man, very handsome, in ten years, the handsomest in the village, or perhaps the one nobody noticed, all according to chance, impossible to tell. He was wearing a thick bubble jacket, black, a black bubble jacket and the rain was soaking through the fabric, making him cold, and he pulled his zipper up higher, hands in pockets.

So, where do you come from? he asked. *Norway,* I answered and he said he'd never been there. But he'd been to Denmark, he'd been to Copenhagen twice. *Tivoli,* he said. *Red hot dogs,* I said. *YES!* he said, *Red hot dogs are nice. Norway's just like here,* I said. *Except with trees. And a few more people. But otherwise the same.* He looked away, to the side, he didn't quite know what to say, it was raining, it was cold, and we didn't quite know what to tell each other, I had no news from the Western Front, so I said *What are you doing out? I'm going to Óluva's,* he answered quickly, turning and pointing down toward one of the houses, a wooden house at the edge of the cluster. *Girl friend?* I asked, out of duty. *Friend,* he answered, equally practiced. Great, we had the formalities over with. *My name is Sofus,* he said. *Mattias. There are fifty-four people in Gjógv,* said Sofus. *That's not many,* I answered. *No,* he said. *Hardly any.* Then he said *Bye bye,* and hurried down the road in his sneakers, shouting out for Óluva when he'd nearly reached the house, and I saw a shadow behind a window that looked out, called back and disappeared. I heard the door open and close. I walked the final short stretch up to the Factory, opened the door and walked in, nobody home and the sound of nothingness.

I was wet again, to the skin. I took my jacket off, hung it on a chair, feeling ashamed, hoping that Havstein wouldn't come back just yet and see my wet jacket, realize that I'd been out, that I'd been on the point of giving up, and I didn't know Havstein as a man, but I felt a huge respect for him, automatically, like the obedient dog I was, a dog that wags its tail when you arrive. I lay on the sofa and played dead, put the TV on with the remote control from the table, but I must have pressed the wrong button, because I couldn't get a single channel, all I got was snow, and after half an hour it was losing its appeal, and I turned it off, looked at the clock. It still said half past seven. Looked at the ceiling, tried to think, but didn't know what to think about.

Havstein didn't return before it had begun to be dark, it was probably already eleven, perhaps twelve. I heard the car stop just outside, the tires crunching in the gravel, the noise of the car door being opened and closed, his footsteps at the entrance, and a moment later he stood in the living room. I lay with my back to him, couldn't see him, but knew he was there, felt a change in air pressure, as though the space taken by his body made the air press itself farther into the room. I waited for him to say hello, to begin to talk, waited for him to tell me what Jørn had said, and what he'd said to Jørn. Wasn't sure I wanted to hear it at all.

He came in. Sat in the chair opposite me. I hoisted myself up, pulled myself together. *Try to look presentable now. Don't get in the way. Be a good guest.*

"Hi," said Havstein.

"Hi."

There was a long pause, as though we were waiting for the day's script to be given to us. I had the first line.

"Did you find Jørn?" I asked.

"Yes," answered Havstein. "I found him. A very nice guy. Have you known him long?"

"Yes, since high school, I think." I was suddenly unsure, problems keeping my thoughts in order.

"Very nice guy."

"He's the vocalist," I ventured, "in Perkleiva, the band I came with . . ."

"Yes, he told me."

"Great band."

We sat like that for a while, Havstein put his hands on the table. I was Mickey Mouse, could only talk in falsetto. Big ears.

"I think you'll be here awhile, Mattias."

And those words felt good to me. Fatherly. Like sitting all day on the top floor of a burning, swaying skyscraper. And then leaping. Knowing somebody has spread out a net.

"Really? Do you think so?" I looked at him, tried to work out who he was, decided to ask later, not now. There was no point, I would be here awhile.

"Yes, I think it's sensible."

"I see."

"There's nobody relying on you at home, I understand. No job waiting."

I had nothing, neither needle nor haystack.

"No."

"So things are all right from that point of view. That's good."

"Is it?"

"I thought I'd call your mother in the morning too. If you think that's okay?"

Mother. Who still knew nothing, but who knew everything. Mother, like all mothers, always the last, yet the most important link in the communication chain. Mother for whom opportunity had never knocked, who was always a step behind. I didn't like it. Didn't like it at all, mixing her in with this chaos.

"Is it okay? To call your mother?" he repeated. I answered that it was, he could just call. But remember to say hello. To tell her I'd call soon.

"It can be pretty good here," said Havstein. "On the Faroes."

He didn't say more, that would have to do as the message of the day. And that was how he was, how he would generally show himself. Calm. Controlled. Practical. Rolled out of the Factory, the new model. *Mr. Practical 2000.* And I liked him already.

We had a kind of improvised night snack, Havstein put out some bread, butter and orange juice on the kitchen table, we cut slices from the bread, shared the butter knife, talked about the weather, tentative, opening sentences, that reminded me of those "getting to know each other" trips in high school, where we'd sit for hours with a bunch of new classmates on a bus up to some summer cabins that the more organized students in the class had rented, and none of us would know each other, there was bingo on the bus, and you could end up next to the most boring person ever, or next to the person that would end up being your best friend. Either way, we hardly spoke, at least not on the bus. We gazed out of the window, in suspense, the lid was stuck firm, unopenable in any other way than through this ritual. We'd have to drink our way to friendship, and so we'd sit in the cabin, on tatty old couches in dusty rooms, waiting for it to be seven, eight, or at least six o'clock, so the drinking could start, the first beer opened. Time yawned, and we tried to kill it by eating, to rev up for the evening when we'd all be introduced. And we'd gaze around the room, and think *I don't know any of you guys, and you don't know me. But tomorrow we will know each other, and then it will seem impossible there was ever a time we didn't. Of course that's Johannes, of course, who else.*

And I felt just that way now.

We sat in the kitchen.

We hadn't started to drink.

Actually, we had no plans to start drinking.

Eventually we ate in silence, looked out of windows that only reflected our own images back now, we looked past each other, a touch embarrassed perhaps, it was Havstein who took the initiative, I was just pleased not to have to. The formalities. I finished my food. Sat with my hands in my lap. Stared at the milk carton. *Mjólk*.

"Have you had enough?" he said.

"Yes, thanks," I answered.

"Come on then, I'll show you to your room."

School trip. Class outing. Sleeping bags rolled out from backpacks. Who will sleep where? Rumors about girls and boys in the same room, even if they were never true.

"Come on. It's upstairs."

I got up, took my plastic bag with me, and followed Havstein into the corridor and to the staircase at the entrance, the stairs creaked and I tried to spread my weight evenly over the steps, to decrease the noise, to make the least possible din. Havstein swung to the right on the second floor, opened the first door on the left. He stood in front of me in the doorway and said *here*, but I couldn't see in, so I moved closer, like a schoolboy, standing on my toes to see over him, and he must have registered it, stood aside and let me into the room, turning the light on behind me.

I didn't know what I'd expected. Something more like a summer cabin perhaps? Paneled hostel walls, fixed wooden bunk beds with dents in the bed slats and names carved in the frame. It could have been a room filled with enthusiastic brass band players, with Scouts, or panic-stricken children trying to solve the life and death problems of who'll share rooms, who'll sleep on top, who'll sleep below? But we were the only ones here. The two of us. And this was where I was going to stay.

And the room was white. White painted walls. Anonymous, like a waiting room, with golden brown floorboards, light-colored furniture. There was a desk in here, a bed in the one corner, a good bed, it seemed, and apart from that there were the usual things, cupboards, spindle chairs, brown carpet covering parts of the floor, a map on the wall, and a big window that stood open. The room was cold and damp, Havstein came in after me, walked over to the window, closed it and put the catch on.

"All right?" he asked, looking at me. "Okay?"

"Okay."

He took a step back, stood in the doorway and looked back at me. I stood in the middle of the room, plastic bag in hand. I had nothing more to say. I was tired, exhausted. I was frightened.

"Good night," said Havstein, turning and going out, I only just managed to answer before he closed the door behind him, I listened to his footsteps descend the stairs, and then sat down in the nearest chair, a spindle chair, stared at the ceiling, I could hear the noise of the track lighting, a steady hum, and there I sat, on a spindle chair in the Faroe Islands and it was nighttime, I should sleep, should go to bed, it would be a long day tomorrow.

Because?

Why would it be longer than any other?

What plans had I made?

None.

Exactly.

I'd stopped functioning.

Yes.

I was out of order.

From today the days ran onto each other, they were just Tuesdays.

From today I was no longer a cog in a machine.

From today I was officially broken.

I wrenched my sneakers off, still wet, damp, rolled my socks off, hung them over the bedpost. Took my clothes off, folded them neatly and laid them on the chair next to the desk, drew the curtains, turned off the light and lay down on the bed, it didn't even creak, as I'd expected, as I'd hoped. It was completely quiet in the room and I wished I was elsewhere.

But I can't get to sleep, I lie on my back, eyes closed, hoping somebody will come, that somebody might suddenly open the door, Mom, that somebody will come through the door with cocoa, with warm hands, that somebody will hold this confused head of mine in their hands, ruffle my hair gently, plump my pillow, sit on the edge of my bed and share wise words of experience, reassuring me that nothing bad can ever happen to me, that I just have to dive in, that everything will fall into place. I want someone to come in and tell me things will be better tomorrow, that the saltwater taste in my mouth will go away if only I get some sleep, that I'll get up tomorrow as always, find my clothes on the chair where I put them the night before, that I'll get up and take a shower, get dressed, go to work, call Helle from work, go up to Valbergtårnet in Stavanger in the evening, sit on the wall if it's warm, watch the cruise ships hum into the fjord, for those with enough money and arthritis, and for the first time in my life I wish I didn't exist.

I thought of Jørn's brother as I lay there in bed. Hadn't we grown somehow closer to each other now? A memory from the summer of '85, we sat on Vaulen Beach together, Jørn and I. Maybe there were other people there too, probably, but Jørn is the one I remember, the only one in the picture. We'd just been in for a swim, we sat warming ourselves on the smooth rocks, it was late, we'd been out for a long time, but it was the middle of summer and we were allowed to stay out for almost as long as we wanted, so long as we reported back when we got home, opened the door to our parents' rooms, woke them up to say *I'm here*, we sat on the rocks drying off, just sat there, staring out into space, and on the other side of the fjord the lights began to go out in the houses, it was getting darker around us and I don't know what triggered it, but I think that was the evening we began to talk, properly, no silly talk, it poured out from some place in my brain, I told him how I talked to my plants, and that I wanted to be a gardener. I went into detail about how the sea was rising and rising, inch by inch, and how it wouldn't take that much, just one yard more, and almost a hundred million people would lose their homes, and then I went on, telling him how I'd decided I didn't need to be the best, the most popular, or even liked, I just wanted to find myself a vacant space and stay there, do my thing, maybe I was just frightened of disrupting something, of knocking the world out of its delicate balance by being in the way, in the wrong place, if I was too visible, tied people to me. And I talked about the Presbyterian Edwin E. "Buzz" Aldrin, Jr., the quiet, reserved astronaut who did everything right, pressed the right buttons, fine-tuned their course, did the sums and reflected on the calculations. The man who brought wine and a chalice with him, held communion on the surface of the moon, impossible to get nearer to God, and we talked about whether it was just a coincidence that the director for the manned mission at the Houston Space Center in 1969 was called Christopher Columbus Kraft, or whether it had some significance. I guess we covered most subjects that evening, that is, I probably did most of the talking, for once, and Jørn sat there, listening, commenting, analyzing, Jorn began to fill in the black holes in my universe, he talked about Petter, his big brother that lived on the other side of the fjord, in Dale, the Dale Psychiatric Unit, the madhouse, a closed unit, there were no holes in the fences around Dale, there were no fences out there, only mountains, water, the fjord. Jørn talked about the times he'd gone with his father to visit his brother, white corridors, cold rooms, green linoleum, worn away by a symphony of slippers, and Jørn told me how his brother would always be sitting in his chair under the window when they came in, sitting quietly in his green chair under that window, and how he'd look away, and hardly ever talk, less and less on each visit. Sometimes they'd just sit together in silence. Listen to the shouts from other rooms, the mumbling, the babbling, the chatter after silence, it wasn't as dreadful as you might imagine, said Jørn, only in brief moments did you remember where you were, otherwise it was like any other hospital, and lots of the patients were very nice, they'd give you toffees and there was always a bowlful of toffees in the smoking room, Petter liked to sit in there when he had visitors, he liked to show the others he had family there, that they'd come to visit, and Jørn described the day they'd discovered something was wrong, how his father had come home from work to find his son sitting naked in the kitchen, with his head on the kitchen table and blood running from his arms. Jørn had been to football practice and when he got home they'd only just been picked up by the ambulance, Petter and his father. The blood had begun to congeal on the wax tablecloth.

"I miss Petter," said Jørn.

"Do you think he'll ever come back?"

"Maybe. I don't know."

It was quiet for a moment.

"Why do you want to be a gardener?" asked Jørn.

"Because it's quiet," I answered.

I don't remember how long we'd sat there, whether anybody else came or went, but we'd talked for a long time and that evening it hit me that Jørn was one of those people you shouldn't lose sight of, one of those people you wouldn't want to find in your photo album years later, when you were looking at pictures of old friends that had vanished from your life, wondering what had become of them. Jørn had always been my man, and he was today too, sitting in Tórshavn with Havstein, and that was a good thought.

And the days that had passed, I tried to play them back, what had I really done in the last few days, in this last week? I'd been in Stavanger, I'd said *Yes, yes, of course I'll come,* I'd sat in the back of a car that day with Jørn and Roar and Tomas, and we'd taken the road to Bergen, driven on and off the ferries, and when we'd finally arrived in Bergen, we met the two other bands, and we'd boarded the boat. Evening had fallen, and then things had started to go wrong. There was a lot of water, I remembered that, but it had been so dark, I couldn't remember what had actually happened. I tried to concentrate, to reconstruct the boat journey across, but I was too tired, too slow in my head, and finally I had to give up, it was impossible, for now at least, maybe tomorrow. Everything was potentially different tomorrow, potentially okay. I was cold. I longed for home. Probably for the first time ever. I longed to be back in my empty apartment. Longed for things I knew. I got up again in the end, took the magnolia overalls out of the carrier bag, put them on. It was something at least. And they fit perfectly. I felt a little more at home. Lay back under the covers. And that was how, lying on my back, filled with fear in the bed in Gjógv, in Havstein's Factory, I slept, on that first day.

LIFE

I

I was woken up by noises from the ground floor. I was lying on a narrow bed, under a duvet with an unfamiliar smell, light coming through the curtains onto a linoleum floor. I wasn't at home. I had no idea where I was. I might be anywhere. And somebody was talking on the floor below, morning voices, a radio playing music I couldn't bear to listen to. I lay in bed, with a head that refused to cooperate and a body that wanted to be left in peace. I felt as if I'd drunk weed killer. By the gallon. As if I'd eaten plaster of Paris. I didn't want to get up. I wanted to stay lying there. Until I knew where I was. Until somebody arrived and sent me back. Collect on delivery.

It was like being a child again, I've stayed the night with the boy next door, and I wake up alone in the room. He's already gotten up, gone downstairs, and he's sitting, eating breakfast with his parents. You wake with the shock of not being at home, don't dare to get up, don't dare to get dressed. Don't dare to go down and say *good morning*.

Just as then, I curled up in my bed now, trying to work out where I was, why I was here. And everything that had happened in the last weeks and months wrapped itself up in a ball of panic that threw itself at my head and I heard footsteps coming up the stairs, a creaking on the treads and a hand that knocked at my door.

"Mattias?"

I didn't answer, pretended to be asleep, fooling nobody.

"Mattias?"

"...Yes?"

He opened the door, stuck his head in, and when he saw me he came right into the room. Havstein. My harbor Havstein.

"Good morning."

"Yes," I answered. "Good morning."

Havstein cast a look at my clothes, they lay neatly folded on the chair despite still being damp, dirty. He smiled.

"How are things with you?" he asked, picking my clothes up, putting them on the desk and sitting down on the chair, doctor-like, all he needed was my file under his arm. Stethoscope.

Which must have been when I started to cry. Rivers of despair ran down and across the floor, completely without warning, the first time in a long time, like a child. I hid my face under the duvet, lay there shaking, fell completely apart at the seams in front of Havstein. And I was despair's puppet as I lay there, everything in total ruin and not one good plan left up my sleeve. So what could Havstein do? Nothing, because there was *nobody* who could comfort this Toffle, and I tried to laugh at the idiotic comparison. But I couldn't, my laughter turned into nothing but low, gurgling, guttural noises.

Havstein sat there in his chair, waiting for me to resurface, he didn't sit on the edge of the bed, didn't stroke my hair, didn't turn into my father, and I was grateful for that, he didn't lose composure and as so many others might when confronted by somebody spontaneously bursting into tears, throwing themselves over one, comfort's fire blankets. Havstein remained in his chair, and slowly but surely I composed myself, let go and peered over the top of the duvet, taking short gasps of air, sat halfway up in bed, dried my eyes with sleepy fingers, feeling embarrassed, naked. That was when he noticed I was wearing the overalls. He didn't pass any remark. Said instead:

"It's hard?"

"Yes," I replied clearly, without giving it a thought. And then, quickly: "But it's a little better now." I sniffed. Havstein was prepared, he handed me a tissue from one of the desk drawers and I blew as hard as I could, tried to drain myself, but with only moderate success. Havstein got up, went to the curtains and pulled them open. It was raining outside. I lay back down again, and I think I slept.

And the days and nights would coagulate in slow motion, like cars seen through dirty windows, now and then I'm awake, in the morning, at night. I'm woken by noises from below, the sound of chatter, the radio, Havstein brings food up to me a couple of times a day, sits next to my bed, talks. But I say nothing in reply, like an oyster on dry land, tightly shut, sleeping sixteen or seventeen hours a day, but I wake up at night, always at night, when the others are asleep. I lie wide awake, listening to the sounds of snoring, of bodies turning in their beds, of the rain outside. I get up, go over to the window, draw back the curtains, open the window, and it's dark outside, the air is damp, I sit and stare out, look at the contours of the mountains to the right, the sea that lies straight ahead of me, stretching all the way to the Arctic, and I squint down at the rocks on the shore, searching for a fixed point by which to check if the sea is rising, but it isn't, apart from at high and low tide, as normal, and I sit by the window until I'm cold, then close it and on the bed again, stare up at the ceiling, trying to run through the last few months, and I don't know what I'll do now. I have no idea. And Helle? What is Helle doing? Helle is asleep now, alone or with Mats, I imagine she's sleeping badly, that she's tossing between the sheets to no avail, because something's not quite as it should be, but she doesn't know what. She's happy with him, surely? Yes, of course. Perhaps it's her job? Isn't it quite what she'd hoped for, how she'd dreamed it would be? But hardly anything is as we think it will be. And I think about Father who's back from Saint-Lô, together with Mother, and Father is waiting for a postcard from me, he walks down to look in the mailbox every day, but there's nothing there, another day and nothing, but you'll get a card, when I have the time, when I've got one, and I think how Father would have been pleased if I'd called, or for me to call him now, bringing him to his feet at the other end, hearing him make himself comfortable, talking with Father, for hours on the phone, but there isn't a phone in here, and Father's asleep now, next to Mother, lying on his back with one arm around her, and his arm has gone to sleep, but he doesn't notice it until he gets up, before he shakes the life back into it in the bathroom that morning, and that's when he sees it, in the mirror, after he's come out of the shower, that there's an imprint of Mother in his arm, a little dip in his arm where she's lain, every night for all these years. I think about Father's arm.

I don't know what day it is. I've lost track. I'm tired, I sleep too much and I don't ask Havstein when he comes in, I accept the food I get, obediently, I am the monk in the highest, narrowest tower of the castle. Doing penance in silence.

What were Buzz Aldrin's thoughts on the night before liftoff? *Tomorrow I will be in space. I will be among the first people out there, we'll find the moon, approach it, bring the landing module carefully down onto the dusty surface, in the basalt. In thirty-six hours I will set foot on the moon, I will walk around up there. Me.* And what were Buzz Aldrin's thoughts when he got back home, after days in quarantine, on that first night with his family at home, after he'd brushed his teeth, gone into his bedroom, got undressed and lain under the covers? *I've been on the moon. I've actually been up there. It was me. I've been up there, and now I'm here again, in my bedroom. Those are my footprints in the carpet to the bathroom, just as they're my footprints in the Sea of Tranquility, nearly four hundred kilometers and another planet away.* Impossible to sleep on such a night. Impossible to slow the brain. After traveling at 40,000 kilometers an hour there can be no talk of putting the brakes on. Collision is the only possible outcome.

More sleep, of the kind that neither starts nor finishes with any marked break, but lies calmly covering your face, darkening the world, a sleep you can't rely on for a second. And laughter. Laughter from the floor beneath, mixed with the radio and the rain, stairs that creak and doors that open, food that is served and my mouth that chews but refuses to speak, refuses to say anything, questions that are asked and afternoons that melt into each other, nights spent wide awake, sitting at the window, not like a bird, but like a sheep, caught with my head in the wire fence, and uneven streams of images projected into my sleep, the ferry trip, Helle, Father, Jørn, synchronized swimmers covering the entire Store Stokka Lake, in circular pulsating formations out on the water, we stand around and clap, tightly packed crowds around Stokka Lake and the synchronized swimmers change formation, turning into swans, sea serpents, flowers, Mother in the middle, wearing her bathing cap, Mother back on the team, and Jørn stands beside me in his brother's room and we try to turn the ceiling light on and off, but we can't break the code, and somebody must tell us to stop, we're wearing the switch out, we're told, and I cut the roses on a slant, put them in a vase and fill it with water, put it on Grandfather's bedside table and he is so happy with the flowers, and now I part the petals carefully with my fingertips, see Helle lying there among the roses, with the courier, Mats, and Grandfather says, *look, how beautiful they are*, and I say, *yes, but it isn't easy*, and we look down among the flowers, *not many things are easy*, laughs Grandfather handing me the binoculars and ruffling my hair, I look at Helle through the binoculars before I lean back, I put my head back as far as I can, see the meteorites gathering speed toward us and Grandfather lays his binoculars aside, down on the ground, *don't you need them anymore?* I ask, pointing at them, and with his head leaning back Grandfather tells me, *no, I don't need them anymore. Not when they're as close as they are now,* and then my sleep turns black again, I sleep for a long time, and when I wake up, my head has cleared, fine weather, and Havstein is sitting in the chair again, the curtains drawn back. Outside, it's raining. Overcast. And yet it is light, and in places the sun almost comes through the clouds.

"Hello," he says.

My voice: "Hello."

"So how are things now?"

"What day is it?" I lie in the bed, my hands clutching tightly to the sheet.

"Friday," he answers.

Pause.

And then: "It might just turn out to be a nice day," he says, squinting out of the window. "I thought you might like to get up today, meet the others. We could go out for trip, if you fancy."

I want to get out of this room. And I want to stay here. To never go out.

"Yes," I say. "Okay."

Okay.

"Good. That's good. You can use the shower down the hallway. I've washed your clothes, they're there," he says and points towards the desk. "We'll meet for breakfast downstairs afterwards, okay?"

"Yes."

Havstein goes to leave, but stops, turning to me in the doorway, as they do in American movies when they're about to impart words of wisdom, to say their doorway exit lines. But he says nothing. He waits a moment, goes out, closes the door behind him.

I was so heavy in my body.

I weighed a thousand pounds.

I had magnets under my shoes.

I folded the duvet carefully back. Pushed my feet over the mattress, out toward the edge. Put my feet on the cold floor. Curled my toes. And there were no birds singing outside.

I just stood there for a moment to begin with. Feeling what it was like to be up, thinking for a moment that I'd returned. That it was over. Imagined that I felt lighter in my body.

But I didn't.

How desperate is it possible to be?

That's something that's never been researched.

There are no statistics.

There are no graphs to compare oneself with.

No diagrams with uplifting figures.

I could still change my mind.

Go back to bed.

It'll sort itself out, all this, I thought.

No it won't, I thought. It really won't.

My clothes lay on the desk ready and freshly washed. I stretched out an arm and took hold of my jeans, lifted a leg and guided it through the fabric. Balancing on one leg. Didn't fall. The next leg, pulled my sweater on, also newly washed, the smell of unfamiliar washing powder. It was raining outside. Wind. Water. Waves. I pulled on a pair of brown socks that lay on the desk. They weren't mine, I didn't know where mine were, but I accepted the ones I was given. Socks. Got my shoes on, they were dry, even the soft insoles.

I scanned the room, turning three hundred and sixty degrees. Bed. Window. Desk. A mirror hung beside the door. I stood in front of it.

But saw nothing.

Laid my hand on the door handle.

Go.

Stairs down.

I went into the hallway and down the stairs to the ground floor. I heard the radio was on. Elton John. Clung hard to the banister. Heard talking. Women's voices. Havstein. Down the stairs.

Step by step. Twelve steps toward rehabilitation.

An optimistic outlook on life is more important today than ever.

The treads creaked.

An optimistic outlook on life is more important today than ever.

I went down the stairs. Held onto the handrail.

An optimistic outlook on life is more important today than ever.

Mattias is going down the stairs. Me. Nothing more.

An optimistic outlook on life is more important today than ever.

More important today than ever.

And then I was down.

I stand in the hall at the bottom of the stairs, right near the solid front door, nobody has heard me come down. My shoes are on. I could run out the door, look for a bus, go down to Tórshavn, out to the airport. I could get away unnoticed. There's nobody to miss me. I could go home. Disappear out the door, walk down to the sea, just keep walking until I'm under the water, just keep going as far as I can manage, until I'm sleeping with the fishes. Or, I could go up again, creep up the stairs, find the telephone. Ring Jørn. Get someone to fetch me. Rescue me. An ocean of possibilities to choose from. I'd selected Helle. And she'd deselected me. Selected another prize from one of the top shelves. Most people have chosen cheap plants this year, but I've chosen to get off a boat at Tórshavn, to disappear into the rain without knowing why, to lie in a bus shelter, to let Havstein pick me up. Because he was the first person to come along. Simple.

And then I decide that I can't bear this any longer.

I decide to begin the journey.

And I walk into the living room, to the others.

One foot in front of the other.

Johnnie Walker.

So I walked into the kitchen of what had once been the Factory in Gjógv. The first thing I saw was Havstein standing at the kitchen workbench, the same generous body I'd remembered from my first hours here, too many days ago, perhaps weeks, and now he was standing here slicing tomatoes, the only time we'd have tomatoes in the house as long as I lived there, they were so expensive, there were hardly any vegetables in the stores, we had to go to Tórshavn to get any, and Havstein was performing a little jig in front of the tomatoes, humming to the rhythm, because somebody had put on a CD of the Cardigans in the living room, Nina Persson gushed from the speakers and little whoops of enjoyment were coming from in there, and Havstein caught sight of me as I stepped into the kitchen, he put the knife and tomatoes aside, came over to me, arms outstretched, and gave me a good hug, a Faroe-hug. I'd lost weight and almost disappeared in his embrace, then he pushed me along in front of him, past the long kitchen table, past the big open windows overlooking the harbor, and the sun streamed in, I remember it was cold in here, but it was the first dry day, an almost cloudless sky, and I could see for the first time how things actually looked by daylight, I saw the blunt, rounded mountains that rose in gentle waves all around, the total absence of trees, the way the green, green grass lay like a carpet over the mountains, the knolls, reminding me of the felt-covered fiberglass mountains on the table in the basement, where Father kept his model railway in the old days, this was Märklinland, the entire view from the window in just two colors, green and blue. Blue sky. Blue sea. Green land. Havstein shoved me into the living room ahead of him, pushed me into the large room where I'd sat on my first day, and there, in the middle of the room were two girls of about my age, dancing uselessly, totally out of rhythm. They saw me, stopped dancing, swung over to me, and I got more kisses than I had had in the last year, vanished in arms and hair and it smelled good from every direction, smelled like perfume, grass, mild shampoos.

That was how I met them.

Anna.

And Ennen.

That was how I actually met Havstein.

That was the day things started to happen.

The day I began to walk.

I remember being given breakfast. Orange juice. Bread. Cheeses and cold meats. I still didn't have much of an appetite, but it was improving,

I ate a slice of bread, struggled with it, swallowed, drank some juice, hadn't had that for ages, probably didn't say much, oranges in my throat, let the others talk, answered when I was spoken to, ate another slice of bread, felt it help, saw I wasn't under constant observation as I'd feared as I'd walked down the stairs. I wasn't a patient. Wasn't some piece of driftwood nobody quite knew what to do with, wasn't a spare part. I fit in. That was my feeling. As though I'd been expected.

We ate breakfast together, the open windows behind us letting a breeze through, they talked in Danish to me, or Norwegian, a sort of mixture, Faroe-Danish, I understood, we talked the same language and then when we'd finished eating Havstein disappeared up to his bedroom, came back down, car keys dangling from his hand.

"Are you ready?" he asked.

"For what?"

"To go out. You don't intend to sit in here forever, do you?"

The two girls giggled, but Havstein hushed them.

"No," I answered at a loss and got up, padded up to my room to fetch my jacket.

We covered the entire Faroe Islands that day. Zigzagged across the country, along roads carved in the sides of mountains. Havstein had a car, a red Subaru, rusted with the damp of two hundred and eighty days of rainfall each year. Ennen drove, Anna sat in the passenger seat, while Havstein and I sat in the back. We drove west, over the mountain and towards Eiði, stopped on the road some miles away, parked the car in a byway on a little plateau, close to a bend, and got out. The local council had put some binoculars up here, a permanent telescope, and I had charge of it and pointed it out over the ocean, looked a long way, to America, no doubt, swung it in toward land and then down towards the western tip of Streymoy, where two huge, sharp rocks lay close to the sea.

"Those are Risin and Kellingin," said Ennen, pointing. *"The Troll and the Witch,"* she said, with the strangest Norwegian accent I'd ever heard. "Those are the most important landmarks, photographed by every idiot tourist that ever set foot here since everybody got cameras." I stared, the two rocks looked matted from the torrential rain, and I gobbled the view up, tourist that I was. We continued down toward Oyrarbakki, crossing the bridge from Eysturoy to Streymoy, and then farther south toward Tórshavn, driving at the foot of the mountains, on smooth roads through the simple landscape, grass-covered hills and dark brown mountains, like driving on a green moon, Mare Humorum, broken only by small settlements here and there, small and large clusters of houses painted in all colors, vivid blue, pink, black, signal yellow, settlements with fifty to five hundred inhabitants, each with their own church, and the odd gas station on their outskirts, Statoil with greasy-spoon cafés and imitation leather chairs at the back, French hot dogs for ten kroner, for whoever wanted them. And the birds, the seagulls, the puffins, that only occasionally appeared, circling the tops of the round mountains, skimming the surface of the sea in the inlets. And sheep. Sheep. Sheep. Sheep up in the mountains.

Driving a car through the Faroe Islands was a unique experience. Like being in a Monaco Grand Prix: a combination of domestic cars and heavy-goods vehicles, and as in any motor race, there was only ever one route from A to B. In fact it was practically impossible to get lost, and if you did it would only be a matter of stopping at a gas station, asking for a road map, and hiding your surprise when you received a fifteen by twenty centimeter map that not only showed the entire Faroe Islands, but every single road too. Generally only one road was built from one place to another. There was *one* road from Eiði to Tórshavn. The one everyone had to go down. As fast as possible. It was the road we were on now, and it was here that I understood overtaking was not a necessity but an extreme sport, an exercise in aesthetic mobility. And if you opened the window allowing the moist air to slam into the car, you could hear the road signs stutter their hopeless messages.

80 km í mesta lagi . . . 80 km /hr at the most . . . 80 km í mesta lagi
Pleasepleasepleaseplease.

Ennen was the youngest of us, two years younger than me, and used
to the traffic. She didn't let herself be daunted by the overtaking of
trailers at bends on the tops of hills, at the entrances of narrow, unlit
tunnels, while I shut my eyes and waited for the collision, for my neck
to be flung to one side, to smash against the side window, for the seat
belt to rip the skin on my chest, for the noise of twisting steel and for
the trailer to drive into the wall of the tunnel, sparks raining as it ran
across the concrete, the smell of gasoline reaching us in those final seconds as we lay trapped in the wreck, bones sticking out in all directions,
a spark igniting the fuel as I waited for somebody to come and cut us
free from the wreck, to the sound of melancholy music. But Ennen
didn't think like that, wasn't bothered by the car two hundred feet
behind ours that accelerated and overtook four or five cars before overtaking us at one hundred miles an hour, only to slam on the brakes, turn
off on a side road and drive carefully down to one of the settlements
we passed, Ennen put her foot on the brakes nonchalantly and took the
car toward the shoulder as she half turned toward us at the back, telling
me about what she saw, pointing and gesticulating out of the windows.
"That village is called Svínáir," she said.
"Look down there, that's how typical fishing boats look," she said.
"Look at those mountains with blunt tops," she said.
"Look at those villages there," she said.
"Look at the sea," she said.
Look. Look. Look. Look. Look. Look.
That was how it was. Havstein. Anna. Ennen. And me. In a Subaru
down near Tórshavn, one day when the sun was high, August 1999.

And, for every hundred yards we drove, there were bouquets of
flowers on the roadside, withered and dry, tied to the road barriers.
"You see those bouquets?" Anna said, and for once Ennen slowed

down to give me a better view of what Anna was talking about. Three bouquets, two almost side by side, the third fifty or sixty yards farther down the road. "One bouquet for every person that's died driving along here," she said. "Every July, families that have lost somebody on the roads put a bouquet where the person died." Ennen accelerated again, these half-rotten bouquets popped up in the most incredible places.

"But that many people can't have died this year, surely," I objected.

"There aren't just bouquets for people that have died this year. Lots of the flowers are put there for people who died ten, fifteen years ago."

Overtaking. Icy roads. Mountains.

I thought about the night I'd spent lying in the bus shelter, in the pouring rain, the night Havstein had appeared out of the gray, came for me. I'd lain in the middle of that road for ages, face down, dark clothes, almost impossible to see. I hadn't known where I was, I'd scarcely been in a state to move, and I thought how flowers weren't like people at all.

Havstein was the first person to introduce himself properly, and he did it that day, as we sat in the car, racing along the road, in and out through tunnels and along one fjord after the other. Havstein was the grand old man of the Factory, almost seventeen years older than me, and close on fifty. He was a genuine Tórshavnite, born and bred in the capital, he'd moved to Denmark at eighteen, an uncle and aunt lived in Århus and his original plan had been to move there, but he'd ended up in Copenhagen instead, studying medicine and eventually getting a job in the Rigshospitalet. He'd worked shifts there while continuing with his studies, taking psychiatry and finally getting himself a permanent position in the psychiatric department. He had sporadic relationships with girls, among them a Danish girl who talked the whole time about him moving to Texas with her, not that he ever understood why. Later he moved in with a girl from Sweden, thought they'd marry, settle down, family, car, house, furniture catalogs in the mail, but nothing came of it. He continued living in Copenhagen until the beginning of the eighties, when one day he suddenly decided to go back to the Faroe Islands, and in the summer of 1981 he was, to the delight of his parents, back in Tór-shavn, and by the spring of 1982 he already had plans in motion for the first long-term psychiatric halfway house in the country, started looking for suitable locations, and finally found a factory in Gjógv that had been empty for two years, that offered almost 2,000 square feet. With the help of state money and a substantial contribution from his father, who'd done pretty well as a fisherman, Havstein began to convert the Factory. He hired workmen. Electricians, carpenters, welders, and plumbers moved through the Factory, and with paperhangers, floor layers, and removal men, they built seven bedrooms on the second floor, as well as a bedroom and office for Havstein. On the ground floor, where the ceiling was twelve feet high throughout, he put in a big, oblong kitchen that led into the three hundred square foot living room. When the money for construction began to dwindle, he was left with a massive entrance hall he didn't quite know what to do with, two old workers' locker rooms on the ground floor that he left more or less as they were, and at the back of the building, the largest room, the factory floor itself. He removed the old machinery, painted the walls, and installed big workbenches and better lighting, since the thought had already come to him, it should be possible to do something here, he didn't want residents sitting and staring at the walls, he wanted them to produce something, anything really, it didn't much matter what. (And it was here we occupied ourselves with the laughable production of model animals, peat baskets and other items that we presumed visiting tourists might think of buying. I never asked who'd come up with the idea first. But I guessed it must either have been Ennen or Havstein, whatever the case, they were the only ones with any real enthusiasm for the work. In fact, Ennen applied herself to the task so diligently that over time a huge number of wooden sheep stood grazing on the shelves along the walls.) Anyway: During the autumn of 1982 the first residents arrived, people that had been discharged for years without feeling they'd made any progress, and people coming straight out of treatment. There'd been a full house that first year, Havstein had had to take on extra help, but things soon flattened out, many people came and went before it began to stabilize, and towards the end of the eighties they'd tumbled in, one by one, Palli, Anna, Ennen.

We sped along in the car down toward Tórshavn, the sun growing warmer and warmer with each minute, that was how it should be, how it never was. Nobody was used to this kind of weather, the closer we came into town, the more people were out on the pavement, T-shirts parading up and down the streets in August, on this island in the middle of the sea, and they hoped they wouldn't have to put clothes back on until long into September.

It was hot in the car. Anna wound the window down on her side allowing the soft air in.

"It is okay to open the window," she asked me, "isn't it?"

"Yes, sure."

"Are you sure?"

"Yes, of course."

"'Cause I can just wind it up again if you're cold."

"No, honestly. It's fine."

"You're not freezing?"

"No, really."

"But you'd say if you were. Freezing, I mean."

Ennen turned toward her.

"I think it's fine with him that you have the window open."

"I just want him to know that he can say if he's cold."

"He's not cold. Are you?" Ennen looked round at me.

"No, I'm not cold."

"You see? He's not cold."

"But I don't want him to *get* cold either, I'm just trying to be nice to him, poor thing," said Anna.

"I'm beginning to get pretty warm," I said.

"I'll put the air conditioning on instead," said Havstein, "then there won't be such a draft."

A cell phone peeped.

"Is that yours, Anna? asked Havstein.

"Wait, I'll see. Yes."

"Is it Palli?"

"Yes."

"Shall we go and pick him up?"

"He finishes at three."

Havstein looked at his watch.

"Okay. We'll drive down to Kollafjørður and fetch him first, then we'll go over to Tórshavn afterward, okay?"

"It's getting a little windy now, isn't it," said Anna, "with the window open and the air conditioning on?"

"Should I turn it off?" asked Havstein.

"Yes, could you? So nobody gets cold."

"Christ," said Ennen and turned around to me again, rolling her eyes, I smiled back, shrugged my shoulders.

Palli was at work, he worked loading and unloading the Russian ships that came into the fjord a few times every month. On the whole they were ex-Soviet hulks that barely held together, ships you'd never believe could float, and which you'd never believe would be allowed to go on sailing. Rust ate its way over their bows, along their sides, over their decks and into the wheel houses, threatening to plant itself in their captains' faces, to corrode their crews, and there seemed to be something sad about working on these ships, since each time you boarded them could prove the last. When they left in the morning, there was a fair chance they'd never come into harbor again, that they'd sink somewhere out there, noiselessly and undramatically, like a cat hiding away to die, and little notices would appear in the Russian papers in the weeks that followed, sole proof that they'd ever existed.

We drove along the east side of Streymoy, along the sound that divides the Faroe Islands more or less into two, listened to the radio,

Ras 2, a channel Anna and Havstein both liked, not that I ever understood why. A girl hosted the program, sounded friendly enough, sweet,
pigtailed, you could imagine her in the studio somewhere or other in
Tórshavn, coming in every morning, apart from Fridays, taking her
seat, slightly disheveled, making herself comfortable in the little studio,
putting the large earphones on, talking into the microphone, playing
her records, the most impossible blend she could come up with, something by Wham! one minute, then straight over to Pearl Jam or similar,
our *Madonna of the Airwaves*, she steered the tempo of the traffic with
the songs she played, and we passed Kollafjørður Center, swung down
toward the quay, toward the giant Russian vessels where Palli stood
waiting at the entrance to one of the warehouses, he waved when he
spotted the car, Ennen honked a couple of times as she drove toward
him and braked as she came up alongside him.

Palli was from Kollafjørður, a small village just far enough away
from Tórshavn for the people there not to be regarded as townsfolk,
but still close enough for them to be subjected to a number of direc-
tives that the capital threw in their direction. This was where he'd been
born, and where he'd spent his whole life, apart from the few times
when he'd taken off to *the harbor*. (It took time before I worked it out,
but *the harbor* was another name for Tórshavn. Local slang, you might
say. When you went to *the harbor*, you went to the capital.) Other than
this, Palli was the person it took longest to get to know, not until weeks
later did he open up just a chink, and talk in more than monosyllabic
words. But the first memory I have of him is of his hands. Palli had
powerful fists. Welder's hands. And as soon as he opened the car door,
flashed me a glance and mumbled a moody *hello* in my direction before
dumping himself down in the seat without a word, I thought he must
be a good guy, even if one of few words. Felt as though he was anyway.
And he went on that way, didn't say a lot, unless he was asked something directly or if something really engaged him. I think that was one
of the reasons I liked him right away. Felt he was somehow on my

team. He was more talkative with Anna though, she had a way of getting him going, he seemed more comfortable talking to her, she could get him to tell her much more than we ever could. Never really understood how she managed it, what she did, what she said. Anna was thirty-four when I met her, she was from Miðvágur, one of the best harbors for pilot whale, she said. She was short, almost stocky, dark, with long hair, big, soft eyes, and a miniscule nose. She could have been a kids' TV presenter with a face like that. But the stuff I heard about her later would have been more appropriate for News Night. She was the only one who'd been to Norway, she'd worked in fish farming, and she was doing that now as well, she worked full time and came back to Gjógv with Palli in the evenings.

And I contemplated how everything had happened so fast. I'd lived through nearly thirty years with barely a couple of friends, I'd avoided other people, I'd snuck away from them or they'd passed me by in silence. And now it seemed new friends were tumbling in, in the space of just a few hours, two women, and two men, and my unwillingness to talk, my unwillingness to accept them, was ebbing away, I was becoming two open arms.

With Palli now with us, we drove some hundred yards up to the Statoil station higher on the slope, found ourselves a parking space and went into the gas station. A little group of men were standing there, truck drivers mainly who crowded around the slot machine against one wall, tripped around in wooden clogs that clacked, waited their turn, cheered when one of them won and the coins clanked down into the bowl. There was a strong smell in here, hot dogs and coffee, and it seemed the woman behind the counter had been put into a kind of optimistic stupor by the stench, she stood rocking backward and forward behind the register, wearing a permanent smile and listening to the radio. To Ras 2. I was thirsty, I crossed over to the fridge to get a soda, studied the various brands, the unfamiliar names, picked a Jolly Cola. Large advertisements for it hung all around the shop. Föroya Bjór's proud drink, with its cheery name. I felt jolly. Hadn't felt that way for a while.

Anna stood at the counter and ordered five French hot dogs, and the smile behind the counter squirted mustard into the bread holsters, the gas station's own spaghetti western. Splat! Splat! Splat! Splat! Splat! Filled them to the top with mustard and drove the sausages in, still with the same fixed smile. Havstein paid, while Ennen and Palli stood by the newspaper racks, investigating the day's headlines. In the past, I might have kept my distance, gone to the counter, paid, and gone outside, drunk my soda by the car and waited for the others to come out. But I went over to the newspapers now, joined them, picked up a paper and started reading. That is, I didn't read, couldn't understand a bit, but I stared at the words, tried to make them my own, and Ennen laughed at me: "Bet it'll take awhile before you get the pronunciation," she said, after I'd read a passage aloud which I thought had something to do with possible oil finds off the coast. Palli looked over my shoulder, read the same extract in his soft voice, a confusion of sounds, like Danish with an American accent, and then Anna shouted over from the counter that there were hot dogs for everybody, and we went up together, I put ten kroner on the counter for my cola.

"Djolli," said the assistant.

"Djolli," I answered and taking the bottle I went out, swinging the door wide so as to let a little fresh air into the room where she stood waiting to make more French hot dogs, waiting for better days or more of the good ones she'd already had.

We sat in the car and ate our hot dogs, kids on a day trip, and Palli talked about his work on the boats, answering Anna's questions. We'd rolled down the windows, the hottest day in man's memory, twenty degrees at least, and it wasn't often that happened. It was usually overcast and damp, and we generally had to drive with the windows half open to reduce the steam that covered the windows with a film in just minutes, and fog often settled over the countryside too, mingling with the low clouds, and we rarely needed to drive more than sixty feet up into the mountains before we disappeared into white nothingness, we couldn't see the road barriers let alone our hands on the wheel. And maybe that's the thing I remember best from this time: the long drives through thick fog, sitting in the car and seeing nothing, listening to the sound of tires on asphalt for proof we were moving, getting somewhere. But now, now it was sunny, and I'd gotten up from my bed, I'd begun to walk, I tried not to think about Helle, that I had a flat in Stavanger with no furniture, that I had a parked car, that there was nobody waiting for me. I'd tried to dismiss the thought that I wouldn't have the money to keep it, that when I returned some day I'd no longer drive down to work, arrive early, sit out in the garden and wait for the others. I did my best to stop thinking about things, and on the whole I succeeded. Once in awhile I felt a stabbing pain, from nowhere, a knife that drove into my spine, as if to remind me that nothing at all had been resolved for real, and that sooner or later I'd notice it. Really notice it.

So we drove to Tórshavn from Kollafjørður, taking the main road toward the tunnel, and Havstein leaned forward to whisper something in Ennen's ear, and as she came out of a turn she reduced her speed, Havstein turned to me, and without a word he motioned for me to look out of the window, I turned to look. I didn't know what he was trying to say at first, so I scanned the landscape searching for something worth seeing. Saw nothing. Just mountains. The fjord . . .

"Do you recognize that?" he asked, pointing to a turning place on the right of the road.

"What?" I answered.

Ennen slowed the car even more, but I still couldn't see what Havstein wanted me to look at.

"You've been here before."

"Have I?"

"This is where I found you, that night."

And I then recognized it. The bus shelter with its long bench. The road. The road barrier. It looked like a beautiful place now. Undistinguished, perhaps, but lovely. A place like any other. This was where I'd lain with my face to the wall. This was where I'd been, without knowing where I was. This was where I'd wanted to vanish completely, and never be found. I'd almost drowned here. Turned into a bouquet. Ennen picked up speed again, and I sat twisted in my seat until the bus shelter was totally out of view and we swung in toward town, past Kaldbaksbotnur and Kaldbaksfjøður that lay below us to the left as we came out on the other side of the tunnel, windows wide and air streaming into the car, blowing away the cigarette smoke from Palli who sat jammed between Havstein and me in the back seat, and the roads here seemed familiar, despite most of the similarity of the landscape everywhere, monotone green, and wet, I had the urge to go and lie on the nearest slope, I thought how moist the grass must be, how I could drink it, suck it into me without fear of it being polluted, spoiled, contaminated by heavy industry or mercury. Just lie there and wait for the rain that would come, sooner or later.

We drove into the center of town, through shopping streets, past the police station on Jonas Broncksgøta, and I couldn't place it, but I knew I'd been here before, in these streets, with Jørn, with Roar, and with the other band I'd come over with. I'd walked down these streets with them, on that first day, but I was erased from my own story, couldn't remember what we'd done, what we'd been up to. We drove on up R.C. Effersøesgøta to the SMS shopping center, where we parked, Havstein needed to go in the Miklagarður grocery store to buy more cigarettes and I used the opportunity to go into the bank. I still had fifteen thousand Norwegian krone in my wallet, without having the least idea why. And the cashier didn't ask either. She changed the money dutifully, efficiently, handed me the Faroese notes, and I thanked her, stuffed the new cash into my wallet and went out to the others.

Then we drove to Café Natúr.

Café Natúr was at Áarvegur 7, not far from the sea, a cozy café with its share of drunken old seadogs who seemed almost to hang over the tables, listing to the side, providing natural buffers between the café's young regulars. In the evening, by contrast, Café Natúr would transform into the hippest bar in Tórshavn, where you might ramble in to hear the year's hottest band play on the miniscule stage in the center of the floor. Café Natúr was in an old wooden house, painted dark brown on the outside, and sort of brown inside too. Or greenish. All according to how you looked at it. And the roof was covered in grass, in a kind of attempt at hiding what was really inside. The fixtures in Natúr had that peculiar quality of refusing to reveal if they were genuine or just plastic or fiberglass imitations, the solid beams and wall paneling all gave off a suspiciously artificial sound when you knocked into them, which was known to happen on occasion. Although it certainly didn't seem to bother anyone. So long as the house stayed upright. And it did. The first floor was generally less crowded, it was filled with an assortment of tables all screwed to the floor, and some seating booths too, and railings to prevent the Islanders from falling down to the floor below through the large opening, through which it was possible to communicate with people at tables below, if you yelled loudly enough at least, or waved in the air with brightly colored clothes and large gestures.

We sat at a table near the stairs leading up, and it was still early evening, it wasn't usually crowded before midnight, earliest, up to then we could move between tables with ease, maneuver over to the bar, order ourselves a beer, Föroya Bjór, always Föroya Bjór. Which cheered me up, I think. And I remember this evening best of all. We sat there, in Café Natúr, on what was essentially my first evening, I was still tired, the nausea and panic still crept up on me, as they would for months to come, letting go isn't done in a day, but I'd already noticed them come less frequently, the gaps between the moments when I lost perspective were growing longer. I was already beginning to relax more, could feel it in my shoulders, things would go all right, I thought, things might work out, I thought. And that was what began happening around me, pieces began falling into place, not because I'd finally bent down to hunt for the pieces that had sailed over the table's edge and disappeared to the floor, but maybe because I'd spent weeks letting go already, giving up on my half-hearted attempts at self-repair, screwing together the bolts without any blueprint handy, sticking myself and the shattered pieces back together, I'd spent weeks lying in bed on my back, or sitting at the open window at night, and slowly but surely I'd created new pieces, an entire new jigsaw puzzle, I'd finally let go, and it wasn't until this moment, here and now, that things started to go on track, and I began putting the new puzzle together, and the pieces looked better than the old ones. Thought of de Lillos' songs that night: *Are you trying to find yourself? What if the man you found, was a man you didn't like, who you'd have to live with for the rest of your life?*

We sat in Café Natúr late into the night. We drank beer, we talked, I talked more than I had in my entire life, my throat was raw, but I talked, truthfully, in the main. It flowed, poured from my mouth every time I opened it, perhaps I was too talkative that night, but I didn't care, it felt good to be able to tell people things, to feel that every story was potentially interesting, I told them about Stavanger, about Helle, about my song at the Christmas Ball so many years ago, about how we got together, how I succeeded in getting the snowball up on the school roof, twice in a row, even though I'd been trying for years before, each time I'd walked past in the snow, and I told them about Father who waited for his science journals and large insurance payouts, about Mother who swam in formation and helped kids, I told them about Jørn and Roar, talked about the moon expedition and Buzz Aldrin, the eternal number two who was barely remembered, about the *Voyager* probe that traveled farther and farther into space with messages from earth to whomever was out there, talked about the trip to Kjerag and about my job, the job that had vanished without trace, and they sat around me, Anna, Ennen, Havstein, and Palli with big ears, as though they'd thought I'd never start to talk, and perhaps I hadn't believed it myself, but here I sat, talking myself hoarse and happy and wishing it would never stop, that the bar would never close and that we'd never have to leave and go home. I talked and they asked questions about Stavanger, because Anna had been there years ago for a conference on salmon farming, I think that was it, but don't quite remember, and I told them about the band, about how Perkleiva had gotten the gig along with the Kulta Beats at a concert on the quay here, and Anna and Ennen said they'd been there, they'd seen Jørn and the band, they'd been good, really good, a great sound, and I was happy to hear that, happy for Jørn, happy things had worked out without me, happy the chain had held together even if the weakest link had snapped at the last lap, and Ennen interrogated me about Helle, what she looked like, what she liked, why she'd left, and how I felt. The thing I didn't tell them was the one thing I didn't know; how I'd ended up out on the Hví-tanesvengur that night, after being in Tórshaven. Why I'd lain in the middle of the road. Why I barely remembered anything from the moment of boarding the boat in Bergen.

And then twelve o'clock came, and suddenly the bar went into chaos. As though the whole town had been pacing back and forth outside, checking their watches, waiting to storm the palace on the stroke of midnight. In minutes the place was completely full, and we had to pull our chairs closer into the table and hold our beer glasses extra tightly to stop them from being knocked over as people walked past. It was Friday, and there was a concert on. One of the local bands would save the world tonight, and they plugged their equipment in and turned all the switches on. And then she started to sing. It was the Cranberries. It was Björk and Motorpsycho stirred together in a bowl, and she sang beautifully, danced back and forth on the stage and shouted into the microphone, and she looked so cute, so sweet, but then, everybody did that day, like Smurfs, and Havstein leaned over the table towards me:

"Sleipnir," he said.

"Eh?" I answered.

"They're called Sleipnir," he repeated. "They're amazing."

"Sleipnir?"

"Yeah."

We didn't get to say more, Telda thundered in with a roaring version of "I Put a Spell on You" and it was Marilyn Manson at 200BPM, a hurricane was let loose and beer rained from the upper floor, lights flashed over the bar, and there was a deafening din, Anna and Ennen disappeared from their chairs, clambered over the audience to get closer to the stage, found themselves an inch of space and began to dance, as off-beat and out-of-rhythm as earlier in the day, although in here it looked right somehow. Or perhaps it was the beer. Hard to tell. Havstein smiled and nodded at me, and Palli sat as quietly as he had all evening, Indian Chief, he tapped the rhythm carefully with his index finger on the table, lit himself a cigarette, Clint Eastwood cool, and watched the girls as they mingled with the rest of the public, and soon this bunch of dancing individuals became a pulsating mass that grew hotter and hotter until the windows were covered in steam and I had to take off my sweater, sit in my T-shirt, which to my surprise bore the words *Please Take Me Home* in big, blue letters against the white fabric, and our glasses started to refill themselves.

We left Natúr for Club 20, a nightclub up by the movie theater, where everything went at double speed, and at five-thirty we finally said our goodbyes and left for home and my ears were ringing, I had problems hearing what people said to me, had to concentrate hard, Anna and Ennen talked at me in loud, precise tones, dragged me between them through the streets in the town center, Havstein and Palli bringing up the rear. I hadn't eaten properly for a month, hardly eaten, and I wasn't sure which way the earth was rotating, but I felt sure it was the wrong way, and they dragged me between them up to the SMS shopping center, where we'd left the car, they got me in and shoved me in the back seat against one of the doors, head jammed against the window, lips and cheeks leaving marks on the glass.

Havstein drove us home that night. He always did; didn't drink beer, drank soft drinks, drank water. That's how it was. *Dr. Driver.*

We drove home. And I was happy.

I was awfully happy.

I might explode at any minute.

Kodak moment.

But I didn't go to sleep. I stayed awake all the way home, was allowed to keep the window open, because it still wasn't really cold, so I lay with my head against the window's edge and looked out toward the dark mountains surrounding us, the still cloudless sky, and it all seemed so endlessly vast at that moment, even though it was a miniscule country. The smooth grass-covered mountains rose around me on all sides, a scattering of birds that had the stamina to fly by night, birds that had gone astray from Norway perhaps, believing they'd flown to Iceland, or worse, the USA, and the waves crashed against the quaysides in the settlements that we passed, and against the rocks below the roadside barriers. The odd car would pass in the opposite direction, and for a moment I'd be blinded by the light until the noise melted away behind me and only the sound of the Subaru was left.

It took a good hour to drive back to Gjógv, which was more or less on the other side of the country. Not a great deal to do. Just to sit quietly. Let myself be taken along, I'd begun to get used to it. And the long drive cleared my head little by little, technical faults were being repaired, and with that everything I'd managed to keep in check all evening came back too, it crept in through the window, and rolling the window back up didn't get rid of it either, it just perched at the back of my head like a much-too-wise owl, hell bent on reminding me constantly how fabulously wise it was.

"Go to bed now? We can't go to bed now, surely? There's no way." It was Ennen talking, we'd just gotten back home and were standing in the living room at a loss, and Palli wanted to go to bed, he was tired, had had a long day at work.

"But Palli," Ennen said, "just look out of the window. Can't you see how beautiful it is? How often is it like that? For more than an hour or two? Hardly ever." I was tired too, in my body at least, my muscles ached, my throat hurt, but my head didn't want to go to bed, it wanted to stay up, so I cheered Ennen on, and Anna joined us, of course, since she had nothing to get up for in the morning. Havstein wandered soundlessly out into the kitchen, rummaged, returned with a bottle of wine for us and was met with exclamations of gratitude. Palli smiled, "I'm really tired, so I'll be off to bed," he said, and padded out. I heard him go up the creaky stairs and suddenly the sound seemed so familiar, as though I had heard it all my life.

We sat in the big chairs and sofas in the enormous living room, under the twelve-foot ceiling, and Ennen was everywhere at once, back and forth between the sofa and stereo system, playing all her Cardigans records for us, *Emmerdale, Life, First Band on the Moon,* and *Gran Turismo,* and she played some of the songs again, the really good ones, the best ones, the ones she knew by heart, and Havstein opened the wine, found three glasses, I struggled to keep my head from drooping onto my chest, it had grown so heavy, filled with all kinds of junk and too much fresh air. Anna sat next to me in the brown sofa farthest from the other chairs, Havstein had pulled one of the big wing backed chairs across, and Ennen stood up most of the time, or moved back and forth across the floor as she sang, hummed, and shook her head in time or out of time with the music.

"Do you like the Cardigans?" asked Havstein.

"Yes. Sure. They're all right," I answered.

"They're the only thing she plays, the only thing she listens to. Aren't they?"

"Yup," said Anna, smiling at Ennen who was standing next to one of the loudspeakers listening for new nuances in Nina Persson's voice. "Aside from the Cardigans, she's completely indifferent to music."

"A kind of song autism," I suggested.

Anna laughed and red wine sprayed out of her nose, blotting the pale tablecloth on the table between us, and Havstein lay a protective hand over his glass, drawing it closer to him. I don't know why, but that was the kind of thing they found funny.

Ennen put "Your New Cuckoo" on and came over and sat in the sofa with us.

"What are you all talking about? Mattias?"

"Rain Man," said Havstein, cracking up even though it wasn't a particularly good joke, but it was very late, or early, who knows, depending on the way you looked at it.

"Havstein and Anna say you only listen to Cardigans," I said.

"*The* Cardigans," she corrected. "And so?"

"Oh, nothing. It's just, well, it's a little . . . unusual. Listening to only one band."

"You should start a Cardigan's Army," said Havstein, pulling himself together, but continuing to snicker, a little schoolgirl in his chair. "Like the Kiss fans did." Ennen was getting riled and began to raise her voice, a finger pointed at Havstein: "I just can't be bothered listening to other bands, when everything I need is in this band. What's so wrong with only listening to the Cardigans, if they've got everything I need? What's the problem, huh?"

"Nothing," answered Havstein.

"Are they that good?" I asked.

"And better." She turned towards Anna: "It's not like I've never listened to anything else. I have, I liked Prince when I was younger. Michael Jackson. Depeche Mode. Stuff like that. But only the Cardigans stand the test of time."

"What about the Beatles?" I suggested.

"Nahh."

"Radiohead?"

"Nope."

"Björk?"

"Björk?" She thought about it. "No. Not anymore. But I really liked her band KUKL in the old days."

"But don't you ever get bored? Of listening to the same songs, over and over again, I mean?"

"No. Not really. What's the point of buying CDs if you're going to ration their use and hold off from playing them? The Cardigans make me happy. I don't get bored of them."

"But we do," laughed Havstein. "God almighty, I don't know how many times I've wanted to hide those CDs of yours, but it must be pretty often."

Ennen looked straight at him.

"And do you know what would happen then?"

"Yes."

"What would happen?" I asked.

Anna laughed.

"I don't dare think," answered Havstein.

"You're probably wise there," said Anna.

"Anyway," said Ennen, "the Cardigans might be one thing, but the stuff you listen to, Havstein, is another disaster altogether."

"True!" burst out Anna getting up and going over to a little pile of CDs next to the stereo.

"Can I, Ennen?"

"Yeah, sure."

Anna took off the CD that was on, found another one, and it went quiet for a few seconds before the room filled with a blend of dance-band boogie, blues, and a caterwauling sound, hardly beautiful, and I suddenly realized this was what I'd been hearing in the mornings, and not the radio, as I'd lain in my room all those weeks.

"Havstein," I said, looking at him and trying to remain serious. "What is this?"

"This is Kári P. The Faroe Islands' big hero."

"Carrie?"

"No, Kári. Kári's a man, can't you hear, *co-ry*."

Ennen sat on the sofa and grinned, giggled, shook her head and shouted over to Anna: "One more time!" and Anna played the same song again. *Góðborgara-shuffle.*

"Play the one with the sax part in it," shouted Ennen.

"*Sangur umflyting?*"

"Yes!"

Anna put another track on. It began with a moody sax solo and was a ballad about how the poor were forced to move out, and the rich moved in, because the world was changing, times they were a-changing, and Kári sang mournfully, a guitar in the background, not as ghastly as the last track, but I wouldn't have wanted to buy it, even less wake up to it.

"This is a tremendous song," Havstein suggested, "It has something really relevant to say. Just look around. There used to be lots of people living around here, and now, there's hardly a soul. The lyrics are bloody brilliant, he really gets in there."

"Yeah, sort of," answered Anna. "It's just he shouldn't sing them."

"Maybe he could have just recited them instead," suggested Ennen.

"Or just printed the text on the cover and released an empty CD, sold it with magazines for housewives."

Somebody passed me the cover, Anna I think. The CD was called *Vælferðarvísur*. The image on the front was a kind of collage, that kind of worked. The background was done in pencil, the right hand side was taken up by mountains and a tiny village that almost seemed to be erasing itself, rising on the other side was a black tower block. An elderly man walked through a door in the middle, and a fisherman, holding a piece of fish wrapped in paper, stooped to get through the low door, stepping onto a chessboard where the black and white squares didn't tally, an impossible game, with only four pawns. Tarzan swung on a liana toward the chessboard, and a man without eyes, mouth, and arms sat in a chair at the back of the room, and down at his feet, three American soldiers held their hands up to shield their eyes. An angel watched over them all, or had forgotten their existence. It should have meant something to me, but it didn't, I got nothing from it, except that it was about things that didn't turn out right, that everything was hopeless, but that nobody cared.

And we listened to the rest of the song, the mournful saxophone reminiscent of times gone by that would never return, things that had gone askew and could never be repaired. Kári believed in what he sang, without a doubt, he did his best, and that was good enough, people moved from their farms, moved into town, into tiny rooms with scarcely room to turn, and Kári lent his voice to the cause, and for moments you could go along with it, until the saxophone forced itself in again, stealing the show with its pathetic cooing, so there was nothing to do but give up, and a moment later we were onto the next track again, back with the *Góðborgara-shuffle* and everyone in the room fell about laughing, while Havstein sat there looking offended, tapping the beat with his foot, trying to keep it discreet, trying to convince himself it was a good CD, that Kári P. was a good man, that it was worth listening to, that it meant something to him, I watched him go through the arguments in his head, there was something sad about it, but I said nothing.

So we drank more wine, our insides turned red and we found each other in that enormous room, snuck closer on the sofa. Ennen put more Cardigans on, it had already been light outside for a long time, sharp sunlight through the windows, a pair of indolent puffins made a few cautious rounds outside, but gave up, thought it was too early, flew back and went back to sleep. I sat here among these people, yet I'd begun to sink away from them. I thought about what I'd do next, how long I could be here, what I'd do afterward when autumn came, when my money was used up. There really weren't many alternatives left, almost none. And I'm not sure I liked any of them.

"It was a collective decision to let you stay here," said Havstein suddenly, and a shock went through me. "I wanted you to know that. We've talked a lot about it. There's no reason for you to go back now."

"There's not a lot to go back *to*," I said. I thought about Jørn, apart from during the weeks before we'd left, we'd barely seen each other in the last years. The occasional evening, a few hours once or twice a month, Jørn was busy with his life, so much to do, things were going in the right direction for him and I'd never wanted to stand in his way. And my parents, they'd miss me, of course, my visits, I knew Father would, he'd be sad that I no longer stopped by, that I no longer stood in the hallway unexpectedly, ready to hear the latest news, to discuss some event or other on the news, to stand in the garage helping him change to winter tires, or to assemble that new IKEA cupboard that Mother just had to have. I was going to miss them, and it was a strange feeling, realizing that the only people waiting for me back where I came from were my parents, and they'd wait for me whatever I did, forever tuned into that station, the frequency of loss.

"But I've got a flat in Stavanger," I said.

"Yes, but it's almost empty," said Anna. "Can't you give it up, get somebody to pick your things up?"

And of course I could. There was almost nothing left there. Barely a cracker. And I wondered if one could do something like that, to be rid of everything one had, not to stop, but to return to Go, collect $200 and start again.

"Perhaps," I said.

"Stay here," said Ennen. "We think you should stay."

I sat saying nothing for a while.

"All I have is the money in my wallet," I said.

Havstein looked at Anna. Anna looked at Ennen. Ennen looked at Havstein. They each looked at each other. Huey, Dewey, and Louie. I was Donald and understood nothing.

"What's your relationship to sheep?"

"A natural one," I answered.

"Then we've got the perfect job for you."

And that was how I got the job, how I came to be Mattias, souvenir maker. Of handmade wooden sheep, covered in glued-on wool. No two alike, which is why everybody wanted to take them home, tourists, Icelanders who wanted to take a symbol back to their fatherland, proof of how the Faroe Islands were still behind them in every way, the Faroese, the people that fought for independence from Denmark, or not, and that went to bed at night and thought about, or forgot the world beyond. Wooden sheep. I produced souvenirs until the grim reaper himself went soft and begged me to take a break. I got up early in the morning, ate breakfast with Havstein and Ennen. Anna and Palli had already left, Anna for the fish farm in Funningur, Palli for the quayside in Kollafjørður. Leaving us to make sheep. The perfect futile activity. Went into the locker room I'd been in on the first day, changed into work clothes, not because we really needed to but because it gave us the feeling we were running a business, we were workers. Finally had a use for the overalls I'd come with. Havstein and I turned the wood, planed it, sawed it, carved and hammered until the animals were beautiful, supple and aerodynamic, the way they should be. The old fish filleting room had been turned into a planing mill, a workshop, an enormous room in the back of the Factory, the only area that still looked like a factory, white brick walls, winches and pulleys hanging from the ceiling, windows covered with shavings and dust, dead flies on the ledge. We packed the sheep into beautiful brown cardboard boxes made by an advertising agency down in Tórshavn that we visited once a week to get supplies. We got support from the state to keep production going, to keep Gjógv going, which was almost deserted now, and to keep us going. We got almost all our income from there. I had the impression it really didn't matter what we made, that we'd have been subsidized for just about anything, the production of tree felling equipment, even, so long as we did something. How we did it was up to us, so long as we gave first aid. But then, you can sell anything, it's only a matter of convincing the world it needs it. Bottled water for example. In Norway. Wooden sheep were just as good, they brought happiness to little children and souvenir hunters. With state subsidy.

August and September came and went before I'd even registered it, the nonexistent trees lost their leaves, and I spent my days in the workshop with Havstein and Ennen, producing wooden sheep and putting them carefully in their tourist friendly packaging, trying not to think about what I was doing, that it was meaningless, that I was contributing nothing of import. Late in the afternoon, Anna and Palli would return, and we'd eat dinner together, they were good times, and gradually, day by day, I began to thaw, I was Ötzi the iceman discovered in the Alps after so many years, and I'd waited so long for this, drank it all in and tried to float more lightly between rooms with each day.

I hold out until one day in October. Then everything comes to a stop. The tape gets screwed up again. Haven't gone out of my room for several days. I don't know why. I'm not eating. I dream about Helle. I dream about plants, about the nursery, and in my dreams I'm the only one at work, the only one who comes in that day. And there's so much to do, so many plants to be delivered. So little time. The clocks wind themselves forward on the walls. The hands scrape the metal surface as they spin. The door into the storeroom bulges outward, threatening to burst open. The storeroom is completely overfilled. I can't get through my list. I'm behind time. Papers piled high on the counter. Orders. Reservations. I start from the sitting room. Lift the first pile of papers. Open the door to the storeroom. The plants come tumbling out, cover the entire floor of the shop. The clocks race on the walls. I fill the car to the brim, sit in the car, and the plants start dividing, multiplying themselves. They fill the whole shop, pressing up against the display windows. Bursting through. Breaking the walls of the building. So that glass and wood and steel and bricks rain over the car, smashing the window screen, denting the hood, scraping the paint. It smells like gasoline. And I drive away from the nursery, up to the first nursing home on the list. I run in. Run down the corridors. Bang on the door. Open it. Enter. But the rooms are all empty, the patients are already dead, taken away, and I have a car full of flowers nobody needs. I stand outside one of the nursing homes, feeling lost, my hand on the door handle. I don't know what to do. Which is when I realize my legs are cold. Wet. I look down. I am up to my knees in water. The sea has begun to rise. It rises to my waist. I open the car door, get in, but the motor won't start. Utterly dead. Just get to see the tidal wave raging toward the car, tearing people and houses with it as it goes, I wake up as the car turns over and the windows smash.

I've shut myself in again. Nobody comes up anymore. I don't know why. Haven't seen Havstein for days. Perhaps I've asked to be left in peace. I don't know. Haven't eaten. Am awake at nights. Tiptoe out, fill my Jolly bottle with water from the bathroom tap and go back to my room. I miss the anonymity. I miss being unwanted. I miss myself. I'm out of sorts. I'd foreseen this somehow. That things wouldn't go so well. I had thirteen years to wipe out. Nobody's got an eraser that big.

But then, it doesn't last as long as the first time. By the fourth day I'm beginning to see the contours of myself in the mirror. My stomach aches. But I'm still here, still living here.

I should call home. At least send a card. To my parents. Give some sign of life. For my own sake, if nothing else. Confirm my own existence.

Day five. It's dark in my room. My sweater sticks to my skin. My socks stink, and are impossible to pull off. It's raining. I haven't been out of my room for five days. I don't know what I'm going to say. I can hear Ennen in the kitchen below, with the others. She's laughing, and when she laughs, the others do too. They're drinking beer, I can hear the cans being opened, a sporadic pfff and a schlup as they try to catch the beer that runs over the rim. Ennen has put the Cardigans on, the *Life* album, *I will never know, cause you will never show*, sings Nina Persson, and I can hear Ennen singing to it, *C'mon and love me now* and

I'm struck by how, for a moment, Ennen's voice blends with Nina's, and then after, a verse goes off on its separate path.

I get up in the end. I decide quite suddenly, get up, stand upright. Pull off my socks, my sweater, go out into the bathroom, take a shower. I stand in the shower and turn the water on, ice-cold at first, in seconds my whole body stiffens, but it wakes me up, I come to, and slowly but surely I let the water get hotter and hotter, until the steam drapes itself softly around the room, and on the walls. I dress, clean clothes, new socks. I open the door, after five days, go down the stairs and into the hallway, come into view in the doorway to the kitchen. I go over to the table, sit down in a vacant chair, say nothing. Open a beer that's put in my hands, drink. Listen to the conversation as it goes back and forth over the table. Havstein turns toward me and says: "We knew you'd turn up sooner or later." And then I start talking again. And from that moment on those two breakdowns will be something I scarcely remember in detail, a vague memory, a barely visible mark on a page.

– – – ■ – – –

"Mattias?"

"Yes?" I answered. Havstein stood in the doorway to the workshop one day, I was sitting in a chair at the table that was covered with half-finished wooden sheep, sitting with my hands in my lap, taking a break, thinking how it was out of season anyway.

"Come with me."

Havstein disappeared into the living room and I slowly got up, nodded to Ennen who was reasonably absorbed in cutting up wool, signaled to her that I'd be back soon. Then followed Havstein out through the kitchen up the stairs and into his office. He sat in the chair in front of his desk. I was expecting anything and nothing.

"I think I've found you a job."

"But I have a job, don't I?"

"I think this one's more suitable."

"Really?" I answered thinking how anything, absolutely anything would be better than what I did now. Havstein leaned back in his chair, lit a cigarette, and for a moment allowed the smoke to hang delicately over him in the light from the sun outside, like an enormous hat on his head, and I thought I ought to take up smoking, if no other reason than to have something to occupy myself.

Havstein said: "I think it's time for you to go back to gardening, Mattias."

"What do you mean?" I said.

"That I have an idea."

Then he told me about his plans, my plans. He'd talked to the local council about how they might get me out doing it again, and I wondered how it was that the local authorities were suddenly interested in me and that things should go well for me. Havstein had organized it, with the hole-punch-and-stamp brigade down in Tórshavn, a whole new career, my own one-man band. I was to be a gardener again.

"A proper position," said Havstein.

"A proper position," I repeated. Right.

"I got you put on the system down there with the local council, which means you can stay here for awhile, as long as I've got reason to say it's better for you here than elsewhere, for example in Norway."

"And have you got reason to say that?"

"Well ..."

"But you've sorted it out anyway?"

"I said you were insane."

The plan was for me to help Faroe Islanders who contacted the local council to get cheap labor, to fix up their gardens, establish winter gardens or plant hedges. I was meant to be a traveling salesman of green shrubs, on loan from the council and the Factory, the nutcase in the garden, loony on the lawn. It would bring customers, and I suppose that was what they'd planned, down in town where they sat by their hole-punchers, researching the number of sheets they could perforate in one go, when they gave the scheme the okay.

So I agreed. I was glad to escape the monotony in the Factory, even though I'd enjoyed working with Ennen, listening to her humming through her entire Cardigans-record collection each day, the things we'd discussed when we were alone and everyone else was out.

I was given my own contact in the council now who passed on jobs, addresses, and telephone numbers of clients to me. He ordered any plants and equipment I asked for, as long as I drove down to the quay in Tórshavn and fetched it myself. This meant we were given a new car at the Factory too, another used Subaru, clearly the car of choice in this country, and I had priority when it came to using it.

Free gas.

A small wage.

I wasn't about to complain.

Havstein was pleased at my new existence, and plotted for how it might develop further, over time, how I might become a national treasure, how much I'd mean to the people I visited, the entire country might undergo a change, growing ever greener from my work and he probably had plans for Gjógv too, initially for the small flower beds outside the front door, around the Factory, and later perhaps I'd be able to make all Gjógv pretty and full of blooms, it was only a question of time in his head before the entire village would be transformed into a botanical garden with its inhabitants hidden among lilies of the valley and tulips. Tourists would stream into the village to see more than just the harbor. That evening I think perhaps Havstein pictured people moving up here because of my work, I didn't have the heart or courage to say that wasn't what I wanted, that I enjoyed my quiet, so I went along with it, played on his team, laid plans with him, which grew bigger and bigger, until weeds grew over the tables and we were lost in tall grass in the living room, had to use scythes to reach each other, and everything seemed perfect that evening, and on the following days, days you could have framed and hung on the wall, pointed at for visitors: *Look, that was how things were for me then. Things were that good.*

Ennen was optimistic on my behalf too and began questioning me on all sorts of things she wondered about being a gardener. She wondered how much water roses needed, and why one should put sugar or lemonade in the water. She wondered why *Emperor's Happiness* was called Emperor's Happiness, which flowers went together and why, and where they came from, and why Holland was famous for its tulips and whether it had anything to do with people going about in clogs there, as she seemed to remember they did, and in the evening she'd often sit in the living room and read *Garden Flowers in Color*, which Havstein had given her. And when I came in and sat next to her, she'd smile knowingly before putting the book down and telling me what she'd just read. She even came to Tórshavn with me in the new car a couple of days later to pick up the plants I'd ordered for my first job for a family in Hvalvík. We sat in the car, and breathed in the aroma of our new used car as we waited for the boat carrying the goods to come along-side the west quay outside Bátafelagið, and I thought how Ennen's gift was the way she interested herself in what the people she had around her were interested in. It wasn't that she engaged with what the other person did for politeness' sake. I think she did it because she wanted to find out why we did what we did, since what we did was somehow who we were, and that was her way of getting to know people, by searching to share the fascination that people she met had for the most disparate things. I've often thought it must have been exhausting. But perhaps it wasn't. Maybe it was blindingly simple.

And after I'd gotten back from that first job in Hvalvík, after Havstein and Ennen had stood outside the Factory to greet me as I drove back, after Palli and Anna had made supper, and we'd switched the TV on because we were waiting for some news item about some-thing, I've forgotten what, and after Ennen and Havstein and I had sat up in my room and I'd chatted on about Steve Martin's stand-up records and said they weren't particularly good, weren't particularly funny, but that was what made them so brilliant because they were the sound of being second-best, and after we'd had one of our long conversations about why we all wanted to be in second place rather than first, and after Ennen had said that what she wanted most of all was Nina Persson's autograph and I'd decided to try to get it, to write to her that very night on Ennen's behalf, though it was January before I remembered it again, and then I forgot it the next day, by which time there were six instead of five at the Factory, and nobody had died yet in the new millennium, after Palli and Anna had joined us in my room for a beer before going to bed early as usual, and pretending they didn't sneak into each other's rooms at night to sleep together, after we'd sat huddled in my little room with the window open so Havstein could have a cigarette, and after he'd talked about how much he loved us all and how happy he was we were there with him and we'd admitted to ourselves and each other that we might never improve, let alone get away from the Factory, and that that was okay, that there was nothing wrong with that, and that there wasn't anyone who could decide how things turned out, after everybody finally left my room, and I lay under the duvet and thought about the job I'd done, what I was going to do over the next few days, after that, I felt everything would work out all right in the end. Absolutely everything. And I was the certainest person in the world that night. Slept like a marmot in its burrow.

The days came on an assembly line, almost identical and perfect on delivery, accompanied by a user manual in several languages and with ready-completed guarantees. We'd eat supper. Anna and Palli would sit in the living room while the three of us stayed in the kitchen, washed up, had some wine, when we'd bought it, or coffee. Havstein would still disappear off to his own room at some point, to sit and read all evening, or all night, for all I knew. I'd sit in my room most evenings, looking at the wall, looking out of the window. Go to bed early and tired, or as time passed I'd go to Ennen's room, or more precisely, she'd come to mine, knock on the door, open it, and drag me out of my room into hers, her room was the farthest away in the southeasterly part of the first floor, the biggest room, light, crammed with old, surplus furniture, stacks and stacks of magazines along the walls, old dog-eared magazines from almost every corner of the world, all colors and shapes, a bookshelf on which she'd squeezed her stereo system and her four CDs, only the Cardigans, and at the back of her room another door, into her bedroom, a solitary mattress on the floor, a wooden chair next to it, an alarm clock on it, nothing more. I don't quite know how it was Ennen who ended up taking care of me most in the evenings, why we started sitting together like this, up in her room, it just turned out like that, and they were wonderful evenings, among the best. Anna and Palli often disappeared into deep conversations together, they worked outside the Factory too, and met more people than I did. Perhaps Ennen and I felt like younger siblings, doing our best to occupy ourselves without being in the way. Or maybe such things are coincidental, incomprehensible, impossible to change.

"So, what do you think of the others, Mattias?" asked Ennen one evening in her room, with *First Band on the Moon* droning on in the background.

"The others?"

"Yes, Anna and Palli, for example. Do you like them?"

"Sure, what can I say? It seems like Anna takes good care of you. And Palli? I think they're good people. Really good people."

"Yeah, they are. Did you know they're together?"

"I had my suspicions," I answered. "Has it been going on for long, or?"

"About a year, longer perhaps. Do you think you and I'll end up together?"

"You and I? How do you mean? I haven't really thought about it."

She scrunched her eyes and squinted at me, God alone knew what that might mean.

"I don't believe you," she said. "The first thing anybody thinks about when they meet a new person, is whether it's possible to fall in love with him. Or her. That's the way it is."

"Really? So, what do you figure? Would you describe my odds as good or catastrophic?"

"I've no idea. But I think you might be the best thing that'll ever happen to me."

"Can you really know that so soon?" I asked.

"Mm."

"Goodness."

"But we're both working on this, huh?" she said, rotating a finger at her temple.

"On getting better?"

"Yeah."

"Sure."

"I don't think I'll get a lot better, by the way," she said.

"But that's good enough, isn't it?"

"Not really."

We fell silent for a minute as we searched for something else to talk about.

"Have you ever thought how human beings are made of almost nothing but water?" asked Ennen.

"No. How much water?"

"72.8 percent. About the same as the quantity of sea in the world."

"Have you ever thought how if you stretch your arms out to the side, the length is the same as your height?" I suggested.

"Sometimes. Not often. But now and again, yes."

"Right."

Music on loop. Or the evenings. The hours. The minutes.

Let's come together, me and you.

La-la-la-la-la-la, your new cuckoo.

And then, one day toward the end of October. I woke to the noise of my own breathing, my own pulse, and a sudden sense of panic coursed through me telling me I'd overslept, and I sat quickly up in bed, began putting my clothes on with my eyes still half-closed, and I was already fully dressed and standing in the hallway dazed when I remembered I didn't have any job to do, and that the day was mine to use as I wanted. Quietly in the Factory. It reminded me of that first afternoon, when Havstein went to Tórshavn to talk with Jørn, but I wasn't frightened anymore. And I didn't have the desire in me to go off into thin air.

I padded down the stairs and into the kitchen, ate breakfast as I counted raindrops on the windowpane, drank orange juice, coffee. Did the dishes from everybody else's breakfasts and looked at the clock over the kitchen table. Half past twelve. I'd slept for almost twelve hours, much longer than usual. Since starting work I generally only slept for six or seven hours each night, was up and around at about seven in the morning, getting stuff done.

I poured an extra cup of coffee and carried both cups through the living room and over to the door to the workshop, opened it and went in. But Ennen wasn't in there. Piles of wool and naked wooden sheep lay on the tables, it didn't seem like she'd been at work today. Since I'd begun as a gardener, Ennen had taken over responsibility for the souvenir production on her own again, she had to run the whole shop, get the materials delivered to the door twice monthly, she worked hard, long hours, rarely saw her before supper, and on some days she'd disappear back in for a couple of hours in the evening. But it took longer when she had to do everything herself, a lot fewer sheep were finished per week, although more than enough still to satisfy Havstein, the local council, and the few tourists who, according to the airport shop, asked for the sheep they'd heard were made on the Faroes somewhere, by old prisoners or patients or whomever. It was an enterprise to make futility itself blush.

Had two cups of coffee in my hands and only one mouth, so I sat down on her chair, put the cups on the table, drank both, and fiddled with one of the sheep, out of habit. Filed and polished. It didn't turn out quite right, I was out of practice, and I'd never glued the wool on before, but it kind of worked, it stuck firmly and was almost sheep-like, if you looked hard enough. I put it aside on her table, and taking the cups I went back into the kitchen and stood there. I pondered what I might do, but couldn't think of anything, somehow. I remembered I didn't have the car that day either, which reminded me that Ennen had told me she wouldn't be working today, she had to go down to the council offices to fill out some forms, and to visit her mother, to help her with something, I'd forgotten what. So there was only me here. Me and my inestimable boredom that rarely led to anything good.

Which was probably the moment I decided to pay Havstein a visit. Even though I knew he wasn't home.

It wasn't so much that I was looking for something, so much as needing something to fill my time with, and a map-less treasure hunt was the best I could come up with.

He who seeks, finds.

I went in Havstein's bedroom. Through the office.

Yes, I know, and I do apologize, I didn't mean anything by it, it's just the sort of thing I do when I'm bored, I open doors, peep in cupboards. When nobody's looking, I'll snoop through everybody's stuff, rummage through your cupboards, putting everything back in place with photographic precision. So you'd never notice. Never know. At all. I've always been smart at it, remembering how things looked. I could have been a spy.

The bedroom was dark. The roller blinds were down. A queen-sized bed placed on the far side of the room. A floral sheet and the same closed in smell as in Ennen's room. Havstein had carpet on the floor, old, brown, deep-pile, wall-to-wall, wow! Shaggy! A big poster on one of the long walls, a map of an island whose location I didn't know but that looked a bit like the one in my room.

A bedside table next to the bed.

I've always liked bedside tables.

The FBI should have a special bedside table division for profiling criminals.

Show me your bedside table and I'll show you who you are.

Havstein's bedside table had a drawer. Without a lock. I sat on the edge of the bed. Felt myself grow curious. As though I was about to be introduced to a new person. My hands ran along the outside of the drawer, found their way to the handle in the semi-dark, pulled the drawer gingerly out so as not to disturb whatever might lie within, thus revealing to the world that I'd been snooping in other people's things. This was, as I've said, not the first time I'd done this. I opened the drawer. But it wasn't full of the thousand little things people usually tuck away. The drawer was totally empty. Or rather, that isn't true. There was a book in the drawer. I took it out, held it in my hands. A travel guide.

Fielding's Guide to the Caribbean plus the Bahamas 1975.
Fielding Publications.
Madison Avenue.
New York.

I don't know what I'd expected to find. Probably just the usual things. Old receipts, small change. Exotic travel guides hadn't featured on my list. I looked at the book again. It was thick, over a hundred pages long, an orange and green cover, with horizontal white stripes and written by the Harmans, who'd met in Haiti in 1949 and married a month later and who, according to the opening of their foreword, had not only researched the islands thoroughly, but actually lived there for over twenty years, with a base on the Cayman Islands. You couldn't ask for more. They had their own slogan: "Don't ask the man who's been there. Ask the man who's lived there." They weren't messing around. The book itself was worn ragged, read to a thread. Havstein had folded the corners of almost every other page, had made loads of notes in the margins, in pen and pencil, had circled extracts, underlined words and sentences. He'd researched. Reread. So that was what he did when he went up to his room early in the evenings, while I sat with Ennen until one of us grew tired and suggested we go to bed. Bahamas Bermuda baluba, it made no sense. Totally hula hula. Nobody went to the Caribbean anymore, did they? Not as far as I knew. Not since the mid-eighties. Perhaps with the exception of American retirees from Tampa, Florida with blue rinses, who did, after all, have the money and opportunity and more free time than they could fill at home in their huge living rooms.

I took the book with me out into Havstein's office, sat on the floor, read my way across the Caribbean Sea, from island to island. I waded through shallow lagoons, wandered through Rastafarian markets in Kingston, Jamaica, took the sea route to the Virgin Isles, visited Montserrat as Christopher Columbus had done in 1493, walked through the center of Plymouth twenty-two years before the volcanic eruption that devastated the south end of the island making it uninhabitable in '97, flew from Barbados to Antigua and was met with the biggest smile ever, took a taxi ($9.50) from the airport to Half Moon Bay by the beach, sat beneath an expensive parasol next to the S-shaped swimming pool behind the reception, played tennis with the proprietor Hipson late into the evening, drank a couple of beers, crept up to my room, lay between clammy sheets in a room without air conditioning in the knowledge I could go exactly where I pleased the next day.

So this was Havstein's plan B. It looked like he'd spent months, years perhaps, reading these pages, over and over again, and every time he'd reread the same pages his notes multiplied. And when there was no space left in the margins, he'd continued on slips of paper, on newspaper cuttings and envelopes that he shoved between pages, his scribblings covering every spare inch of almost every page. I attempted to work out what he'd written but it was largely indecipherable, either because he wrote in Faroese, or simply because his writing was so small, so tight and scrappy that the letters slid into one another, turning into long lines that wanted to leave the pages and go over to a new island, on the other side of the ocean.

I drank my last imaginary Hawaii Surprise with its parasol at six that evening, sitting in Havstein's office chair with the book in my hands, a heavy head and yawning mouth. I looked at the clock. Then I crept quietly back into his bedroom, as though I was frightened of being discovered by someone who might come home as I sat there engrossed. I opened the bedside drawer carefully with my right hand and was about to put the book back where I'd found it, when one of his notes fell out, landing soundlessly on the floor. I snatched it up quickly, looked at it, but it was impossible to read what was written on it. Couldn't remember seeing it before, and had no idea where it should go. I leafed carefully through the book looking for a place that looked as though it had something missing, but it was impossible, there were several pages without any notes in the margins or on paper slips. Shit! Finally I flicked to a random page, hesitated for a second, then shoved the sheet of paper in, put the book back in the drawer, shut it and went out.

The brain is a strange contraption. A library with a messy librarian. And in the floors below, in the cellar, there are vaults, filled to the ceiling with books and journals, dissertations and papers that are scarcely ever asked for. I stood in the bathroom brushing my teeth (another therapy when bored), when I suddenly got a tooth-brushing-thought. I remembered the poster on the wall of my room. I'd never given it much thought, but now I realized that it didn't hang there by chance. With a mouthful of toothpaste I left the bathroom and went into my room, switched the light on and looked at the poster of the Caribbean Islands on my wall, an enormous map in gray and white.

Montserrat. The island that almost vanished in the volcanic eruption.

That was when I got the inspiration, the librarian straightened up his archives. I went into Ennen's room. There was a map of Grenada on the wall. The poster was exactly the same size, and in the same gray and white print. I crossed the landing to Anna's room, opened the door and went in. Saw the poster on the wall. Trinidad. Continued to Palli's. Poster there too. Map of Antigua. And then I went back into Havstein's bedroom one last time, switched on the light, looked at the poster on the wall. St. Lucia.

I understood nothing. Or everything.

I went back and finished brushing my teeth, as I tried to make sense of Havstein's big project. I couldn't figure it out.

Anna and Palli slammed the car doors shut outside the Factory at twenty-five to seven and Havstein arrived half an hour later with Ennen, by which time I was already standing in the kitchen with Anna cooking pasta. I gave Ennen a hug and asked if everything had gone okay.

"Yes," she answered. "No hitches."

"And your mother?"

"She's really well. I think she's found herself a new guy. At last."

We talked for a while on the subject of this new man and the mother who I'd never met, before Havstein came over to me wanting to know if I'd had an okay Friday.

"One of the best," I answered.

"And what have you been doing?"

"Not much. Watched a little TV. Drank coffee. Counted raindrops. Read."

"What have you read, then?"

"Oh, just magazines, newspapers. *Garden Flowers in Color.* Stuff like that."

"I'm glad to hear it."

"What?"

"That you haven't been bored."

"Oh no. I've been fine. A real summer holiday."

That night I slept as never before, my dreams were hot and sun-kissed, I wandered along the water's edge of an island where there were no other people. I was lighthouse keeper on an island where the waves continually crashed hard against the rocks, preventing the inhabitants of any neighboring islands from rowing over, and I'd only go out in my boat once a week, knew precisely where I had to set out from to get past the breakers, the corals, to row over to one of the other islands for provisions, a cup of coffee in a restaurant, or a beer. And the other customers didn't talk to me, didn't see me. Although when I looked the other way, I could feel their gazes all around me, hear their voices. They talked about the boat that had only just managed to come into harbor yesterday, in the terrible storm that crept toward becoming a hurricane. This large boat had finally managed to maneuver between the jagged rocks, by the light of the lighthouse.

It had begun to get colder, windier, hurricane gusts, and I was sitting up in Ennen's room one evening early in November. I hadn't got around to sending a card to my parents, and *nobody* had sent me any mail, either: Nobody had called. Nobody had written to say Helle had thought better of things, or that I should go back home, that flower sales were on the rise. I still knew nothing about what Havstein had said to Jørn that evening, and to Mother on the phone the next day. I assumed he'd tell me, when the time was right; I was outside the coverage area and that was fine by me. I was sitting on Ennen's sofa as she stood over by the window with a roll of tape in her hands, pulling long strips out and laying them along the edges of the windows, blocking the cracks and insulating her room. We'd done this in our rooms over the last few days, because the windows were old and drafty, and frost had begun to form on the inside of the glass, making it impossible to see out, impossible to see anything at all. Ennen was playing *First Band on the Moon*. It was still the only thing she ever listened to, even though she didn't do it every day, and slowly but surely I'd begun to like the Cardigans too, didn't have that many alternatives really, and it was fine to listen like that, Nina Persson's voice singing its way from Stockholm and over the sea, soft and clear, in through our frozen windows on the Faroes, and around and around in the room where we sat and Ennen standing with the tape in her hand, humming the melodies as they came out, tapping the beat with her foot, *Never Recover*. I sat with the white CD cover in my hands, gazing at the blurry concert photo on the front, looked as if it had been taken with a water-damaged single-use camera, indistinct figures under strong spotlights, and as far as we were concerned the Cardigans were the first band who really could have made it on the moon, Nina Persson could have popped out of one of the craters with the band, I told Ennen, had they existed when they sent men up there, and the astronauts from *Apollo 17* could have seen them as they got out of their landing vessel, sat down in the moon rover. Wouldn't that have been great? A band who played with no sound in a zero atmosphere, and who didn't mind playing an encore. *Lovefool*. And Ennen said she was sure Nina would have slung her microphone out into space after the concert and that it would have just traveled farther and farther, inward, outward, with the final notes of their finishing number. And so we talked on. It would have been a wonderful moment, unscheduled broadcasts from all over the world, fuzzy pictures from the earth's telescopes that stood pointed toward the front side of the moon, percussion, guitarists, a vocalist singing and singing in a soundless vacuum.

I got up from the sofa, put the CD back on Ennen's shelf and helped her finish the last window, lay double tape over the gaps, the half-rotten timber. Then we sat there, on the sofa, on either side of the table, coffee cups between us. And Ennen looked up at her bookshelves.

"You've put it in the wrong place."

"What?"

"*First Band on the Moon*. It should be farthest left."

"Don't *Emmerdale* and *Life* come first?" I asked, I'd started to learn.

"That's not how it works," she said. "They go in the order I bought them. It's quite important to me." She got up and adjusted the order on the shelves, *First Band on the Moon*, *Life*, *Gran Turismo*, *Emmerdale*. Better.

"Don't you think it's a better system for keeping your CDs, in the order of when you bought them? So you can see the path you've walked, what you've thought and how you've developed, chosen CDs according to mood."

"Perhaps," I said, thinking how she only had four albums, hardly difficult to keep track of. But it was a good idea. A CD for every chapter, every paragraph of your life. Or in her case, a CD for every volume.

It was mid-November before I'd heard Ennen's whole life story, and how she'd ended up in Gjógv. She told me quite a bit herself, during those evenings spent sitting in her room, gave me lengthy explanations about where she came from and how things had evolved along the way. The rest of the information came from Havstein, and Havstein's version was pretty different, or it filled in the colors that were missing in her picture, so that I was left with a more or less complete Polaroid of her, fuzzy at the edges.

It turned out that Ennen was born and brought up in Greenland. Her mother was a genuine Greenlander, born and bred in Nuuk. When she was eighteen, she'd moved to Narsarsuaq to work at the international airport. That was in 1970, when Narsarsuaq was no longer the buzzing place it had been during World War II and the Cold War years that followed. In April 1941 Denmark had signed an agreement with the USA allowing Greenland to be used as a supply base for the allies, and that July the Americans had, virtually overnight, established the base Bluie West One with an airport attached, and huge bomber planes had flapped out of the sky to refill their tanks before flying on to do their worst over Dresden, Berlin, Dortmund, or wherever. By the end of the war the base at Narsarsuaq had become the biggest settlement on the island, with over twelve thousand inhabitants whizzing about on the edge of the ice. The initial plan was for the base to be wound down after the war, but during those first Cold War years it grew instead, expanding proportionally to the fear of the Soviet Union, and it wasn't until the early fifties that it closed, with surplus equipment being sold at knock-down prices to a miserly and needy Norway. The following year the Greenlanders built a civil airport there, and Narsarsuaq began filling up with people again, although in considerably smaller numbers. The odd American still passed through, pilots mainly, flying cargo planes over the Atlantic, and it's one of these pilots that Ennen's mother meets at the airport one evening, perhaps while she's putting the paperwork away for the day, on her way home. The American flies from Pittsburgh to Paris three times a month, stopping off at Narsarsuaq. As the autumn progresses there are fewer and fewer flights, his stays in Greenland get longer and in the following spring, by which time Ennen's mother is already pregnant, he takes a job as a commercial pilot instead, on the internal flights between Narsarsuaq and Nuuk, Kangerlussuaq, Ilulissat, Kulusuk and Qaarsut, and the like. The eighties bring a decline in population and the number of tourists, and Ennen's father finally gets the sack in January 1984. Only months later he is offered a job on the Faroe Islands, so they have to move, they pack up the contents of their home in one weekend and transport them, and themselves, across the sea to Iceland and on to the Faroes. Ennen is thirteen, and they move into a house on the windblown island of Mykines on the west coast. Her father flies, shuttling to and from the island and Ennen tries to settle down to school again, to find new friends, to find herself a place in the storm. Mykines is one of the most beautiful of the Faroe Islands, and the increasingly famous sheer cliffs attract hoards of tourists with tents, camping stoves, and bags stuffed with Kodak film each year. But unfortunately Mykines is also barely inhabited by the eighties, and this isn't improved by the fact that boat connections to the mainland are dire and dependent on good weather conditions, and that the island acts as a buffer to just about every storm and fogbank to roll in towards the Faroes, nor by the fact that Ennen only gets to school every other week, when the teacher comes by helicopter. Things aren't made better either by there being only two other children on Mykenes, nor by the fact neither of them gets along with Ennen. She goes in circles at home, sits in her room, listens to music, dances around on the wooden floor, is thirteen, and during the autumn of 1984 she's increasingly absent when the teacher comes over, she's struck down by various illnesses, practically stops eating, disappears into herself, curls herself up and packs herself in brown paper. In the winter of 1984, just after Leonard Bailey transplants a baboon heart into a baby girl who only lives twenty-one days, as Arne Treholt is arrested for spying at Fornebu Airport on the way to Vienna, after Carl Lewis runs faster than anybody in Los Angeles and the DNA code is broken, as Bill Murray catches ghosts in New York and only months after Gallo and Montagnier isolate the HIV virus as the cause of AIDS, the year before the microchip is launched and Madonna releases her first album, as Prince makes girls' hearts cry holes in the wallpaper of their rooms over the purple rain that falls that year, when Ennen hasn't been to school for almost two months, without anyone being able to say quite why, after she's lost forty-six pounds, she's sent to Tórshavn, to a Danish psychiatrist who has his practice there. After some long conversations with her, he finds she is deeply depressed, has anxiety problems, and has developed severe anorexia. His somewhat vague conclusion is that Ennen is suffering from a sense of being completely forgotten, that apart from her parents there is nothing around her to confirm her existence. No friends. And not even the Dane can rescue her. Weeks later she's transferred to the psychiatric ward for the first time, and over the coming years she becomes a regular there, for months at a time. She tries to go to school in between, sometimes it holds for a month, a year, or just weeks, but never for long. Eventually her parents move to Tórshavn, and she lives at home with them most of the time, but it doesn't seem to help much. Toward the end of 1991 she's spent so much time in institutions, either in Tórshavn or Copenhagen, that it's difficult to get her out again. But they manage, with her parents' consent, she drags herself away from the white corridors, out into the fresh air and on April 8, 1992, Ennen stands outside the psychiatric unit in Eirargarður, more or less healthy, more or less back to her ideal weight, a suitcase in her hand, and no plans. She stands at the crossing for a moment, wondering what she will do. She has a check in her suitcase, the first of the monthly support payments she will get from the state, she has a key and an address for a flat in Bakkahella. She can do anything she wants. So she takes the bus.

She takes random buses. Whatever comes. Sits at the back. Looks straight ahead. She meets the gaze of people as they get on, young men and boys who can't take their eyes off her and who sit alone on the bus dreaming of lovers they will never have, the occasional girl who notices how gorgeous she is as she sits there, with that little suitcase on her lap. And she meets every glance that comes her way, looks down, looks up again, waits, looks at the men who take a peep at her, the men who feel a sting in their groins when they see her. And then, just before they dare to come over, before some boy or other dares to get up and walk over to her, she gets off. Takes another bus. And so it goes on. She pops up all over the country, she's the person everyone of us meets, sooner or later, on a bus, a train, a plane, the person you don't notice until you've sat down, whose eyes you meet suddenly, so you blush, so you go hot, because it shouldn't be possible to fall in love as quickly as this, that sort of thing shouldn't be possible, just on looks, in the flash of a gaze, but it is, and you sit on the bus and think how you should go over to her, you should say something, you think, you should get off at the same stop as her, because you'll never meet a more wonderful person than this. And if only you dared, if only you said something, got off together with her, went over to her, hugged her, then you'd perhaps, perhaps or for certain, meet the one person in the universe who can make you the happiest person ever. But you don't. You hardly ever get off at the same stop. You don't get up from your seat. You don't say anything to her, or to him. You both go on sitting there, looking at each other, or looking away, until one of you gets off and a few hours later you've forgotten anything ever happened, until one morning, ten, twenty years later, when you suddenly feel the same pang, you manage to see her before you, and you know that you should have pulled the bell that day, you should have said something. You didn't do it, and the only thing you're left with is the knowledge that you have, at least once, been loved, without reservation, unconditionally. For one single moment, a snap of the finger. Melodrama.

Ennen gets it into her head that she is, in fact, that person, that person from nowhere, the person who looks at you that way, on a bus, on a train, or catching a plane, the woman you never see again, she's convinced that anybody who mentions such an experience, has in fact seen her, which is why she doesn't exist, why she has to slink up and down the Faroe Islands, making herself into the person you meet on the bus, whom you'll never get to know, letting herself be discovered over and over again, she seeks out the people she believes need it most, the people that sit with their heads against the bus window, the driver who now and then looks at her in his mirror, she always selects one person on the bus, and gives that person all her attention. Boys, men, girls, old women who miss husbands that met dramatic deaths at sea decades ago, and who sit in their mackintoshes and hats, holding ratty string shopping bags, galoshes on their feet. She looks at them, smiles, believing that her smile will lodge itself in somewhere in the spines of those who notice, a shudder, a shift of body weight in the seat, and everything is a little easier, on that particular day.

But the Faroe Islands is a small place, and sooner or later she's doomed to end up on a bus with some of the same people, and in the end she sits on a bus and looks at the wrong person, one who interprets it all sexually, and things go disastrously wrong, he gets off at the same stop as her, and then she doesn't know what to do, it's never happened before, it pulls the carpet from under her, for one moment perhaps she thinks she's been discovered at last, but she hasn't, not in that way, because she's beautiful and he's too old for her, he starts pawing her, her clothes, it's raining and they're standing on a road without a bus shelter, and he wants to put his hands under her clothes and she doesn't know what to say, doesn't know what she expected, so she puts her arms around him, hugs him close, and with all her strength drives her knee into his crotch, she hears the sound of testicles crunching against her kneecap, he sinks before her, pukes up, and she hitches a ride with the first car that drives past, goes home, packs, and the next day she's on her way to Copenhagen, one year later, London, then Stockholm, Oslo, Berlin and Reykjavík, she takes casual jobs, as a postal worker, as a shop assistant, things do improve, but then she slips back for longer and longer periods, takes the U-bahn over the whole of Berlin, the T-bane in Oslo and Stockholm, so you never can be sure if you really are loved there and then, by the person who looks at you, or whether you're being observed by a psychiatric patient on an outing without aim or purpose. Ennen sits right at the back of the bus from Reykjavík to Akranes, making herself into that person of your dreams, and it takes its toll, she grows iller, thinner again, eating almost nothing, returning finally of her own freewill to Tórshavn, stands on her mother's doorstep, and her father has left, left last year, went to London to look for her, but never came back, sent her mother postcards next spring, *Sell the house, sell the car, sell the kids, I'm never coming back, forget it!* (But that's only what I imagine to be written on them.) And Ennen is admitted again, improves quickly, but this time they keep her in for a long time, extra long, on her mother's request, and one day Havstein stands there, in her room with its yellow walls, and he has an offer for her, another place, in the North, Gjógv, both mother and the institution support this move and she says yes, okay, she says. Then takes the bus.

And so there we sat. Evenings with Ennen. Me and the person you've always wanted to meet. And she played the Cardigans *ad nauseam*. And I thought, I should have met you years ago.

All those evenings. Spent in the rooms of Ennen and Havstein, and sometimes Anna and Palli. For the first time I had several friends I could go to at any time, and they were always happy to see me. We spent the weekends together, went to Tórshavn, sat in Café Natúr. One afternoon when the weather was fine, we drove south to Vestmanna, Havstein had phoned ahead and made an appointment with Palli Lamhauge, who took tourists out in his boat in the summer on a two or three hour trip to the Vestmanna bird cliffs. Lamhauge took us with him outside season, early one afternoon in the biting cold, and I sat in his open wooden boat, Fríðgerð, plastic helmet on my head and hands tucked under my rear to keep warm, squeezed in with Ennen, Anna, Havstein, and our own Palli. They'd already undertaken this trip themselves long ago, but it seemed more or less part of the required curriculum for all residents.

Hajj.

Kaaba.

Frozen fingers and high waves.

Birds whizzing about, just inches over the water's surface, skimming the waves and flying straight into the fog over the sea. I wasn't keen on going. Not at all. I've never liked being at sea. I hated baths as a child. And here we sat in an open boat, with Palli Lamhauge pushing it as hard as it would go, it sounded as though an old bus engine was mounted right under the deck, and it took an hour to come far enough out, I could feel myself turn green inside, wanted to go home, to go back. But I didn't dare say anything. I didn't want to spoil things.

Then it happens.

We round the headland.

Head the boat straight toward the vertical cliff face.

And I have a near-nature experience.

Thousand-foot cliffs, sharp as awls.

And the birds. I've never paid them much attention before, filthy pigeons always waddling around the Breia Lake. But now the puffins swoop from the top of the cliffs, dive bombing us, as though they were in free fall, but they're not. They're in full control. Kamikaze-like. And this is no performance just for us, they do this even when nobody's here, because you can have a good time even when nobody's watching. Then Lamhauge looks upward, points to the cliff tops with a chubby finger.

"What?" I ask.

He lays a heavy hand on my helmet, tips my head backwards in the right direction.

"You see that white patch up there?"

I look. There's an eighty-foot patch of snow on the top.

"Four sheep graze up there in the summer," says Lamhauge excitedly.

"Up there?"

"Yup!"

On that precipitous slope, more than a thousand feet above us, four terror stricken sheep graze for months at a time.

"And another two go on that peak there," he continues. "And there, up on the left, five more." I look at Havstein. He shrugs his shoulders.

"Extreme sports."

The others are leaning back in the boat too, staring up.

"Apparently the meat's extra tasty at that height."

"But how do they get the sheep up there? And down?" I ask.

He smiles.

"They hoist them up. And hoist them down again. They're pretty hard to catch, they're so shy. At least one person per sheep, attached by a rope so they don't fall."

"But don't they ever fall?"

"Well yes, it happens. And the sheep too. But it's a test of manhood of course. Want to try? You'll be famous!"

"Some other time," I say.

"Maybe. In the spring."

Laughter in the boat. Waves. Rain. The car trip back. Sent a card home that day. A picture postcard of one of the bird mountains, the biggest. I don't remember what I wrote, but I think it was about birds. And the sea.

The bombs fell a week later, I'd just gotten back from work, from spending four days in Funningur making a winter garden for an elderly widow, when Havstein shouted down to me from the first floor of the Factory to come up. Obediently, I kicked off my shoes and went up to his room, stood in the doorway, still in my overalls, compost on my hands.

"Yes?" I said.

"Sit down," he said.

"Is something wrong?"

"Sit down, I said!"

I sat down. I didn't sit at ease.

He didn't take a dramatic pause, didn't lean back in his chair and gaze momentarily out of the window. Instead he said: "Why have you been in my bedroom?"

"What do you mean? I haven't been in your bedroom."

"Do you like it here? Do you like living here?"

"Yes."

"Why are you acting like a jerk, then?"

I didn't like that one bit.

"I don't know," I said.

"Why have you been in my drawers, Mattias?"

I could think of nothing to say, except: "I was bored."

"You were bored?"

"Yes."

"Did you think I wouldn't find out? Did you think I wouldn't find out that you'd been rooting about in my things? Did you think I'd find it okay for you to sneak into my room?"

"No," I said.

"That's breaking and entering, you do know that?"

I said nothing. Looked at the floor. Ashamed. Ashamed from here to China.

"You're all the fucking same, the whole lot of you," he said. "You just care about yourselves, and let me sit here like an idiot." And then added: "I'm disappointed. Really disappointed."

I wanted to say something to improve the situation, for his sake mainly, it isn't the worst thing to be the accused, to be the criminal, it's far worse to be the person who's disappointed, who's been tricked into thinking Christmas is canceled, the person who can no longer trust anybody and has to take on the burden of being angry instead. But there was nothing I could say to rescue him.

"I'm sorry."

"That's not good enough, Mattias. Just not good enough."

We sat in silence awhile before he said anything more. I didn't dare to leave. Didn't dare to get up. Didn't dare move a single muscle.

"That book," he began, "is the most important thing I own. That book is who I am."

Havstein was the Caribbean. I was an idiot. That's how it was. The distribution of roles seemed fair enough.

"All of us have something that's terribly important to us, Mattias."

I thought about the box of space books in my flat in Stavanger, the book I'd got for my tenth birthday. It wasn't the moment to talk about it.

"I was working at the Rikshospitalet in Copenhagen when I bought that," he went on. "I was living with a Swedish girl called Maria, was terribly fond of her. I think I was going around with plans of marriage and all that. But nothing came of it. She disappeared in the end, out of the house, out of town, out of the country, I think. There might have been lots of reasons for that. But I remember we weren't having a very good time toward the end. We barely spoke, even though we both had a lot on our chests. Didn't know where to start somehow. So we said nothing, just tried to play for time, hoped it would pass. And then one day on my way home from work, one of the last days before she left, I walked into a bookstore just to see if there were any books that might take my mind off the silence at home. There was snow in Copenhagen that day, a rare occurrence, it never settles at least. But that day it snowed, December

1980, and a bland version of *Silent Night* was playing over the stereo system to get us into the mood, and I felt it had to mean something, so I walked around looking for something to read, and then I found this book on the bargain table. *Fielding's Guide to the Caribbean plus the Bahamas.* It seemed such an inappropriate time to be selling a book of that type, that must have been why I picked it up and looked at it. It was already five years old, but the sales pitch on the front and back promised it was the best book on that region: *The Best*, it said. *The Best, Washington D.C. Star. The Best, Fort Lauderdale News. The Best, Miami News.* I had no idea if they were big or small papers, I just believed what they said. *Informs you how to avoid trouble spots in paradise,* it said. Precisely what I needed. A guide to paradise, a book about something thousands of miles away. I'm not sure whether I seriously thought such a book could help us, or whether it was just a symptom of my feelings of hopelessness that I chose to put my trust in it, there and then. But I bought it anyway and took it home, and we didn't talk that evening either. I stayed up into the early hours, and it was summer in my living room that night, I almost got sunburned, read from cover to cover, from Antigua to the Virgin Islands. Then I went straight to work. And when I got back that evening, she was standing there ready to leave. It was just as well maybe, I don't know, things were going nowhere between us. I went on living in town, working at Rigshospitalet, worked a lot, met other women occasionally, but nothing much ever came of it somehow.

"So I moved back to the Faroe Islands, in the summer of 1981. Brought the book with me, read it now and then, I was always rather fond of it. It brought me a touch of summer. We don't get much summer up here. On the Faroes. And after moving to the Factory, I began to read it regularly, a little bit each night. I tried to keep it updated, looked for all the information I could find about the Caribbean, entered the changes in the margins, added information I was given, things I read elsewhere. I wrote to the authors, Harry E. and Jeanne Perkins Harman to ask about things they'd omitted, I even called them once, and they invited me to visit, but the time never seemed right. I'm not sure that I would have felt comfortable if I'd gone anyway. Harry had been an athletic star at Atlanta University, was a World War II veteran, he'd been a high ranking officer on a destroyer on the Pacific, Iwo Jima, Saipan, and Jeanne used to write for the New York *Herald Tribune*, *Life*, the *New York Times*, *Business Week*, was the regional correspondent for *Time* and had received the highest accolades from the governor of the Virgin Islands. And there was I, a Faroese psychiatrist who'd never ventured beyond the Nordic countries."

Havstein paused, probably waiting for me to say something. But I had nothing to contribute. He looked down.

"This book means an enormous amount to me, you understand?" His voice was milder now, perhaps he'd given up being angry with me. "I've had this book nearly half my life."

"Yes," I answered. "Yes."

"How on earth did you end up coming into my room anyway? And opening my bedside cabinet?"

"I don't know. I was bored. I do things like that. And I wondered what you always went up to read, night after night, while Ennen and I stayed behind. I suppose it was going around in my head."

"You could have just asked."

"I guess I'm not so good at that. You should get yourself a padlock."

"Maybe. Or you should get yourself some handcuffs."

We laughed. I was pleased to see him smile for the first time in what seemed like a hundred years, I dared to move again, just the merest squirm where I sat in my chair.

"Have you ever been there? To the Caribbean, I mean?"

He gazed around the room. Whether he was despairing over himself or the question, was difficult to tell.

"No. Not yet. But I'm preparing myself."

"Still? Twenty years later?"

"When I go, I don't intend to go for a vacation. I intend to go for good."

"Why?"

"I don't know." He gave a little sigh. "Which is probably why I haven't gone yet."

We didn't mention it again that day, nor on the days that followed, even though he must have realized I was thinking about it, even though I couldn't get it out of my head that in many ways I'd taken one of the few things from him that he had for himself, and that the magic of sitting in his office, evening after evening, with his pen in hand and the Caribbean laid before him in words and pictures, must have diminished a little that day. Perhaps that was what made him come to me with the book one evening, as I sat talking to Ennen, he handed it to me and I accepted it quietly.

"I think you might need this. If you want to borrow it."

"Thank you," I said. "Thanks a lot."

He was about to go, when I plucked up the courage at last to ask: "How did you know it was me?"

"Because the others have already stolen it before you."

"All of them?"

"One by one."

And from that evening, every day, after I'd gone to bed, there was light and warmth and a blue sky on the ceiling of my room, my ears were filled with the sound of bathers, transistor radios, and small tropical storms.

And then I remember, one day in early December, an afternoon, I was sitting in the living room with Havstein. He was reading the papers and asked out of the blue: "Have you made any plans for Christmas?"

Had I made any plans for Christmas?

Had I made any plans?

"No," I said, hesitantly, I'd thought I was going to stay here, I'd thought we'd all be celebrating Christmas together. "I don't know, what do you think I ought to do?"

Havstein went on reading the papers. Talked without looking up:

"Have you considered going home?"

Home?

Now?

Now that I'd started to function again at last?

"I thought perhaps you'd like to celebrate Christmas with your parents."

"Do you think it's a good idea for me to go back home right now?"

He looked over at me, as if to reassure himself he'd reached the right conclusion, or perhaps because it was a stupid question.

"I think it would be fine."

"I'm not so sure," I said.

"You can buy a return ticket, of course. And come back here, I mean."

"I suppose so."

I sat and thought about it. Going home. Christmas. Christmas in Stavanger, the conversations over dinner tables, in living rooms and bars that always centered on the lack of snow in town, the sleet and storms in Vågen. Christmas trees with bags of clothes under them and the Salvation Army collecting boxes and winter coats, and Christmas lights suspended between the buildings in the shopping streets, I thought how Helle and I would always buy a Christmas tree on Little Christmas Eve, never earlier, even though the choices dwindled as the prices rose, how we'd stand around what was always a scruffy tree in the living room and decorate it with our limited collection of Christmas decorations, how Jørn would want me to go out for a pre-Christmas drink at Cementen, how I'd never go. And *The Butler and the Countess* would be on repeat. Merry Christmas and a Happy New Year.

"Perhaps," I said.

"Think it over," said Havstein.

I waited a couple of days before doing anything, sounded out the terrain. Havstein was going to be with his family in Århus, he generally went there every other year, and every other year his family came to

Tórshavn. Ennen was going to Tórshavn to be with her mother. Anne was going home to Miðvagur and Palli always went to a big family gathering in Kollafjørður. If I stayed I was going to be alone. Wasn't sure I wanted that. I wasn't the best company.

I made two telephone calls. One to Atlantic Airways in Vágar; yes, they still had some seats available on the last flight to Stavanger before Christmas, on Little Christmas Eve, it went at a quarter past three. I had twelve thousand krones in an envelope in my room. I said I wanted to pay with cash when I picked up the tickets. She wished me a Merry Christmas over the phone. She had a nice voice, like a soft package under the tree. The other call I made was to Father. Didn't want to make it at the Factory, didn't want the others to hear, I put my coat on, turned the collar up and went out into the wind, into the sleet, huddled in the telephone booth outside the shut down shop.

"Hello?"

"Hi."

"Mattias?"

"Yes."

"Mattias? Is it you, Mattias?"

"Yes, it's me."

"Well, well, how are you?"

"Fine, I think. I'm fine. Did you get my card?"

"Yes, I did. Thanks. It looks nice over there. Wide open spaces."

"It is nice. You should have been here."

"I've been so worried about you. *We've* been so worried about you."

"There's no need. There are so many other things to worry about."

"Like what?"

"The Balkans, for example."

"What are you talking about, Mattias?"

"I was thinking of coming home."

"For good?"

"For Christmas. If that's okay?"

"Of course you can come home, Mattias. Any time. We've missed you. And everybody asks about you."

"Everybody?"

"Yes, your aunts, your uncles, Grandma. Jørn. Helle."

He said the last name and instantly regretted it, he tried to suck the last letter back in, but couldn't, the vowels had escaped now.

"Helle? Have you talked to her?"

Father hesitated.

Double or nothing.

Thefortyeightthousandkronequestion.

Sorry, but your thinking time is over.

"Well, yes, I . . ." mumbling across the Atlantic. He won the silver platter and the consolation prize. "She's come over a few times. We've talked a bit. After you'd left. When you didn't come back."

"I see. What did you talk about?"

"About you."

"Only good things, I hope," I said, in an attempt to be amusing. He didn't laugh.

"It hasn't been easy for her either, Mattias."

"Hasn't it?"

"No."

"What can I say?"

"You just left, you know. She had no idea what had happened. You just disappeared."

"She was the one that left."

"I know that, Mattias. I know. But—"

Beeps over the connection. My money had run out. I had to rummage in my pockets for coins.

"Hang on—"

Put two more ten krone pieces in and the line went quiet again. Our breathing traveling through the air and into the receivers in our hands.

"I'm coming on Little Christmas Eve. The flight arrives at Sola at four."

"Do you want me to come and pick you up?"

"Could you?"

"Of course. I'm so pleased, Mattias."

"Great," I said.

"Do you want a word with your mother too?"

"Can you just say hello from me? And we'll see each other next week?"

"All right."

"Okay. Bye, then."

"Bye, Mattias. Look after yourself."

"I will."

Pause.

Click.

I went out of the telephone booth and straight home, and nobody noticed I'd been out.

The others left on the Wednesday of the following week, in the morning, before I'd even gotten up, one after the other they came knocking on my door, I lay in bed getting hugs, we wished each other a happy Christmas and Ennen brought up some cocoa, we sat on the edge of my bed, cups steaming in our hands, as though we were on a hike, the only thing missing was a Kit Kat, and Havstein came in three times to make sure he'd written down the right day for my return, and to drill me again on what I had to do when I locked up and left, which lights had to be left on, what needed turning off, turning down, turning up, switching on, and to check I knew which buses I had to catch to get down to Tórshavn and to the airbus that left the quay two hours before the flight, that would make it one fifteen, *was that right? Yes, okay, good.* More hugs and Christmas wishes, and then everybody was out of the door and I lay alone in bed, the last person on the moon.

But the bus didn't come the next day. Not when it should. It came late, I'd gotten up early, or perhaps it was the other way around, I was packed and ready to go, sat in the hallway watching the hands of the clock go slowly around. The bus came almost an hour late and it was twenty past two when I got off at Oyrarbakki to wait for the next bus for Tórshavn, and forty minutes later I sat in the backseat of a taxi that did everything it could to drive faster, we raced through the tunnel under the Vestmanna Sound, then Sandavágur where we'd been to a village festival in the late summer and watched a boat race and Miðvágur flashed past on the left and I looked at my watch, stared out of the window looking out for my plane, but saw nothing, and as we passed Vatnsoyrar, coming in toward the airport, I saw my plane taxi along the runway and pick up speed. I got out of the car and sprinted toward the entrance.

There I stood in the Vágar departure hall, watching my plane take off from runway 18, and disappear into the clouds, on its way to Stavanger, and the presents for Mother, for Father, for Jørn, the things I'd bought in Tórshavn during the months I'd been here, suddenly felt heavy and bulky in their bags. There was nothing I could do. I paced the departure hall hoping an idea might come to me of what I should do. Went into the souvenir shop and found our sheep, rows and rows of them, at sky-high prices. They sold horses too. And cows. A veritable barnyard. But only the sheep were ours. I bought myself a cup of coffee in the café outside. Waited. No idea came, snow came, and sleet, an announcement of the four-hour delay of a flight to England. My cup was enormous, and I really didn't want coffee.

There was a married couple at the next table, about my age. They looked sad. Had that green tint in their faces that only English people have, always a giveaway, mint-green faces, indisputable proof of acid rain and eternal miners' strikes during childhood. Here they sat, at an international airport with no tax-free shop or bar, quarreling. Here of all places. He'd obviously forgotten something. Difficult to tell what, they talked fast, quietly, and in some dialect you don't hear on the BBC. He tried to take her hand, but she kept pulling it away. *I'm sorry,* he said. *I'm sorry. So sorry.* I drank my coffee. I was sorry on his behalf. Tried to picture them at home in their own surroundings, somewhere in England, maybe Scotland. Edinburgh maybe. Or Swansea, Wales. Tried to picture him tomorrow, if things didn't improve, how he'd sit on his own in the living room that night, when she'd gone off to bed. She'd have told the kids, that daddy daddy daddy hadn't been nice, that if it hadn't been for you we'd have separated, and daddy daddy daddy who's in the living room messing with the wrapping paper, fumbling with tape, daddy daddy daddy who never quite makes the grade will still try to make things right again, decorate the tree, put up the Christmas lights, and he stays up all night in the living room, he drinks tea, tries to put the lights up, but there's one not working, one of the three hundred and twenty-five bulbs isn't screwed in properly, so he tightens them all, until his hands ache with each turn, and then, as he reaches the very last bulb, it happens, the living room lights up, they'll have lights for Christmas Eve, and then, cinematically-America, Happy Hanukkah, she stands behind him, arms crossed, his wife, Doris, to whom he's been married for so long, the girl he met in school, they were twelve, she was the only one who looked good in the uniform, and it took years to capture her, four years on the rowing team because he thought she liked boys that rowed, but she didn't, she'd only waited around for him, and he got her one evening, with fumbling faltering helpless childish movements and an unsure move toward her blouse at that party in that room, and the kids who are sleeping now and whom he adores are half him and half her. And now, there she is, standing in the doorway, she's been standing there for half an hour, watching as he did everything in his power to rescue his family's existence. He turns, looks at her, and the radio is on, in the background, a suitable song, Bing Crosby, probably, and they dance across the floor and she's unsteady, hasn't danced for years, but he's light on his feet, swings her around, and now the children have come down, they stand at the doorway in their pajamas.

Eyes sparkling. Snow in their hair.

Kodak moment.

Right now they were quarreling. I drank my coffee, drank up the last slurp, the dregs, got up and walked toward the exit, placed the carrier bags filled with presents for Mother and Father and Jørn at his feet.

"There you go," I said.

"Pardon?"

"Lighten up, squirt," I said, and went out.

It had stopped snowing, or hadn't begun yet, not easy to say.

I stood there at a loss for a moment, before I went back in and over to information, told them I had missed my plane, that the bus hadn't come. That I was stranded.

"There aren't any flights before Wednesday," she said. "Next week."

"I know," I answered. "I didn't catch Christmas this year. It came a bit suddenly, don't you think?" She looked at me. Not understanding what I meant. But she smiled, and she had such white teeth. Perhaps she stood in front of the mirror every night and polished and polished the enamel with an iron file, as the tears ran.

"But do you have somewhere to stay? For Christmas, I mean," she asked. She cared. Or perhaps she was just being nice, worried she might find me frozen stiff in the parking lot, worried she'd have me on her conscience.

"I have a factory where I can stay," I answered. "In Gjógv." And that might not have been the right answer. She looked at me sadly.

"It looks like you might not be on your own. The flight to England probably won't leave because of the weather. So . . ." She hesitated, a little shame-faced about saying it: "Perhaps you could ask somebody here if they could help you with somewhere to stay. There are lots of friendly people around."

"Yes, and so many pleasant Englishmen," I answered. "But I'll manage. Things will be fine. They're a lot better than they were."

"Oh, really? There aren't many people living out at Gjógv anymore, are there."

"Barely any," I answered.

She tapped away on her keyboard, back and forth, staring near-sightedly into her computer screen, as if there might be a minuscule departure she'd overlooked.

"No," she said mostly to herself, and shook her head. "Sorry."

"Don't worry."

"Merry Christmas, then."

"Sure," I answered. "Merry Christmas."

I went back to the souvenir shop at the other end of the departure hall, bought a postcard with a picture of Tórshavn on it, so they wouldn't think I lived somewhere without stores. Wrote my parents' address on the back, with a few short sentences saying I hadn't been able to make it home for Christmas after all. Wrote that I was fine. That there was nothing to worry about. Wrote *Merry Christmas.* Wrote *Happy New Year.* And *love from Mattias. Still on the island that can't sink.* I don't quite know why I wrote the last sentence, perhaps because there was just enough space.

Then I took the bus back to the harbor, sat in the Burger King at the SMS Shopping Center, ate a Christmas burger, the Whopper had gained an extra ounce in honor of Christmas, for the same price. But they didn't have a Christmas drink.

The wind was blowing sideways when I came out, it was dark, and it was Little Christmas Eve. The store was closed, so I got my shopping done at the Statoil gas station up in Hoydalsvegur, before I went back down to the town center and sat in the bus shelter, like an obedient dog, waiting for the bus to Gjógv. Rummaged in my suitcase, opened a bottle of Fanta, a chocolate bar, Merry Christmas, and it was cold, I had summer shoes on, my fastest sneakers, and a jacket that was way too thin, but the bus was on time, and the driver looked jolly as I got on, I don't know why. Sat right behind him, drank my Fanta, and wondered whether to ask him about Ennen, to ask whether he knew who she was, but didn't. *Do not disturb the driver,* it said. And I did as I was told.

Got off the bus at Gjógv, it turned and drove straight back to where it had come from, whizzed up the slope behind me and gathered speed around the bends. I was already wet as I rounded the corner and saw the Factory, I was walking into the wind and it was raining horizontally into my mouth, cold rain with ice at the edges, hard rain, and the Factory was dark, only its outside lights on. Noticed that I started walking faster, automatically, that I held my bag a little tighter, even though I knew there wouldn't be anyone else there, that they'd already left the day before, that it was going to be a long week.

Alone.

Without food.

Without people.

Christmas. Rain. Snow.

I stood in the middle of the kitchen. Everything was so quiet. Empty. A day for singing, with no audience. It was as though a thin layer of dust had settled on the table during the course of the day. I stood there in semi-darkness, flicked the light switch on the wall, light flared over the kitchen counters. I'd have liked it if I'd just woken up in my room upstairs, listening to noises coming from downstairs. People. Not even the rats and children had followed me out of town.

2

Afternoon. Evening. Darkness. I sat in the huge living room, in front of the TV, watched the news without taking much in, and the telephone rang on the first floor. I knew who it was.

Dad was calling.

Dad had gotten up from his sofa in Stavanger, he'd stood in front of the telephone on the hallway table, looked at the note stuck on the mirror, dialed the number, and it was ringing in Gjógv.

I got up from my chair, went into the hallway, up the stairs, turned on the light in the corridor and went into Havstein's office, where the telephone was, but before I could reach it, the ringing stopped.

I could see Dad before me in Stavanger, standing next to the telephone in the hallway, Mom at his side, leaning toward him, as though she thought she'd be able to hear me, even though I hadn't picked up the receiver, as long as she could get close enough to the phone. Minutes passed. I didn't call back. Then he called again, I lifted the receiver.

"Hello?"

"Mattias?"

"Yes, it's me."

"What happened, Mattias? I was waiting for you at the airport."

"I missed the plane."

"What do you mean? You missed it?"

"There isn't always another bus . . . That's just what they'd have us believe."

I could hear Mom in the background, even though she didn't make a sound, I could still hear her anyway.

"I waited for ages at the airport, Mattias, until everyone had collected their luggage. I had to go to the desk, ask to see the passenger list. Your name wasn't on it."

"I got there ten minutes late. It can happen to the best of us," I said.

"But why didn't you leave a little earlier, Mattias?"

"It wasn't me that was late. It was the bus that was early."

"But," he took the plunge, "when are you coming home, then?"

I decided there and then.

"I don't know. Not for a while, I think."

"But Mattias—"

And I interrupt him and say *Dad, you should come up here some time, you've got to come and look at the sea, there's sea for you here, Dad,* I say, distracting him, and he says that he really should, without a doubt, he must take a trip over, and we make vague plans and both of us know that he'll never show up, not because he doesn't want to, but it's the kind of thing that never happens, he's got a job to take care of and he hasn't been anywhere without Mom for years, over twenty years, and he isn't much of a traveler, likes it best where he is, and I say he must come up here for a trip, I say it many times, and he tells me he will, we make vague plans and they'll all come to nothing, and we both know it, because I'm his son and my life is so distant from his at this moment, and he thinks that if he were to do it, if he were to come, he'd be an intrusion in my life and be in the way and that I'd be embarrassed when I see him, when I introduce him to the people I spend my time with, but it isn't true, and I don't know how to tell him, that it isn't true, that I want him to come, that there's nothing I want more than that he should come and visit me here, see how I'm living, and then Dad disappears and Mom takes over the receiver.

"Mattias? When are you going to come home? When's the next flight?"

"Not until well after Christmas."

"I see, okay, but—but are you going to come then? Home? For New Year?"

"No," I said. I said it more shortly than I'd expected to.

"We've missed you a lot, Mattias. We wish you'd come home."

I was missed.

I was wanted.

I was elsewhere.

I was a fax someone had forgotten to send on an all important Friday. An appointment that went down the chute.

"Is there any snow back at home now?"

"Do we have snow, here? In Stavanger? No ..."

"Thought not."

"Why not?"

"It hardly ever snows in Stavanger. Not surprising, really."

"What do you mean?"

"So who's coming over? For Christmas?"

"There's, there's the usual. Your aunts, Uncle Einar, Grandma."

"How old do you think Grandma is now?"

"How old? I don't really know. Old."

"Grandma worked at Ellingsen Foto until she retired, didn't she?"

"Yes ..."

"Took pictures of people, developed photographs."

"Yes, she did. She was a very skilled photographer, your grandma."

"But there are no more than a couple of photographs of her, maybe. Almost none."

"Maybe so. I guess so. Why do you ask?"

"Nothing. It's funny the way things end up."

"Why are you talking about this?"

"I don't know. Just came to me."

"When are you going to come home? Are you coming for New Year?"

"No. I think I'll be staying here for some time."

"But do you have money? And your apartment, what will we do with it? Your dad's paying the rent every month, but he can't keep doing that forever. You're welcome to stay with us for a while."

"Everything's fine. You don't need to worry. I've got money. I've got a job here. I don't think I'll be needing the apartment. You can probably just give my notice."

"So you've got a job, what kind of job?"

"First I was making sheep. Wooden sheep. For the tourists. But now I'm a gardener again."

"Sheep out of wood?"

"They're very nice. I can send you some."

"I wish you'd phone more often at least."

"I sent a card."

"What?"

"I sent a card. A Christmas card. But it doesn't have a Christmassy picture on the front. Doesn't have quite the right seasonal feel, maybe. But anyway."

I could hear her giving up.

"I'd better be going now, Mattias, if I'm going to have the scrambled eggs and speke-ham ready in time—and Vidar Lønn-Arnesen's special is on TV soon, we always watch that, you know . . . so . . ."

"Merry Christmas, then," I said. I didn't tell her that I'd be here alone.

"Merry Christmas, Mattias," she answered. "Take care of yourself."

I lowered the receiver, placing it back in its cradle, and in the instant before it clicked into place I could hear Dad, in the background, wishing me a *Merry Christmas*, but I didn't manage to answer, didn't manage to wish him a Merry Christmas, before the connection was broken. And I didn't really want to call him back, just to say that.

And so there I stood. In Havstein's room. My shoes on. Without plans. Christmas Eve, 1999.

So what do you do? Watch TV? Make a good dinner? Sing Christmas songs to yourself in an echoing room? There aren't any handbooks for people spending Christmas alone. Only TV guides. Ready-made dinners.

Havstein's room. The Office. A large desk in the middle. Solid wood, of course. This was where the telephone was. Two chairs turned toward the table. Twelve big filing cabinets side by side against the wall. The bookshelf behind the desk. Another one against the opposite wall, by the door into his bedroom. Havstein had furnished his room like the films he'd seen. It was like a stage set in here. *The Psychiatrist's Office.*

Which might have been why I spun around and walked to the first and best filing cabinet and pulled out a drawer. Because I expected to find it empty, for all the drawers to be empty. Or filled with blank paper. But they weren't. The drawers were filled to the brim with papers, and the papers were filled with text: neat, handwritten notes, almost illegible comments scrawled in pen, and endless pages of typewriting. This was the great archive. The great drain. Detailed journals on everybody Havstein had met over the years. Everybody that had ever lived at the Factory, or patients from all over the country, collected together, not easy to say. They were all in here somewhere, Ennen, Anna, and Palli, logged and with notes that aimed at understanding. I knew I shouldn't look. I should close the drawer, go back downstairs, sit in a chair, watch TV, get into Christmas mood, find a beer in the fridge, eat nuts. Pack presents I hadn't bought. Call a friend. But I can turn thief, I can have the longest nose around, I can sniff my way to you blind, open every cupboard and drawer, let the skeletons tumble out so they cover the entire floor.

I was at it again. I wasn't to be trusted.

I lifted some bundles out.

Began leafing through the papers, going through the drawers, hundreds of journals, of varying length. See attachment 1-9, see photograph 2F, see accompanying CT-transcript. See it all. And I saw.

I sat in Havstein's chair with heaps of journals, read and leafed through countless admissions, discharges and re-admissions, eternal revolving-door patients and others who'd been cured, who'd left the clinic one day and never needed to walk through its doors again, people who were out there, getting by, who looked like anybody else. The pilot of a plane coming here. The captain of the boat. The woman who makes your bed in the hotel. The woman who delivers your mail without reading it first. The man who makes sure your boat will float. They might be anybody at all.

And then, among them all, I found what I was looking for.

No. 12. VMF.82/05/32914/1–15.04.1980

Poulson, Palli Jóannes. Pers. ID ▓▓▓▓ Born March 12 1962. Signabøur, Kollafjørður. First adm. April 15 1980 on req. of par., ▓▓▓▓ and ▓▓▓▓. On adm. patient 18 yrs, not in a rel. no previous hist. of ment. ill. Uncle on father's side schiz., ▓▓▓▓. Pat. childhood appears adequate, gen. good, father fisherman, away long per. during childh., stay at home mother. Childh., see Appdx. 1. Pat. went to sea age 17, sailed in foreign vessels, but had probl. settling down on any of them, worked on 6 ships during this per. Often exp. fatigue, low concentration, several casual sex. rel. when ashore. Returned from sea age 18, par. think they detect some sympt. from that time. Moved home, insomnia, restlessness, lack of initiative (progr.), complained that the neighbors were out to get him, that they controlled his thoughts and broadcast them to ships he had worked on. This has incr. rec., Lately pat. unable to eat reg. Believes food poisoned by neighb. and family, complains of threatening voices. Interv. 1, acts calmly, adqu. groomed, adqu. cooperative, does not interrupt and usually answ., though answ. short and incompl. Pat. adm. to clin. dept. Tórshavn, 8 wks, medic. neurolept. Klorpromazin (Hibanil) (. . .) Pat. adm. 2nd time, Jul 2 1980, following interrupted treatm. (Pat. discharg himself, went home to parents, reassured them on improvement), cont. treatm. with therapy and Klorpromazin for 11 months after satisf. impr. in sympt., (see appdx 2) (. . .) Pat adm. 6 times, now with longer per. of partial/near complete rem. Adm. 6. 6/12/1989, Pat has rec. (approx 4 yrs) functioned satisf. in own apartment with weekly visits, light work at harbor, described as easy going. Adm. due to slight det., treated with low dose Haloperidol 2mg, 12 weeks. Transf. aftercare Gjógv under Dr. Havstein Garðalið 7/13/1989, near compl. remission, cont. treatm. w low dose neuroleptic or sim. on det. ICD–10 F20.x3. (sign.)

No. 33. FHTYE.82/530/1929/7-22.01.1989.

Anna Kambskarð. Pers. ID: ███████. Born June 17 1965. Miðvagur. Adm. first t. Jan 22 1989, upon req. of father, ███████. Pat. is on adm. a 24 yr. old female, unmarried. She is clear abt. time/place and current sit. During conv. alternates betw. despair, anger and apathy. Pat. seems suspicious, answ. Psych's qus more or less fully. No prev. adm., but conv. with parents indicates two siblings w sim. cond. Childh. partially stressf. Pat. descr. as introvert and over-sensitive, but helpful. (See Appdx. 1). Childh 0-16. Dur. period 18-22 pat. empl. at the post off. in Eiði, where she claims to have felt at ease with tasks and colleagues. At 23, laid off without warn. due to restructuring, moved to Tórshavn. Exp. diffic. in leaving her community and friends, in her pres. environ. she has only been able to estbl. friendship with one pers., an old classmate she met by chance. Hist. outlined below supported by pat. and parent. First sympt. traced back to Nov 1988 and indicates incr. degr. of disquiet, dissoc. probl., conv. sympt., feels that "someone" (non-spec) is out to get her, descr. voices that communic. with each other that she receives by mistake. The voices belong to sailors that are planning to kill her. Father also descr. visual halluc./delusions he was told by pat., who is unable to recog. these as delusions. In the main these concern "dead seamen who stomp around in my kitchen in the day, stand next to my bed at night whispering, and dripping with water." (pat. own expl.) The constant pres. of these imagined beings results in fear of mov. outside house, fear of eating, sleeping etc. The spec. episode leading to adm. on Jan 21 1989, pat. att. suic., discovered by a friend, ███████ who came to visit at her res. in ███████. Together with par. she was transp. to em. clinic at hosp. in Tórshavn, transf. to this clinic follow. morn. Instg. treatm. with anti-psych. and psych. therapy, treatm., 4 weeks. (. . .) 2/19/89: Init. diagn. Ganser syndr. (ICD-09 F44.80), this is now repl. by React. Psych. with schiz.sympt. A cond. the causes of which we know rel. little about, but indications are biol. fact. may have greater sign., in conj. w cerebral bio-chem. reactions. Conv. w pat. and parents reveals that on the day bef. suicide att. the pat. attended an exhib. together w ████████ where they saw paintings by the Faroese artist Samuel Mikines. Acc. to ████████ the painting *Returning from the funeral* esp. caught the att. of the pat., which acc. to ████████ made a strong impression on her. This ep. may be the trigger for the timing of the ep. even if it is too early to say if the ep. was the main trigger in isol., but cf. poss. supp. by research by French prof. of psych. Hérve Muller (cf. *Séance de rêve éveillé, 1984).* Pat. treat. w neuroleptica (Klorprotixen). Compl. 8 months. 9/03/1989, pat. discharged, weekly obs. Satisf. remission. See appx. A. 3/7/1990, det./relapse, adm. 3 months (Appx B) 9/16/1990, adm. 5 months (Appx. C). 11/29/1991, adm. neur./psych, 7 months, transf. 2/08/1993 Aftercare in Gjógv under Dr. Havstein Garðalið, appar. compl. remission. ICD-10 F23.1 / F23.2.

It's been a bad day please don't take a picture.

Palli and Anna. So that was who they were. I suddenly felt a mild attack of bad conscience for having snooped around in their lives, reading things almost nobody knew, and I put the records back, solemnly.

For a while I hunted for my own name in the archive, I was pleased not to find it, it was reassuring that I couldn't be traced back to this place. Hardly anyone knew I was here. That I even existed.

I'd put almost all the records back into their drawers, when I discovered the envelope with my name on it. It lay at the edge of the desk, on the other side of the telephone, threatening to tip off the edge and onto the floor. A white, oblong envelope. On it, in gold calligraphy it said; To Mattias. My hands went to it, picked it up. I tore the paper carefully, not knowing what to expect.

Dear Mattias! If you come back before us, we all wish you a fantastic Christmas. You'll find beer in Cloakroom A. Just wanted to say that we are ever so happy you are with us. This is where your sanity gives in and love begins. Without you we move at random.
Love from NN, Havstein, Anna & Palli.

I stood there holding the Christmas card in my hands. She'd made it herself. Crayons. Drawn Gjógv. The mountains. Cut photographs from her magazines and stuck them on, with our names underneath: I was Prince Albert. It would seem. Palli was Johnny Depp. Havstein was Vígdís Finnbogadóttir, Anna was Audrey Hepburn. And she was Nina Persson. Prince Albert? Prince Albert?!

I look down at the Christmas card and that's when it suddenly clicks. It's as though my ears have been plugged all this time and I haven't heard a single sound. It was like being under water and not understanding what they meant when they told me the rain had stopped. Her name isn't Ennen. It's NN. Of course it is! Nomen Nescio. No Name. Ennen. NN.

Why in the world didn't she use her name? And why didn't any of the others use it? Didn't anybody know it? Not even Havstein? I put the Christmas card back on the desk, walked over to the filing cabinets, began searching through the files again.

What I was looking for was a folder without a name, or a file of a woman born in 1971, admitted for the first time in the winter of 1984, and containing symptoms or signs similar to those that NN and Havstein had described. The files were organized exclusively by name, making it impossible to pull out files quickly that began in the present day, I would need to go through all the cabinets. It would take time. A long time.

I was still sitting in Havstein's office at half past eleven that night, reading through his files. I shuttled back and forth between the desk and the twelve filing cabinets, replacing one bunch of papers, pulling another out. There were six drawers in each cabinet, about a hundred files in each drawer, seven thousand files in all, plus or minus. Far too many cases for them all to be Havstein's patients. Even if he'd worked as a psychiatrist for over twenty years, they couldn't all have been his patients. Besides, it didn't fit, several cases went back to the fifties, 1953, the year he was born, and there were stacks of files from the beginning of the century and upwards, from both Denmark and the Faroe Islands. An entire national history of psychiatry gathered in one place, X-files. Some people collect stamps or dried butterflies, napkins or beer mats. Havstein collected patient files. An indexed collection of every screwed-up and confused head from the past fifty years, and I'd decided to read the whole mess.

I'd passed file number four hundred and fifty when I decided to go out and get some fresh air. Replaced the last pile of papers before I went out of the room, down the stairs and put on my jacket, went out into the cold air. The rain from earlier had turned to sleet, and I buttoned my jacket all the way up to the collar, not that it helped much, wandered down the street, past the graveyard, and the little white church just down from the Factory and farther down toward the harbor. It was completely dark, outer space dark, and no streetlights, only a lamp in a window here and there, so I had to walk cautiously, hands out in front of me, before my eyes adjusted. Gjógv had gotten its name from the natural harbor it had been built around, the harbor that lay close into the mountain on the northern side of the settlement, a three-hundred-foot long, sixty-five-foot deep vein that sheltered fishing boats from the ocean and poor weather. It was this harbor that tourists came to see. When they came. If they didn't go elsewhere, to see something more exciting. Tórshavn. The Faroese National Gallery. Nordic Center. Or take one of Palli Lamhauge's boat trips. Or grow a beard and wait for the whale slaughter in Miðvagur. See Klaksvík and die. I made my way toward the harbor, walked around it and up the steep slope to the left, scrambled up onto the mountain, in the sleet, stood leaning diagonally on the slope close to the edge, clinging to an old chicken wire fence, trying to get a glimpse of Kalsoy out there, on the other side of the deep sound, only miles below. But there was too much fog, and it was dark. I could see nothing. Not a yard ahead of me. But I was very bored. Remembered a story Anna had told me about this harbor. About how it had filled with water one day. A tidal wave. It had taken seconds, but that had been enough for half a village to disappear in its wake. An earthquake somewhere out in the ocean, friction between continental plates and there'd been nothing anybody could do, no way to be prepared. I imagined the sea roaring in over the land, heading straight for Gjógv, smashing its way through the narrow natural harbor, splintering every boat in its path, and the houses above, the sea sucking the women into itself as they ran out of their houses to see what the men were shouting about, to see why seconds before the water level had sunk down to almost nothing. And the silence that followed. Gentle waves crashing idly in toward land. I closed my eyes, sleet in my face, and for a moment wished another tidal wave would come. Now. That I'd be torn down from these cliffs, dragged into the North Atlantic before sinking some place out there. Havstein, Anna, Palli, and NN would maybe hear about it on the radio. TV. Think what a good thing it was I hadn't been there. And then come back after Christmas, after good food and loved ones, come back and see that I'd been there after all, search and not find me. But he who waits for a tidal wave generally waits in vain.

And then I sang. Right there. There was nothing else to do. Christmas carols, I think, *Silent Night,* and it was such a beautiful sound, my voice carried way out on the wind, spun out across the water, sideways toward the mountains, before it returned to settle calmly in my pockets, in my mouth. And I started to walk.

I struggled back down along the narrow path, clinging to the chicken wire, walked back toward the Factory. Thought of Helle as I passed the Factory. Hadn't thought about her for a long time, in fact. Had stopped having visions of what she was doing at every moment. I didn't think about what she might be doing now, at that moment, but thought about Little Christmas Eve thirteen years ago, the evening I'd met her outside the school in Stavanger. It had snowed, I'd thrown a snowball. I'd thrown a snowball onto a roof and won myself a girl-friend. I looked at the slope. Sleet. Slush. Bent down and filled my hands with this slushy stuff. Tried to make it into a ball, unsuccessfully. Squeezed the water and ice together, aimed at the church roof. Threw. And it disintegrated before hitting its target, and ice rained over the church roof and the loneliest of the eighteen Faroe Islands.

Christmas Eve. I woke early. There was no Christmas cavalcade. No nuts for Askepott, no smell of Christmas Eve dinner and unopened presents, no perfume or clacking stiletto heels in the early afternoon, no freshly ironed clothes ready to put on. It was cold in my room. I got up, dressed quickly and went down to Havstein's room, straight to the filing cabinets, and began where I'd left off on the previous day, a new round of faltering lives in my hands. I read through stack after stack, a rumbling stomach under the files, and the sun rose and came in through the window for a few hours, before it vanished and it was dark again. It was Christmas and here were more people who no longer dared to go out to meet others, who couldn't sleep at nights, or couldn't face getting up, who had changed beyond recognition or took long walks and had to be fetched back in the evenings. Anorexia and self-harm, nightmares and recurring visitations of dead sailors in the bath, the woman of forty-two who got it into her head that her husband, dead for eight years, still came to dinner every Tuesday, and who always put out her finest china, silver cutlery, prettied herself with lipstick and rouge, a dress and smart shoes, and was just as disappointed each time he didn't turn up.

At around six in the evening I took a break, lent back in the chair and wished myself a Merry Christmas.

"Merry Christmas, Mattias," I said.

"Thanks, same to you," I answered.

Went down into the kitchen, rummaged around in the fridge, found the chicken and French fries I'd bought in Hoydalsvegur the day before, it more or less made itself while I sat in the living room, the TV on, watched some carol singing from one or another church, the Faroese Boys' Choir sang Christmas in, solemnly and slowly, in my own tempo. Wandered into Cloakroom A, found half a case of beer at the back, took some bottles back with me and put them on the kitchen table. Tiptoed up the stairs and stood for a moment outside NN's room, my hand on the doorknob, as if I was frightened of being discovered, before carefully opening the door, and going in. It had that closed in smell already, after just a few days. But it also smelled of NN, soft and calm, soap and fresh towels. And the stillness in here, like a theater set at night, when you return to it hours after the performance is over, but the doll's house still stands, the piano is still there, the drawing room, the little cornet filled with macaroons is still on the table. I went over to her bookcase, took one of her CDs. The Cardigans. *Life*. It had the most Christmassy cover, a smiling skate-queen Nina Persson surrounded by pretty pale blues and white.

So I sat there.

In the kitchen. The last Christmas night before the future. My first Christmas without people.

Ate chicken.

Drank beer.

French fries.

The Cardigans.

C'mon and love me now.

And I was fine.

Yes, I was.

But could have done with a few more people here.

Thought how living rooms all over the country, in Scandinavia, the Nordic countries, Europe, the world, were filled with people who sat eating, at this very moment, families gathered around the table, children impatient on their chairs, *don't want don't want don't want to sit here anymore*, want to leap from their chairs, to run to the tree, but it isn't allowed, not yet, they'll have to wait until everyone has eaten, until coffee is drunk, until the cakes are on the table, and elsewhere, in other time zones, the gifts are already in the hands of small children sitting in their pajamas, cross legged, in front of the tree, if Christmas trees are the tradition there, a big red fire engine in a child's hands, vroom vroom, and for the spoiled children of Texas, the time is only noon or one in the afternoon, and the presents won't be opened until the next morning, Mother has overstretched herself and with tears in his eyes Father packs the brand new rifle, a carbon semiautomatic home-assault rifle, home protection, life membership in the NRA and red lingerie from Victoria's Secret for his wife, because that's the done thing, and Buzz Aldrin stands in his garden and watches a shooting star in the sky, makes a wish for something, I don't know what, has wrapped an exact replica of the moon-landing module for one of his grandchildren, it's thirty years since he walked on the moon and he still remembers that Christmas, the Christmas of 1969, it snowed so much that year, and I think of Havstein and the others who will soon be unwrapping who knows what, of the English or Welsh family from the airport and the Christmas lights that finally work, of Helle who gets everything she wants, and all the people who sit on their own in front of their televisions because they have to, because there's nobody else, of Jørn and Nina who will go to town in a few hours, to Checkpoint Charlie, and my parents who are sitting with our relatives now, chatting happily if one ignores those moments in which Father grows distant and excuses himself, says he's going to the bathroom, but doesn't, goes into the hallway instead, to the phone, several times in the course of the evening, a hairbreadth away from calling me up here, but he doesn't, nothing comes of it, and he goes back in, sits with the others, unwraps something from Black & Decker, always something smart from there, my presents have been put aside, put up in my old room, on the bed perhaps, timeless gifts perhaps that I can have next year, because I'll surely be home by then? Yes, I think I will. I expect so. Probably.

Ninety minutes and forty-two seconds later. I'd played the *Life* album, done the washing up from dinner, was sitting in the living room with a beer, watching TV and feeling something was missing. It wasn't Christmas somehow without the trashy frills. I missed having the money-grabbing shopping center to despise, the mechanical Christmas elves, silently, repetitively performing behind newly cleaned shop windows, the gaudy Christmas lights hanging over streets, and the crackly Christmas wrapping at the counter. I missed the Christmas tree that dropped its needles, spiky and painful to walk on in stockinged feet, the Christmas carols really meant for other days and songs about Jesus who we'd long since given up waiting for, and who, if we were honest with ourselves, was born at a completely different time of year, the cards you forgot to send before it was too late, the Santa Claus who was really only an uncle in a red bathrobe. I missed Dudley Moore in the afternoon, a Christmas matinee, *Arthur*, or *Santa Claus: The Movie* in which he played Santa's little helper, Dudley Moore, actor and concert pianist, didn't appear in films anymore, didn't release records, nobody had seen him for ages, Dudley had melted into the crowd and was only rarely seen out, at a party he particularly wanted to go to, and he got embarrassed looks, he stammered when he spoke, staggered when he walked, it wasn't funny anymore, but Dudley Moore wasn't drunk, Dudley Moore had a parasite eating into his brain, nanometer by nanometer, but nobody knew, nobody asked, and a few years later, in the autumn of 2002, he died, he refused to see his children in the last months, didn't want them to remember him like that. And Liza Minnelli cries wherever she is. *Arthur on the rocks.* I missed Christmas. I missed Dudley. And for the first time, I missed the others. All of them.

That evening, and well into the night I was back up in Havstein's room, reading my way through filing cabinet after filing cabinet. I found nothing on NN, there were too many, it could be any one of them, I gave up at some point or other, I just wanted to have read the files, have the feeling I'd done something useful, that I'd cared about these people, given them a thought, Christmas—a time for reflection—I did what I could to make a contribution, read my way through the archives, and around me Christmas dissolved in all directions.

_ _ _ ▪ _ _ _

It wasn't until the Wednesday between Christmas and New Year that I went outside. There'd been some light snowfall during the night, but not enough to settle. A thin film that disappeared as soon as I stepped on it. I went into the street and drew in the cold air, killed time with my breath and feet, stamped my way through the day and it was completely silent in the village, nothing to go out for, its few permanent inhabitants used the day to visit friends and relatives in other parts of the country, took their cars and went away for a few hours. I shuffled back and forth, happy just to be outside, and to think of something other than the patients that had worn down the linoleum of hospital corridors. And the moment I'd managed to release that thought, my head filled with another; what I was doing here, why I wasn't on a flight home. There'd been a flight today. I hadn't booked it. I'd decided to stay. "Stand at ease."

Because I was doing just fine here, wasn't I?

Yes. I was better at least.

I panicked for an instant; maybe I was digging my life deeper and deeper into a ditch with every second that I did nothing, shovelful by shovelful. Did I have plans at all for going back? Had I decided to stay? Or was I here for no other reason than because I'd come? It wasn't as if I was stranded here, like some Robinson Crusoe arriving on the Faroes in distress, after a relationship had run aground, had sunk dramatically and violently.

But when I thought about it, there weren't any reasons for going home.

I had no job in Stavanger.

Had nowhere to live.

Jørn managed perfectly well without me, with many people around him.

But my parents. I missed Father. He'd have preferred me not to be so far away.

But still.

All I wanted was to be useful, didn't want to be in the way, and right now I'd be useless in Stavanger, I'd end up living stressfully at home with Mother and Father. Restless, jobless. It was unthinkable.

I was doing something here. Fulfilling a function. Repairing winter gardens. Later I might find something else, in town, if I needed to. Or I could leave. Whenever. Wherever.

But you couldn't build Rome before you knew what you wanted. What to build.

And perhaps most important: I wasn't in the way here. I left no tracks after me. I wasn't there, almost.

I thought.

But even an invisible person will be seen in the end, as a white aura flickering through nature, and there are no places to hide. Whoever hides by creeping into a hole will pop up again, in the spring, at the opening of another. A tiny mole.

I tramped about in the thin, slushy snow, up over the slopes, out of the village and down again, staying on the move and burning calories I probably ought to have saved. It was a small village and I had to walk back and forth if I was to be out more than a couple of minutes at a time. And I went on walking, in circles, tracing my own steps with a tailor's precision.

I'd passed the harbor for the fifth or maybe the seventh time when I heard the sound somewhere behind me of a front door being opened and slammed again, I turned to see Sofus coming toward me with the hurried steps of a child. He'd got a new bubble jacket for Christmas, that was obvious, bright yellow, it glowed as he came towards me and the label still hung from one of the lapels, the sort of jacket a popular kid wears on the first day of school in Tórshavn after Christmas, so big they'd see how many people could pile in at once. I stopped and waited for him on the slope down to the harbor, and he half-ran the rest of the way.

"Hi," he said when he'd reached me. I stretched a hand out to greet him, and he hesitated a moment, looked at my outstretched hand before taking hold of it and shaking it carefully, businesslike, then he gave a deep bow and laughed.

"Hi there, Sofus," I said. "Did you get a new jacket for Christmas?"

I pointed to the expanse of yellow fabric. Sofus could get all his friends into that jacket and still have room to spare.

"Yup."

"It's great," I said. "Yellow."

He flapped his arms up and down, but the chicken couldn't fly. So we stood there not knowing what to say to each other.

"Why are you alone?" he asked suddenly, out of nowhere.

Did he know I'd been alone all Christmas? Was it common knowledge in the village? Had I been watched for days from behind curtains?

"I missed my Christmas flight."

"What?"

"It was flying too fast. Couldn't catch it."

"Were you going to Norway?"

"That was the plan."

"Are you sad then?"

"In what way?"

"That you have to be alone here?"

"I'm not alone."

"Aren't you?"

"Well, *you're* here."

"Yes."

"So, Sofus, did you get any other nice things for Christmas?"

He nodded. Vigorously. He'd had some other nice things for Christmas.

"What?"

"A car."

"A car?"

"Remote control."

"Great."

He nodded.

"Mum wants you to come and eat dinner with us."

"What?"

"Mum asked me to come and ask if you'd like to come to our house to eat dinner."

I understood nothing, or too much. I'd obviously been the object of investigation that Christmas, and now they wanted to check if their assumptions were correct. I imagined the entire family dressed in white lab coats, gloved hands, asking me to lie down on a cold steel table in the middle of the living room. Out with the scalpels and clamps.

"Did she? Are you sure?" I asked.

"Yes. Do you want to?"

No. No-no-no-no-no. I did not want to. Not at all. There was nothing I wanted less.

"I don't think I come today. I'm a bit busy today."

"With what?"

"With . . . things."

"Don't you want to eat with us?"

"It's not that I don't want to," I said. "It's just . . ."

"Oh, please come."

"No, really, I think…"

"Mum said you have to."

What could I say?

I gave in.

"Okay."

"Yippee."

"All right. Yippee."

He turned and began to walk quickly homeward, with me in tow. I'd not had a shower for days, had been in the same clothes for ages, had had smarter days, but I followed obediently toward his red house, walked in the door, took my shoes off quietly and stood in my stockinged feet in a strange house, sniffed the smell of the family, the food they usually made, the smells of their bodies, the unique signature you find in each home. Sofus sat down on the floor and began fiddling with his laces, the knots were hard and difficult for him to undo. He held a foot up to me, and I took it, began teasing the knot loose, and that was how I made my entrance into that house, standing in the hallway with Sofus's foot in my hands as his parents came out into the hallway, Herr and Fru Faroe, windblown faces and broad smiles. I fiddled with the lace, finally undid the knot and stood there with his boot in one hand, and his father's hand came whizzing across and put itself in the other.

"Good evening," he said, looking directly at me. "Óli Jacobsen."

I said my name, loud and clear, turned towards Sofus's mother.

"Selma."

My name once more.

"And you've already met Sofus," she said, tousling her son's hair. Sofus immediately smoothed it back down. Tousled hair had no place here! And he flung his other foot forward, another knot. I'd have offered to untie that boot also, but Herr and Fru beat me to it, bending over their son in unison and each grabbing a lace, this was cooperation, teamwork, and pretty swift too. Sofus's parents were shorter than I'd thought when

I first saw them. They both seemed to be of equal height, a head shorter than me perhaps, and I was, more or less to the inch, the average height of a European man. Óli Jacobsen had short, brown hair that stuck out in all directions, and Selma's wasn't very different. An enchanting pair. Good-luck trolls. Tourist publicity material. Óli was clearly a solid working man, a sturdy fellow with big fists and a chunky wool sweater with three gold buttons on one shoulder, and coarse trousers. Selma was slimmer, had made herself smart for dinner, Christmas was only just over and she'd gone right to the back of her closet, I could see her digging the Marks & Spencer bag out from eighteen months ago, she'd been on a shopping trip that summer to Scotland and England, she couldn't pack all those clothes away again yet, she had to get proper use out of them. This might be the last chance anyway. Next Christmas, perhaps already by summer, it would be too late, there'd be new clothes in the stores and more Christmas garments to stash in the back of her wardrobe. So perhaps she knew it was the last time she'd wear them, and she loosened Sofus's boot and he ran into the living room in front of us.

Socks padded over the wooden floor of the large living room, and then we sat at the Formica dining table, and I was the nice guest from nowhere, the spy who came in from the cold, to the family Jacobsen and partook of their lasagna. And the living room was like the others I'd seen in all the houses around here, light colored walls, landscape paintings, and an arrangement of leather sofas and carpets from the second half of the eighties, a time when people had had more money, when the country had still been on track, before the crisis and massive unemployment of the mid-nineties that had come in the wake of fishing quota changes and which threatened to strangle a country dependent on its exports. The Faroes were beginning slowly but surely to work their way back up now, krone by krone, and by the summer it might be out with the old sofa and in with IKEA. The TV with a plant on top, placed to give the sofa's occupants the best view.

Óli spoke softly, Danish with a Faroese accent, the occasional word I didn't recognize, but it mostly went in, they prodded and questioned me, were kindly and polite, they'd apparently seen me going back and forth over Christmas, up and down the streets, and they'd seen me a bit before that too of course. And they'd figured I lived with Havstein and his friends. That was how they phrased it. *Havstein and his friends,* like the title of some cartoon, and I wasn't quite sure if that was a good or bad thing.

"You're on vacation here, are you?"

That was a question I asked myself too.

"Not exactly, I . . . well . . . it's not that easy to say, really."

There was silence for some seconds, none of us sure how to proceed. Óli cleared his throat, Selma took the hint, but picked up the thread again.

"So you're not on vacation, then?"

So I explained how things were. Said how times were hard for gardeners in Norway, how the shopping centers had won the terrain, I said, the new millennium is approaching and everybody wants to hide behind their plants, but nobody wants to pay more than they have to, and I told them I had a friend who'd played in Tórshavn during Ólavsøkan, and they seemed to find that interesting. I told them I'd met Havstein outside town, which was true in a way, and that I'd accepted his offer of a job, that I liked to make myself useful. I didn't talk about Helle, or my parents who wanted me to go home, with whom I'd almost broken contact, or how I'd spent weeks in my room upstairs. I gave them the cut version. PG rated. The suitable Disneyland version. Didn't mention any catastrophes, bloodied hands or envelopes that appeared from nowhere filled with large amounts of money.

"Yes, you make those . . . what are they? Up at the Factory, I mean." She turned to Óli, talking to him in Faroese, and he mumbled something in answer.

"Tourist gifts," I said. "Souvenirs. Wooden sheep and that sort of thing. And then I started work as a gardener again. Havstein organized it."

"Yes, quite. And is that going all right? You find it all right?"

"Everyone's got to do something," I answered.

Óli agreed. These were words to his liking, true wisdom, and he nodded approvingly as he went out to the kitchen to mix up some more blackcurrant cordial.

"I think it's so nice that there are young people who want to live in Gjógv," said Selma. "There aren't so many of us left."

"No?"

"Well, apart from you lot up at the Factory, there are . . . let's see now," she shouted some sentences out to Óli in the kitchen and he shouted back, I made out that he said *four or five* and Selma continued where she'd left off—"yes, Óli thinks there are four or five houses that are occupied now. There was an old man who lived right down the road here, but I'm not sure if he's moved into a nursing home or not. This isn't the place to be old."

"No?"

"Not at all," she said almost brusquely, "not with the stores so far away and the weather being so dreadful in the winter. It's better to live down in Tórshavn. And we get snow up here too sometimes, and then it's almost impossible to go out on the roads to Funningur with those sharp bends, you know. Before the plow comes. Although it generally comes pretty fast. And a couple of people around here are so old they're not able to drive no matter what the conditions, so we generally drop in to ask what they need if we're going shopping in Funningur or Tórshavn."

"That's kind," I answered, taking the plates that were being continually sent around the table, supper in orbit, Jupiter lasagna, Mars bread, Neptune butter on the table before me, and at the farthest edge of the solar system—me, an astronaut who couldn't get enough of anything, but devoured the planets one by one as they came my way,

"Only ten, fifteen years ago we had a lot more people living here, we had our own shop, our own school, the men worked as fishermen. And quite a few scholars came from Gjógv even. Professors. The Bishop. But now? No. Now we feel more or less forgotten by the rest of the country. But it's still a good place to live, don't you think?" She said this last thing with her gaze glued to mine, as though she wanted me to say she was right, to confirm her statement, and by doing so turn it into an incontrovertible truth.

"Yes, absolutely," I said. "There's no better place. The best."

Óli came back in from the kitchen at last after preparing the cordial according to time-honored tradition. He placed the jug in the center of the table, and was about to help himself to more food when he got a sharp look from his wife, she let out a little snort which instantly made him put down what he had in his hands and pour me some cordial.

"Thank you," I said. And I said the food was lovely, best I'd had in ages. I told them how I'd missed my plane home, the Christmas flight, somebody had messed it up, I'd meant to go to Stavanger, but hadn't, I said, these things happen, and that I'd had to rush to get the basic necessities from the Statoil station up in Hoydalsvegur. They laughed and told me the tourists always complained about the opening times too, that everything closed so early and it was impossible to get beer except at Rúsdrekkasøla Landsins, the state outlet, and you had to rise with the sun to catch that, and I felt a bit offended that they saw me as a tourist rather than somebody who'd come to settle, felt I didn't fit in with the community, I was a sore thumb on this country's hand glowing crimson as it waved to the world, but that was okay, all in all, it was fine. Somebody had to be a tourist. Somebody had to do it.

Sofus sat on his chair restlessly, he'd been quiet through the entire meal, saying hardly a word. He'd glanced at me occasionally, then glanced down at the floor, listened to his parents talking to me, and suddenly I got a feeling I'd never had before, a big brother feeling, a sudden sense of protectiveness that shot out from nowhere.

His parents got up almost in unison, there was a rhythm in their bodies, they were finely tuned to each other, they combined forces and cleared the table, signaled that I should take a seat in the leather-department of the living room and disappeared into the kitchen. Sofus looked at me. Sat swinging his legs. I should say something. I glanced at the parquet floor. Small wheel tracks, rubber marks next to the sofa.

"That car you got," I said. "Is it around?"

And a smile went right around his head. I was okay.

"Yes. In my room."

"Have you tried it out? Is it water resistant?"

"No. I don't know."

"Go and get it, and we can see."

Sofus jumped down from his chair and ran to the kitchen, said something to his mother and disappeared into the attic, coming back down a minute later with a huge radio controlled car in his hands, a racing car with big rubber wheels, yellow too. They were all the rage. Bright colors. Like the colors they painted their houses out here on the Faroes, bright blue, red, pink, colors that broke up the monotone green of the summer and the gray landscape of the autumn and winter. I was given the racing car to hold, I turned it this way and that, it seemed watertight. Sofus handed me the box, the text was in English and said the car was *all weather fun*. Okay. If it could take water, then it could take some slushy snow. There's no such thing as bad weather, only bad radio-controlled cars.

"Do you want to give it a go? Outside?"

"Now?"

"Yes."

"Is it waterproof?"

"Yes," I said, "it seems like it."

Selma and Óli came back in, put the coffee on the glass table between the sofas. But we didn't want coffee. Neither Sofus nor I. We had other plans. And I saw the smiles come to their faces as Sofus announced we were going out to try the car, big smiles you could hang on a wall and look at.

That evening I had a purpose. Filled an empty space. A small green dot on a blue painting. I was the lone island that makes the ocean look so big.

Sofus carried his car in his arms, walking ahead of me across the road. Over to the church. I walked alongside him, holding the remote control. And then he put the car down next to the little gate into the cemetery, switched the electric current on, and I handed him the control, so he could show me what the car could do. And the electric buzzing of the car radiated out of the plastic, rose into the damp air and slammed into the mountains all about us, as the car vanished down the road ahead until it was almost out of sight, then it turned and came back like a boomerang, like an obedient dog, like me.

That evening we created racetracks along the slushy asphalt, small obstacles for the car to negotiate, a little jump, and we raced each other, alternately, against the clock. I went over to the Factory and into Cloakroom A to fetch a stopwatch and some chocolate. Sofus was achieving the best times, his fingers manipulated the controls with ease and he anticipated every hump and how to get over it in the quickest time. I got the hang of it after a while, got better, even got ahead of him sometimes. But I generally let him win, and he ate the victor's chocolates with sticky fingers as he steered the car through the slush.

Kodak moment. Again.

"Your turn," said Sofus, handing me the remote. I took it and gave the stopwatch to Sofus, who gave me my marks, *ready, set, go!*

As I stood there steering the car, I suddenly thought of the friend he'd been on his way to visit the last time I'd met him, on my first day. Óluva she'd been called. I remembered. I'm good with names.

"Where's Óluva, these days?" I asked as I swung the car around one of the boulders down the slope.

He glanced at me as though we were old buddies, and as though he assumed I knew her well.

"I don't know," he answered.

"Don't you go over to her place very much?"

"No."

Pause.

"She's moving."

"To Tórshavn?'

He shook his head.

"Copenhagen."

"When?"

"In January."

"That's a shame."

"Yes."

The car hit the jump and hung in the air for a moment then landed with a thud, and the rubber tires softened the impact before I swung it back to us.

"You liked her a lot, didn't you?"

He didn't answer.

"I'll get private teaching when she's gone," was all he said.

I thought about NN, and the teacher who'd defied wind and rain to get out to her on Mykenes, to teach her history, to teach her that there was always a war some place out there, at all times. That the world around her spun ceaselessly at a speed that made it almost impossible for her to orient herself, impossible to hold on, and that was why the waves were so big here, the winds so strong.

"Would you move, if you could?" I asked.

"No."

The car came buzzing toward us, slush spraying out to the sides.

"Somebody's got to stay behind, otherwise it won't work," I said, to myself most of all.

He leaned forward so as to see the finish line more clearly, to get the precise time that the car came over it. She was leaving, which was why he didn't want to be with her any more. Then he could start to forget her.

"You really liked her, didn't you?"

The car passed the finish line and slammed on the brakes at 1:23:22.

"Yes. Should we go back in now?"

"Yes."

Sofus picked up his car and brushed the worst of the slush off with his jacket sleeve and we trotted back to the house. His parents were sitting in the living room watching TV. Sofus sat with us for a quarter of an hour, before being told it was bedtime, and he padded out to the bathroom, through the wall I heard the sound of yawning and teeth being brushed.

"It'll be lonely for Sofus," I said, "Now that Óluva's moving."

"Has he said something about that?" asked Selma.

"Just that he liked her a lot."

"Yes they've been together since they were born. More or less."

"Why are they going to Copenhagen?"

"Jens Henrik's got a good job there," said Óli.

"Her father, Jens Henrik," added Selma, "and they have family there too."

"Aren't there any other children here?"

"In Gjógv?"

"Yes."

"No. Not any more. Sofus is the only one left."

And Sofus came into the living room in his pajamas, got a kiss on the forehead from both parents, and I was given a handshake, the full treatment.

"Bye bye," he said to me before turning.

"Good night," I answered.

I stayed there late into the evening. It was still Christmas. Óli got out a bottle of cognac and we sat on the leather sofa with a glass each. Óli talked about the fish factory in the village, the fishing, about boats that sank or that never returned and were just reported missing. He talked about the memorial garden for seamen that was next to the church. I hadn't seen it. Hadn't been there.

"Take a walk there one day," said Selma. "It might perhaps help you to understand a bit more about the Faroe Islands."

"Maybe so," I said.

And on we talked. Relaxed, agreeable, post-Christmas chatter. Óli had a good rowboat down in the harbor, and by the way, we must feel free to use it, if ever we wanted to take it out to go fishing or whatever. It was ready to go. No need to ask. Simply borrow it. And later, just as I was about to break up the party, we talked about Sofus again. I was in the hallway tying my laces and Selma and Óli stood in the doorway and waited, I got up and stretched a hand out. Selma shook it.

"He really appreciated your playing with him today," she said.

"My pleasure," I answered.

"I could see it in his face. I haven't seen him like that for ages."

I said nothing.

"It's not good for him to be alone so much, you know. Or just with us. He needs friends his own age. He needs friends."

"I could come here more often."

"Would you like to?"

"Of course."

I was useful. I had a function. I was a good investment.

"He'd like that so much."

"I've got plenty of spare time."

And then I left. I thanked them and wandered home over our wheel tracks and into the Factory. And it was only now that the feeling of Christmas hit, flowed into me, like an actor walking slowly, step by careful step, across the stage floor on a postponed first night, finally ready to deliver his first line, after a long pregnant pause:

"Christmas."

Didn't get to sleep that night. At all. Lay in bed awake and counted the beams in the ceiling again and again. There were forty-two. I thought a lot that night, about Sofus who wanted friends, but who had none left. I thought about how lonely it can be to be a child, how tough it can be sometimes, like squeezing a blue whale into a photo booth, and around the corner of every single house you run toward you can bump into the greatest happiness obtainable, a happiness to make you explode, or the darkest abyss you never knew existed, the kind that makes you sleep with the light on, makes you think that nothing will ever be okay again, that nothing can be made good. And you crawl to school, hands out before you, because you're a reptile and you're not doing well, you've got lousy grades, and you think if you can't make it now, you never will, because that's what they've told you, that you'll always be an outsider. And even when it doesn't turn out that badly after all, on adult reflection, with the benefit of hindsight: things still won't get easier. You don't escape it even when you're a grown-up. It'll go on demanding every scrap of strength, wrecking you almost entirely. At least that's how it will feel, as though nothing's changed. But in truth it has. Everything's changed. And then you feel it one morning, one afternoon, one Sunday in February, an otherwise dreadful day, you sense things are different, because you know you'd never want to be a child again, not for the world, and you think how you really couldn't bear to go through it again, and then you realize that something's lost its grip on you. It's as if you've gone to town for the first day without winter boots. In soft sneakers. You're nearer the ground. You've got a better foothold. Something's released you and you're capable of thinking the thought: *Things aren't so bad.*

04:23. Click. 04:24. I switched the light on. Got up. Dressed. Went down the stairs and into the storeroom in Cloakroom A, fetched a couple of beers, went up again.

Stood on the landing. Was cold.

Looked at the different doors.

Wondered a bit what I should do.

Two bottles of Pils in my hand.

Disheveled hair.

I walked into Havstein's room.

I stood in his office, as I had many times in the last few days. My second sitting room. I switched on the light, walked over and sat in his office chair, opened a beer and welcomed fictive patients who never came, never needed diagnosing, and were actually surprisingly well.

Then I got up, walked back and forth, stopped at the bookshelves, read the titles. On psychology. Psychiatry. Self-help literature. *Marital Brinkmanship. How Not to Kill Your Husband / How Not to Kill your Wife. Three Ways of Staying Happy. Problems & Solutions.* Quackery mixed in with professional literature. Didn't really feel like opening any of them, I'd read enough psychiatric files to last me a year or a lifetime now, but I stood there wondering for a moment if I should get on the bandwagon and write a book myself. *Survival Strategies: Basic Model For a Long and Happy Life.* A-three-step program.
Breathe in.
Breathe out.
Repeat as required.

Something happens to you when you've been alone for a few days. Home alone. It's like when your parents have left you at home to go away to Denmark for a holiday, a week in Ebeltoft. You develop new habits, your body gets new rhythms. Imperceptibly you turn troglodyte, a Robinson Crusoe at home, and your steps create new paths in the house, you sit in different chairs, in Father's chair, you pursue absurd activities because the boundaries have practically disappeared. You can sleep on the living room floor if you want. Sit up all night. Nobody will ever know. In a matter of days you're beyond any structure, any previously walked trail. And you almost stop going out too. And then when your parents do return one day, it seems to come on you so suddenly. You always seem to be caught unprepared. No matter how hard you try, how much effort you make. You are Robinson Crusoe, with a big beard and clothed in an animal hide you hunted yourself. The trash, the glasses, the plates, the cushions you forgot to straighten on the sofa where you lay one day, they all reveal where you've been, what you've done. And as they open the front door and walk in, you meet the culture clash at the door and even your own voice sounds strange, unfamiliar, almost new.

I was sleeping when they arrived a couple of days later. It was the day before New Year's Eve and I was woken by a face uncomfortably close to my own. I opened my eyes and was staring straight into somebody else's.

"Hi," said Helle.

I squinted at her. Didn't believe my eyes,

"What are you doing here?" I whispered.

"Have you slept all Christmas, or what?" she laughed. "I'm back. Did you miss me?"

I rubbed my eyes and opened them again. NN was sitting on the bed next to me, eyes close to mine.

"Have you slept all Christmas or what?" she repeated.

I didn't have time to answer. A second later Havstein came tramping in, together with Anna and Palli, at the rear as usual, he stood there in the doorway.

"Merry Christmas!" they shouted.

"Merry Christmas," I mumbled.

I tried to shake my head awake. It wobbled on my shoulders.

"Has he been lying there asleep all Christmas?" Anna asked NN.

"Yes!" she answered grabbing hold of me, dragging me from the covers. I made myself heavy, held tightly to the warm duvet, but she didn't give in. "Come on! You've got to get up. We're going to Klaksvík. It'll be 2000 tomorrow night. Wild, isn't it?"

"Yes," I answered apathetically, as I let her tear the soft, warm duvet from me, inch by inch, until I sat in my underwear on the edge of the bed, feet on the cold floor and goose bumps over my entire body, the warmth of a Caribbean map on my back.

"We'll wait for you downstairs," said Havstein. "We ought to get going as soon as possible, so we catch the stores. And the boat. Okay?"

"Ten minutes," I mumbled. "And I'll be ready."

"Fantastic."

Palli turned in the doorway and disappeared with Anna and Havstein in tow, tramp tramp tramp down the stairs and into the kitchen where I heard them laughing loudly, and my name being mentioned.

"Did you have a good Christmas in Stavanger?" asked NN as I started getting dressed.

"I didn't go."

"What?"

"Missed the flight.

"Where have you been then?"

"Here."

"Here?"

"It's as good a place as any."

"But what about food? There was almost nothing left here." A maternal instinct coming to the surface. I liked it when she cared like that.

"The gas station in Hoydalsvegur," I said.

"Wonderful selection there, I'd bet."

"You can't imagine," I answered and gave her a big hug. "Welcome home."

"Thanks."

Then I told her about the plane that left and the bus that didn't arrive early enough, and about Sofus who'd be all alone when his last friend left.

"There's always another bus," was all NN said.

"Almost always," I answered.

I put my jacket on, yawned, not quite awake, took some money from the envelope that lay in the drawer of my desk and put it in my pocket, and we went out of my room and onto the landing.

"Thanks for the card, by the way. It was so nice to get it."

NN looked at me and frowned.

"Card? Oh yeah, that. But I forgot to put it out . . . I was going to . . . have you been in Havstein's room?"

No handcuffs or sirens, a brutal arrest nonetheless. Didn't know what to say.

"The telephone rang one day," I said. "I thought I should answer it. And then I saw your card on the table. On his desk."

"So who called?"

"On the phone? Nobody."

"Nobody?"

"Wrong number."

"Havstein doesn't like us going into his room."

I looked down. "No."

"You've been in his archives, haven't you?"

I couldn't lie. I said nothing.

"He'll be furious if he finds out."

"He won't," I said.

"No?"

"Not unless you tell him."

NN lifted her hand to her lips, turned an imaginary lock and threw the key over her shoulder.

"Thanks."

"No problem." She signaled for me to follow. But I didn't move.

"I couldn't find you in the archive," the words tumbled out. "Your file, I mean."

She stopped. Looked at me. I don't know if it was a good or bad sign.

"No, I know. I've removed it."

"Why?"

She looked round the room, then back at me.

"No Name?"

"That's right."

"So, what's your name?"

"Come on," she said. "We've got to go now."

She turned heel and went out the door. I went on questioning her as we went down to the others, pressing her as to why she'd taken her file out of the archives, and whether she knew that there were century-old cases lying in those cabinets, I wondered whether she knew how Havstein had come to collect all these papers, but she wouldn't answer my questions, brushing them off and steering the conversation to other subjects, either because she didn't know what to say, or because it bored her. I didn't intend to give up though, I just held my tongue, and decided that I'd get it out of Havstein one day, I'd ask him directly what he was up to. And from that moment, not a day passed when I didn't think of doing it. Not one day.

It was almost cloud-free that day, and a couple of degrees above zero, we crammed into Havstein's little Subaru and drove down along Funnings Fjord, crossing Eysturoy in the middle and continuing down the famous Skálafjørður fjord. This was, according to those in the know, the country's best harbor, used by the British as a marine base during the war. There'd even been talk in the mid 1700s of making it the center of political power and trade, but then people had got distracted, forgotten it perhaps, who knows, but it had come to nothing, even though it would have been a good idea. Instead the region around the fjord had grown into the most densely built up area of the Faroes, a Scandinavian Tokyo, a microscopic megapolis with over five thousand inhabitants. Yet possibly the least interesting place I've ever seen, and as I sat squashed up against the car window, next to Palli and NN, I thought how if anybody had come here to take photos for a picture postcard, nothing would have appeared on the film, it would have been unexposed, because there wasn't a single thing to look at.

It wasn't until we approached Leirvík, where the ferry was, that I began to wake up properly and my hearing returned fully. I'd been leaning, half asleep against the car window almost the entire journey from Gjógv, so my ears only vaguely registered the conversation that circulated in the car, Christmas reports, the presents everybody had been given and from whom, and somewhere, as though packed in cotton wool, the car stereo played the Cardigans, and now and then NN sang to it, tapping the rhythm with her fingers on my jacket. We drove into the quay just in time to see the *Dúgvan* floating off toward Klaksvík, loaded with the cars and passengers that had gotten here on time, and there was no alternative but to park and wait the hour it would take for the boat to return. It wasn't a big deal. It was a nice day, on a day like this we could just stay in the car, button our jackets up, open the windows, and enjoy the cold, clear winter air on our faces and hands, close our eyes and imagine it was spring. Which is what we did. We parked the car on the quay, first in line, and sat there, windows rolled down, leaning back in our seats, not needing to say a word. I lay thinking about the new millennium that would be upon us in less than thirty-six hours, wondering if it would be different, or if everything would just go on as though nothing had happened. I wondered whether all the world's computers would go out of control, lose count and collapse, revolt against themselves. I wondered what would happen if we had to start all over again. Would we start making video games everybody could program? Would Commodore 64 make a comeback? Would my watch, that had stopped one night in July, start again? Impossible to tell. Out in the world professors wrote articles explaining how the world was at knife-point, this was the battle against the clock, at precisely the zero-point of the new millennium all the banks' debt records would be wiped out, interest rates would soar, our bank accounts would either vanish or expand. Underdeveloped countries would become developed. Time for fairer trading. It would be impossible to tell when the semi-skimmed milk was beyond its use-by-date, or how long the pizza had been in the oven. The car might explode when you put the key in the ignition to drive across town to see your girlfriend. The gas tank would catch fire from a spark caused by a short circuit in the car stereo, traveling via a myriad of wires and devious routes, that single millennium spark would work its way into your gas tank, light the fuel and explode out of the tank, through your dash board, setting your body alight, and your face would melt, you'd be fried in your own fat in your fake leather car seats. That was how they talked, wrote. And at home in Norway, the biggest newspapers had already printed a whole page in which the prime minister pronounced that precautions were in place, there was no need for panic so long as we all stayed calm. Although, for those of us whose fear was of the prime minister himself, no guidance was given.

We'd been sitting in the car for half an hour, barely saying a word, when Anna decided to get out and go to the supermarket next to the church and buy herself something to drink. She asked if anyone wanted to come too, but none of us wanted to move, so we stayed in our seats. *Does anyone want anything?* she asked. No, we were fine. She opened the door and started walking across the quay, I changed my mind, went after all, bounded over to catch up with her.

"Changed your mind, Mattias?"

"Yes," I answered, "I was getting cold in the car."

"Great."

We walked around the little supermarket, Anna first and me a step behind. She was the kind of person who you'd just assume, if you didn't know her, was leader of the group. I thought it was something about the way she moved, the straight back, a gaze that seemed constantly searching to get an overview, eyes that scanned the product shelves or the workplace, separating the unimportant from the interesting at a glance, she walked firmly in seemingly predetermined paths, steered us past the canned foods and skerpi meat to the soft drinks, hidden away at the back of the shop.

"What do you fancy?" she asked, taking a bottle of water out for herself and pointing at the rows of various bottles and cartons in the fridge before us with the other hand.

"Have they got anything with apple juice, do you think?"

"Let's see . . . apple, apple . . ." Anna examined the shelves and found a little green carton with a straw. "Here."

"Is that nice?"

"It's okay. It almost tastes like apples."

"Good."

I took the apple juice and we made our way to the register, paid, and went back out into the cold sunshine, threw away the packaging, searched for something to say. I knew so little about Anna. Apart from the fact that she no longer visited galleries, the details I'd secretly read in Havstein's archives. She was only the second oldest of the three ex-patients I lived with, but she'd automatically been assigned the sort of responsible mom role, and she kept an eye on us when we turned our backs on her.

I drank my apple juice. It was pretty all right. Like apple and plastic. Looked across the quay where the rest of the gang sat at a loss, waiting for the ferry to come back.

"I hope you don't take this the wrong way, but I just wanted to tell you I'm glad you're looking after NN."

"Looking after her?" That wasn't how I'd thought of it, not at all. She was perhaps one of the best people I'd ever met. I'd not been looking after her. It was more a case of her looking after me, wasn't it?

"She's really lit up since you arrived. So . . . listen, I'm asking you to be careful what you do. Okay?"

"What do you mean?"

"You know exactly what I mean, Mattias."

I nodded hesitantly. Drank my plastic apple juice. Looked over at the car, looked like they'd all gone to sleep there. And out in the fjord the ferry came sputtering over.

Anna squinted at me.

"Did you really think you wouldn't be noticed here?"

I considered it.

"Yeah," I answered, and meant it.

"Well, you've failed completely then."

"Perhaps."

She gave me a hug.

"Come on now, you miserable Norwegian. Or we won't get to Klaksvík."

"And would that be a great loss?"

She laughed.

"No, not really."

So we walked back to the car, as the ferry prepared itself to dock. We got in, NN was dozing in the backseat and woke up as I moved over to her and settled into the seat. Havstein turned toward me.

"Did you buy anything?"

I held the apple drink up. He frowned.

"Are you drinking that? Plastic apple juice."

"Plastic fantastic," I said.

The ferry hit the quay, the bow opened and we started the car up, rolled on board, we were almost the only passengers, there were just a couple of cars more and a trailer, and a little family on foot.

I buttoned my thin jacket up again and once the ferry was out into the fjord I went out on deck, hanging on the railings while the others sat inside in the little café at the front of the boat. It wasn't the season for tourists, and there was a strong wind, so I got to be more or less alone, except when the odd sailor rushed past on his way to the engine room or the bridge. We were right in the fjord now, and snuck around the edge of Kalsoy where jagged mountains shot sharply above us, small and pathetic in our floating tub. I thought about what I'd been doing for the last few months. Waiting, mostly, without really knowing what I was waiting for. Better times? To get my job back? For Helle to turn up one day and fly me home? Or for the arrival of a new millennium when people might suddenly start buying flowers and plants wholesale? I hadn't done much. Almost nothing. But then, it seemed plenty of people were able to live lives like that, doing more or less nothing. Taking things as they came. And when I thought about it, it didn't even seem so bad, really. And anyway I'd started working again now.

I was back on track.

I'd stopped waiting. Hadn't I?

A puffin came sailing down over the boat. It made a little swing astern and continued onward along the ship's side before rising and circling me a couple of times, as though wondering whether to land or not. But I saw in its eyes that it had decided against it. And it flew off.

Havstein came up on deck through the double wooden doors. He stood next to me, resting his arms on the railings.

"Well?" he asked. "What do you think?"

"It's lovely out here," I answered.

"Yes, isn't it." He pointed at the island we passed. "That's Kalsoy. That's what you can see from Gjógv sometimes. And over there," he continued, leaning over the rail and looking forward, "is Kunot, with the pyramid."

"Pyramid?"

"Ranndalur, a mountain. It looks like a pyramid. Wait and see."

I looked around. Naked islands in every direction. Almost gray. I thought how different things looked now, in contrast to when I'd arrived in the summer. Everything had been so green. Almost copper green. Now the colors were faded, nature had shed its skin. A winter coat of fur on the mountains.

"How was your Christmas?" asked Havstein.

"Not bad. Quiet."

"You didn't get home, I heard. To Norway. NN told me."

I longed to ask him about her, what her real name was. I longed to ask him about the archive and why he kept it. But didn't. I couldn't go telling him I'd been rummaging among his things again. Instead I said:

"Gjógv is as good a place as any."

"Didn't you want to go home?"

"I missed the flight."

"But did you want to go home?"

A pause. Another bird passed over the boat, not that there was anything dramatic about that.

"I don't know."

Havstein didn't answer.

"I can't believe we'll be going into the year 2000 tomorrow," was all he said.

"Yeah, feels weird."

"I remember thinking how strange it was when we went into the eighties. And the nineties. As if the future was about to begin. But now? I don't know. It feels like entering a new room, blindfolded. And we've got nothing to hold onto."

"We have each other, don't we?"

He looked away. Gazing far out, into the fjord. It wasn't easy to guess what he was thinking. I thought about whether it was an advantage or drawback that we walked alone. Or whether it had any effect at all.

"Yes. We do. And we should be grateful for that."

"Yes, we should."

"But don't you think it's strange, Mattias? Think about it, here we are, five people, all over thirty, and none of us married, none of us with partners. Family. Kids."

I thought about NN.

"Perhaps marriage is just a buffer against loneliness, or perhaps we're just special people. The exceptions on the margins."

"No," he answered. "There are lots of us. Hordes. And we're all equally lonely, or maybe we're not lonely at all, maybe that's the problem, we're too self-sufficient. We just want to be left in peace. That doesn't make children, Mattias. It doesn't make families."

"Maybe there are enough families?"

"There can never be enough families. Never."

He looked away.

"Fear of contact, Mattias. I had a lecturer in Copenhagen who talked about it. The fear of getting too close to other people. That thing that makes us all move a little farther away on the bus seat when somebody sits next to us. It's the fear of belonging, the fear of dying."

I wasn't quite sure where he was heading, and I was going to say something more, but he beat me to it, suddenly changing the subject.

"Did you know that the Americans were here in the sixties, to train for the moon landing?"

"Wasn't that Iceland?"

"Here too. I saw him myself."

"Who?"

"Armstrong. Aldrin too."

"Here on the Faroes? When?"

"The mid-sixties some time. The summer of sixty-seven, I think. Up near Slættaratindur. We'd been on a fishing trip, or maybe we were on our way to go fishing, I don't quite remember. By Eiðisvatn. A couple of friends and me. And then we saw it, a column of vehicles coming over the hill and parking at the side of the road."

I didn't know whether to believe him, whether he was telling the truth. I'd never heard it before. It could be true. A carefully guarded secret that only few people knew, left out of the biographies for any number of reasons. Or perhaps he was only saying it so I'd forget what he'd just said. Perhaps he didn't want me feeling bad on the last day of the millennium. But no matter. It was a great story anyway.

"There must have been fifty of them," he went on, "all with big bags, carrying suitcases, with equipment in tow. Then they took everything over to the gravel area, up toward the mountain. And we followed them, keeping a good distance. Hung in the background so as not to be noticed. They went on for ages, organizing this and that, a big ring of people in the middle of nowhere. And then, when the ring finally opened up a little, we saw these two astronauts lurching about in huge suits, performing various tasks. It was hard to make out quite what. But I remember one of my friends had a pair of binoculars with him, and we took turns with them. Lay on the ground, hiding in the grass, spying. Eventually they took their helmets off and it was possible to see their faces. And one was Armstrong. For certain. I recognized the face two years later, I've always been good at them. Faces.

"Did you see Aldrin too?"

"I think so. But I'm not sure. Didn't take so much notice of him, how he looked and stuff."

"Not many people do," I said.

"Look over there," said Havstein, pointing. "Look at that."

I lifted my head, and saw Ranndalur, straight ahead, and it certainly did look like a pyramid, but covered with grass and a thin, speckled layer of snow. It loomed over the port of Klaksvík, like a layer cake, like a stunning community project made by nature or by the people of Klaksvík, and I had to lean almost right back to see the blunted top, almost lost my balance, and I thought that I could have had a camera, have photographed it, captured it on film. But I rarely had my camera with me, not on any of the trips I'd been on. Wasn't sure who I'd show the prints to even if I'd taken them.

We turned from the mountain, its image imprinted in our minds as we crossed the deck, went back in to the others, took the stairway down and got into the car as the ferry docked in the quay and opened its hold, and then we drove into Klaksvík. Havstein dropped us off at the bridge and we arranged to meet him a few hours later. He was going to drive up to Múli and visit what he referred to as "the other group." The "other group" was made up of people like NN, Palli and Anna, institutionalized people who for various reasons wouldn't or couldn't fit in with society, without its leading to more problems than happiness. From what I understood, this unit had more residents than our little Factory, and some of them weren't even as healthy as my gang, as us. Because of this they were only allowed partial freedom of movement. Even its location hadn't been a coincidence. It hadn't been until 1994, when the last local inhabitants had left forever, that the state granted money for the building of this house, due mainly to Havstein's persistence, apparently, and if we felt isolated in Gjógv, that was nothing compared to Múli.

There hadn't even been a road there until the nineties, inhabitants had had to go by helicopter in and out, or take the boat to the neighboring island from where they could cross the bridge over to Bordot, and travel the final five or six miles from there into Klaksvík.

We strolled away from the quay and down toward Nolsoyar Páls Gøta, found a bakery and bought ourselves a bite, I got myself a currant bun and a bottle of Jolly, and was content, Palli had a French slice that went down in a couple of gulps, something was troubling him, preoccupying him, as though the new millennium was approaching too fast and he hadn't been able to prepare himself. We walked down the street, making for a shop on the other side, farther down the road. Anna and NN were determined to get me a new jacket, I was still using the one I'd arrived in that summer, a thin Fjällräven jacket without any padding and with pockets that were totally falling apart, and even when I zipped and buttoned it up, and pulled the hood over my head, it still didn't keep me warm. This jacket's days were numbered, and I was freezing slowly to death, the beginnings of permafrost across my back, ground frost in my arms, it couldn't go on.

The purchase itself went quickly, I didn't care how the jacket looked as long as it was warm and did its job, so I let NN and Anna choose, and after some going back and forth NN found a huge, brown wool jacket, double-breasted with a big collar and handmade buckhorn buttons, that made me look like a captain. Or a pilot. Not that I could navigate.

I delved my hand into the pocket of the jacket I was wearing, hunting for my envelope of money, but NN beat me to it and spoke to the proprietor who nodded at me and took her fingers away from the register. NN turned to me and laid a hand over the worn envelope.

"Don't worry, she'll send the bill to Havstein."

"But why?" I answered, feeling embarrassed. "I don't want him to have to pay for it."

"He won't. He'll get reimbursed, of course."

"Who by?" I asked, confused.

"By the government." She handed me the bag holding the jacket. "Put it on. Then you won't have to freeze all day."

"Thanks."

"Don't thank me," she laughed. "Thank the Faroe Islands."

"Or Denmark," came Palli's voice from behind us.

"Yes, for that matter, thank you to Denmark, from Denmark with love."

Because the Faroe Islands were Danish soil, however independent, and Denmark supported the Faroes with a yearly billion, and the Faroes supported Havstein, and Havstein supported me, I was on welfare, so to speak.

And then we were out of the shop.

We strolled down over Biskupsstøðgøta and I was given a guided tour of Klaksvík, we walked around the harbor, went into all the stores, into the video store, I walked beside NN, I think we talked about the New Year, and Anna and Palli walked just behind us, lost in a long conversation, talking over each other, laughing, they were good times, and I thought how the next year might not look so bad, things weren't perhaps as hopeless as they seemed, even a plane with a damaged motor can land on a disused airport, so long as you take time to plan, and keep cool.

It was Palli who suggested we go up to Christianskirkja while we were waiting for Havstein to return from his "home visit." I was up for anything, I was a tourist for the day.

But Anna objected. "Come off it, Palli, we visited the church last time we were in Klaksvík."

"So?"

"So we've got a church right opposite the Factory and you never visit that. Why not? That's a church too."

"It isn't the same."

"Isn't it?"

"No."

The connection was probably better here, I thought, perhaps there wasn't any coverage in Gjógv and God was only contactable by fax during office hours. I looked at Anna, Anna looked at NN, but she just shrugged and since the rest of us didn't have any strong objections, we turned and walked up to the church, Palli in the lead.

The church stood on the slopes high above the main road, much larger than the wooden churches found in every single little village. This was sixties Faroese architecture, it had walls built of stone, reminiscent of the old ruins on Kirkjubøur, and large windows like the ones in the old Faroese boathouses. We sat on one of the pews, there was nobody else in the church, Palli sat next to me, eyes shut, the only one of us who could really call himself religious, the rest of us sat with our heads leaned back, gazing up at the ceiling and gables, covered with as many stencils as an old Viking hall. Óli had told me how most of the churches in the country had a miniature ship hanging from the ceiling to protect the sailors, bless them on their way, and one was hanging from the ceiling here, but this was no model, it was a full-size eight-man rowboat, and it appeared to be floating on a windless sea getting nowhere. Palli came to, it was between him and God, he opened his eyes and looked at the three of us who sat there waiting, cricks in our necks.

"An eight-man vessel," he said. "An eight-man . . . boat."

"It looks like it's floating up there," I said. Suddenly I had the sense we were all under water.

Palli gazed up at the boat. Air bubbles exiting his mouth as he breathed, seaweed on the rows of pews.

"The clergy used these boats in the old days. To go from island to island. And this boat never sank. It was the only one that didn't. It stayed afloat. It was out with three other boats from Skarð village, Christmas 1913. The weather was terrible, and all three boats sank. Seven men vanished in the waves and never came back. This was the only one to make it back. All the men of the village died that day, apart from a seventy-year old man and a fourteen-year old boy who'd been left ashore. And it was Christmas too. Their wives couldn't get by on their own, so they took their belongings soon afterward and moved to Haraldssund, leaving Skarð deserted. Nobody's moved up here since."

None of us said a thing.

We gazed up at the boat.

The sea seemed to swallow man and mouse in this country. And everything is water if you just look long enough, even human beings.

A vibration went through the bench. Anna was the first to say anything.

"Hang on," she said and disappeared.

A couple of minutes later she was back.

"That was Havstein," she said. "He's in Klaksvík again, down by the jetty, I arranged for us to meet him down at the brewery.

"Now?" asked Palli.

"Yes."

"Great," said Palli. "It would have been nice if you didn't have your cell phone on in church."

"But I had it on silent. And I did go outside!"

"Even so."

Anna looked at him in irritation.

"Do you think God will be mad?"

"I'd just have preferred it if you'd turned it off while we were in here," he said.

We got up and strolled quietly out of the church into the raw December air and toward the brewery, on the lookout for Havstein driving down the road.

Palli couldn't stay offended for long. It had all been forgotten by the time we met Havstein again and stood in the Föroya Bjór sales hall, waiting for our orders. He'd looked forward to this all day, and waited impatiently for this visit to the brewery, he'd worried it might be closed by the time we arrived. We were normally happy to go to Rúsdrekkasøla Landsins where we could buy wine and liquor as well as beer, but since we'd come all the way to Klaksvík, we'd agreed we should make our purchases where the beer was produced, and they generally had a better choice here than elsewhere. Besides, they sold Föroya Bjór merchandise here too; T-shirts, shopping bags, hats, and towels, all bearing the brewery's logo, and Palli wanted a fresh supply of everything, of course, despite the fact the motifs and designs never changed and he already had more than he'd ever use. This was clearly something Palli did more out of habit than necessity. The instant he saw Palli, the sales assistant put an example of each product out on the counter beside the three cases of beer we wanted, and as seemed routine, he didn't ask for any payment for these additional items. We were good customers, and the assistant was on chatting terms with everybody, it was a long time since they'd been here last, so it took time, Palli had a lot to talk about, and he stayed with the assistant as we carried the cases out to the car, Palli talked about the boats that had come and gone in Kollafjørður, about things that had happened in Tórshavn, and of course, about me, the new resident, as he called me. Palli waved me over and I had to go up to the counter to introduce myself properly, say who I was, where I'd come from, and then I had to taste the beer. It was against the rules, of course, and the assistant peered nervously around, but there was nobody else in the hall. He lifted the counter up quickly and let me in, opened a bottle of very dark beer, poured half a glass and gave it to me. I lifted it and took an enormous swig as the assistant and Palli eyed me closely. It tasted like rancid socks brewed on a soggy sheep and then dipped in petroleum.

"Not bad," I said and looked at the assistant.

"Black Sheep."

They shook their heads and laughed, the assistant relieved me of my glass, adding that not many people liked it the first time they tasted it. Then he made a remark to Palli I didn't understand. I waited for Palli to translate.

"He says you've got some way to go before you're a true Faroe Islander," said Palli.

"I thought so."

Nevertheless I felt certain the adaptation process had begun. It was definitely underway.

We bought groceries at the store in Klaksvík, I bought two postcards of the Ranndalur Pyramid, scribbled a few sentences about how things were, how things were fine, better than for ages, added a *Happy New Year* and *Love to all* on the last remaining inch before writing my parents' address on one card and Jørn's on the other, then I put them in the mailbox outside the store. We drove back to the jetty and waited for the ferry to come to town again and take us back, I sat squeezed in the backseat of the car with NN and Anna, contemplating what an idiot I'd been to think the Faroes were a good place to disappear, since information about me traveled quicker round here than sound. We were recognized in the strangest places, because there were so few of us and because we were obviously odd, between psychiatry and reality, like soft, cuddly mascots, I thought, and I continually found myself being introduced as the latest ex-lunatic, a role I played as best I could, although perhaps there was no longer any need to play it, I don't know. All I know is that I left tracks behind me reluctantly everywhere I went, despite treading as softly over the ground as I could. I'd been an idiot to think I could disappear here, I was making myself more noticeable than ever.

Still, I was a reasonably happy idiot.

I began to recognize myself, and my hands did my bidding.

I was on the edge of being loved.

I slept well at night.

I don't think I really missed anything.

Probably never had.

Apart from Helle, perhaps.

Yes, I'd missed her. For a long time. And a lot.

But now?

I didn't know. It had begun to pass.

Somebody had begun to fill the cracks, hang wallpaper over the peeling paint.

I was being renovated.

Finally warm in my jacket, driving home in the car, I put an arm round NN in the backseat, she said nothing, just let me rest it there. We crossed Eysturoy and disappeared up into the mountain and back down into Gjógv on the other side. We stowed the crates of beer and food in Cloakroom A, filled the fridge and that evening we ate dinner together, for the first time in ages, and it was a good supper, I don't think I thought about how many people we were that evening, just that it seemed natural, as it should be, everything in its right place. Havstein didn't disappear up into his room as he usually did, and Palli talked more than ever before, about his job, about plans he had for building his own boat, he was in good form in his T-shirt from the brewery, we were homeward bound astronauts in the quarantine bunker, and NN played the Cardigans, and I opened one beer after another and was the only one drinking, my brain stuffed with cotton wool as their voices grew muffled, warm, a deflector shield against the rays of the Death Star, I talked about Jørn in Stavanger, about my parents, told them I had no intention of leaving, and it almost saddened me to see how happy they were to hear it, how fast people grew dependent on each other, how much I already meant to them, and inside, somewhere deep inside, I knew I'd suffer for it, since it went against everything I'd decided, I'd opened myself up, open for anyone who wanted me. And tomorrow the future would come to the Faroes.

3

There are two things I really can't quite explain. The first is why gravity is not constant on the moon, but variable between poles, causing worried expressions on the faces of NASA's engineers in the sixties who sat hunched over their calculations trying to find safe places to land. And the second is the night a person came to us from across the sea.

He seemed to come from nowhere, just as I had six months earlier. He, too, came in from the cold, and this is perhaps the night I remember best, as we entered the millennium. Elsewhere on the planet, people burnt millions of dollars of fireworks in an attempt to hide their anxiety that everything they believed in might be taken away, or to underline their joy that everything would be wondrously different. We celebrated the New Year in a more subdued manner. We weren't waiting for anything special. Didn't expect much. We'd take things as they came. Nonetheless it's this that stays in my memory. I remember sitting in the kitchen with the man who'd arrived from no-man's land, the man from 1999, he sat wrapped in blankets, bearded, water running off him, almost six feet tall, and strong, and I remember thinking how completely absurd this was. But I think he had to come, sooner or later. If he hadn't, we might still be sitting there, Havstein, Anna, Palli, and I. In the kitchen in Gjógv. Sometimes one doesn't know what one needs before one has it.

I sat up in NN's room on New Year's Eve, the clock on the wall showed five and she was of two minds as to whether to wear the black dress or the navy one. She vanished into her bedroom, emerged wearing one, stood before the mirror and began a detailed analysis of what gestures and poses brought out the best in the dress or herself, before she resolutely disappeared, only to return wearing the other dress, new poses, fresh assessments, I sat on her sofa and watched a fashion show of limited repertoire as it went in a loop.

"What do you think?" she asked.

"They're both fine."

"But which do you think I should wear?"

"That one."

"This one?"

She studied herself in the mirror, then grew bored.

"Or the other one," I said. "I really don't know."

"You're not exactly helpful, are you?"

I smiled. It reminded me of evenings with Helle when we were going out. I always liked it when she tried different clothes on, asking repeatedly what I thought, for my opinion. *Can't you just choose for me*, she'd say. And sometimes I would, though she'd rarely end up wearing what I'd suggested. It was like watching the weather forecast on TV, you can have any opinion you like, but at the end of the day you have no power over what really happens. And now, new place, new person, new dresses.

"How about the blue one?" I ventured.

"Do you think so? The blue one? Hmm . . . maybe."

"How about just putting a tracksuit on?"

"Mattias!"

"I'm sorry."

"Aren't you changing, Mattias?"

She looked at me. I looked the same as ever.

"I don't have a suit," I answered, pondering the idea of putting my overalls on. Or making a space suit for myself.

"You don't have a suit?"

"No, not here. I have one in Stavanger." And then, I don't know whether she heard it or not, I added: "But I hadn't expected to stay this long."

Havstein called up from the ground floor. My name. I called back.

"Maybe I should go down to him," I said.

"Okay."

I left the room. Stopped on the landing, opened the door a moment and watched her, the most beautiful person you'd ever meet, trying out gestures for an imaginary party in the mirror.

"The black one," I said, and NN looked over at me. "It's got to be the black one."

She smiled.

"Thanks," she said. "You can do it when you want."

"It's a shame I want to so rarely."

I found Havstein in the kitchen. Bent over the pans. He'd gotten up early that day, I'd been woken by the sound of him singing in the bath at eight o'clock that morning, and he'd been puttering around the Factory all day ever since, cleaning the living room and kitchen, preparing dinner, setting the table with the best china and things. Palli and Anna had taken the car and driven down to Anna's mother to wish her a Happy New Year, and we all went around discreetly peering at our watches, waiting for their return, in time for supper.

"Potatoes," said Havstein.

"Where?"

He pointed at the bowl on the kitchen counter full of potatoes. I got out the potato peeler and filled the sink with lukewarm water, stood beside him and began peeling potatoes. Havstein had three dishes going, turkey, pilot whale, and skerpi, a Faroese speciality of cured mutton. The turkey smelled delicious in the oven, the skerpi and whale meat stank, but that was how it should be, and we said nothing, just got on with our tasks, looked out of the big windows, down toward the beach, tried to stare straight into the sun, couldn't. An almost cloudless sky, a steely chill in the air, yet the windows all stood open, a final airing before New Year, and the floor was cold, cold underfoot, it felt like the first day of spring, when you fling the windows open and release the submarine air you've lived in all winter.

It's just the way of things. We do everything except what we ought. I was horribly afraid. Of everything. And I was so glad that I knew nothing about it. I didn't put my potato peeler aside and go up to her. Instead I stayed and finished the potato peeling, and Havstein and I said nothing until Anna and Palli came into the kitchen half an hour or so later, returning from their car trip, fresh cheeked, yes, I know it's a strange thing to mention, but it's what I remember, their fresh cheeks as they walked in. Like teenagers returning from a mountain walk they've been forced to go on, against their will. All that exuberance, that ruddy health. The excitement they try to disguise, but that their faces exude, because it's been such a fantastic day after all.

Do you remember those days?

When it was like that?

I remember them all.

And half an hour later Havstein took the turkey out of the oven as NN came into the kitchen, wearing her navy blue dress, we looked at each other, then away, Havstein looked at us both and gave NN a hug, I said she looked great, *you're lovely,* I said as we sat down, carved the New Year's turkey, on the 10,756 day of my existence.

- - - ∎ - - -

I've looked through my mental photo album so often, replayed the corny films, and to begin with it's always in slow motion, we've eaten the turkey, a great meal, the skerpi and whale, we've drunk wine, beer, we've chatted, one of those great conversations, and then we stand in the hallway, put our shoes on, because it's nearly midnight, and Palli has bought a rocket, and we follow him out into the courtyard, walk around the Factory and down to the stony beach. And we stand in a semicircle on the patch of grass above the harbor, watching Palli as he looks for a good place to set up his wine bottle with the rocket in the neck. It's raining lightly, I stand next to NN and she's wearing my jacket, it's too big for her and I'm freezing, but act as though it's nothing, and Havstein cracks a joke, I can't work out what he's saying, but we laugh, we all laugh, and Anna shouts *Happy New Year* and NN shouts *Happy New Year* and Palli sets to his task, strikes the match against the side of the box, the little stick sparks, hesitantly catches fire and flares up with a crackle, and then his hand guides the flame toward the fuse on the rocket, Havstein opens his arms, big arms, and we all melt in his embrace, and Palli's hand ignites the rocket, then he gets up carefully and steps back toward us and we all stand together as the rocket lifts from the bottle, gathers momentum and disappears upward, ignorant of the faces that turn up toward it, waiting for it to reach its peak and watching as it explodes against the background of outer space, our eyes fixed on the point where glistening sparks are flung out in pre-ordained patterns, almost like synchronized swimmers, and it's only when almost all these points of light have fizzled out that we see one single red light shoot up from somewhere beyond and hang in the air, and from this moment time moves noticeably faster, and I think it's Anna who opens her mouth to say:

"What's that over there?"

"An emergency rocket," answers Palli. "A flare."

"Can you see anyone out there?" asks Havstein.

Palli says he can't. Havstein runs back up to the Factory for a flashlight as we stand there, squinting into the distance.

"It's just a false alarm," I say. "New Year's Eve. There's never a New Year's when someone doesn't do that."

"What do you mean?" asks NN.

"There's always some jerk in Stavanger who can't get enough, even after he's sent all his rockets up, always ends up digging an emergency flare out from the garage."

"There aren't any garages out here," says Palli sharply. "There aren't even any boats. You don't send a flare up for fun if you're in a boat."

I say nothing. I stare through the darkness, but can see nothing. I move swiftly down the beach, as if a few feet might make a difference, as though I'll see everything more clearly from there, and Havstein comes running back down again. And behind me I can hear everybody talking at once, Havstein shouts wait wait wait and brings the binoculars up, scans the area out there and we all go quiet as he does so. I see nothing. Then he says, there's something out there! And my legs turn my body toward him, I race across the few feet to where he's standing, ask him to show me, and before he gives me the binoculars, he points with one hand in the direction I should look in, and I take the binoculars, bring them to my eyes and begin searching in the direction he's pointing, but can find nothing, where? I ask and Havstein guides the binoculars with his hands, to the left a bit, up a bit. There.

And there is something out there. Something small. Vaguely reflected in the red light of the flare.

Hard to say what.

It could be anything.

But it can't be good.

Which is when I remember the boat.

Óli's boat in the harbor.

"The boat," I say, "over here."

And I start running. I run through the wet village streets, and I'm actually a bit drunk, but I run faster than ever before, and Havstein follows close behind, *wait!* he yells behind me, but I don't wait, I run, run past the houses where almost no one lives any more, from where the people have vanished, moved, died, where everything that could happen has happened long ago, and my legs carry me down to the harbor where I put my back to the bow of the wooden boat, shove it away and watch it slip over the logs and out into the dark waters of the deep, narrow inlet, and Havstein comes up from behind, running, only just managing to get aboard before I push away with one oar, pushing us out, and I sit in the middle of the boat, oars down in the water, and start to row.

Havstein sits in the aft, shouting rhythmically: *Come on!* he shouts, *Come on!* And I row, and he urges me on, and I row beyond my capability, out, out through the narrow channel, past the first breakers, I can see nothing, sit with my back to the sea and Havstein commands me to the right and left and the rain falls at a ninety degree angle, it fragments to all sides, fills my eyes and I keep them shut, I row on, and Havstein tells me I'm close, and my arms are tired, but I go on rowing against the stream, I descend from the crest of a wave and shoot forward over the water and the flare has gone out, only Havstein has the course now and he knows where he's going, and as he shouts to me to row faster, I turn for a second to look over my shoulder and glimpse a yellow rubber dinghy and a man struggling to stay upright, fumbling for his possessions as the waves lift them lazily and they escape from him, sinking into the sea, and the dinghy starts to sink too, and he's up to his knees in water and I manage to swing the boat around in a single movement, put all my strength into one oar, yell to Havstein to take over, stand in the boat, turn toward the dinghy, and dive in.

The instant I'm underwater, the brakes go on, all the clocks in the world stop, the sound is turned off. I glide patiently on through the water, dragged on by the current through a mass of water and it isn't black here, as I'd imagined, not black, but a blue darkness, colors of blue, and there are fish swimming toward me, they stop half a foot before me, part to the sides and allow me to glide past, and I look up and see the rain as it explodes in rings on the surface, watery craters, and I have to get up there, because that's where I'm needed, for the first time in my life somebody actually needs me, I'm the only person in the world in motion now, and I remember it all, crystal clear pictures projected in the water, I am four years old, standing on a chair blowing the candles out on my cake / Father comes home with a new used car and I'm allowed to go with him for a test drive / I am twenty, drinking beer on the balcony of a stone building that overlooks a large swimming pool / I am at the movies watching *Back to the Future* / I sit on the bus on my way home and a girl at the front looks at me, I look back and she turns away / I throw a snowball onto a roof / I learn to dive in Østlandet and I am nine years old / I sit in front of the television watching an episode of *Colargol* / I come home from school, stand outside in the rain, I've lost my keys, my bag on my back / Mother reads from *Mio, My Son* and I'm ill / Mother is pregnant, I look forward to having a baby brother, or a baby sister, but the birth never happens, Mother cries in the bedroom / there's a TV series about space, and I've been bad, so I'm not allowed to see the last episode, but Father comes to get me from my room, just after it's begun, I sit on his lap and watch Buzz Aldrin emerge from the *Eagle* / I'm underwater, for a long time / I lie in the middle of a road waiting to be run over / I think of NN, she's standing back on the shore where she can barely see us through the rain and dark, and I think of how NN lived on Mykines and dreamed of somebody coming over the sea to her, and now it's happening, somebody's coming, somebody has found us here, discovered us and sent up a signal, but we don't know who it is yet, and maybe that's another reason for my pushing my way through the water to get there so fast, maybe I finally want more people around me again, and I kick out as hard as I can and break the surface, come up into the pouring rain, and in those first seconds it still feels as though I'm underwater, see the dinghy that's filling with water, sinking, and I swim the last lap over to the huge person who sits motionless in what remains of the worn-out rubber, he sits totally motionless and lets himself sink, water up to his neck as I grab his arm, and for a split second he looks at me, the bearded face looks at me, with surprised eyes, before he turns toward the remains of his baggage, that floats from us and sinks, and Havstein has the oars, guides the rowboat toward me and the man whose arms I grip and whose head I hold above water, and we bob on the waves, the millennium's first flotsam and I'm tired, exhausted, and barely notice as we are dragged on board, and as life's tempo returns to normal again, 720 km/hr, and the beach grows larger with each stroke of Havstein's oars.

That was how he came to us. The man from the sea. The last survivor from the past.
Long Distance Man.
He said nothing.
Although, that isn't quite true. We'd gotten back to the beach, we carried him up to the Factory, wrapped him in warm blankets in the kitchen, sat around the table looking at him, he stared into the tabletop, blindly before him, as Havstein asked him questions using every language in which he could form a sentence. That was when the man finally said something. In English. He said: "Happy New Year. I'm Carl."

----■---

It's strange how we can get used to almost anything, and how normality and routine demand their place in every existence. Only a week later, Carl, the newcomer, had gone from being a shipwreck to a permanent fixture at the Factory, on an equal footing with the rest of us, and without us seeing anything dramatic about it. Havstein asked us early on what we thought he should do, and after some discussion none of us suggested we send him down to Tórshavn, away, or anywhere. So he stayed. He seemed happy enough with that. None of us knew where he'd actually been heading.

Like me, Carl was put into a spare room after a few hours in the kitchen on New Year's Day, so as to rest, but unlike me he was up and in apparently good form by the fourth day. I was sitting in the living room with the others when he came wandering in, and for a split second I saw myself; he walked into the room hesitantly, just as I had on that first occasion, then he sat with us and began talking, in English again, and to judge by his accent he came from somewhere in America, and I remember he talked a lot, even if a little quietly, the only thing he didn't want to talk about was why he'd ended up on a lifeboat in the middle of the Atlantic, just before the start of the new millennium. On that subject, he refused to say a single word.

"I don't want to talk about that yet," said Carl politely with a ruler-straight smile, and it would be another ten months before he told us anything, but by then it would be October, when the leaves had fallen from the non-existent trees, and somebody had died.

So in the meantime we learned to avoid the subject of the rescue, integrated him into our world, and he seemed happy with that, we spoke English to him and to each other when he was around, before like me, he learned a fair bit of Faroese, or a kind of Faroese, enough to keep a conversation going. Havstein gave him a job with NN in the Factory and they worked well together, Carl proved extremely clever with his hands, and after a short time working with the wooden sheep, the wool and peat baskets, he began to experiment, and develop new merchandise for the souvenir shop down at Vágar, Havstein got hold of a second-hand lathe, and soon bowls, plates, and candlesticks emerged from Carl's hands. And he sawed off the legs from the wooden sheep, drilled holes and pulled steel wire and springs through them, making animals with movable limbs, achieving far more than we'd done before, and our sales rose, still not enough to earn huge sums, but enough to raise the level of enthusiasm, and NN seemed happy with her job again, she stopped talking about finding something else to do, entered into her work, sketched new ideas with Carl and me in the evenings. And I remember the days with Carl standing in the kitchen after dinner with rubber gloves on his hands as he did the dishes, nodding in time to the Swedish pop that NN had on in the living room, shuffling his feet from side to side as though he was dancing. Then he'd turn, nod at me and smile. He smiled a lot in fact.

From the day he got up, which was probably why none of us suggested we report his entry into the country, nobody rang the police, the immigration authorities or the like. And it sounds strange now, maybe, but in the beginning I was convinced his mere presence might erase the last dregs of the sickness I'd dragged with me to the Factory, offer us all an alternative to the crises and mental breakdowns we all went around in fear of, but the truth was, he probably only put them on pause before we slipped imperceptibly back into our individual medicalization, the gently calming tablets, the talks up in Havstein's room, and the perpetual roundelay of recovery and regression, until we almost began to think that feeling well was a symptom of the illness itself. But meanwhile we were pleased with our newly extended family and to have somebody else to concentrate on, like having a cat that padded gently about making the world harmonious in its wake, and we didn't mention him to anyone, simply took him into our improvised world, and waited to see how things would turn out.

Although, that isn't wholly true.

Particularly for Havstein. He grew increasingly uneasy that winter, as though he was on his guard all the time, he spent a lot of time on his own and became less good humored than he'd once been. And the backwash of this was, I think, that much of the security he'd given us melted away, without his realizing, and without our being able to put words to it.

Havstein did his best to ascertain that Carl didn't need acute psychiatric help and to be sent down to town. They spent a lot of time together, Havstein sat behind his desk and tried to get him talking, took notes, something had to be done after all, no sane person would cross the Atlantic in December in a rubber dinghy, that much was clear. But since Carl wouldn't budge, the rest of us avoided pressuring him, even though we discussed it among ourselves when he and Havstein weren't around, coming up with our own diagnoses or bills of health, that changed from week to week, not that we had much to go on, apart from the fact that he complained of nightmares, and was happiest by day, when it was light. He was neither more nor less sociable than the rest of us, and he beat us all at chess and Scrabble, so in the end we couldn't be bothered to play against him. Later that winter, Havstein got hold of one those computerized chess sets from the eighties, but our new family member didn't prove a genius after all. As far as I know, he never beat the computer on the highest level. Maybe the rest of us were just bad at chess and had problems concentrating for any length of time.

Whatever the case, none of us knew what was wrong with this man.

Apart from the fact he'd come over the sea in a lifeboat.

On New Year's Eve.

During those first days after his arrival, I took Carl with me to the memorial garden across the road from the church, the one Selma had recommended that I visit. It seemed appropriate somehow, now that I too had been a hair's breadth away from becoming an engraved statistic, and I hoped he might open up as we sat there, that he might say something about why he'd been so close to going under on the coast here, why he'd turned up in the middle of the night in a single yellow lifeboat, exhausted and with several weeks' growth of beard.

We put our rain jackets on and crossed the road, opened the gate and went up the path, crossed the little bridge to the asphalt square where seven plaques bore the names of people from Gjógv who'd perished at sea. We sat on the bench staring at the uncredited iron sculpture in the center of the square; a mother, with her daughter on her lap, her sons sitting by her side. The mother looked out to sea, as far as she could, of course, and her daughter looked blankly ahead while one of her sons cast a skeptical glance toward the harbor, just days maybe, weeks or months before he would go out too, picking up where his father had left off. It was, I thought, the most serene sculpture I'd ever seen, but if you looked long enough it was as if you could see tiny movements, hands shifting carefully, then coming to rest. We looked out, a choppy sea, waves torn against the sharp mountainside and the sea spray rising many feet high toward us, not weather to be out in, even if one of the country's best fishing grounds was only a short distance away, I wouldn't dream of setting foot on a boat today, under any circumstances, just the noise was enough to convince most people it would be a crazy thing to do. For every wave that came thundering in and climbed those last few feet there followed a rumbling sound, a slow boom that didn't stop before the next wave came and overtook it, a continual thunder guaranteed to give you tinnitus if you stood there for long.

Carl looked at the plaques.

"Lots of names, eh?" I said.

"Way too many." He got up and went over to the plaques laid in the grass behind the statue, he crouched down and squinted at words he couldn't read. *Deyðir av óhappi. Deyðir av vanlukku. Deyðir á veg til arbeiðis. Deyðir á veg úr arbeiði.* I stood behind him and tried my best to translate these tragic deaths. The dates stretched backward and forward in time. 1901. 1920. 1954. And on April 30, 1870, the day that sixteen men were lost: *Fórust tann stóra skaðadagin.* The boats had gone down with every man and mouse in these parts. And children. There were several children, fifteen, sixteen years old. Some had been on their way to Iceland, others on their way home, some had barely made it beyond the headland before drowning. A crystal clear picture emerged here, that it was no laughing matter to settle in such a place, to keep going in a country like the Faroes, hundreds of miles from the mainland. Living in Gjógv, perhaps even snowed in and cut off in winter, romantic notions of a quiet and peaceful life of leisurely fishing trips with everybody singing on board, weren't what it took; it was hardcore self-preservation that paid the bills here, you'd have to accept it or leave it. No wonder they left, those who could no longer take it, no wonder they gave up and found other ways of getting by, in town or in tranquil villages. But I thought I understood those who stayed as well, those for whom this was home despite it all, those who knew every turn in the mountains, who sat on the grassy slopes high above the harbor in summer, of an evening, on calmer days, when their work was done, when things were as they should be, wife, kids, all together, promo-brochure days, they happened too. You just had to look hard enough.

He didn't say anything about what I'd hoped, instead we discussed the memorial garden, the names on the plaques, he talked about how it must feel to drown at sea, to realize your boat was capsizing and to end up in the icy water, to know you'd never get on board again, never get back to land, to feel your clothes dragging you down and the cold water stealing all sensation from your arms and legs, so you couldn't swim, couldn't stay afloat, yet he constantly talked as though none of it affected him, as though he'd never been out there himself and close to drowning. That moment of history had, it seemed, been completely blown away on the wind, and this doubtless had its reasons.

_ _ _ ■ ■ _ _ _

NN and I grew closer at the start of the New Year; I think we really found each other. Of course it wasn't so much a case of her finding me, as the reverse, I'd been discovered long ago, but my head had been stuck in the sand and twisted around, with my feet stuck up like two useless signposts. But something had happened that night six weeks ago, the night of New Year's Eve when I'd dived into the sea. The things that had come to me as I'd pushed my way through the sea were more than mere random thoughts. I think I'd finally fallen in love, there and then, as I was swimming. Because although there may be nothing new under the sun, it's an entirely different ballgame underwater.

But I haven't planned to tell you a story in which people finally come together and kiss under the trees and the camera moves up and disappears into the sky leaving lovers standing on a hill, locked in an embrace, united at last and all that. I'm not even sure that I'm using the words *in love* correctly anymore. Maybe I should use other words, I don't know. Maybe it would be closer to the truth to say that we reached another point, that we reached the end of a long year, I don't know. But I liked being with her. I think I fell in love with spending time with her, not necessarily with her, herself. Perhaps I was just so desperate for somebody, that I'd have stretched my arms out to anybody, sooner or later. Or worse, perhaps I thought I was.

Anyway, we grew closer and everything changed. We talked more often, for longer, took trips together, in the afternoons when we had the car to ourselves. We often went to the woods. We'd drive down toward Tórshavn, to the end of Hvítansesvegur, where on one side of the bridge, in a big field, a cluster of trees had been planted, one of only four places with trees I ever found on the Faroes. The trees stood, randomly placed, to give the illusion of something accidental, natural, and we used to park the car and walk down to them, then putter around in circles to get the feeling we'd been for a long walk, in the woods in a treeless land.

And on one of these afternoons, after we'd spent an hour in our woodland and were practically dizzy, we sat in Café Natúr, just the two of us. And NN said:

"I don't know how long I want to live here."

"What do you mean?"

"The truth is, I'm getting fucking bored of this place."

I hadn't expected to hear this. Of all of us she was the one person I assumed would never move away, unless pushed to it, her enthusiasm for the Faroes was generally exemplary.

"So what are you thinking of doing?"

"Don't know. I'll move, I suppose."

"But where to?"

"Sweden, perhaps. Stockholm. Copenhagen."

I didn't want her to move. Not at all. Change was the last thing in the world I wanted.

"But do you know of a better place to live?" I asked, half joking, half serious. I flung my arms wide and looked at the café around us, but still wasn't offered a job in the travel agency.

"You've lived here for six months, Mattias, of course you still think it's fantastic here. Or maybe you've just begun to think it? Try fourteen years. Then you'll probably want to leave too. Then you'll probably want to walk in the woods for more than twenty feet before you have to turn around and go back."

"But," I began, and was relieved when she interrupted, I couldn't think of any good arguments.

"I want to do something, don't you see? It sometimes feels as though I'm just going around killing time, it's running between my fingers and all I do is sit and watch. I want to do something too, don't you understand? I had plans too, you're not the only one who fell down at the fork in the road." She was almost angry now, or desperate, and it was so sudden I was completely unprepared. "I'm doing fuck all here."

"You've got a job," I said.

"Making wooden sheep? What the fuck do you mean? Seriously. You think I'm meant to be satisfied with that? That's what I should do, go on doing that?"

"No."

"I want to do something I enjoy, something meaningful to me, for once. I'm shit tired of waiting to get better, when it's never going to happen. And even if I did get better one day, I wouldn't even notice, because there's no difference anymore."

I didn't know what to say, what to suggest. It was awful to realize I'd never thought of her doing anything apart from what she did now: keeping up the production in the Factory. Did I really believe she couldn't do anything else? Or did I just want things to be predictable?

"Do you think what I do is any more sensible?" I began. "I make gardens for strangers, in midwinter, planting flowers that'll freeze to death in just days."

"No, of course not, but for you it's just an in-between thing. Sooner or later you'll go back to Norway, you're just using this to get over a relationship that you knew in your heart of hearts was over years ago, and now you're here because—well—why are you still here now, really? Because you're a coward. You're here because you're a coward, Mattias, nothing but a coward. You're not so sick or tired that you need to be here anymore, you're here because you're too much of a coward to go back and pick up where you left off, for fear it'll all go to hell again."

A coward.

She'd said it four times.

So it had to be right.

"The difference is, Mattias," she continued, "that I can suggest things you could do, I can imagine you working as something other than as a gardener, I have no problem seeing you working with kids in a nursery, being a musician, a builder, a teacher, whatever you want, I can imagine you doing just about any job. Now, tell me: what job can you see me doing?"

There was quiet at the table. I thought about it. I never had before, not about that. And I didn't dare to say it straight, that I had no idea, that I'd never imagined her doing anything else at all.

I thought for a long time.

I said nothing.

Stared into the tabletop, heard the seconds pick up their jackets and leave demonstratively through the door behind us.

"Maybe it's not true that everybody's good at something. Deep down you haven't even thought about it, have you? So long as the world around you behaves as you expect it to, you're safe, aren't you? So long as you can be useful? So long as you can be one of those damned cogs you keep talking about. Well, why don't you want that for others? Do you want to be the only cog? That's cowardly, Mattias."

Cowardly again.

I didn't answer, wished I was far away, crossing the desert with nobody watching.

"That's what I thought," she said.

"I—," I began, but she brushed me off, gave a heavy sigh and drank her coffee.

"Just don't," she said curtly, and the café noise of the customers and the stereo in the corner drowned out our silence, the unsaid things, and neither of us spoke again until our cups were empty, until we'd walked out to the car, until we'd got in and were on our way back and things fell back into place and we started talking to each other again, hugs in the car and sunshine from nowhere.

I think that was the first time we came close to quarreling, and during the weeks that followed we had a few days like that, when she was miserable about not having seen enough, done enough, when she'd wonder what she could do with herself, and I didn't know if this was a sign she was on the road to total recovery at last, or if it was the start of a relapse. But even though on that first day she made it clear she was angry with me for letting her see I hadn't given a thought to what she might do with her life, these moments of anger, these quarrels generally revolved around her own disappointment in herself, and the fact she didn't know what to do with herself. And they were also about the frustration that inevitably had to come after Carl had entered the frame, because even though I'd liked him from the instant I'd brought him in from the ocean, even though I soon realized he'd fallen in love with NN and that it was probably deeply mutual, there was no doubt it had disrupted the balance between us, and the days were an accordion, nobody knew who played it, but NN and I were pushed together and pulled apart from one another as the music went on playing and everything was all right, really.

Because NN and I didn't become lovers, we didn't sleep in the same bed, didn't stand kissing as the sun set and the whales sang on command in the coves, it was Carl that found that side of her a couple of weeks later and I was pleased, pleased for them, it gave me some sort of pride even, I know Anna's shoulders relaxed a bit when she saw them together and what was going on. When it came to Carl and me, we'd gotten along well from the beginning and as the year passed he became my closest friend, we had a totally different relationship from the one I'd had with Jørn, who slipped slowly away from me, day by day, despite my hope that he wouldn't, and in a way, it was thanks to Carl that NN and I became such good friends. Still, it took time to get used to it, to reconcile myself to the new situation, and now and again it was a bit painful too, when I let it in.

They were altogether strange times in the Factory at Gjógv that winter. A totally different feel from everything six months before. And despite the fact that the mood was lighter after we'd received our gift from the ocean, I couldn't quite shake off the question that NN had posed, why was I still here, why hadn't I left for home long ago? I thought a lot about it. Thought about how I still had nothing to do in Stavanger. No friends who sat and missed me anymore. Not even Jørn, I thought. I didn't want to go back. I wanted to stay. And I thought about it until I could fathom the reason, and I remember being surprised when I understood it. I think it even scared me. I wasn't going back home because I'd begun to grow dependent on these people. I'd grown too fond of them to leave. And then there was my being needed. Havstein needed me, I just didn't know why. Carl needed all he could get. And NN needed me. But the best or worst thing of all was that I needed them even more than they needed me. So I stayed. At ease, sir. I did my thing, turned the little cogs, those I could reach, helped where I could. Post-psychiatry's grand tourist.

And then the day came that we'd all been waiting for and that I dreaded perhaps more than anybody, because it put my resolve to stay to the test, and now, with the benefit of hindsight, I can say it wasn't unnatural that I disliked it so strongly, because it was the beginning of the end, proof that nothing lasts, and that nothing you take for granted, everything you love and or that makes you happy, everything you spend time and energy to get, will all be taken inexorably away from you. It's just a question of how long you're allowed to borrow it.

One Friday afternoon, right at the beginning of March, I stood on the steps and rang Óli and Selma's doorbell, and the instant Sofus opened the door to let me in I knew things weren't quite right, even though he didn't say it at first. I'd been coming around two days a week since Christmas, just as I'd promised, I'd spent time with Sofus so that he wouldn't have to spend so much time alone, we'd sat in his room playing computer games, or I'd helped him with his homework, we'd spent all January assembling a model he'd gotten for Christmas, a space shuttle, to my delight, an exact model of the *Columbia* with miniature astronauts who could be glued into their seats in the cockpit and tiny stickers for the wings. NASA. The shuttle was hanging from the ceiling by a fishing line when I came into his room, I gave it a little tap as I passed by so that it sailed aimlessly back and forth for a moment, in useless circles that went nowhere. Building the shuttle had been a success, we'd had a great time together during those days, bent over the plastic pieces, with stinking tubes of glue in our hands and three table lamps clamped to the desk to give us a good working light. I'd been in charge of diagrams and instructions, Sofus had been the glue-boss, the builder. Now that we had a taste for blood we'd gotten ourselves another model, it lay on his bed, still in its plastic packaging. I sat on the chair at his desk and Sofus sat on the edge of the bed, lifted up the model and studied the box.

"It's from the *Apollo 17* expedition," I said, and pointed at the box in his hands that showed a picture of a lunar rover with a big parabolic antenna at the back. *Lunar Rover Vehicle*, it said on the pack, white writing on a black background of the universe.

He nodded.

"That was the last expedition of the Apollo Program," I said. "It was all over after it. People began to lose interest in the moon."

"Why?"

"It's not easy to say why. Maybe because there was so much wrong on earth that needed putting right."

"Hmm."

"Did you know, by the way, that I was born on the same day that they landed on the moon for the first time?"

"Is that true?"

"Yep. At roughly the same moment."

"Imagine if it was their fault you were born. The men on the moon."

"You never know. But I doubt it."

And then I added:

"But it probably means nothing. Did you know that the astronauts played golf on the moon too?"

"Is that true?"

"Completely true."

"Why did they do that?"

"For fun, I suppose. And the golf ball, well, it just disappeared out into space. It never stopped."

"How many people are there on the moon now?"

"There's nobody there now. Just lots of stuff they've left behind. Buzz Aldrin's moon boots, and other things. But twelve people have been up there in all."

"Those twelve people must have been very famous."

"They were, for a while at least."

Sofus fell silent, for a long time.

"Mattias?"

"Yes?"

"How big is space?"

"I don't know," I answered. "But pretty big. Millions and millions of times bigger than the Faroe Isles."

"If I stood at one end of outer space and you stood at the other end, and then we began to walk toward each other, do you think we'd ever find each other?"

"Maybe if we walked long enough. And had good shoes."

He pondered over that awhile, tried to picture it, but couldn't, it was impossible.

I nodded toward the model. "Should we build it, or what?"

Sofus shrugged his shoulders.

"There's no point. We'll never finish it anyway."

"What do you mean? Come on. You can be the glue-boss."

"I'm moving next week."

So that was it. I'd been waiting for it almost. But I hadn't expected to feel so sad about it.

"Is that certain? Where to?"

"Tórshavn. Dad's got a new job." He flung the box aside and lay back against the wall.

"But that's good, surely. You'll probably make tons of friends. There are lots of kids your age in Tórshavn, you know."

"I'm okay now. Here."

I couldn't contradict him.

"And you're here with me," he added.

"It'll all work out. Things always do. I think you'll have a really good time down there. There are girls and everything there, I've heard."

"Mom and Dad said we might go to Denmark in the summer and visit Óluva."

"Sounds good. Are you looking forward to that?"

He looked at the wall, exaggerated the gesture designed to demonstrate that he was practically indifferent. "Yeah." Then he grew serious again, stopped trying to be more grown-up than he was, he was just Sofus, and anxious.

"Will you forget me too, when I leave? Like the spacemen?"

I looked at him.

"I've never forgotten them," I answered. "I still remember them. So I won't forget you either."

"You can have our address in Tórshavn, if you want. Mom must know it."

"Of course I will. You know, I've got Buzz Aldrin's address too, in the USA."

"Have you ever sent him a letter?'

"No."

"Promise to send me a letter if you get my address."

"Of course I will."

I talked a bit with his parents when I left that day, thanked Selma for the delicious meals I'd had on my visits to Sofus, and got their address in Tórshavn, thanked them for making me feel useful, talked with Óli, about his new office job down in town. Talked about Gjógv. And we agreed it was good that at least some people stayed, they'd have preferred to stay themselves, but it was impossible, there was no money in it, and things would get worse, he thought, if the Faroese went ahead with their demands for independence from Denmark. And so we talked. About trivial things and the political ideologies that dogged our country, nothing ever changed, and I finally told him how I'd taken him up on his offer, how I'd borrowed his boat, and I told him about New Year's Eve and the person we'd hauled from the sea, and I could see Óli was pleased that I'd told him, that we'd used his boat that night, that it had been possible to save a life simply because Óli lived there and owned a boat, that when it came to it every bit helped and everything linked together. He smiled:

"Use it as much as you want. I'll leave it here. Just in case."

"Won't you take the boat with you?"

"I hardly ever use it anyway. So I'll leave it. It can be useful to have a boat."

But we never used it again. Didn't touch it. The rowboat would lie in the harbor until the day we vanished for good.

I shook his hand, thanked him and said goodbye, went out and down the steps. Then Óli opened the front door and shouted after me.

"Why don't you sing anymore, by the way? I haven't heard you in forever."

"Because things are on the way up," I answered and left, and I'd thought of showing up on Wednesday the following week to say goodbye to Sofus, to Selma, I stood in the Factory kitchen watching them pack the final things into the big moving van, but I was beaten to it, by the time I'd put on my shoes and gone out into the courtyard the van had already gone, the birds had flown, and Gjógv had three less inhabitants.

I had gone on until March with the work Havstein had set in motion, planting gardens for people I didn't know, and then one day, God help me, a journalist called, desperate to write an article about this stupid Norwegian who was planting gardens for people in the middle of winter. I wondered how they'd found out about it down there in the editor's offices of *Sosialurin* or *Dagblaðið*, Havstein obviously must have tipped them off, thinking it was good for me to see it was useless to hide away, that it was better to take the bull by the horns, as he said.

Fuck no, I said.

Forget it.

No way.

Snowball in hell.

But when you're living in post-psychiatric care, decisions are not yours to make, and on the following Monday I sat in the car next to a hungry journalist from the biggest newspaper on the Faroes, I hadn't come up with any complicated strategies for the interview, merely decided to make myself impossible, I was determined to fly over the cuckoo's nest.

I insisted, among other things, on having the car radio turned all the way up while I drove, so that Útvarp Føroya blasted out of the windows, booming against mountain walls on the bends in the road down toward Funningur. He objected valiantly at first, but then I told him, very seriously, that I was allergic to the sound of rubber against asphalt, and after that it was fine, totally fine, he must have thought I was totally insane, exactly my intention.

I drove down toward Vestmanna, taking the longest route, with the stereo so loud the whole time that the journalist could do nothing but sit in silence next to me, fumbling with the camera in his lap, as though he might, at any moment, take the world's greatest snapshot of me. And as we passed Streymnes and he was still sitting with his camera at the ready, I turned the volume down on the radio.

"No Kodak moment today," I said.

"Sorry?"

I turned the sound up again, even louder this time, rolled the window down, still in Streymoy, as the ice-cold air blasted into the car and I pretended everything was normal, while the journalist made himself small in his seat, not daring to protest.

I was on my way to plant a garden for some wealthy person by the name of Magnusson, just outside Vestmanna, he'd made his money from fishing, and I didn't know why on earth he was so desperate to have a miniature Japan in his garden, but that was what he'd asked for, I'd received clear instructions on both contents and design, Havstein had helped me order the goods, a time-consuming process in itself. So Japan it would be. Maybe this Magnusson had known this would get *Sosialurin* interested. Maybe he wanted to be interviewed and photographed, so he could saunter down to the shop the next day, buy a newspaper, take it home, and make a show for his family of working through the paper from the front page onward, until it grew increasingly difficult to resist leafing through to the last pages where the interview would be. And when he finally got that far, to page thirty, and saw himself standing there smiling beside his bonsai tree, he'd spend just seconds skimming the interview before uttering an indifferent *well, well,* and leaving the paper on the table, hoping his wife and children would pick it up and read it. And then that evening he'd go out to the bin where the newspaper had been thrown, take it back in and cut the interview out, put it in a plastic sleeve with a dark cover entitled *Magnusson's interviews, articles etc.* Then later he'd take this one clipping, copy it, and put it in a file, in case the original should go missing.

I pulled into the driveway of Magnusson's big house and turned off the radio, rolled the windows up and got out to open the trunk and back door, started to take out the plants and equipment that I'd squeezed in to make enough space. The journalist hung around me like an abandoned child and was clearly uncertain whether he should start his interview with me now or wait, and for a moment I wondered if I should ask Mr. Magnusson for a saucer of warm milk and somebody to stroke my journalist passenger's fur while I worked.

I felt bad for a moment and stretched my hand out to him, gave my name and presented myself politely.

"Olaf Ludvig Bjarnason," answered the journalist.

"So, Olaf Ludvig, do you have a strong pair of arms?"

He looked at me. Mr. Olaf Ludvig didn't know what to say.

"Do you think you could take those slabs?" I said, pointing at the big slabs of rock in the boot. "Come on."

We walked up to the house, myself in the lead, Olaf Ludvig stomping after.

Magnusson was a nice man.

Without a doubt.

Dressed in a Japanese kimono as he was, one didn't quite know what to expect.

But he was congeniality itself.

We had to sit on the ground around a little table and drink tea first, while Magnusson talked about the green plains of Japan, at great length, I pitied this journalist, he'd accepted this garden assignment to have a peaceful day. Now he had to decide which of his two subjects was less crazy. It was a tough contest, and when we'd finally begun work on the winter garden and Magnusson had disappeared inside to do whatever he did with his days, it seemed as though the media man grew a little calmer, and went back to his notebook. Ready, set, go.

"So, you're Mattias. Mattias . . . ?"

I repeated my whole name, slowly, so he could get it down, and then sat down to inspect the plans for the garden layout. Garden designer. I'd moved up in the world, and had to work out where everything would go. I began with the rocks, the patterns, doing my best, and apart from the presence of the reporter who'd already spent more time than he'd hoped with me, I was pleased, liked making it nice, giving Kimono-Magnusson the garden of his dreams.

"So, Mattias, you're from Norway, aren't you? And you're a gardener, I understand. When did you first come to the Faroe Islands, and why?"

I laid the rocks in a semicircle around him, and he moved out of my way.

"It was in the morning, I think. I came for the climate. Doctor's orders. I suffer from reverse rheumatism. Sun and warmth are bad for me."

"Havstein Garðalið told me that you'd been here since last summer."

"Yes."

"That he found you outside, one night."

"Somebody told me it was going to be a fine, starry night. But they lied."

"And you've lived up at the home in Gjógv ever since. As a guest."

"Yes."

"That must have been a special meeting. What's it been like living there, in an post-psychiatric home like that, what's it been like living with the other residents, and what's it been like living in a village like Gjógv, so remote and almost deserted?"

"Great."

Pause. He tried again.

"So do you plan to live on the Faroes permanently?

"No."

"How long do you think you'll stay?'

"A quarter to fourteen days."

"What do you think of our little country?"

"It's green. And gray. Grass and grit. In the winter everything's gray."

"Can you tell me something about what you're going to do here today?"

"I'll plant plants."

"What else can you tell me about what you're doing?"

"The plants are Japanese. Which isn't always the case. Sometimes they're Norwegian. Sometimes you don't know where they're from."

Olaf Ludvig gave a heavy sigh, poor man, stroked a hand across his face and concentrated hard on burying the desire to punch me on the nose, he was hot and red in the face, and I was the most childish man in the Western Hemisphere. I went on doing my thing, set the rocks in place so I could get to the part I'd looked forward to, the difficult task of planting Japanese plants I'd never seen before, plants I'd had to look up in gardening books to see how they should be handled. The reporter changed tack now, began photographing me, from every angle, a shimmer of petals each time the flash went off. I avoided looking at the camera, turned my back, but couldn't escape, he followed me around continually, stomping through that little winter garden without looking left or right, until I suddenly exploded.

"Stop it, for fuck's sake! Stop! You're trampling the whole flower bed! Can't you fucking get those god-damned pictures taken so I can do my work around here! There's nothing to look at, I don't want to be interviewed, why are you taking pictures of me! MAGNUSSON!"

I screamed for help.

I screamed for a man I didn't know.

I screamed for Kimono-Magnusson and he came into view in the doorway seconds later, saw me down on my knees before the journalist who stood there, terrified, hands hanging helplessly at his sides, camera round his neck, looking as though he'd been caught in the act of tearing my clothes off and raping me. Magnusson in his kimono scratched his head, unsure what to say, so he said:

"It's looking good already. Fantastic! Would you like some sake?"

Olaf Ludvig nodded desperately.

I stared straight ahead, on the verge of tears.

"Excellent." Magnusson disappeared inside for the sake, I got up and took a step toward the journalist who still stood there like a poker, staring at me.

"Is it so difficult to understand?" I said. "I don't want to be in your newspaper, I want to read it. I've never been interviewed before, and I never want to be. I didn't ask for this. What, who, where, why, how, and not least, how long, they're all my business, and they have nothing to do with anybody else."

"You could have said that up front," said Olaf Journalist. "Do you really think I wanted to do this damn garden article for housewives? Can't you see that I'm doing you a favor? I'm trying to help you? Or are you so out of it, you can't even see that?"

"What is it you really want?" I said, limply. "Are you under some illusion I'm a patient too, is that it? That it's all gone totally down the pipes for this Norwegian, and that's why he's worth writing about, some columns on a man who's making good, against all odds, a feel-good story, dandelions breaking through the asphalt?"

"Oh, forget it. I wanted to do something for all of you, up there. That's all."

"For us? We're doing just fine, thank you."

"Yes, that's obvious, I must say."

There wasn't time to say more before Magnusson came back out, smiling and carrying a tray with three cups and a bottle of sake, he put it down on the ground and sat next to it, filled the cups and began talking, sunlight itself.

I spent most of the next three days at the Faroese-Japanese man's house, only going home to sleep, talking to nobody, leaving at about five in the morning, before the others were awake, letting myself into the winter garden, and Magnusson would come out later in the morning, following my work eagerly, excited by each bit of progress, he asked questions and was curious about the plants, we read the gardening book together and talked about compost, and now and then it felt as though I was back at home in the safety of the nursery in Stavanger, a thousand light years behind, and by the time I left him on a Wednesday, Magnusson was standing in the loveliest Japanese garden in the country, a flash of green in a wintry gray, enclosed by pretty glass walls with dark brown ornamental wooden frames, purchased from a firm that built winter gardens, and I realized I was sad the job was over and that I'd have liked to stay longer, to perfect it, I saw how much it meant to him, how he stood in his garden and smiled, it could have been Japan, and I waved as I drove away.

But when I parked outside the Factory, I turned the motor off and sat there.

My patience had run thin.

My precious patience that I've always prized. I was fuming inside, and for a moment I glimpsed a quite different Faroe Isles, a place where you can never slip away, where you're constantly being watched, where you're not allowed a moment's peace in the day.

I fling open the car door, reach for the last remaining plant that I hadn't found space for, a little bonsai worth 2,000 kroner in a ceramic pot, get out, slam the car door behind me, go up the stairs, into Havstein's office, he smiles as I come in, rises from his desk, walks towards me asking *Well? How did the interview go?* Before he realizes I'm not smiling, and the corners of his mouth straighten, and we stand face to face on the soft carpet.

"What did you do that for?" I ask quietly.

He says nothing.

I'm on the verge of tears. Quaking inside.

"What do you want from me?" I yell, and I throw the tree, chuck the plant into the wall behind him and the ceramic pot smashes against the brick wall and soil rains down over his office and in a split second

I'm terrified he'll kill me, I've never seen him like this before, neither have I seen myself like this, but then he softens, controls himself, pulls himself together, clasps his hands psychiatrist-like in front of his chest, and talks as though nothing has happened.

"Mattias," he starts.

Pause.

"Mattias, I thought it was time you came out of yourself. Time you met the world. You're clever. You know that? That you're good at what you do? Has anybody ever told you that? I'm proud of you, Mattias."

"What do you want from me?" I repeated. "Who the hell gave you the right to make decisions over my life?"

"Who gave me that right? You. You, Mattias, gave me that right, from the moment you arrived, from the moment I found you in pieces down in Kollafjörður, when you didn't get up for weeks, when you chose to stay because you couldn't face going home, then you put everything you had in my hands, and I'm doing the best I can, Mattias, don't you understand? Was I supposed to let you rot away here, like NN, like Palli and Anna? To let you believe, as they do, that this is just an in-between place, before everything turns out all right again, before everything sorts itself out, before the world looks different one morning and you can just pick up your bag and leave, all possibilities open, no fully booked flights? Unlike them, unlike with Palli, Anna, and NN, things haven't gone so far that you've got to be sick forever." He was silent for a moment. "But they will go that far if you don't unlock yourself soon. *That* much I can promise. So to answer your question, what do I want from you, Mattias, the answer is frighteningly simple, I want you to pull yourself together, because you're about to vanish into yourself."

"Why do you think everybody's so frightened of being forgotten?" I ask quietly.

"Is *that* what all this is about? Then I can tell you now you're going about it in completely the wrong way. Because you're not trying to be forgotten, are you? You're just trying to get away! And if you think you'll make yourself invisible like that, you're mistaken. My god, you're more and more visible with each day! And you're not fitting into the system either, you're creating a new one, and then you're forcing everyone else to follow it. I know what you want, and this isn't the way to go about it. You're just being a big spoiled baby who thinks the world's done him a huge injustice, but it hasn't, it's been on your side almost all the way, you've been the damned captain of this team! I didn't let you live here so you could turn into a snot-nosed brat who cries because somebody's taken his toys."

Which is when I lash out.

I punch Havstein in the face, as hard as I can.

I punch him because he doesn't take me seriously, because his arguments don't ring true.

I punch him because he doesn't know how I feel.

I punch him because the words he's saying are getting to be true.

And Havstein's head jolts backward, he loses his balance and staggers towards the desk, instinctively I've closed my eyes, and only hear the sound of his body as it meets the table, his body, arms dragging down the files, telephone, and cup of ballpoint pens, and when I open my eyes he's sitting on the floor with soil on his face, strewn with pens and documents from lives that have been rescued, mine excluded.

I held my aching hand against myself, and walked carefully over to Havstein who was pulling himself up by the desk, I helped him to his feet and sat him back on the table, he held a hand over his nose, blood running out between his fingers.

"I'm sorry," I said.

Havstein wiped away the blood with the back of his hand.

"That's fine."

"I just want some peace. That's all I want."

"I know," he said. "I know."

"You've never asked me why I want to be alone. Ever. As a *psychia-*

trist you should know how to *relate* to people like me. You've read all the theory; you know what questions to ask."

"No, Mattias. It's *you* that never told me that before."

I was angry for a long time. Fucking furious. But more than that I was getting scared. Because it couldn't possibly be recommended in any book that I should be subjected to the events of the last few days. It couldn't possibly be good therapy, unthinkable. So, why had he done it? Doubtless from the goodness of his heart. But suppose this heart no longer knew what was best for anybody? Then it was Havstein who was coming unstuck, and with him we were cracking bit by bit too. He'd lost his grip, surely, there certainly wasn't much left of the doctor who'd fished me up that night from the drenched asphalt of Hví-tanesvegur, and I no longer felt sure who he really was, wasn't sure at all.

Yet after we'd shaken each other's hands and reassured each other that things were still okay between us, after he'd said he loved me, and after I'd gotten some toilet paper for him from the bathroom, and been shouted at by NN who'd come in and seen us, and after I finally left his office and closed the door behind me, I caught sight of him hunched over a little dustpan and brush, alternately sweeping the soil and remains of the plant off the carpet, then plugging his nose with fresh tissue, then I felt the stab of conscience's deep-sinking nails; this wasn't how things should be, and I'd made the world harder for all the people around me who had more than enough to do holding their heads above water.

It ended as you'd expect, of course. The interview. The journalist wrote a long article, a double-page spread in the paper four days later. Its main focus was Magnusson who'd finally fulfilled a dream with his all-year Japanese garden in Vestmanna. Magnusson clearly liked talking and had nothing against being the focus of a big report in the papers, quite the opposite, he'd talked about Japan, about his life, his riches and family, all his businesses and where the best silk was made, the journalist had written a gushing article, and Magnusson had thrown himself into it, sake flowing, opening himself more and more to this nationally acclaimed reporter. But there was more than enough about me too. Of course the journalist had taken umbrage at my outburst and did what he could to describe me, not in the best, but under the strongest light. He used the brief interview he'd extracted from me in its entirety, verbatim, and I was consummately portrayed as a genius gardener who lived in a post-psychiatric ward. Additionally, he'd filled the greater part of one of the pages with a picture of me, over the caption: *God's gardener in full swing*. The picture showed me in an absurd pose in a flower bed, halfway down on my knees and trying to avoid the camera. An idiotic picture and not included from any affection, so far as I could see. Neither the picture's caption nor the parts of the article dealing with my purportedly supernatural gardening skills were meant to be complimentary, they were there because he knew they'd raise the number of phone calls, create an explosion of inquiries for gardening work and give me exposure, everything I didn't want, everything I wanted to avoid. But it didn't matter. I'd made my decision. I'd done my last gardening job on the Faroes.

‒ ‒ ‒ ■ ‒ ‒ ‒

Since Havstein had arranged all the necessary paperwork, had got everything stamped and approved, and creatively reproduced any documents that had been refused, it would be relatively easy for me to get a job, so I went down to Tórshavn a week later, went into the local government offices and half an hour later left with a new job, and the following day I was in full swing planting trees on the Faroes, three days a week. A lumberjack in reverse, I worked on extending the woods by the field at the end of Hvítanesvegur, together with two other workers from Kvívíkm, Herluf and Jógvan, my age, they'd worked for the local government for years, and we planted, laboriously following the laws of art and nature. Most of the trees would never grow, they'd be so much stillborn driftwood due to the saltwater spray, the wind, or sheep, but it was an okay job, and I also seriously started getting myself together, opening myself up and growing more sociable, I drove into Tórshavn and ate lunch with Herluf and Jógvan, went into the office once a week and talked to the secretary, had coffee with the boss, was lovableness itself, polite and obliging, could have sold sand to the Saharans, but I don't know whether I was just acting or whether I'd really shifted gears, as Havstein had suggested, opening myself up and making a point of being seen.

Some afternoons I'd take Carl for a drive, take him on trips, show him various places in this little country, he'd huddle up in the front seat of our small communal car and we'd drive uphill and down, crisscrossing the country, this way and that, and all on the orders of Havstein who was convinced I was the man for the job, he figured two foreigners in a car had to find something of interest to talk about sooner or later. The truth was we talked a lot on these trips, I pointed things out, explained where we were, everything I'd learned, why the mountains were so round in the South and had sharper peaks in the North, I showed him the intricate patterns of fjords and rivers, the unique sprinkling system, explained why the trees didn't grow here naturally, and what a battle it was to get the ones we planted to take, I showed him the cafés where he could check his e-mail if there was anybody he wanted to contact, I took him on a boat trip out to Vestmanna, the bird cliffs, we took the helicopter out to Mykines and barbecued sausages in hushed silence. I talked about Norway, Iceland, the Faroes, and about the cod wars, about why Miðvágur was the best harbor for the pilot whale slaughter, and how it was carried out, tried to teach him as much as I could, hoping all the while that he wouldn't tell me to stop, tell me he already knew these things, or that he wasn't interested. All I wanted was to contribute. To be useful again and again, and in doing this, find a purpose. And he didn't come up with any objections, instead he listened, asked questions that I answered as best I could. NN came along too sometimes, in the afternoon or the evening, sat in the back seat as I talked and gesticulated, helped me with the occasional phrase when I couldn't remember the English, and we usually drove around until it started to get dark, and we'd stop off at the ruins at Kirkjubøur, the courts in Tórshavn, the NATO radar base at Sornfelli, places like that, before driving to Café Natúr to drink coffee as the room slowly filled up, voices and music drowning out the sound of the rain.

I think I heard the expression from Havstein first, and I've seen it in numerous books since, hunting through the reference books I've found, but I'm still looking for a satisfactory explanation. Havstein called them trigger factors, minute, dormant firecrackers in the brain that can go off without warning given the right stimulus, so we're never the same again. We all have them, and they're each differently coded, so it's impossible to know what might set them off before it's too late. As yet we still have no possibility of un-experiencing what happens in our lives. The majority get through their lives without ever setting off these electrical mechanisms that cause us to think so differently, turning us into totally different people than we once were, most of us will experience tiny shifts at worst, a spark or two that's quickly extinguished without recourse to anything more dramatic than a short period of sick leave, half a year on Prozac, a weekend on Valium, or with good friends who are there when needed. Most people never give a thought to the giant catastrophe that might hit and cause the brain's ultimate meltdown. But for some of us, these trigger mechanisms are more sensitive, more vulnerable to impulses, and eventually they go off, one, or all of them simultaneously. It can happen at any moment, we can be on the bus, on the way home or to work, we can be in the supermarket waiting for the new checkout girl to remember the code for celery so we can pay and leave, go home and make dinner. It can happen when we've ignored warnings for weeks, going steadily downhill, after we've received complaints that our work's not up to scratch, we're not doing a good enough job, we're arriving late, missing meetings, staying at home, curtains drawn, TV on. Or it can come like an explosion from nowhere, when we're with a best friend, and we're in our prime, only twenty-three and we've gone to the Faroese National Gallery, and we stand in the first room, before Samuel Joensen Mikines's greatest painting, *Home from a Funeral,* which was when it happened to Anna, that was the moment those microscopic electrical charges went off in her brain, so small that even nanotechnology would seem clumsy in comparison, Anna stood in front of Mikines's dark painting and exploded, an event totally invisible to her friend and probably to herself, but she noticed it when she got home, by the time she got to bed that night she knew it had happened, and for Anna the damage was irreversible. Since then she's never dared go closer than five hundred feet to the gallery, never looked at a single work by Mikines again. Because sadly, it isn't over when these triggers are released. In the tiny little craters in which the damage is done, new triggers are formed, with even more intricate release mechanisms, and even if you recover, if everything gets sorted out, if things go well, there'll always be something there, ready to return, to be released by either the same or some new factor, and then they'll explode again, the firecrackers you never asked for, this time they'll spin out of the initial crater, and out to new places where it'll be even harder for the emergency crew to reach you in time. So you live on your guard, avoiding the triggers you think you know, like a migraine patient avoiding red wine, chocolate, or whatever, you avoid the situation you've begun to fear, friends you no longer understand, your workplace, your apartment, the sound of helicopters, large crowds, or something as innocent as a Faroese painting from the first half of a long-gone century.

It's strange. But that's how it is.

I spent a lot of time thinking it over. About what might have caused them to fall ill. NN. Palli. Anna. Carl. A stupid attempt at self-diagnosis, there's no way around it, and I'm probably not the first to have tried it, but I believe that if only I can find out what went wrong with the others, I'll be able to work out how to repair myself, classic really, the patient who thinks he can escape if only he dons the doctor's coat. And I'd been thinking about that since I sat there that first evening with the files, and read about Anna. The National Gallery. Its pictures. It was time to see them. If a painting could make you ill, I wanted to see what it looked like.

No, that's incorrect.

I burned to see that picture.

So, anyway: I secretly went to the National Gallery with Carl one Sunday when it was raining and the fog hung particularly heavily over the islands and there wasn't much else to do. I don't remember what we said to the others, so they wouldn't want to come with us, maybe I got Carl to say we were going fishing, something we did often, for hours at a time, nobody but Carl ever wanted to go. Yes, it's likely we said we were off fishing. But the fish we were after were for looking at, not to be caught or grilled or eaten.

We parked the car in the back and walked around the building looking for the entrance, but changed our minds halfway since it seemed we were on the wrong path, we turned and tried walking the other way, it wasn't easy to find the front of this place, we managed to get drenched in no time and ran the last few feet before finally locating the entrance and going in through the glass doors where we were met by a receptionist who sat in defensive mode at the register, barely able to see us over the edge of the counter. We must have looked rather forlorn standing there, with steam rising from our jackets and gazing around, not knowing quite what to do, because the girl behind the counter immediately sat bolt upright and asked if she could help us at all.

"We just wanted to see some paintings," I answered, wiping the rain from my face. "Mikines. You have his paintings here, don't you?"

Her face lit up. "Yes, of course!"

She crept down behind the counter again, prepared two tickets, twenty kroner each.

"You've been unlucky with the weather today, haven't you?" We looked as though we'd been underwater.

"We left our umbrella at home," I said.

"Excuse me?"

"Oh, nothing. But it's a nice day indoors."

"Yes. It's nice in here."

She gave us our tickets, then emerged from behind the counter, crossed over to the information stand and took a couple of pamphlets, and now I saw there was nothing wrong with her height, it was the counter that was odd, and I thought how embittered the carpenter must have been to build such a creation.

We were given two pamphlets about Mikines, one in English and one in Danish, which she placed solemnly in our hands.

"Samuel-Joensen-Mikines-is-the-father-of-Faroese-painting," she said mechanically. "It-is-impossible-to-overestimate-his-importance. Many-people-consider-him-to-be-the-first-professional-painter-in-this-country. Mikines-was-born-in-1906-and-died-in-1979."

We thanked her, bowed and waved at her with our pamphlets as we wandered into the gallery, and she padded back to reception and was gone.

As we rounded the corner and disappeared out of view, Carl suddenly turned to me.

"Mattias? Is there something wrong?"

"No. What do you mean?"

"Why didn't you want the others to know anything about where we were going? Why did we lie to them?"

"It's Anna," I said. "Anna was here and saw this painting shortly before she fell ill."

"And so? What does that have to do with us?"

"Don't you ever think it's strange that things turn out as they do?"

"What do you mean?"

"I don't know. Maybe nothing."

So I didn't tell him about the things I'd read about Anna in her file, the dripping wet sailors who'd stepped out of the picture and into her house for years. I said nothing, not even to Carl, since I was uncertain he'd be interested, but I made it clear he mustn't tell her where we'd been, nor the others, *she's got problems with this gallery,* was all I said, and Carl nodded, *best to keep it quiet.* He had no problem with that, was probably only happy to keep well away from any problems, while I, I couldn't stop thinking there were connections out there, there had to be.

We found Mikines on our first attempt, hardly difficult, his paintings looked like nothing else hanging there, I stood before a self-portrait and looked at Carl.

"Does it say anything in there about the picture?"

"Let's have a look," he leafed through the pamphlet.

"This self-portrait is from 1933, right?"

I bent down toward the little white label.

"Yes, that's right."

We stared at the picture. It was Mikines in person. It was dark. His face almost melted into the picture, and it looked as though he was thinking about things he shouldn't think about.

"Apparently Mikines was often ill, it was difficult for him to get a proper education since it was constantly interrupted, and it says here that it was in periods of good health that he tried to paint, but it wasn't until an international visitor came to the islands that things opened up for him. Mikines was seventeen or eighteen when a Swedish bird painter called William Gislander visited the island. It says that Mikines grew totally obsessed with this man's work, and literally followed Gislander everywhere that summer, collecting all Gislander's used tubes of paint and using the leftovers for his own attempts, and he soon began working with a definite aim. He was accepted by the Academy in Copenhagen in the following year."

"Right," I answered, walking on down the line of self-portraits, each painting darker than the previous, each face more anguished. Carl read my thoughts and dipped into the pamphlet again, no need for a tour with him at my side, a born tour guide.

"It says here Mikines's work can be divided into roughly two periods. The dark and the light color-wise, that cover, among other works, the well-known whale slaughter paintings. His dark period begins in 1934 when two boats were wrecked on their way home from a fishing trip near Iceland. Forty-three men are lost, among them nine from Mykines, which naturally hit everybody in the tiny community terribly hard. Added to which his father died that summer too, bringing the dark undertone, which became characteristic of all his paintings for the next ten years. The year after the accident and his father's death, he began work on the large canvas, *Home from a Funeral* and . . ."

I recognized the title immediately. Anna. It was Anna's picture.

"Where's that picture? Is it hanging here?"

"Yes, it should be here—"

"I think we should find it right away."

He looked at me uneasily. "Yeah, okay. No skin off my nose. Come on."

We continued down the hall, took a right turn, into the biggest room, a large, square, white room, into which light poured through a glass roof, hitting the wooden floor and the wall in front of us, a gigantic picture, more than five feet tall, in a frame of what looked like old timber. This was the painting I wanted to see. Carl and I stood stock still in the middle of the room. It was the creepiest picture I'd ever seen. The paint was cracked, lines scraped in all directions, as though it had been dragged across several battlefields or transported over the sea in an open boat. It reminded me of Munch, but where his paintings and the angst they portrayed ought to be easy for us to identify with, considering our condition, this was something else. The angst encrusted in this paint was different, even more powerful, because there was no sickness in it, it was impossible to explain away. There was no fear here. Just an oppressive, monumental sorrow. It stood out of the painting like a deep, deafening thunder, and was at the same time frustratingly soundless. The painting showed eight people sitting huddled together astern a boat, forming an irregular pyramid. All dressed in black. Brownish-black. It seemed as though they rose up from a wave, and all that was visible behind them was a disturbed night sky of gray, and the sea, all in the same dark tones, the opposite of a Kodak moment. Their faces stared out at me bitterly, lozenge-shaped, oval faces with sharp edges that seemed to grow longer with each passing second, narrowed eyes, I felt the desire to ask their forgiveness, to tell them it wasn't my fault, it was beyond my control, that there was nothing I could do to help them, but I said nothing, I sat on one of the seats in the middle of the room, unable to take my eyes from the canvas.

Carl stood in front of the picture for a minute or two before boredom overtook him and he shrugged his shoulders. He moved to the end of the room with me in tow and continued on his own personal introduction to the artist's life and art, with almost dogged determination.

"Mikines's-output-was-uneven-and-viewed-by-some-as-disjointed-but-this-has-to-be-viewed-in-the-light-of-his-numerous-long-hospital-stays-and-breaks-from-his-work.-For-long-periods-Mikines-also-drank-excessively-and-took-drugs-railroading-him-from-his-artistic-work.-The-word-schizophrenia-is-often-used-to-describe-his-mental-state-but-he-was-never-diagnosed-as-such.-However-he-oscillated-between-a-superiority-complex-to-overwhelming-feelings-of-inferiority,-and-is-recorded-as-saying-that-if-it-was-up-to-him-85-percent-of-his-paintings-would-be-recalled-and-destroyed-by-him-personally. We-must-be-thankful-this-didn't-happen."

He looked at me for acknowledgement, but I was no longer following. My mind was elsewhere.

"Should we go?" I said, walking swiftly toward the exit, with Carl on my heels, his nose still in the artist's biography.

"But listen to this, Mattias: Mikines had an appalling temper, and this was often a terrible burden to him. During his enforced stay in Denmark during the war, when all communication with the Faroes was broken, he joined the Danish Nazi party one evening, probably as a result of being drunk and excitable. But unlike Knut Hamsun, he woke up the next morning and regretted it, and immediately withdrew his membership. Do you think that bears any significance?"

"No," I answered. "No significance at all."

It was quiet in the car as we drove back home to Gjógv that afternoon. I kept it to myself, but a thought had taken root and wouldn't shift. NN also came from Mykines. Was that somehow relevant? She wasn't the only one from the island who'd had problems besides Mikines. Could I totally exclude the possibility that there was something in the air there, that the experience of loneliness there was more oppressive than elsewhere? Not entirely. And more, if one could be driven crazy just by looking at a painting, or by life on an island, or by taking buses, what other things might lurk behind every corner? How could one guard oneself when surrounded by such uncertainty? I hadn't a clue, no idea what had triggered my problems, it could have been anything or nothing, Helle, the nursery, things that went farther back. But most of all, I was worried for the others, for their so-called well-being, it seemed that it took so little to tip the balance, and more than anything I wished I could talk with some of them about this, but that was impossible without tearing everything up from its foundations, without any guarantee of being able to put the pieces together again, I couldn't even say anything to Havstein, as it would reveal I'd been snooping in his archives, and if I did that, we'd both have to tell each other everything, and I had no idea where I'd start or where I'd finish. There were so many things we didn't know, and most of them would have been horribly painful to acknowledge.

4

Four days later NN died. On one of my days off. We were going to take the bus down to Hvitanes, NN, Carl, and I. I was going to show them the trees I'd planted, NN and I hadn't taken a walk in our minimalist woods since I'd began working there, she'd barely been out of Gjógv of late, stayed in a lot. We were going to have a beer later, meet Havstein and the others in the evening. But Carl had changed his mind at the last moment, wanted to work for a couple of hours instead, come down to the harbor on the late afternoon bus, he had a new idea for something to make, so it was just NN and me. She went on ahead, I was going to change into a lighter jacket, she walked up to the bus shelter, sat on the bench, and waited.

Then, as I come out of the Factory door I hear the bus coming, I hurry across the road keeping an eye on it as it makes its way downhill toward us, I round the corner and call to NN, but can't see her, until she suddenly comes into view, she takes a couple of steps out of the shelter, at the same moment the bus driver tries to brake, and she's hit from behind, crumples up, disappears under the bus.

Hydraulics.

Brakes as the bus finally stops.

Her arms don't move.

The bus driver stares straight ahead.

The sound of my shoes on asphalt as I run to her.

Droplets of rain hit my face as I frantically try to pull her out from under the bus, one of her hands is under the front wheel, the bus driver has to compose himself before starting the bus and inching forward to free her.

The bus moves. She screams.

Blood floods from the almost torn off hand. From her belly.

Panic. Puking. Panic. Puking.

The bus driver is sobbing and rips the sleeve from his jacket, ties it around her wrist.

The passengers sit motionless in the bus, looking down into the floor.

She screams, then she is suddenly still. I hold her, telling her it'll all be all right, you'll get help soon, just hold on, be patient.

I shout and Carl comes running, his hands full of wool, we drive her in our car to the hospital in J.C. Svabosgøta, Tórshavn, because we have no time to wait for an ambulance, I watch her in the mirror all the way, talk to her, Carl holds her, tries to keep her conscious, comforts her, ties more fabric around her arm, her belly.

By the time we arrive NN is already wandering carefully through coma's vague gardens, and they operate on her immediately as we sit outside in the hallway waiting, we call Havstein, get him to come, and there we sit, waiting, while NN is operated on, and we think everything will be all right, that we got here fast enough.

NN doesn't die that day, even though it feels that way, she lies in the hospital for almost six weeks, and when it's over, much has changed, trees have grown, and I'm on the way home.

– – – ■ – – –

Quiet days at the Factory after NN was gone.

We gave each other a wide berth and got nothing done, it was hard keeping the simplest routines going. We got up as usual, went to work when we had to, came home at the usual times. But the simplest things,

the meals, evening activities, were all absent, fell apart. We had diffi-
culties talking about it with each other, everybody reacted so differently
and nobody knew where to begin. Carl stayed in the Factory mainly,
continued from where he'd left off on the day she'd been run over, as
though he could change events by pretending nothing had happened.
I sat with him in his room a lot, but he rarely talked about her, changed
the subject every time I broached it.

"What do you think about this?" he'd ask, holding up one of his
latest inventions.

"How about this?" he'd ask, showing me horses he'd carved, cows
he'd made, the patches of brown he'd painted on their white bodies.

"Think we should make more like that?" he would ask and point at
the sheep.

And once in a while he'd say: "Can I borrow the car tonight? I want
to go down to the hospital."

"Of course," I'd answer and let him borrow the car, I never asked to
go with him, never asked what he did down there, what he said to her,
or if he said anything at all. Avoided the subject, talked about other
things, figured he'd talk when he was ready, and the only thing to do,
until then, was to wait.

It was different with Anna and Havstein, Anna took it hard, barely
ate, barely slept, and was irritated by little things around her, bread-
crumbs on the kitchen counter, the shower curtain not being pulled
back, messy cupboards, and scruffy flower beds, she grabbed onto trivialities and they kept her afloat, meanwhile Havstein spent a huge
amount of time analyzing what had happened, chance's tragic lottery, I
had to describe to him what had happened over and over again,
moment by moment, frame by frame, like a film, answer all his questions, tell him what we'd talked about during those evenings we spent
in her room, how Carl felt, how I felt, and this last question was always
the hardest to answer, almost always answered: "I know it wasn't my
fault. I don't think I was to blame."

"Good," he'd say. "Good." And then the conversation would die.

Even Palli changed during those days. He sat with us more often in the evenings, helped out where necessary, asked Carl and I out on fishing trips, and we'd go with him almost every evening, we'd stand along the beach fishing without saying much, he'd help me with my equipment, selecting my spinners for me and taking my rod over when I got my hook stuck at the bottom, he taught me how to manipulate the spinner in the water, when I should tug on the line, when I should reel in, showed me the best places to stand. We caught a lot of fish on those evenings. And if the weather was right, we sat outside, in thick wool sweaters, grilling fish, three stooges on a rock, and all the fish in the world couldn't change a thing.

So NN lay in the hospital in Tórshavn seeing nothing, hearing nothing, saying nothing. Received visits. From Carl. From Havstein, Palli, and Anna, they went there in the afternoons a couple of times a week. And me. To begin with I went almost every day after work, taking sandwiches with me. Things to read. Talked to her a lot. About everything, really. Anything that came to me. Stuff I'd read in the papers. Told her what had happened to her, and that we were all looking forward to her waking up. How it almost always turned out all right in the movies when beautiful people lay in comas for ages, that the longer they lay there, the bigger the chance they'd come back. I told her she was possibly the most beautiful thing that ever happened to me. I said that we could all go on vacation together when she woke up, to Denmark, perhaps. That would be nice. Or England. London. New York. We could take the bus. If she wanted. We could take the bus in every country. I promised green fairy-tale forests, filled to the brim with fresh fruits and exquisite flowers, gentle animals in soft teddy-bear fur with no dangerous small parts for kids. I talked and talked, and by the time I left in the evening my words were left strewn, on the walls, from the ceiling, on the floor, in disorder. I stopped it in the end. The talking. Sat and listened instead. For changes in her breathing. For her to suddenly wake up. But on the whole I just read. Or listened to the radio. Or something.

And then one day her mother came to visit too.

She entered that light room one average Monday afternoon, bright sunshine and April warmth in the air. She was petite, with long, dark hair and an enormous handbag. I'd been sitting with NN for an hour, an hour and a half maybe, with Havstein's book about the Caribbean on my lap, I was sitting in the hospital reading my way through the island kingdoms, I'd gotten caught up in Grenada for some reason, I tried to memorize population figures, twenty-year-old hotel recommendations, sights that might no longer exist, lengths of swimming pools that might already be filled with sand. She gave me a little nod before hanging her jacket on the hook beside the door, sat in the chair beside me, looked at NN. We sat like that in silence for a moment.

"Are you going to go traveling?" She pointed at the book in my lap.

"No, no," I answered. "I just like to know what I'm missing."

Silence.

"What do you think she's thinking about?" she said, almost to herself.

"I don't know. Nothing, maybe."

"She's a beautiful girl, don't you think?"

"Yes," I answered. "The most beautiful person I've ever met."

"Did you know she used to take buses all around the Faroes, going nowhere, for no reason? That's what made her sick. All those buses."

"Yes. I've heard."

"You're Mattias, is that right?"

"Yes."

She gave me her name and shook my hand. "She talked a lot about you."

She had? What had she said?

"Really?" I stammered.

"When she stayed with me at Christmas. She showed me pictures of you. I think she was almost getting well enough to leave Gjógv. Was that something she talked about?"

"Some. Not a lot. But some."

"I don't know where she would have gone. Do you? Denmark, maybe?"

"Maybe."

She rose from her chair, went over to the bed and held NN's hand, stroked her head, she was tiny in the sheets, melting into the white, and there was nothing but cables and the monotonous bleeping from the ECG tapping her rhythm into the room.

Air conditioning.

Traffic outside.

Springtime.

Her mother turned towards me.

"Was she with that . . . Carl?"

"What . . . when it happened?"

"No, were they together?" She almost blushed. "I mean, were they a couple? If you know what I mean?"

I nodded.

"Yes. I think so. Didn't you know?"

"She said so little about it. I only knew that he existed, and that he was American."

"We don't know a lot more ourselves," I said.

"It was you she talked about, you know. Goodness, what a to-do." She laughed, tentatively. "As though she were studying for a test on you. It was you, day and night, it was like having a teenager in the house again."

"I didn't know."

"Are you sure?"

I waited.

"Yes," I said.

"She didn't say anything about it?"

"Not directly."

"And you?"

"Me?"

"Did you love her?" She corrected herself: "*Do* you love her?"

"Yes," I whispered.

"Good."

"I'm not sure that helps."

"Or maybe it's the only thing that helps?"

"Helps with what?"

"Everything."

It was quiet for a moment and we sat and turned the thought over, and neither of us knew if it was true, or if it was just something one said: that it helps to be loved. NN was breathing evenly and the clock hands moved on undisturbed, second by second, I thought about outer space, that if I were to go now, for example, to the middle of the Milky Way, at the speed of light, it would take twenty years for me to arrive, while for NN, lying in her bed, 30,000 years would pass before I returned. But nobody can travel that fast.

That's the way I'd think when I was sad.

It was Einstein who made sure we'd never travel too far from each other.

A nurse came into the room, nodded to us and took the readings at the side of the bed, pushed a button, turned a switch, made notes in the margin and disappeared again.

NN's mother looked at the clock, checked it against her watch.

"I really should go."

That was when I realized. It was now or never.

"Can I ask you something?"

"Of course."

"What's her name?"

She looked at me as though she didn't understand the question.

"You don't know her name? What do you mean? Hasn't she told you her name?"

"Nobody at the Factory knows it." I answered. "Apart from Havstein. He might know it. It has something to do with those buses of hers, and not wanting anybody to know who she was, what her name was. So we've only ever called her NN."

"No Name?"

"Exactly."

She looked at her daughter in the bed. A bird might have flown past the window, a faint smile might have crossed her lips, revealing so much. But it didn't. Nothing happened.

"Sofia. Her name is Sofia."

Then she got up, took her jacket from the hook, buttoned up the buttons, turned to me again.

"Do you think she'll get better?"

I thought about it. I knew what she wanted me to say. But I didn't say it.

"No," I said.

I continued visiting Sofia as often as possible, several times a week, but never saw her mother again. Perhaps she stopped coming, perhaps she just chose different times, other days, but our paths never met, never a trace of her when I came in the room.

The woods near the driveway into Hvítanesvegur was somehow never the same after the accident. It just shrank, no matter how much planting we did, and in the end there were hardly any woods there at all, just a cluster of ragged trees that most people drove right past, and the work was reduced to a couple of days a week, if the town council called us at all. Otherwise I sat at home at the Factory and waited, went to Palli's job with him some days, helped out in various ways, did some welding, carried crates of fish, went in the van with the drivers taking fish into Tórshavn, then took the bus home.

Or I read.

I read *Fielding's Guide to the Caribbean plus the Bahamas*.

Seven hundred and ninety pages and not a single photograph.

Havstein's endless notes, underlinings, and added slips of paper.

Didn't it ever occur to him that all the information was completely outdated? That Montserrat had been almost completely obliterated by the volcanic eruption in the nineties?

That Baby Doc no longer ruled Haiti?

It didn't seem to make any difference.

Not really.

Strange how the whole Factory was quieter after Sofia disappeared. Not that it had been noisy before, but we all started to move around more quietly now, trod with lighter feet, avoided making the stairs creak, as though any loud noise might result in catastrophic consequences. We didn't walk on pins, we walked on memories and we all wore invisible memory-cleansing suits, masks, helmets, and bullet-proof vests, we were beyond each other's reach, when we talked it was about trivialities, about the weather, the car that needed fixing, a few brief exchanges about Sofia. Nobody suggested cleaning her room out, nobody said what we all knew, what we all thought, that whatever happened, she'd never come back. And that whatever happened, the Factory would never be the same. Neither did anyone say what Havstein must have thought all along, that he'd have problems the day the government contacted him about placing anybody new up here. Because it would be impossible for anybody new to come now. Without our noticing, or thinking about it, the boundaries had slowly glided out, further and further out, until they'd finally disappeared, and somewhere along the way the divide between institution and home had been completely eradicated by the great nothing. There was almost nothing left of the post-psychiatric home I'd come to that previous summer, where Havstein watched over us like a father. It had become nothing more than an oversized yet ordinary home, where we lived on the generosity of a state that still believed it paid for a functioning institution. As to Havstein, he spent most of his time in Múli, left each morning and came home in the evenings, was often tired, said less and less. I began to cook again, dinner when we were all there in the evening. Carl usually came in and helped me put out the plates, silverware, glasses, water, before everybody else came into the kitchen, took their places, ate from their plates, drank from their glasses.

And the days went on as though nothing had happened, rolling indefatigably on until one early afternoon in the middle of June, I was on my knees in the field at the end of Hvítanesvegur, with the sun burning on my neck and my fingers burrowed deep into the wet earth which I was preparing for the day's tree planting. Herluf and Jógvan had driven in to the council to discuss the vacation schedule for the next month, unlike me they were employed full time by the council, doing a variety of work, tree planting, road work, anything required, and I was alone in the field, apart from the even stream of cars passing by up on the road, and the occasional sheep wandering past on the lookout for better grass. Herluf and Jógvan often went off on errands like this when we worked, so I was used to working alone for long stretches, and when they said they had to take a trip to town I was only too pleased, I could work at my own pace, concentrate on what I was doing, until nothing existed beyond my two hands as they worked in front of me, fingers stretching and closing on the earth before me, the small patch that changed appearance moment by moment, while the big landscape was reduced to a vague backdrop somewhere in the distance. Even the sounds around me entwined themselves into one amorphous hum of cars, birds that sang or only cried wishing they didn't exist, the wind or the rain in the grass.

Maybe it was because it broke so sharply with the rhythm that I heard the sound of the car so clearly as it stopped on the bend above. Cars didn't usually stop there. Car doors opened and shut. A trunk opened and shut. My hands were in the wet ground, and I knew who it was before I'd even turned.

Hadn't I expected him to come sooner or later?

I turned to see Father walking down the slope toward me, a huge suitcase in his hand and a taxi disappearing back toward town. He zigzagged slowly towards me between the waterlogged holes in the field, clinging to his luggage, the only thing he knew that was safe from home.

Good God, how Father hated to travel.

I loved him then, in that moment, as I saw his face with that anxious expression, that worried brow, how much it had cost him to come here, to sit on a plane, to call Havstein to find out where I was, to talk to people until he found somebody who could drive him out here to find me, all the thoughts he'd had about what might happen when the taxi set him down and I was nowhere to be seen.

I stood up with gardening gloves on my hands and watched him as he walked toward me. I didn't go to meet him. Nor was it necessary. Father crossed the field and the boundaries, one foot before the other, in calm, rhythmic steps as he looked around in all directions.

Yet I think he smiled as he walked.

I'm almost certain of it.

And when he finally reached me, I gave him a hug, suitcase standing on the grass beside us, I hugged him hard and said nothing. Thought then about Sofia, who slept and thought of nothing, about Jørn who I hadn't spoken to for more than a year, about Helle, about whose whereabouts I knew nothing, nor who she slept with, about all the people I'd hidden from over the years.

I stood with Father before me.

"You came after all," I said.

"Of course I came. I would have come sooner or later."

I wanted to say so much, but couldn't think what.

Looked up at a totally blue sky.

"Good flight?" I asked.

Father shook his head.

"Horrible, I thought we'd never get here."

"You can take the boat the other way. To Bergen. It takes twenty-four hours, but it's a nice trip. You like the sea better than the air anyway."

"True. Mattias? What are you are doing here?"

"I'm planting trees," I said, knowing that that wasn't what he was asking about.

"Why don't you come home? Mother misses you very much."

"And you?"

"Me too."

"Maybe I'll come home this summer," I said.

"You promise? Not like last time, when you said you'd missed the flight?"

"I did miss the flight!"

"All right."

"I'll come soon. There are more flights during the summertime."

He wanted me to come with him there and then, in a day or two, for us to take the boat back together, he wanted to be on the safe side, and I explained why I couldn't leave yet, told him many things, not yet everything, that had happened these last months, since I'd last talked to him, all the things I'd left unsaid in my postcards.

"I, we broke the lease on your apartment. Since we didn't hear from you." I could hear from his voice that Father had a bad conscience. "It seemed stupid to keep paying for it, when you weren't there, don't you think? So we brought your things back home. Your car's there too."

"That's fine. I was going to move out anyway."

Tried to make a joke of it, but neither of us found it particularly funny. I picked up the thread again. "I don't know if I can live back at home again. I might be a little too old for that."

"We've talked about that, and we thought you could live at the cabin, until you find a flat."

"In Jæren?"

"Yes. I've talked with some of the neighbors, and we could probably get you a job at one of the local farms for the summer, if you want."

Father had thought of everything.

I'd barely thought about anything.

When Herluf and Jógvan came back half an hour later, Father and I were sitting against one of the tree trunks in the field, squinting into the sun and feeling okay, I explained the situation to Herluf, who thought it was just great, he was a soft-hearted guy, and it was fine if I wanted to take the rest of the day off, so I took Father over to the car, put his suitcase in the trunk, drove us through town, and stopped off to do some shopping at the SMS Center, and Father bought a book of knitting patterns, some souvenirs for Mother and a white T-shirt with a picture of a goat and the words *I Love the Faroe Isles* in blue, he put it on right away, and we got back into the car, drove toward the Factory in Gjógv, me contemplating how to explain my life up there, how things had changed when we'd pulled Carl from the water, after Sofia had been injured and things had darkened at the edges, and why I still hadn't changed my mind and come home.

As it turned out, Father needed very little explanation; Mother and he had been updated a great deal more than I'd imagined. Already during that first phone call to my parents, Havstein had explained what kind of place this was, and how it might be better for me to stay for a while. Which was why they hadn't called. But Havstein hadn't stopped there, he'd filled them in during the autumn and the spring, calling once a month or thereabouts, telling them how things were with me. Which was why they hadn't pestered me.

Now Father's visit took the shape of a parents' evening.

We sat out on the rocks overlooking the harbor, Havstein, Father, and I.

We discussed things.

Cleaned out the engine, you might say.

"Do you feel we've gone behind your back, Mattias? By not telling you I've talked with your parents so much?" Havstein asked.

"No, not really," I answered. "Maybe it was a bit extreme."

"I didn't want you to have to think about it," said Havstein.

"Did you ask Father to come over?"

"No," interjected Father, and smiled proudly. "That was my idea."

"It was a good one."

Havstein flicked through his imaginary psychiatry textbook and came up with a suggestion.

"Maybe you two would like to be alone for a little while?"

"Thank you," said Father, taking Havstein's hand and giving it a long, firm shake.

"Quality time," I said.

So we sat there. Father and son, on the grass overlooking the harbor, with a view as far as the North or South Pole for anybody capable of looking over the globe and beyond the horizon, hadn't thought we'd ever sit like this, here, that I'd have this feeling of being taken care of by my father again.

"Do you want to talk about Sofia?" he said.

"Sofia?"

"She's in the hospital, I understand. An accident?"

"That's right. She could die at any time. We'd better sit still."

"What?"

"The butterfly effect," I said. "The beat of a butterfly's wings can change the weather."

"You're in love with that girl, aren't you? With Sofia?"

"You don't need to do this, Father. I'm not fourteen, you know."

"No, that's true. That's true. You're right. My mistake."

He was quiet for a moment. Then he said:

"What really happened to you, Mattias?"

It was funny to hear him say it like that. *What had happened to me.* It made me uneasy. My heart beat harder in my chest, and I was frightened he might notice.

"Did you know the sea level is constantly rising? By a centimeter each year. It's true. And the land only rises an average of four millimeters a year. The figures don't balance. Don't you think that's scary?"

"Mattias."

"And Iceland lies directly over two continental plates. Which is why there's so much volcanic activity there. The country could be ripped in two at any moment. Don't you ever think about that?"

"Mattias, what's happened to you? Why are you talking like this?"

And then I said it:

"I think I just fell apart a little."

"Because of Helle?"

I shrugged my shoulders.

"Not just that. It was everything put together, I think. So much happened. Karsten had to give up the nursery, then Helle left, and Jørn got me over here, tried to get me involved with the band, one way or another. By the way, did you know more and more nursing homes have started to buy their flowers from supermarkets? Well, they have. That's not exactly going the right way." I looked at Father, before adding: "I was about to be discovered again, can you understand that? Just when I'd managed to disappear. But I'm better now. Thanks for asking."

Father seemed troubled. He put a hand behind his head, massaged his neck and sighed.

"Mattias, it's impossible not to leave tracks behind you. There'll always be somebody to see you. Always somebody that loves you. Almost always. That's just how things are."

"It's not that. It's not that I don't want to leave tracks, I just don't want them to be visible to the whole world. I don't need to leave my handprint in the cement. I don't need to be interviewed about what I do. Is that such a problem? Not needing to be seen? We don't all want to be in the front row. Somebody has to choose to be number two."

"But why does it have to be you?"

"Because the world doesn't go around in any other way."

He shook his head, took my hand.

"Have you heard of Olga Omelchenko?" I asked, knowing he hadn't. "She was field doctor for the 37th Guard Division in the Soviet Union, she saved a life in 1943. She'd survived one of the biggest battles that year, and when the bombardment eventually stopped, she crawled over to a soldier who lay close by, his arm was a complete mess, and she knew she had to amputate if he was going to live. But she had no anesthetic. She had no knife, no scissors, nothing." I paused briefly. "So she used her teeth, gnawed through the flesh and bandaged his arm, and he lived into old age."

"Mattias!"

"It's true." And I reeled off all the other names I remembered, the facts I'd been collecting since I was a child, stories about Emmanuel Bove and Nino Rota, about Maria Oktiabrskaia whose husband was killed at the front, who used all her savings to buy a T-34 tank and went to join the war against Germany, age thirty-eight, about Tenzing Norgay, the sherpa who reached the top of Everest with Sir Edmund Hillary in 1953, but whom almost nobody remembered, I told him about Jack Purvis, the eccentric American jazz musician who traveled to Europe with his band but deserted them on the first night, climbed over the roof of a Paris hotel in his stocking feet, later he played with the great Coleman Hawkins and Higginbotham, then went to California and worked as a chef, then wrote the music for a one-hundred-ten piece orchestra for Warner Bros. before going back to playing in small clubs in New York, he vanished again, only to pop up in the US Army, later he sat in prison for armed robbery in El Paso and broadcasted concerts from inside. He failed to turn up to meet his parole officer after his release, was jailed again, and when he eventually got out again, it was 1946 and the war was over. It's less clear what happened next, some said he began work as a commercial pilot, and others thought they'd seen a man who looked like him sitting in the garden of the king's palace in Honolulu, playing *Flight of the Bumble Bee*, alternating between trombone and trumpet. He was also observed in Baltimore working as a carpenter, as a cook on an international ship, he lived under numerous aliases, always avoided being connected to his name, didn't want to be recognized, got a job as a radio repairman in San Francisco, and so I went on, an encyclopedia, an ancient scroll flowing with forgotten biographies, and the more I talked, the more I remembered, they tumbled out of my mouth, like pearls on a string, all the lives you forgot, but that somehow touched you, I talked about how Armstrong, Aldrin, and Collins decided they shouldn't have their names on the insignia for Apollo 11, because their mission was greater than any one man, I talked about the athletes that came second to Carl Lewis when he won four gold medals in the 1984 Los Angeles Olympics, Steve Ballmer, the man who worked under Bill Gates at Microsoft, and about President Paul von Hindenburg, who, weary of everything, relinquished the struggle to hold back the pressure, resigned, and gave a much younger upstart the place he screamed for, named him Chancellor, and disappeared himself, and Adolf Hitler, forty-two years younger, took the power in 1933.

"But why do you always have to give up," said Father, "pass up all your chances? Can't you just accept that people want to spend time with you? That you make people around you happy? Is it that dangerous to have a little focus on you? You don't have to be world famous because of that. I just can't understand why you have to take all the world's sins on your shoulders and go into hiding from the world, and work in some kind of penal colony."

"You don't understand. There are no chances to miss," I said. "I haven't lost out on anything, I haven't given anything up. Think of the people that collect the garbage outside your house, the train driver who takes you where you want to go, the projectionist who stands in the control room and makes sure everything's set when you and Mother go to the movies. The ambulance driver. The woman who cleans your hotel room after you've left. You don't see them. You don't know them. But you appreciate them doing their jobs, don't you? That they take care of you? What if that's all I want to do? Take care of someone. I just want to do something right."

"Yes, of course—"

"What I do is important, isn't it?"

"Yes—"

"I contribute to the gross national product too, don't I? I do just as important a job as most people. It's just that I don't want there to be so much fuss because of it. I just want to be left in peace. Haven't you ever liked the thought that you were one of thousands of cogs in some massive machine, that your contribution was worthwhile even though nobody saw it?"

"But you don't work for a Japanese production company. You're not a machine, Mattias."

"No. I'm not. Do you know what I'm most afraid of?"

"What?"

"That I'll be useless. The movie of the week on a defunct TV channel. That I'll only be in the way and get nothing done. That terrifies me," I whispered.

I could see I'd upset Father, he sat closer, put an arm around my shoulder. "You'll never be useless," he said, giving weight to every word. "You are the most meaningful thing I have. You are all that is good in my life. You, and Mother. But you should just relax a bit. Things will work themselves out, you just need to take it easy, at first."

And I believed him.

"It's just that this has gone on far too long now," he continued. "You've become more and more closed off in the last few years, didn't you notice? In the end it wasn't even possible to live with you. And even now you can't see that there are people desperate to be with you. Sofia, for example. Don't you see that?"

I said nothing. Kept mum. Zipped my mouth.

"Your cog needs repairing, Mattias, that's all. You've just been ill again, it's nothing to be scared of, and it'll all turn out all right in the end, you're in safe hands, I understand, and—"

"What do you mean 'again'?" I interrupted. "That I'm ill again?"

And so it came. Father's big avalanche. And I realize now that I must have known about these things all along, but that they'd simply been erased from my memory as I grew older. They'd been repressed or simply stored away, packed in rough boxes and taped down with brown carpenter's tape.

Something serious had happened in 1983. I was fourteen, and then one day when Mother and Father returned from work, the door to my room was locked. I refused to come out. They tried everything, but I locked myself further and further into my room. All they heard was the sound of me barricading the door and windows with furniture. I didn't eat for a week. Crept out of hibernation, out into the bathroom at night, when I knew they were asleep. Somebody came to talk to me, a voice I didn't recognize, pulled a chair up to my door and talked to me, asked how I felt. I didn't answer. Not until late into the second day of his sitting there. Finally I gave up. Moved the desk and let him in, it was a doctor that Mother had got hold of. Don't remember what we talked about, don't remember what it was. Just remember that I never wanted to come out again.

But I came out. Or, at least, not voluntarily. I screamed. I ranted, but they dragged me out, and I sat in the backseat of the car, huddled up under the window, and we drove through the streets, and I didn't want to be seen.

1983. Autumn in Stavanger and I only wake up on Tuesdays, don't know why. Apart from then, I sleep. I sleep through the weeks and when I wake up the sheets are always freshly washed, it smells like soap in the room and there's never any dust on the windowsill. The room is hot, I want to open the windows and let in the fresh air, but I'm not allowed. I'm informed that it's aired when I'm out. I don't know if that's true. Then I fall asleep again, and my dreams are always the same, but I never remember them. Father comes on alternate days. On the other days I do nothing. Father brings tea in a thermos. He's never drunk tea before, I don't know why he's started now, I'm not even particularly fond of it. But we sit in our chairs, and drink tea and talk about the streets outside. *They're still the same,* he says. *They're all waiting for you, they have all the time in the world.* I try to picture them, and then Mother comes through the door. Hangs her coat on the coatrack by the wardrobe, sits on the edge of the bed.

"Well?" she says, always the same word, it's meant as a question and I give the same answer every time.

"I'm okay. Thanks for asking."

I'm a polite person.

None of us says anything. There are no conversations left to be had. Several times. I look at the clock over the door. It's going backward, and I think how in backward-land anything might happen, they're all equally crazy and strange there, all of them. And I am in backward-land. There's no doubt about that. And it's raining outside, it's been raining since I arrived, it'll reach the window sill soon, it'll flow between the cracks and lift the beds from the floor, sweep us out and down the hallway, if nobody does anything.

Suddenly I get up, walk to the wardrobe. I take out my jacket, put it on, search for my shoes.

Father: "Mattias, where are you going?"

Me: "I think it's time to go, isn't it?"

It's the same each time they come. That's just how it is. I want to go home. But it's too early.

Mother comes over to me, hugs me, takes my jacket off. I sit back in the chair, drink tea.

"Don't make things more complicated than they already are," she says.

"Do you think they're complicated? That's really not the intention."

"We're all victims here, Mattias. This is difficult for everyone."

"Is it?"

"Yes."

I look out of the window. The snow is heavy on the trees, a branch gives way, snow gushes down the trunk.

"Look," I say. "The snow came down. That means a man just fell off his bicycle in China. Or somebody's won the lottery."

"Does it?"

"Yes, it's the butterfly effect. It's true."

"I didn't know that."

"That's how things are."

I go home for the second weekend. Out on loan. By the hour. Handled with care. And that evening I'm transported back as though I were plutonium. I get presents I don't know what to do with. In the communal room there's *Elvis—Aloha from Hawaii* on TV. I go back to my room, hide under the covers, and when I creep out again, time has jumped forward, I don't know how it's happened, but I've missed over three weeks and Mother is standing next to Jørn beside my bed, and she asks where I've put my jacket.

At first, I don't understand anything, nobody's said anything to me, not as far as I know, but it seems this is the day I'm to be let out, and Mother gets my jacket from the wardrobe, while I sit on the bed doing nothing, she places it beside me, excuses herself for a moment, leaves the room. Jørn sits in the visitor's chair searching for something to say, but can't think of anything, we don't know each other very well, Mother must have contacted him, we don't have a lot to say to each other, so I say:

"I hear you've started a band. What's it called?"

"Perkleiva. Best band ever. Better than Feige Knep. You've got to come and hear us one day, we've got some shit-hot stuff going on."

"Great."

Mother returns with one of the nurses, they stand beside each other, both with arms crossed, looking like old friends.

"I think we're ready to go," says Mother, but I don't know whether it's me she's talking to, or the nurse. I get up anyway, obediently, put my jacket on.

"It was nice to meet you, Mattias, good-bye for now," says the woman in white, as I follow Jørn and Mother out of the door.

"Nice to meet you too. Have a nice weekend."

"It's Tuesday, Mattias."

"One can never be too early."

"True. Look after yourself."

We stand outside the large brick building while Mother looks for her car keys and exchanges pleasantries with Jørn. I feel like a stuffed animal, on the way between two exhibitions, automatically taking the pose I assume they want me in, but I don't think either of them notices.

Mother asks Jørn if he'd like a lift, but he lives nearby, has a bicycle, it's not far, but thanks. And then, to me:

"I'll call you, in the next day or so. Maybe we can do something."

"I'd like that," I answer.

He nods to Mother and is about to go.

"Jørn," I call after him, and he stops.

"Yes?"

"Will you call?"

"Yes, of course. See you."

"Yes," I say, mostly to myself.

Then he goes. Again.

I prowl at my mother's side over to the car, she's practically parked the car in the middle of the road, frightened of it being blocked in by other cars. Clutching my plastic bag I wait. She opens the door, gets in and opens my side, I get in, pull the seat belt across my chest, check it's fastened, Mother starts the car and we drive through town, through the streets, and home.

But that's in November 1983, a long time ago, I should have remembered it, and if I did know about it all along, I should have mentioned it to Havstein ages ago, or I should now at least, later tonight, explain the real situation to him, explain that this had happened before, and that I hadn't known what it was then either, that things like that just happen. But I didn't. Since this was, after all, different, bigger. I said nothing. Stayed mum. Was embarrassed. Full of secrets you wouldn't want to know about.

"Father?" I said after a while, "Do you remember the moon landing?"

"Of course I remember. It was a Sunday. July the twentieth was a Sunday. I was so frightened that night. That something might go wrong, with you. We'd waited so long."

"For the moon landing?"

"For you," he answered. "And for the moon landing too, I suppose."

We leaned our heads back, but there was no moon. Only clouds. Approaching rain.

"But do you know what I remember best?"

"No."

"The first American to orbit the earth."

"John Glenn?"

"John Glenn. February 20, 1962. He orbited the earth three times. We sat glued to the radio. John Glenn made three orbits of the earth before he was forced to return in his capsule, what was it called? Something to do with friends, I think."

"*Friendship 7.*"

"Yes, that's right, *Friendship 7*. That was dramatic, I remember, part of the heat shield loosened, they didn't know whether he'd be able to pass through the atmosphere on his return or whether he'd burn up. But it went okay. And over two hundred and fifty thousand Americans went to meet him in the rain on his return. I remember *that*."

"I've read about that," I said. "The oldest astronaut on the Mercury Program. A really good guy, I'd bet."

"A fantastic person. For sure. What happened to him, I wonder?"

"I don't know. But did you know that all the inhabitants of Perth switched their lights on that night, so he'd see them as he passed over the west coast of Australia?"

"Yes, that's right. I'd forgotten that. Do you know if he saw them?'

"Definitely."

"A wonderful thing to do. Wouldn't happen today."

"Probably not."

We said no more on that subject. We went in to the others instead, and it was one of those evenings you never forget, an evening when your father blends in with all your friends, and it seems somehow natural to see him sitting in one of the armchairs in the Factory, and he slips so naturally into the picture and you want to tell him all the stories you've been keeping to yourself because you thought that they'd be of no interest, that he'd be unable to relate to the life you live, that he'd think the things you care about were unimportant, but as you start talking, explaining, you see it's not like that, although you know the distance between you will return tomorrow, a closeness, yes, but distance, a natural barrier, so you hurry to say all you can, to fill out the picture of yourself, and the conversation spreads to everybody in the room, Havstein, Palli, Anna, and Carl, all of them join in, and you fetch some beers from Cloakroom A, give your father a beer and he opens it with a lighter that lies on the table, you've never seen that before, thought he could only open beers with a bottle opener, you see yourself in him, as you'll be, it makes you smile, because there's some security in that, and it hits you that it's these details, these nuances, that define the people around you and that your ignorance of them and their routines are the price you pay for holding yourself on the periphery, where you've thought, and continue to think that you can't get hurt, that you're invulnerable, bulletproof. And so you consider what you've missed, how you'd have liked to go on vacation with your father, just the two of you, boys on an adventure, you could have gone anywhere, could have discovered things together, shared the same experiences and when you'd got back home, you could have continued talking about all the experiences you'd shared, and years later you'd have been able to start sentences with *do you remember that crazy woman we saw in Tennessee that morning, on that corner, by the old store?* But it won't ever be like that, there are always these distances in the long run, big distances, we're pulled in so many directions and don't take enough care of each other, and what remains is the memory of an evening like this, carved in stone, a family's wall relief, but it isn't sad, this is how it should be, your father, your very own Man in the Yellow Hat sitting in the chair beside you.

Father stayed until the Saturday that week. We fitted a visit in to Slættaratinður and to the place where Havstein had watched Aldrin and Armstrong train in the sixties, we got the British weather forecast on Útvarp Föroya Radio and managed to organize two seats on a helicopter trip from Tórshavn out to Sofia's and Mikines' island of Mykines on Thursday, watched the Gulf Stream passing below us, keeping us warm, watched the big ships that passed the islands far out on their way to Europe, and Father talked about how things were at home, about Mother, about what he did, trivialities, insignificant events that were nice to hear about, didn't mention Helle at all, Jørn had called a couple of times after Christmas apparently and they'd talked a little, good old Jørn, Father liked him, always had. We visited Tinganes, where the Parliament had once met, looked at the few buildings that had been left standing after the catastrophic fire of 1673, Father took pictures, documented every nook and cranny of his trip, and I had to stand up straight in every picture, look into the camera, smile, that was the way he liked it. We visited Sofia in the hospital, she lay as she had during the last weeks, no change, but I wanted Father to see her, and we sat next to her bed as I explained what had happened, sentence by sentence.

What else did we talk about during those days? I don't remember, but I remember that it was nice having him there, that we all went to Café Natúr before he left, and Father told Carl jokes, he doubled up over the table with laughter, I didn't know Father had it in him, but he certainly did, had the gift, we didn't discuss the possibility of my traveling home, not before Father and I had some moments alone outside the Factory when we came home that night, I promised I'd come that summer.

"Of course I'll come," I said.

"When?"

"Soon."

"Are you sure?"

"Yes," I answered. "Very sure."

I drove Father to the airport the next day, with Havstein and Carl in the back. We made a trip out of it, and Father promised to come back to visit us again, and bring Mother this time, guaranteed, nothing ever came of it of course, and it was never mentioned again. A year from now there wouldn't be anybody left at the Factory anyway, nobody to visit. And we'd leave our tracks in the village, in the streets, but they'd stop where the land stopped and the sea began. We just didn't know it yet.

----■----

I stand in the bathroom in Gjógv brushing my teeth, put the radio on above the sink, listen to the news with half an ear as I stare at my face in the mirror. It changes from day to day. Some days more than others. Not a lot, of course, but if you look closely, train yourself, concentrate, you'll see minuscule changes in the skin, a wrinkle on the brow that's changed overnight, by just half a millimeter, maybe, but you can see it, with practice. Your contours grow finer, your silhouette weaker. But you're still not quite gone. It takes time. Years. But you're vanishing. Vanishing from yourself, transforming into another, every day, so you're no longer the person you were. The microscopic cells that formed your face in the photograph your parents have hanging in their living room are gone, exchanged for others. You're no longer who you were. But I am still here, the atoms may swap their places, but nobody can control the dance of the quarks. And the same applies to the people you love. With almost stationary velocity they crumble in your arms, and you wish you could cling onto something permanent in them, their skeleton, their teeth, brain cells, but you can't, because almost everything is water, impossible to grasp. And gradually every trace they left is gone, the house they once lived in, the drawings they made for you, the words they wrote on scraps of paper that vanished. And you're left with memories, and they too finally fall away, like old wallpaper, and with time the same will go for this planet on the edge of this utterly peripheral galaxy, and it will be impossible to answer the question: was there life there? Did anybody live there? On earth? And my thoughts run on.

I was sitting in the passenger seat in a car outside Tvøroyri on Suðuroy when I was told that Sofia was dead. The Thursday after Father had left. An average afternoon, the kind of day nobody remembers once its gone, one of those days when it doesn't rain, but the weather's not too good either. And later, when the police interrogate witnesses about their whereabouts that day, none of them can remember.

I hadn't visited her for four days.

There wasn't any particular reason, things probably just hadn't worked out that way.

I regretted it now.

Havstein had been to some guy's house to pick up some papers, I never asked what they were, I'd just come for the ride, never been to Suðuroy before, and when he came out of the house with his cell phone in his hand I knew something was wrong, something had happened over which he had no control.

He sat in the car.

"Sofia died today," he said, simply.

I wasn't surprised. I'd expected it. Sooner or later. Nevertheless I had a sinking feeling, this was the price you paid, I thought, for growing attached to people.

Nothing is more irrevocable.

Absolutely nothing.

I said nothing. Gazed out the car window. Maybe it was raining. Maybe it wasn't. It made no difference.

"When?" I asked.

"This morning," he answered. "Quarter past eight."

I thought about what I'd been doing at that precise moment. I'd been in the bathroom, brushing my teeth, an unremarkable moment. Had I been thinking I should go and visit her again? That I loved her? No. Not then. Later that day, maybe, almost certainly. But not at that moment. I'd done nothing special. Almost nothing.

It had been a completely ordinary day.

Maybe that's the way it is, maybe those are the days that people die. Ordinary days.

"Was there anybody with her?" I asked.

"Her mother was there. It was her that called. She was there all night I think."

For a moment I was hurt that nobody had called me in the night, told me and asked me to come down to the hospital.

But I couldn't expect that.

"Do you know when, when the funeral is?"

"Tuesday. One o'clock. In Saksun."

"Saksun? Why is she being buried there."

"I don't know. Because it's nice there? Her mother wanted it."

"Why?"

"I don't know. That's how it is."

Havstein started the car and we moved off in the direction of Drelnes to catch the seven o'clock ferry back to Tórshavn. I sat there beside him, and as we drove on board I imagined Sofia, who had, quite unaware, begun to die early that morning, without resistance, while her mother sat at her side losing the last of her family in the country.

I thought about things I'd read. That when a person's dying, they lose their senses minutes before. One after the other. First the sense of taste, later the ability to smell. Then their sight goes. Their sense of touch. Hearing. The sensation of pain. Like turning out the lights and leaving the office for the day, locking up after oneself, and losing the key on the way home.

I didn't go all the way home with Havstein, instead I got out at Tórshavn and took the bus home instead, as Sofia had hundreds of times through the years. I thought she deserved that. Then I remembered the patient files. Was she dead because she'd removed her record from the archive? Maybe she'd already erased herself there, removed herself from the larger community? Wiped herself out. Or was it the trigger points, the loneliness, the isolation that was already there from the outset, or it might have been because she came from Mykines, just as Anna's painter had, or that a puffin had flown past one day, looked at her with narrowed eyes, or simply changed the air stream around her by a fraction with the beat of its wings, starting the whole thing off? Nobody knew. I stood at the bus stop, waited for a bus, chose the longest route home, it took almost two hours to get to Funningur, then I walked the last miles, went up the footpath that wound tightly back and forth to Slættaratindur, and then took the long, gently sloping road from there and down toward Gjógv, and when I got down to the Factory and went in, they'd already gone to bed, all of them, not a sound in the house, only my quiet footsteps up the stairs.

GRAN TURISMO

I

Borrowed a black suit from Palli for the funeral the next Tuesday. It rained. I wish I could have said that the weather was nice that day, that as we drove down to Saksun the Faroes looked completely different than they had during all the months I'd been there. I wish I could have told you that there was something in the air that day as we crammed ourselves into the Subaru, in our black suits and dresses, that the wind was unusually mild in the hour it took us to drive, that it felt as though the entire country held its breath. But it didn't. It was the most ordinary day of all, the kind of day when there were only repeats of repeats on TV, and the clouds were the same as they'd been for days, for 99.4 percent of the population it was a day nobody would remember, except for people who had birthdays, or who were fired from their jobs, or who'd finally left home or the country, people who'd remember this date forever as the day things changed, for better or for worse.

It was a Tuesday. That was how it was.

Averageness's own day. The wasted days' parade.

I got up early, got dressed, sat at the breakfast table, ate my breakfast in my suit and read the medical dictionary, I'd found it up in Havstein's room. Read about death. I'd never really thought about it before, nobody close to me had ever died, I'd been to hardly any funerals, apart from Grandma and Grandpa who'd died ten or twelve years previously, I remembered it being sad, missing them. But that was still different. It was harder to comprehend that Sofia was never coming back. Grandma had been a lovable but peripheral person, but Sofia had filled every room around me. If I closed my eyes, I could still bring back the feeling of my arm around her on the day we'd sat in the car from Klaksvík, the feel of her ribs against my fingers. I thought about how she'd never sit at the kitchen table again, never reach for the orange juice, pour it in a glass with one hand, rest her head on the other, elbow on the table, and sigh. Never again would I get frustrated about her sitting on my bed and scrunching up the duvet that I'd just smoothed out so nicely. She'd never take that plane to Copenhagen, and I thought how there'd forever be a spare seat on that plane, each time it flew, and no bus would ever be full. Nobody would ever lie in her bed. Nobody would play the Cardigans. There was one person less to report microscopic events to, one Christmas present less to think about. One more person who could never disappoint you. Time would force you to live as though she never existed.

I went up to Carl's room, found him sitting in a chair in the middle wearing his pajamas.

"Hi," I said.

"Hi."

"You all right?"

He sat up straight in his chair and brushed his thighs.

"Yes, I'm okay."

"You sure?"

"Yes."

"Good, maybe it's time to get dressed?" I said, and gestured toward my own suit.

"You're probably right. What's the time?"

"A quarter past ten," I answered.

"And how's the weather?"

I saw that his curtains were pulled back. He sat, half turned toward the view.

"It's raining."

"Thought so. I thought it should rain today. Didn't you?"

"Maybe. I don't know."

"Have you seen my suit?"

"It's hanging in the bathroom," I answered.

"It's probably time for me to put my suit on."

"I think you're right."

"Five minutes. I'll meet you all downstairs in five minutes, okay?"

I said *fine*, went back down, Anna and Palli were sitting in the living room, Havstein was standing in front of the kitchen mirror doing his tie.

"I can drive if you want," I said.

"No, you don't need to. But thanks for the offer."

He got his tie straight, looked at himself in the mirror. Then he looked at me.

"Have you decided what you'll sing in church?"

"Yes," I answered.

-- -- ■ -- --

Funerals on the Faroe Islands aren't like the ones in Norway, where you can barely fill the front pews, but where the pews at the back are filled with curious retirees determined to keep themselves updated, and where the priest alternates between three or four ready-written sermons giving you the sense that all he's done is fill in the dead person's name and geographic location, a formula, *and he who believes in me will live on forever dead or not, have a good trip, and our loss is great and terrible* and so forth, and the priest pats the coffin, uses the first name of the person he's never met, proclaims how much they loved life, *he had so many friends, there was so much more she wanted to do, he had so many plans*, nobody knows where the Lord might jump, his ways are as mysterious as the rush hour traffic in Rome. It's like fortune telling in tea leaves, vague presumptions that are only roughly right.

On the Faroe Islands you didn't need to ask your boss for time off to go to a funeral.

People went because for each person that died there was one less inhabitant, one less person to meet on the road, one less person who spoke the same language.

And once everyone was in, there was barely space in the church for a hymn.

Over three hundred people came to Sofia's funeral. Two hundred and forty more people, I thought, than she'd talked to during her entire lifetime. The inhabitants of Saksun, and the surrounding villages. Visitors from Gjógv, Mykines, Tórshavn. Family friends. Neighbors. Neighbors' friends. Fellow villagers. We had no idea where they'd all come from. Most couldn't get into the church and stood outside in the rain, listening through open windows. I saw Sofus and his parents too, as I walked down the church to the front pew, tried waving, but he didn't see me, sat looking at the floor, fiddling with his jacket.

Saksun was one of the loveliest places on the Faroes, a tiny village of old, black wooden houses with grass-covered roofs mixed in with new houses that lay at the bottom of the valley where the river flowed out into Lake Pollur, which stretched out to Vestmanna through the narrow gap between two green mountains. And the minuscule church stood on higher ground, a panoramic view.

It was when we drove around the corner that we saw the huge crowd, a heaving carpet of black umbrellas processing toward the church. Havstein lowered his speed, and we rolled gently past them as far as we could, found the parking place that had been reserved for us and melted into the crowd, sat in the front row, and that was when I saw her again, Sofia's mother. She was sitting on the pew to the right, with two other women of her age. I got up and went over to her, and she recognized me instantly.

"Mattias."

"I am so sorry," I said, and gave her a hug. I greeted the two other women briefly, one was an aunt from Denmark, and the other was one of her mother's friends. Neither had much to say.

"She was so tiny that last night," said her mother. "I could almost have put her into my bag and gone." And then, almost as though she'd really considered the idea for a moment, she added, "But I didn't have my bag with me that night."

I wanted to say something, but could think of nothing, just stood there and waited alongside her for a moment, as the church continued to fill with hushed people, little coughs, the creaking of pews, shoes scraping the floor. Havstein came over to us and gave Sofia's mother a hug.

"Thank you for taking care of all this," she said, and gestured around the room. "For organizing all this."

"The least we could do," he answered.

"And for the beautiful flowers."

"Yes, they're beautiful, aren't they. I thought you might like to come up to Gjógv one day, to see how she lived, there might be something you'd like to take back with you."

"That would be nice." Her face vanished into a handkerchief, which flapped as she blew her nose. I stood there between Havstein and her, uncertain what to do with myself.

"Mattias is thinking about singing something," said Havstein.

She took my hand again.

"Sofia said you were very good at that. But why don't you sing more often?"

"It hasn't been necessary," I answered.

"But you must never stop singing, Mattias. Everybody who can sing, must sing. It's no good otherwise."

"Really?"

"Yes."

It goes quiet.

"She talked so much about you."

"So you said."

She took a pause.

"Do you all miss her?"

And for the first time I saw that Havstein found it difficult to answer, he just nodded, his expression blank, turned and walked across to the flowers, shifted a few wreaths, brushed off a little dust, came back and sat down.

"More than we know," I answered.

The priest gave a good sermon, the same priest who'd worked in the hospital where Sofia had stayed in the eighties and early nineties. He talked about buses, a beautiful speech. There was always a bus, he said, but then, there were many buses that never came too, or that didn't follow the schedule, that arrived too early or too late, he talked about taking random buses, about taking bus routes one hadn't tried before and how rare it was to get where one wanted. He used simple images, maybe that was why I liked him. He didn't try to make things more complicated they were. He didn't say Sofia had lots of plans. He didn't say how many things she wanted to see. Places she wanted to go. He didn't say she'd be missed by so many friends. He said that the few who knew her, would miss her as one misses a nation that disappears, a country that sinks into the ocean. And I thought of an old song, a song about a little glass marble, and Sofia was that marble, the tiniest of God's many colored marbles, and it had disappeared from the rest, God had lost it in the sun and now he was on his hands and knees looking for it, but unable to find it. I think that was going through my mind. But I may remember wrong. It's possible that I sat there thinking nothing at all.

And then I sang.

I got up, walked forwards and sang.

And what's important isn't what I sang, but that I did it, and the sound carried in the room, it forced its way several times around the church and through our heads before it squeezed its way through drafty walls, the steeple, and half-open doors and the people outside were warmed for a moment, and they took down their umbrellas in unison, stood motionless as the sound rose above their heads and settled over Saksun like a mist nobody had seen before, and I heard people crying, I heard people unable to hold things back any longer, and the priest turned away for a moment, Havstein held Carl, and Carl sat with eyes lowered, not daring to look over at Sofia's mother, and Anna put her arms around Palli and Palli stared straight ahead, and Havstein smiled at me, and Sofia's mother closed her eyes, and I sang with more power than ever, tried to lift the roof, tried to wrench the beams loose, to pry open the entire building, I wanted the model boat that hung from the ceiling to sail out, and the organist struggled to keep up, scrambling up the scales as I drifted further and further out into the song, and finally I abandoned the entire melody as it should be sung, the organist followed, we abandoned both melody and text so there was nothing left but sound, and the sound wrapped us in a warm wool blanket and took us aboard unsinkable boats, and I transported us across the sea and brought us to land someplace else, and held the final note for as long as I had strength, and then came the silence and you could have heard a bacterium drop from the ceiling and land on the floor.

Not even God could have walked unheard through that room.

And after the funeral we took ourselves to Café Natúr. We had carried Sofia out of the church, placed her on a lowering apparatus over the open grave, lowered her and shoveled the earth back, then we'd stood under our umbrellas while Havstein had a cigarette and thanked everybody that had come for their kindness, shaking people's hands until his wrists ached. We stood there for a while, the remaining five, we looked at each other and hugged each other, before the priest locked the church behind us and we walked over to the car, in silence.

And I said nothing, but I'd already decided. I was going home tomorrow.

– – – ■ – – –

That night at Café Natúr I got drunker than I'd ever been. It felt like the only sensible thing to do. Because I'd decided, enough was more than enough. It was time to go on the big offensive, I wanted to go back, I wanted to be the person I'd once been and I wanted to be the new invention that made all previous models obsolete, I was sure, convinced that it would be all right this time, it was just to turn around and approach it from the other side. I, Mattias, would open myself to the world and reconquer it, no more quietest and nicest boy in the class, rather the invisible man who suddenly appears in the middle of the motorway causing cars to slam on the brakes and skid to the side where they stop, steam rising from their engines, as their drivers sat gawking behind their wheels. I was going back to Stavanger. To Jørn. I might even discuss plans for the band with him, if he was still interested in a new vocalist. So I drank everything I could find that night, until there were no more clean glasses and every bottle was empty, I was a pillow stuffed with fluffy cotton in a soft pillowcase, I wrapped my problems in dreams and sent them away, slipped them into bottles and mailed them off to the waves, to be picked up by trawlers in deep water and cruise ships off course.

A little after midnight, I took Havstein aside and I told him my plans.

"I'm going to Norway tomorrow."

"You're leaving now? Don't you think it would be best to wait a little?"

"I think it's good for me to go home for a while. Father wanted it so much," I answered diplomatically.

"But you'll come back?"

I thought before answering. At length.

"Yes," I said. "In the fall."

Then we went back to the table, and on Havstein's prompting I told them my decision, a murmur went around the group and Carl looked almost despairing, he probably didn't want me to leave now, but didn't dare protest, could see I'd made up my mind, it was time to go, before more of us were damaged. And it was high time for me to leave.

I didn't go back to the Factory that night, didn't go back home with the others. Maybe it was just one of those coincidences that hits blind, maybe God had an interfering hand in it, placed obstacles in my way, placed a girl at my side as I went to buy a beer.

Placed a girl with talking lips in my field of vision.

Her name was Eyðis.

I'd seen her here a few times before, she usually sat at a table near the stairs on the ground floor, with her friends. About my age, maybe a couple of years younger, she had millimeter-short hair, and a tight denim jacket she never took off, and one of the country's weirdest noses, it went sort of up and to the side, and whenever she leaned over the bar, her nose led the way, as if she was sniffing her way to what she wanted before stretching a small hand into the air and ordering.

We stood next to each other.

I was in a good mood. Laughing at everything.

I was deeply unhappy but I didn't know it because I was so happy all the time.

And before I knew it, I was kissing her in the backseat of a cab on the way out to Kollafjørður, long after closing time. I don't know what came over me that night, it just seemed like the only sensible thing to do at the time.

To go back to her place.

The cab stopped on a road, in the middle of nowhere it seemed, I fell out of the backseat with Eyðis, and she had to drag me along, haul me down the path, across a ford which I still managed to flop into, I fell on my back and lay there getting soaked in the water before she got me vertical again, and I wondered why on earth she wanted me to come back with her in my present state, but there you go, for all I know I was a bundle of charm as I reeled happily in front of her along the path that skirted the lake and led up to the summer house at the foot of the mountain. I was malnourished, starving for closeness, a hugs Biafra-child, ready for anything that came my way.

Eyðis lived six months of the year in a summerhouse without electricity, but with running water and a propane stove in the kitchen, a huge living room and two bedrooms. It was nestled in the valley a couple of minutes by car from Signabøur, on the way to Stykkið and Leynar, the view was like a postcard for nature lovers, a heavy mist hung over the mountain on the other side and lay across the road, reducing the cars to moving points of light that came and went. Eyðis took a couple of beers from the fridge and blankets, and we sat up by the waterfall behind the house, talked, listened to the cows that sang or just mooed out there in mist-covered fields. She was, I discovered, three years younger than me, wanted to be a landscape architect and I pondered that there was a lot to wrestle with here, an entire country apparently left to its own devices, just grass and gravel, and there was so much she wanted, and that night I was drawn into all her plans, sounded smart enough, her ideas, sounded sensible, she wanted to open the Faroes up to tourists, wanted to break away from Denmark, show off the Arctic landscape, and it struck me that what she really wanted was for the Faroes to be Iceland, all lava and volcanoes, Björk and Halldór Laxness. It was as though an inferiority complex festered inside her, an idea that wouldn't let her be, constantly telling her she'd been born on the wrong island, hundreds of miles too far east. The price you pay for being born in a country so frequently omitted from the world map, when even the islands of Bouvetya, Jan Mayen, Shetland and Orkney are precisely marked. She talked and talked, about all the things she wanted to do, and I listened dutifully to everything she said, and as I sat there on a rock beside the stream I realized that I'd fallen in love with the Faroes, like a teenager, with all the accompanying traumas. I realized there and then how things stood, if the USA saw itself as a big brother, and most other countries saw themselves, to a lesser or greater degree, as involuntary little brothers, then the Faroes was surely the first foster child, turned out from its family, hidden away, a country you barely think about until one day you come across a brief article about it and suddenly think *well, well, so you really do exist, where have you been in all the confusion? I'd practically forgotten you, and yet I've always missed you.* And then you think you'll never forget it again, from today forward you'll care, from today things will change. But they don't, the instant you turn the page the thought is gone again. I sat contemplating this, and thought: if only you came here, to the Faroe Islands, you might find everything you were looking for, all the things you'd lost, all the keys, important phone numbers, lottery tickets, all the flashy jackets you'd bought abroad, cats that had disappeared and birds that had flown out of windows, people who'd left their apartments one morning never to return, kids you'd been at school with and who you'd never said goodbye to until the last day when you walked through the gates, when you were so certain nothing would ever change you, that you'd always be friends and never lose touch, maybe you might find them here, an entire country for everything you'd forgotten, everything you'd lost, everything that had slipped from view along the way.

Eyðis got up, went into the house and came back out a minute later carrying a cassette player and set it down in the damp grass next to us. Pressed play.

Tuneless vocals and guitar strumming out through the loudspeakers.

"What's that?" I asked.

"Nico. *Chelsea Girl?*"

I shook my head, didn't know it.

"She's from Germany. She was with the Velvet Underground at the start."

"Oh."

So we sat listening to Nico, who'd played in Fellini's *La Dolce Vita*, who'd been a model and who'd been involved with a couple of albums, Lou Reed had written songs for her, she'd been friends with Andy Warhol, and then she'd gone away, died on Ibiza in 1988, aged fifty. She didn't sing that well, but that didn't seem to matter. It was meant to be like that. *I've been out walking. I don't do too much talking these days. These days I seem to think a lot about things that I forgot to do. And all the times I had the chance to.*

True enough.

But it was a bit late to change one's mind now.

That train had gone. And no plane could catch up with it.

It was growing light. Mild rain through mist.

"Come on," said Eyðis getting up. She took the cassette player in one hand and with the other she pulled me into one of the bedrooms, then she took off my clothes and wrapped me up in the narrow bunk bed. Finally she took off her denim jacket, folded it neatly on a chair and crept in beside me, and I clung to every bit of humanity I could grab, in terror it might slip away and that I might wake up nowhere on drenched asphalt again, I floated between the sheets, disappeared into the mattress, slept to the sound of cows that held their breath in the field outside.

I woke up first, and I woke up suddenly. I was lying squashed up against the feeling gone in one arm, I wriggled it free and took a few minutes to get the life back into it. The room was hot, almost oxygen-less, and I wanted to evacuate it immediately. I hesitated for a moment, before deciding not to wake Eyðis. Grabbing hold of the slats in the top bunk, I lifted myself from the mattress, and then wedging my feet between the slats farther down I hung over her, Spider-Man with a bad conscience. I shifted myself sideways toward the floor and got out of the bed without waking her, gathered my clothes and went into the hallway, shutting the door gently after me. I dressed quickly, looked at the clock, half past eleven, went out into the living room. Found Eyðis's cell phone on the living room table and without thinking rang Havstein, just wanted to say I was leaving. He was already up and on his way out.

"Where are you?"

I said where I was, and what had happened, the short version.

"Heavens."

"I'm going now," I said.

"Home?"

"Yes, home. To Norway."

"Do you have a ticket?"

"No."

It was quiet for a moment.

"I'm going down to the harbor now. I can drive you to the airport if you like."

Then a pang of bad conscience hit me because I'd given so little notice, hadn't even told them I was going until last night at the café, and I'd vanished right after, I hadn't even said goodbye to Eyðis, I was just disappearing. I'd gotten pretty good at that. Going off.

"Great," I answered.

"I'll pick you up in just under an hour, along the way."

"Thanks."

"No problem."

"Havstein?"

"Yes?"

I was about to say something, but said something quite different.

"My passport is in the drawer in my bedroom. Can you bring it. And my money?"

"I'll take care of it."

I hung up and crept carefully to the door, fox's tail between my legs, I walked up to the stream where we'd been sitting the previous night,

I sat on a rock and waited. *Two hours from now, I'll be on my way home. Tonight I'll be in Stavanger again.* Strange to think, the time that had passed, one week had turned into a year, that was all, but it had gone so fast, and everything was so far away, and I had no clear idea where I'd start when I got back home. All I knew was that it was time to go back, clear up the mess. I ought to call Jørn, tell him I was coming, suggest we do something. But I couldn't remember the number.

The mist had receded during the course of the morning, and green mountains and fields stretched in every direction now, interrupted only by the road, a straight line drawn straight across the valley and connected to a tunnel into which passing cars vanished. I counted red cars. None came in fifteen minutes. I felt ill, nauseous. I'd drunk a whole bar. I bent down, stuck my head in the stream, held it underwater until I felt the weather clear in my head. Then I heard snorting behind me. A cow came up to the wire fence beside the stream, brown and white, a genuine milk chocolate ad. It stood there close to the fence, staring at me. I stared back.
"Good morning," I said.
I got a vacant look in return.
"And the grass is still green?"
Gaze. Like a camera out of focus.
"Moo," I said.
I was being eyeballed. For a long time. And then it spoke:
"What are you really thinking of doing now?"
I stared at the cow.
"I'm going home," I answered.
"Do you really think that's going to change anything?"
"I'm not sure."
"Why are you going?"
I had no answer. I tore up a fistful of grass, held it up in front of the beast. But it was full. This obviously wasn't the time for lunch. The days were probably long.

"Do you know about Buzz Aldrin?" I asked.

The cow looked away. Snorted.

"Do you think Aldrin was lonely?"

"Why do you always want to be number two?"

"The freedom it gives, maybe."

"What freedom?"

"The freedom to go where you want, and do what you want afterward. The freedom of not being remembered for your achievements. What did you want more than anything when you were a calf?"

"To be a cow."

I nod cautiously.

"Even those who are number two can be disappointed, Mattias. There's no such thing as invisibility."

We stared at each other. I was looking into two enormous eyes.

"Know this, Mattias, we love you—we hold you in high esteem. Know this—you are loved. Do you know this? That you're always seen? That there are people out there who would give everything they have to be with you?"

I patted the cow on the muzzle a couple of times, then it turned, lumbered across the field and stood next to another cow, impassive now, and started grazing. I looked down at my watch. It really was time to leave the country.

A quarter of an hour later the Subaru came to a halt in front of me on the road below. But Havstein wasn't alone in the car. They were all there. Carl in front, Anna and Palli in the back. I got in next to Anna and got a hug.

"Christ," I said, pleased to see everybody. "The whole nuthouse!"

"You didn't think you could just go off like that, did you?" answered Anna, as Havstein started up the car and headed for Kvívík and the underwater tunnel to Vágar and the airport.

They said their goodbyes in the departure hall, hugs and exhortations, they asked when I'd be back and I hesitated a moment before answering October, I'll probably be back in October, I said, and then I asked them to wait while I went to the ticket office. The woman with the pearl-white teeth who'd sat here the last time I was here had been replaced by an older model, a stocky woman who'd had a bad day and barely looked up when I addressed her.

"I'd like a ticket to Oslo or Stavanger," I said.

She looked at me as though that was the most idiotic thing she'd heard all week.

"We don't fly to Norway today," she answered.

"All right, then. Copenhagen."

I pulled the envelope from my jacket pocket, took out the money. The woman behind the counter surveyed me as she considered whether she felt like sending me to Denmark or not.

"When do you want the return for?"

"I want an open ticket. My return will be sudden."

She looked only half satisfied with my answer, but she smiled faintly, or I thought she did. Then she tapped in the appropriate letters and digits.

Ticket in hand I returned to the others, and we all shook hands, hugged one more time, and said we'd see each other soon, time I had a vacation, we said, and I said they could just drive back now, and Anna wished me a good trip, and Havstein told me to look after myself, and call him, and Carl said:

"Make sure to come back. Don't just disappear."

And I said:

"Of course not."

Then we parted ways.

I bought some T-shirts, a couple of wooden sheep and a video about the Faroes in the souvenir shop while I waited for the plane to start boarding.

Made a phone call home. Said I was coming via Copenhagen.

Then my flight was called.

I stood, boarding pass at the ready.

There weren't many of us. I boarded the flight, and we had to distribute ourselves evenly throughout the plane, so there'd be no imbalance in the accounts.

We taxied out onto the runway, gathered speed and vanished into the mists, and for some minutes it was gray outside the windows before we came up over the clouds and I leaned toward the glass, gazed out, the sun was so sharp I had to squint to see anything, I saw blue sky above us, sea, sea, sea in all directions, and below us, a country entirely veiled in mist, haze, and rain that just kept falling.

2

Do you remember Sergey Korolyov? He was a cosmonaut on *Mir*, the space station that had been continually manned since 1986. When he returned to earth on March 25, 1992, he'd been in space for 311 days. Korolyov had been sent up when the Soviet Union was still in existence. When he came down again, everything was gone. The Soviet Union had become Russia, Leningrad had become St. Petersburg and Mikhail Gorbachev was nowhere to be found.

That was how I felt when I got back to Norway. As though somebody had changed all the bricks while I was away, had shuffled the cards and come up with totally new rules.

I stood at the baggage belt at Sola Airport waiting for nothing. I had no baggage, at least not the kind you can show for inspection. I had a plastic bag filled with things I'd bought at the airport at Vágar, a bottle of vodka, some Danish peanuts I'd bought on the flight and some souvenirs. I went through the green doorway, nothing to declare, and nobody flung themselves onto me with gloved hands and triumph in their eyes. In fact, hardly anybody looked at me at all.

And as I came out on the other side, Mother and Father stood there waiting. Their faces lit up as I passed through the doors and it struck me that they looked more or less exactly as they had when I'd left them a year ago. Mother was perhaps a little thinner, a little smaller than I remembered, but it might just have seemed that way, because a lot had changed in Stavanger while I'd been away. Not only had houses been torn down to make way for a new hotel, but it felt as though somebody had pulled the entire town apart, only to put all the streets and houses back in place, almost exactly where they'd been before, but with tiny changes, a road placed slightly differently than I remembered it. And there were people everywhere. People, people, people. And cars. And trees.

I was hugged, kissed, taken out into the sunshine and to the car, put in the backseat, transported home and placed with care on the sofa. And there I sat, as though nothing had happened.

Mother could barely get over her joy at having me back, and just to prove it she came bearing all the cakes in the world, shuttling back and forth between the kitchen and living room, a regular bakery, and I obediently ate everything on offer, drank a glass of Solo orangeade that Father put before me, and leafed through some old newspapers. Saw that C. Walton Lillehei had died at around the time I'd left for the Faroes, nearly fifty years after he'd performed the first successful open heart surgery. The commander of *Apollo 12*, the third man on the moon in the autumn of 1969, had done the same. Charles Conrad, Jr., had driven to his death in a motorcycle accident, maybe he'd been knocked back to the moon, who could tell. And babies, hundreds of babies had been born here in this city since I was here last. And the sea had risen and the land had risen, an eternal balancing act nobody had control of.

Father peered over my shoulder. Asked me if there was anything interesting in the papers. His good-hearted, clumsy attempt at starting conversation.

"Edward Craven Walker is dead," I said.

"Who was he?"

"He invented the lava lamp."

"The lava lamp?" His voice was almost fearful. "I'd all but forgotten those. That must have been about twenty years ago. You had one, didn't you?"

And I had. Once. I'd been one of the first to get one, I think, early in the seventies. They were called Astro-lamps then, and I'd have killed for one.

"Yes," I answered. "It's still up in the loft."

Mother came in with more coffee, put it on the table, and sat beside Father.

"What are you two talking about?"

"Lava lamps," Father and I answered in unison.

"Oh yes, I saw it up in the loft the other day, I think."

That decided things.

We went up to the loft. All three of us. Mother rooted around for a while before getting the scent and digging out what we were looking for from one of my old boxes.

And Mother found the lava lamp.

And Father found an extension cord.

And I found a bottle of wine.

And then we sat on soft-drink crates in the loft, one lovely July evening, and while we watched the warming fluorescent paraffin wax and the oil floating in the water filled container, we drank wine, a superb family to belong to, and we talked about everything that had happened in the last year, without reproach, we talked about why I'd left, how happy I'd been when Father came over, and Mother put on the old cap she'd worn for synchronized swimming, and we laughed, Father held Mother close and gave the cap a gentle tug, before taking pictures of me and Mother. Afterward I went and brought in the plastic bag with the souvenirs, gave them the Faroe Islands video, the T-shirts and wooden sheep, and when they went off to bed I stayed up there, sipping vodka as the lava flowed quicker and quicker up in the loft. Eventually I turned the lamp off, took the bottle and clambered down the ladder, went into my old room to a freshly made bed, posters on the walls, lay under my duvet and slept the restless sleep of a sixteen-year-old.

"Do you have everything you need?" It was Father who asked.

We'd loaded my car up with my things next morning. Wasn't much. I put the box of old space books in the trunk, together with some old newspapers I thought I might read out there, a box of food and some clean clothes. Apart from that there wasn't much to take. The few things I'd left behind in my flat, that Mother and Father had fetched and stored in the loft some months earlier, could stay there as far as I was concerned.

I nodded, said I had everything.

"And you'll come back on weekends?" said Mother.

"Yes, don't worry."

Hugs all around.

It rained as I drove down Seehusensgate and swung toward the stadium where the Viking players were warming up with their coach, I came out onto Madlaveien and joined the motorway going south towards Jæren. Felt good being out like this. Sitting in the car alone, with just the radio playing songs I'd nearly forgotten, window wipers never quite hitting the beat, and fields, fields that stretched across the landscape as I rolled on toward Varhaug and its beaches.

We'd had a summer cabin since I was fourteen, since Grandpa had been promoted to the nursing home and we'd taken the place over and started calling it "our cabin." Although it wasn't so much a cabin as an ordinary house, and Grandma had lived there for large parts of her life, as far as I knew, the smell of Grandpa and her still hung in the walls, impossible to clean away, the smell of old people sitting side by side in their chairs staring out of the windows, content with the way things were, the boulders and fields, waves and bad weather, a storm in Grandpa's hair as he went out to fetch the morning papers.

Because it's windy in Jæren. More than you'd think. And the trick, I've always thought, is to hold yourself upright, to lean into the wind with all your weight and take aim for where you're going before setting one foot in front of the other. Like living in a wind tunnel, almost, with sideways gravitation, I pictured the farmers tethering their cows to the ground, nailing down their roofs, taping themselves to their chairs and waiting for better weather. I remembered things Grandfather had said when I was little, when I went there every summer and we'd go for walks, the hoods of our rain jackets tied tightly and rain falling straight in our faces, and how when I complained and wanted to turn back, he'd always say I ought to be proud the weather was so bad out here.

"It's like this, Mattias," he'd say, "nearly everybody knows that every single eel, European and American, is born in the Sargasso Sea. What they don't know is that every single wind is born here, right here."

And I never doubted it for a moment. It wasn't my place to doubt Grandfather; that was a job for other people, other people's everyday business. And then he'd rest his large hand on my hat and turn me into the wind and we'd gaze out into the North Atlantic like two old seadogs, watching the ships that carried the strangest things to the most remarkable places, and Grandfather would call me his little Christopher Columbus, even though he must have known deep down that I'd never discover anything of note in my lifetime.

So I leaned into the wind as I got out of the car in front of the cabin and carried my few belongings to the door, dug out my keys and let myself in for the first time in over ten years. It smelled closed in, dusty, Mother and Father didn't come here often either, they filled their days with other things. I pulled back the curtains and opened the windows, letting the rain and air in, the curtains flapped and I unpacked my things onto the small living room table, placed my box of books on the floor, went into the kitchen with my food. I pondered whether or not to ring Jørn right away, probably should, tell him I was home, that I hadn't changed, we could meet maybe, have a beer, we could find something to do, catch up with the year that had gone, get a head start on the clocks.

But I didn't call. I stayed in my chair by the window and picked the summer's dead flies off the sill, sat in the sofa and stared at the wall, found an old Rubik's cube in the newspaper rack and in four and a half hours I solved three sides, gave up on the fourth, turned the radio on. Shipping forecast. There was rough weather to the west and everybody was advised to get their sea legs out. I put some coffee on because it felt like the only sensible thing to do, but didn't drink it. I took my old space travel books out of the box on the floor, stacked them neatly on the table and went into the kitchen to make some pasta, and that was when I thought of it. No idea what triggered it, but that was when I thought of him; Sofus.

I hadn't taken the time to visit him in Tórshavn after he'd moved, nor had I written to him as I'd promised. Did he wonder what had happened to me? Or had he forgotten me, found new friends, new playmates in the neighboring houses, even a girlfriend perhaps?

I had his address. I'd written it down in the notebook I'd bought in Klaksvík. As the pasta boiled, I dug out some paper and a pen from the activity shelf that Father had put up for me once, light years behind me now, and I sat at the kitchen table and wrote as I ate.

I don't need to say what I wrote, just it was largely about why I'd decided to go back home for the summer, and how we had to do things like that sometimes, return to GO even if we didn't get to collect $200, I hoped he was well, that he'd made new friends. And then I promised again, promised him I'd come and visit. In the fall. Hopefully that wasn't too far away.

Over the following weeks I began to look like myself again in the mirror. I called home once a week, sometimes more, visited once in a while, when things panned out that way, for Sunday lunch. I worked with Gunnar on the neighboring farm, drove the tractor, painted the barn, worked in the cowshed, helped out where it was needed. Gunnar was sixty, he'd taken over the farm when he'd barely turned twenty, and I remembered him from all those summers as a child, I'd get to sit on his lap on the tractor when he went out in the fields. He still had the same tractor, one of the few who still ran a Gråtass model, and on a bad day this could mean two hours of repairs and tinkering for every hour of work done. But it was all right. There was little hurry, the potatoes had been dug up long ago, the strawberries were picked by the youngsters from the neighboring farm, and the cows stood in the field obediently and waited. I usually had supper with Gunnar and his wife, Ebba, I'd sit and nod with a mouth full of broccoli as she told me the latest news about their son who'd made his fortune from manufacturing tennis balls in Newcastle. Not the most fascinating story ever, but it was okay to hear her voice as I ate, like having the radio on quietly in the background, a kind of accompaniment to the food. Gunnar himself talked about the weather mainly. Always found so much to say. There was sun, there was rain. It could be fine or it could be abysmal, who could tell. But he kept himself updated, listened to the forecast, and noted the day's outcome in the weather journal that hung by a string from the wall. Gunnar had records of the weather going back forty-five years. The fourth of April, 1951? Mild rain that day, with a gentle breeze from the northeast. Good temperature. But their conversation would stop on the rare occasion that a car drove past outside, and they'd fall silent for a second, stretch their necks to the window, and Ebba would squint to identify who it was before they reached a swift conclusion and returned to their conversation, picking up exactly where they'd left off, mid-sentence. Pretty impressive.

It was Jørn who called me, in the end. On a Friday in early September and I was conscience-stricken from the moment I heard his voice, and I could swear he noticed it from the moment I answered *hi there*, so I could hardly have expected anything else but that he'd exploit it.

"So you're still alive," he said, in a flat tone.

"It only hurts when I laugh," I answered, trying to be funny. But failing.

"How long have you been barricaded in, out there at Jæren?"

This certainly wasn't how I'd anticipated things would be. I'd run through this a hundred times, our first conversation, how it might go. But Jørn wasn't following the script.

"A few days," I answered.

"Or a few weeks?"

"Maybe."

"I'll come out there this evening, around seven."

I didn't manage to answer. Jørn hung up and all I could do was wait, put the coffee on, even though I knew it wasn't the coffee he was coming for.

I went in circles as I waited for his arrival. This was my chance, my opportunity to put everything right that had gone wrong, to start afresh. Somehow I hoped he'd walk through the door, sit down in one of the old chairs and that the conversation would flow naturally over the walls, as it had before I'd left. I wanted everything to stand still, like last year's dust on the sill. But hardly anything stands still. Because the mountains rise, the continental plates shift every year, and old friendship rusts in the rain.

Jørn's index finger hit my doorbell at five minutes and thirty seconds past seven. I'd missed that finger, I'd hoped it would do its job and ring countless times. But now I feared what it might bring with it.

Things began well. They began as they always had. The sharp tone he'd had over the phone was gone, and to the untrained eye everything looked as it always had, but deep inside I knew, from the instant he took off his shoes and walked into the living room, that this could be the last evening we'd talk.

He didn't ask me about the Faroes. Didn't ask me to explain why I'd been away so long, why I hadn't been in touch for more than a year, although I knew we'd have to touch on the subject sooner or later. We talked about Jæren, about Perkleiva's new album that had sold relatively well, we talked around the bush, around the houses, mumbled about old times, unable to quite reach each other, fumbled in the dark, it couldn't be otherwise, and we were both relieved when Jørn suggested we take a trip to Checkpoint Charlie, and what did I think, we could drive into Stavanger, get a couple of beers for old times' sake, Friday and stuff, and I answered *yeah, of course we can.*

The car ride in. The hour it took to drive. A gulf of silence between us all the way.

We walked in the open door of Checkpoint Charlie in Nedre Strandgate at just after nine, it was already getting overcrowded, they had cheap beer on Fridays, people crept out from under their stones and planted themselves on the stools around the bar, all the week's ghosts. I found a little table in a corner at the back, sat there as Jørn went to buy the beers. I recognized a couple of faces at the other end, you always did here, Checkpoint lived up to its name. If you wanted to know what had become of them, your old acquaintances, old friends, people from school, the people who put your clothes in a bag and gave you the receipt in H & M, if you were looking for an update, this was the place to come.

I clocked in.

I was in place.

Out among people.

Jørn padded back with two beers, and then we sat there and waited for something to talk about, while the loudspeakers crackled and the bartender played old Garbage songs whose words nobody knew anymore, as ever more people piled into the venue, turning the air heavy and clammy. Some of Jørn's friends turned up during the evening, first

Roar, and not even he asked me what had happened, then later more arrived, a whole gang, and I was displaced, sat squashed between Jørn and a long-haired, bearded guy with a Trøndelag dialect, didn't recognize him straight off, but I'd met him before, his name was Jørgen and he was in the other band that had come to the Faroes, the Kulta Beats. Jørgen talked a lot, talked fast, one of the nicest guys I'd met for years. They'd given a concert on the previous day, up at Folken, together with Perkleiva, it had been wild, he said. I'd almost reached the bottom of my third beer and finally found something to say, excused myself and leaned over to Jørn and bellowed into his ear through Prodigy pouring out of the loudspeakers:

"Did you play yesterday? At Folken?"

"What?"

"Did you play at Folken yesterday?" I yelled.

"Yeah, you should have been there, Mattias!"

"You should have told me," I said, and the moment the words had left my lips, he shot me a piercing look, the look I'd been dreading all along, he wanted to kill me, take my life there and then and put me out of my misery or something. Instead all he said was:

"You know you'd never have come, anyway."

"How do you know? I might have," I answered, injured.

"Like you give a shit."

"What do you mean by that?" I could feel this was going to go wrong, very wrong.

"You know exactly what I mean. You haven't called me in over a year! I have to call your parents to find out where you are, what you're doing. I can't fucking trust you an inch. You just fuck off somewhere! Or just don't turn up. What the hell are you doing? Is it that stuff with Helle still? Is it? Are you still so fucking sore? Maybe it's time to move on, stop behaving like Kurt fucking Cobain. You've got to see she couldn't stay with you when you were so desperate to hide away all the time."

"What's your problem?"

"No, Mattias, what's your problem? I don't fucking know anymore.

Okay, listen. You say you don't want to be in a band, you don't want to sing, even though you're really good, and that's fine, that's really fine, but then what do you go and do? Yeah, you get drunk on the boat to the Faroes, and yell across the whole nightclub that you're going to sing, you say you've changed your mind, you want to be our vocalist after all, and I'm so pleased, of course I am, I've always wanted to play with you. And then I offer you a thousand kroner if you go up on stage and sing with the band on the boat. But, oh no, you want more, fucking prima donna, you don't want a thousand, you don't want five thousand, not even ten, you want fifteen thousand kroner. So we all pitch in, put all the cash we have in an envelope for you, just because I really want the others to hear you, and okay, you sing, you do, and it's fucking amazing, you still have the best voice I've ever heard, but afterwards you go AWOL, you refuse to give the money back. Fuck me. What do you do? Here's what you do: when Christopher tries to take the envelope back, you run away, up to the deck, and you knock him down, you fucking punch him in the face, more than once. Did you know he had to go to the hospital? Eight fucking stitches in his face. Almost lost his hearing in one ear."

The envelope stuffed with money.

The blood on my knuckles.

Havstein must have known all this, surely? Jørn must have told him when they talked in Tórshavn, I couldn't imagine otherwise.

But nobody had said a word to me.

Marilyn Manson on max at Checkpoint, *rock is deader than dead*, and I can't hear my own thoughts and only fragments from Jørn's lips as they move, as I take long swigs of beer. I shout the lyrics to nobody in particular, shout them out of tune, and act as though my actions might have some kind of adequate defense.

"And then we're forced to strap you down in the cabin until we get there, and I have to tell Christopher what's been going on with you, so he won't report you to the police. They had to cancel their concert, for fuck's sake. And then you, you just disappear as soon as we land, wander off from everyone and everything. Jørgen here had to do the sound for us, Kulta Beats were canceled, Christ almighty, Christopher couldn't sing with a smashed face. You should have gone to jail, do you realize? Or at least been put away. You're sick in the head, do you know that?"

"Just like your brother. Maybe he and I could share a room?"

"That's enough. Put your brakes on." He pointed at me with the same index finger that had made contact with me at five past seven.

But the brakes were off now, and there was only one way to go, downhill. The rest of the table sat silently and pretended they weren't listening, it felt like the whole bar had shut up, as I watched all the conversations we'd shared through the years, everything we'd done together, blown away with the wind.

The bartender puts on the music from *Jaws*, or maybe that's just something I imagine, anyway I get up to go to the bathroom and notice Jørn following me, I try to shake him off in the crowd, but it's a laughable attempt, because he's heading for the bathroom too, and I stand before the urinal and pull down my fly, try my best to look unruffled, but nothing comes out, my system has come to a full stop and the bartender plays *Imperial March* from *Star Wars*, or something that sounds like it, and Jørn grabs me by the jacket, tears me away from the urinal, and I fumble for my zipper, while other customers evacuate the room and Jørn shoves me up against the wall, same index finger between my eyes but with a different message.

"You're running out on me again?" he bellows. "You've got some fucking nerve!"

"I had to pee! I . . ."

I search desperately through all the sentences I might say, but can't find anything useful, because everything comes out wrong, and I want to tell him I don't remember anything about what happened on the boat, I want to tell him I'm ill, that I've been ill but things are better, I'm back, it'll be better, but I'm not sure that's true anymore, and I've lost all perspective. Jørn punches me several times in the chest, although at half strength, and I sink to the ground before him, mumbling something about how he's misunderstood me, and then two bouncers arrive, ask if there's a problem, and despite us shaking our heads and Jørn saying *no*, nobody believes us, and we're dragged through the door, down the hallway and out of the bar, dumped on some steps outside and told to get some fresh air, lots of fresh air, a few years' worth.

We say nothing for half an hour. Just sit next to each other, staring into the ground.

But we don't leave.

I don't walk off.

Fuck no.

Finally I say something:

"I'd have liked to be at that concert. In Tórshavn. I don't know what happened."

"You vanished."

"Everyone's allowed to vanish once in while."

"Yeah, but not many people vanish permanently. Why didn't you call at least?"

"I was beyond coverage."

"What do you mean?"

"Have you ever seen the Big Dipper?"

"What?"

"I used to like sitting on the beach at Jæren trying to pick out the constellations. The Big Dipper was always the easiest to find. It stands out, very clearly. But if you go on looking, everything looks like the Big Dipper in the end. How can you be sure that the Big Dipper you see is the Big Dipper you're meant to see?"

"I don't get it."

"Does your brother still live at Dale?"

He shook his head.

"No, he's back home. He's living with our parents."

"Is he better?'

"He sits and stares at the wall. Sometimes he switches walls during the course of the day. But that's mostly what he does. What did you do on the Faroes?"

"I was on vacation."

"That was a long vacation."

"Yes, I missed the boat."

"For a whole year?"

"Time flies. And that's not just something we say."

"I heard you were committed."

"No, but I was out of action. Suspended."

"So why didn't you call me? For a whole year? I'd have come and visited you, if you'd wanted. I'd have been there to help, if I'd have known."

"I hardly remember anything. From the boat trip over, I mean. From those first days. All I remember is lying in a road, it was wet, raining, and I was walking against the wind. You should always walk against the wind, or you end up in the sea. And then I met Havstein."

"Havstein was the man who met me in Tórshavn. Who said we could just leave without you, that you'd follow as soon as you were ready? A psychiatrist, wasn't he? So you were committed over there?"

"Kind of. But I even didn't know that myself."

"Why were you committed?"

"I was trying to hide. And that wasn't allowed. Have you ever been to the Caribbean?"

"No. Why?"

"No reason. I just wondered. I want to go there."

"You're welcome. I called your parents sometimes, now and then, just to hear if you were back. They couldn't tell me a lot."

"I don't need a caseworker."

"Don't you need any friends either?"

I didn't answer that. And he didn't pursue it. There was a moment's silence, before we changed the subject.

"They were good times," he said quietly. "I read an article about Buzz Aldrin a few months ago, by the way. It said they carried out rigorous psychological tests on Aldrin before the launch of *Apollo 11*, they wanted to make sure that in eagerness to be the first man on the moon, or even possibly from shame of having to be the second, he wouldn't shove Armstrong aside at the crucial moment before he stepped out of the LM."

"I don't believe he could have done that."

"What if I told you he thought about it?"

"I wouldn't believe you."

"He did. For a few seconds he contemplated the consequences of doing it."

"No."

"In this article they called him *Business Aldrin*. He never disappeared. That's just something you believe. He works for loads of organizations, makes tons of money writing books, giving talks, that sort of thing."

I was speechless. It was news to me.

"And there are model toys of him, and he promotes Apple and JVC, Givenchy, Nortel Networks, Mastercard, massive companies, and he's appeared on the David Letterman show a few times and lent his voice to *The Simpsons*. And fuck me if he isn't contracted to four, FOUR autograph companies who take $400 for his autograph on some crappy press photograph! And then there's that film, you saw it too, *Toy Story*. *Buzz Lightyear*. Sounds familiar, right? Maybe he never vanished after all. Maybe he did the opposite."

I sat as stiff as a poker. Business Aldrin. The man who played his part and then vanished. I stared straight in front of me while Jørn went on about all the things Aldrin was involved in and how highly he seemed to think of himself and I felt myself getting angry, then I got terribly sad and I put my head in my hands, closed my eyes, thought how it wasn't Aldrin's fault, it was just the price he'd paid for subjecting himself to the world's attention, of course it was impossible to vanish after that, when half the world was out to get as much as they could out of the second man on the moon. But it changed nothing. He would always be number two. It was me who had to become better at hiding away.

Jørn realized he'd said too much. Lit a cigarette and tried to be casual.

"So what did you think of the Olsok Festival on the Faroes? Pretty good, right? It was the best party I've ever been to, total chaos, Wild West in the Atlantic."

"I don't know."

"Didn't you get to go?"

"I didn't go out much."

"The whale slaughter, then? Did you get involved?"

"No. I watched one though," I lied. "There haven't been many pilot whales in the fjords during the last few years." And then I made up some story about how Havstein had run into Sofia and I, one September day, yelling that pilot whales were on their way into one of the fjords, and then as the lead up to this story, I had to explain about Sofia and the Factory, and about Palli, and Anna, and I told him everything, though not from the beginning, and my story rambled on and on, it was the only way to tell it, I answered his questions, telling him what had happened that year, and the clocks ticked on and people staggered out of Checkpoint and the other bars and went home or to private parties while we were back in an evening down by the shore so long ago, and I thought how I mustn't leave anything out, because this might be the last time we'd talk, I wasn't sure why I felt it, just that I feared it.

"Fucking hell," said Jørn when I'd finally finished and told him just about everything, sandwiched in the description of a whale slaughter I'd never seen.

"And you'll get your money back." I said. "The fifteen thousand I mean."

"Don't worry about it."

"But, of course, you should have your money back."

"They were good times," he said again. "Don't you think?'

"Yeah," I said. "Good times."

Jørn looked at his watch. It was late, time to pack up and go. We got up and stood there, both worse for wear.

"We'll talk soon," he said, shook my hand quickly before walking in the direction of the post office.

"We'll talk," I said and stood watching after him.

"Mattias!" he shouted a little way down the road.

"Yeah?"

"Look after yourself!"

I lifted a hand in reply, and then he turned again, went up the steps of the post office and disappeared behind the buildings.

I stood swaying in the alleyway, leaned forward until the air grabbed hold of me and I blew with the wind down toward one of the taxi stands near Vågen, stood nicely in line and waited my turn. I wasn't the only one who wanted to go home. Almost everybody did. Home. But I was the one with the farthest to go. And I was standing there like a lemon, hands hanging at my sides, looking down at the ground when a hand slapped me on the back and stuck a half-eaten hot dog in my face.

"Well, well," said the face that belonged to the hot dog.

I turned and saw Geir and a couple of other ghosts who'd been in my year at Hetland, some fifteen years ago. I was semi-embraced, the kind of hug nobody wants.

"Hi."

"Well, well, well, what do you say?"

"Not a lot," I answered.

"Christ, don't you even say hi when an old classmate says hello?"

"I just said *hi*."

"Are you trying to be funny, or what?"

"Do you know my name?" I asked.

"Yeah, yeah, but fucking hell, we've got to stick together, old class-mates and all. What are you up to these days?"

I could have said anything, it made no difference.

I said:

"We weren't in the same class."

"What? Of course we were. Come on, man, what are you doing these days?"

"I'm in the French Foreign Legion," I answered. "I've exterminated whole villages. If you only knew."

He staggered back and forth as his brain decoded the information.

"Right. There a lot of money in that?"

"Do you remember my name? Do you realize we've never talked before?"

"Why are you going on about that all the time?" Then he pondered for a while. Time passed. He grew an entire beard. He'd been found out. He jabbed a finger in my chest. "Thomas? Right? Huh? That's it, isn't it?"

"Yes," I said. "Thomas from the Foreign Legion."

A taxi came. It was my turn. Geir grabbed me again, his last bit of hot dog slopped down his shirt and landed with a plop on the asphalt in front of him.

"Shit! Wait!" He leaned forward and scooped up the remains, then clambered up my jacket, returning to a more or less upright position. "Maybe me and Oddgeir can bum a ride. Where you going?"

"A long way away," I answered, slipped into the back seat and slammed the door, the driver took a U-turn and drove in the direction of the Atlantic Hotel, I gave him my address and smiled, I was one big smile as I sat in the back seat there, because I'd truly succeeded, there wasn't one trace of me left in this whole city now, I was the snow that had fallen last year, or the year that so much had fallen everyone lost count, and we drove up over Madlaveien and swung off onto the motorway, past the house where earlier that evening Jørn had told me Helle and Mats lived now, and I could have sworn I saw her at the window for a second, and that she looked happy too, and lifted a hand and waved and I lifted my hand and I'd have waved back but didn't get the chance before the car swung off the main road, and I had to turn to see where we were driving and check we were going in the right direction.

--- - ■ - - -

Was it a rash decision?

Was it cowardly? Like migrating birds, ditching the whole program at the first sign of winter?

No. There are times we simply have to go. Times when we have to burn all our bridges and take the sea route instead.

And only captains who fear for their reputations go down with the ship.

I was ready to go in the lifeboat. To go back to the Faroes for good.

I staggered into the living room that night, gripped tightly to the door frame and crawled over the floor to the sofa, pulled myself up onto the sofa and sat there and stared at the books still neatly piled on the coffee table. I laid my hand on the top book. Buzz Aldrin's autobiography.

Read until my eyes were sore.

A lot had gone wrong for Buzz Aldrin too. Things had gone downhill quickly and in the end his was a steeper decline than anyone could have dreamed. But it had begun tentatively, sneaking over his shoulder only weeks after the space trip with *Gemini 12* in 1966. He'd felt tired, drained, had barely managed to crawl into bed and laid there for almost a week before getting up, he and his wife both felt it was natural he should be exhausted, he had, after all, been in space, had trained so much, it had all gone so fast. It was obvious there'd be a price to pay. But it would pass, surely. But actually it was his nervous system sending out faint waves of warning, but nobody saw them, they were written too small, and he got up on his feet again, returned to work, and the new

Apollo Program was set in motion, men were going to land on the moon before the seventies, there was no time to lose, Aldrin was told he'd have a place on *Apollo 11*, and he started training again, alongside Armstrong and Collins, but behind closed doors he told Joan that given half a chance, he'd have pulled out of the later expedition, so as to have less attention on him, so he'd be more involved in pure research work, but he could say nothing to anybody. Not a peep. Because nobody had ever pulled out of a mission before and if he'd made that decision, the other two astronauts would have been removed from the posters too. So off he goes. To the moon. And back. He gets to watch the American flag keel over slowly in the Sea of Tranquility and to whisk up the dust as they lift off from the surface and start their homeward journey, then comes the flood of attention on their homecoming, everybody wants to talk to him, to congratulate him, to ask questions, *what was it like on the moon, what did you think, what did you feel, what's it like to have been on the moon,* but their reception isn't always positive, the astronauts are bombarded with tomatoes on university campuses, because the moon landing cost twenty-four billion, 1969 dollars, that could have been used for other things, it's the middle of the Vietnam War and nobody can agree on anything, nobody has perspective, but Aldrin finds himself pushed onward and upward, and before he knows it he's on a plane together with Armstrong and Collins and their wives, traveling from the USA to the rest of the world on NASA's massive promotional tour, he hasn't asked to be dragged along, quite the opposite, he's felt pressured by NASA, and just the thought of being a salesman for American space exploration terrifies him, but he goes, reassuring himself that if it's too bad he can always pull out, vanish into the Apollo Program, escape the publicity. But putting the brakes on a world tour is not easy and the going gets tough, there are too many people, they're crushed in the crowd, strangled with attention, the press spews out unverified and inaccurate articles about him, claiming he has lunar sickness, that he fears a virus from the rocks they brought back, Aldrin and Joan have a hard time, but they survive as best they can, smile, accept the keys to various cities, greet people, give speeches, the tour doctor gives Aldrin some pills to calm him down, but the panic doesn't ease, it only gets worse, and it seems that in Norway, of all places, it finally comes to a head. They've arrived in Oslo as their only destination in Scandinavia, they've eaten lunch at the palace with a jocular and blustery King Olav, they've been paraded up Karl Johan with the public standing cold and unenthusiastic on the pavement, clapping and waving mechanically, at least that's how he's experienced it, and it depresses him, he has ancestors from Sweden, this isn't how it should be. They're taken by helicopter to an old farm up in the mountains, and it's here, during the evening, that the bubble bursts. He fails to come down to dinner, stays in bed, and when Joan returns, she tries, but can't comfort him. They drink whiskey. They talk about how things can never be the same again, he feels like a counterfeit of himself, everything's spinning out of control, Joan is his emotional Red Cross, but it's no good, the hours pass, there they sit, Mr. and Mrs. Aldrin, in a quaint peasant-style bedroom in Norway, getting drunk on whiskey for the first and last time during the tour. And they cry. Aldrin cries, he doesn't want to go on, wants to go home, to vanish and never be found again. And that night they sleep like two frightened children, clinging to each other and keeping the wolves from the door. But they go on with the tour, they get through it. Behaving as though nothing had happened.

Now things get really hard.

Crisis time.

Because he's been to the moon, and nothing will ever be the same.

Difficult times. Dreadful times. The specters close in, and Aldrin creeps into bed, only getting up to watch TV, his moods swing unpredictably from moments of euphoric excitement to long periods of paralyzing misery, depression tightens on him like a vise, only his family know, and when the family doctor tells him he needs urgent psychiatric help and medication he decides to foot the bill himself, so NASA won't find out, he is treated with Ritalin and continues holding lectures, until one afternoon he breaks down, sobs in a hotel lobby immediately after a banquet appearance. And that's when Buzz Aldrin stops. Everything stops. He continues going to the office in the mornings, determined to get his work done, but he sits in his chair, looks blankly out of the window, for hours, before he gets up and leaves, gets into his car and drives to the beach, walks for hours until he knows everybody's gone to bed, and only then does he come home to sit in front of the TV, drinking whiskey, and gradually more evenings are spent this way, until they all are, and he sinks deeper and deeper into despair, stays awake all night afraid of sleeping in the dark, and all he wants is to stop feeling anything at all, and he gives a damn now whether NASA knows or not, he just wants somebody to help him, before things go dreadfully wrong, and his psychiatrist understands the gravity of the situation, agrees to send him to San Antonio, and Buzz Aldrin tells his father he's seriously ill, but his father refuses to understand; how can this man, who's always been so successful, think so little of himself now. And his father suggests he wait, not bring NASA into it, wait, not take sick leave, so long as he maintains the mask he can have any job he wants, and Joan screams at Aldrin's father not to interfere because Buzz is ill, and she is prepared to stand in anybody's way who tries to stop her from taking him away, physically if necessary, and she also tells the psychiatrist, with Buzz Aldrin sitting passively at her side, that she's considered separation, but that this is no longer an option, not while he's so ill, maybe afterward, when they can sit down and talk things through properly, but while he's ill she's willing to fight this one through, even though it's only tolerable at home when he's away, and she says all this, with her husband sitting there, hands calmly folded in his lap, staring into the carpet and hoping that some one will come and put the brakes on for him.

And then one evening, when Joan and the psychiatrist have finally arranged his appointment in San Antonio, they pack Buzz Aldrin's suitcase as he watches on from the doorway, puzzling over what these people are doing, and how it involves him.

Edwin E. Aldrin, Jr., is admitted into Wilford Hall Hospital, Brooks Air Force Base on October 28, 1971. He has therapy sessions twice daily and is treated with tranquilizers and the antidepressant, Thioridazine, gradually things move forward, the doctors ask Aldrin if he thinks he might attempt suicide, his mumbled reply is that he isn't even in a state to choose a method, this is a man incapable of lifting a hummingbird without getting tired, but things move forward, with each conversation with his doctor things improve, and above their heads astronauts are walking around on the moon or floating in orbit and from their perspective the earth looks uninhabited, as if no wars were covering large areas of it, as if there were no buildings, people, problems.

And it's three years now since he walked on the moon, and he's been admitted into Lackland Air Force Hospital in San Antonio, Texas, he stands by the window and looks up at a perfect full moon and it's here that he decides to begin afresh. Buzz Aldrin stands in his hospital pajama top in front of an open window and talks to himself. *You have been on the moon. You did it. First. It can never be done again, not by you, not by anyone. So get the hell out of here and live the life you've wanted for yourself.*

It was a long journey.

The melancholy of all things done.

The Apollo Program is closed down early.

NASA is on the decline and Aldrin has resigned from his job there.

He leaves his work as leader of the test pilot base in Texas, after more than twenty years in the Air Force.

And Buzz Aldrin is forgotten, gram by gram. Disappears into the confusion.

He's sad. And the passing years don't improve matters.

He drinks. It all comes to nothing, things don't go well.

Things couldn't be worse.

And his family is torn apart. Joan Archer walks out of the door and never returns.

And nothing is as it might have been.

And yet it couldn't be any other way. Everything is in its place.

And I've searched and searched for that moment, but failed to find it, though I know it exists, that particular second in which he realizes it doesn't matter at all, that he'll never travel farther than he already has, that it's of no significance, that he'll never get out of this corner like this, that every drink gives him a slap around the face, rather than what he's hoping for, that it should reduce him until he's so small, so microscopic, that he could vanish between the threads of his own coat and evaporate. I try to trace the moment when Buzz Aldrin finally pulls himself up by his bootstraps and dares to think the thought to its conclusion:

It takes vast willpower, luck, and skill to be the first.

But it takes a gigantic heart to be number two.

Which is why you will also come back from nothing, Aldrin, there will be easier days, everything will get easier, all of it, because one can be all right even when nobody's watching, one can be smart even if one isn't remembered, and you've done your part, done important work, the big cog so many forgot, and so, little by little, things improve, and you stop drinking, start working again, in small ways to begin with, then things build up, you get remarried, you do what you can, work on great projects, hold lectures, you want to send us all back into space one day, so we can see for ourselves what you saw, and for that, I think, you'll have good times again, everything will be forgiven, because there'll be a protective hand held over you as you dive for coral off the coast of California with your family, with your children, as you sit and watch TV, when you wake up, when you take your new wife in your arms in the bathroom in the evening.

-- -- ■ -- --

I went on working for Gunnar, but he could see that I was already preparing to leave. I was restless. We'd agreed that I work for him until the end of September, but when I started talking to him about the situation, he quickly saw where things were. He'd have preferred me to stay out the year, he said, but there was no way of convincing me. So I was free to go when I wanted. I started preparing myself. And then I noticed how I'd begun to miss people again. But it wasn't Jørn I missed. I missed Havstein. Carl. Anna. Palli. I missed the sense of having something in common with somebody. And I missed Sofia.

I felt bad about Jørn, and every morning I'd decide to call him after work. But never did.

Because there was no longer any reason to stay.

I thought a lot about Jørn, in fact, the things we'd done, things we'd talked about. They'd been good times, as he'd said, hadn't they? Yes, they'd been some of the best, they'd been the days when you grow up, and Jørn had dragged me by the hair through so many of them, the best friends you could have, Jørn, Roar, Helle, and I. But it felt as though I'd been away for light years now, nothing was the same. I might just as well have been in another galaxy. And I was suddenly frightened about what Father had said on the Faroes, that I'd been ill before, that I'd fallen ill again. Did Jørn know perhaps? Did Helle? Had they known all along, walked on eggshells around me, treated me like a patient? How long had it been going on, had it spiraled during this last year, after Helle had left, after Karsten had gone bust, or had it been that way all my life, since I'd been small? Because something had happened that evening Father and I talked, hadn't it? Something had changed in me, and I could no longer remember how I'd been before that moment, it was no longer possible to process that film.

And then one night the panic finally grabbed me, the panic about everything I'd ruined. It came spilling over me like the noise of cheering in the world's biggest football stadium, except, of course, nobody was applauding. No, it was more like the Normandy landings, flames raging all around me, sounds of catastrophe and turmoil. I couldn't lie still, had to crawl out the veranda door and into the air, into the wind. Stood there, feeling fragile, on the veranda like a fool, and I think I cried that night, or maybe I was only on the edge of tears, and I remember thinking I had to do something, because if only I could make myself useful now, the accounts would be rebalanced, the poles would right themselves and the birds would be able to reorient themselves and find their way South when the time was right, so I rushed down toward the shore, wrenched rocks out of the ground, lifted boulders and carried them down to the beach, laid them out in a big square, and then into the square I shoveled more sand, filled it up, worked until my hands were raw and morning came, worked through the night as the massive transport ships passed each other out on the horizon, and I remember I was convinced that as long as I finished before light, no ship could collide, there would be no shipwrecks, and I went up into the summer house for an iron bar and rake, walked farther up into the field, rolled three of the biggest rocks I could find down the slope to the beach, then using the bar I levered the rocks inside my stone square, then raked the sand into perfect patterns, watching all the time for passing ships, and there were no collisions, not a catastrophe to be seen, then I relaxed, put down my tools and lay in the center, slept inside Jæren's only Japanese rock garden, dreamed of Kimono-Magnusson and outer space, and in my dream I was an astronaut, I'd gone astray, didn't know where I was, but went further and further out, until I found a planet that was unmarked on any chart, or maybe it was just a star, and I landed softly on the outskirts of a town where nobody lived, and when I got out of my ship, I noticed how weak the gravitational force was, I could almost fly above the town, and there was nobody around, not a soul, but there were houses, and cars parked in the streets, and then in a side road I met somebody, Peter Mayhew who played Chewbacca in *Star Wars*, and he was carrying his hairy costume under his arm and gave me a hesitant nod as I passed, smiled and said I was welcome, and I asked whether he'd ever felt sad that nobody knew he was the man that played Chewbacca, that nobody had ever seen him, and he answered *I never worried about those little details,* and then he pointed toward a building farther down the street, and I went there and I went in a restaurant, drew myself a beer at the bar and sat down, and I thought here, here was a place I could live.

I was woken by the rain and by sand in my shoes. It was cold. I looked up. Darkness. Then a face came and placed itself before me.

"Mattias, what are you doing out here? Are you all right?" Gunnar looked worriedly at me.

"Yes," I mumbled, rubbing sleep from my eyes.

"But what are you doing?"

I lay there and talked. An extraordinary situation.

"I wanted to make you something." I got up carefully and brushed the wet sand from my clothes. "I've made you a garden."

"A garden?'

"It's a Japanese rock garden," I said. "To achieve Zen calm. It requires almost no upkeep at all. It's extremely simple."

Gunnar looked uncertain. "Really?"

Then I took the rake and drew patterns in the sand, waves from one rock to the next, then turned the rake in the sand and made two small circles.

"That's what you do. It creates harmony in the world. I learned it on the Faroe Islands."

He looked as though he didn't quite believe me, but I handed him the rake and reluctantly he made some hesitant strokes.

"You'll get the hang of it with time, no worries."

"Are you leaving soon?"

"Yes, I'm leaving tomorrow." I nodded, and he put the rake aside.

"Back to the Faroes?"

"Yes."

He looked almost sad. A heavy sigh.

"Good luck, then. It's been great having you here. You're welcome any time, you know that? Whenever you want."

"Thank you," I said and started to walk up to the house. "Don't forget to practice," I shouted down to him and nodded towards the garden, "it takes a little time." Then I went in and began packing my things. Some clothes. A box of worn out books about places where nobody lived.

Gunnar called Mother and Father of course, and they arrived that afternoon with troubled faces, sat down seriously on the couch and didn't want coffee, didn't want anything, wanted me to talk. And I did, reluctantly at first, but then with more clarity, more detail, presenting my thoughts for them like a prospectus, describing the episode with Jørn and how I missed everybody at the Factory, and to my huge surprise they didn't come with any big objections. They said they understood. That they'd prefer it if I lived here, but that they understood. And they'd come and visit, it was so nice there, Father had said. The only thing I didn't mention was the rock garden. That would be between me and Gunnar. He'd have to work that out himself.

The last evening. I packed my things in a bag and a backpack. Father had called and ordered a plane ticket, Mother ironed clean shirts even though I said it was unnecessary, but she wanted to do something too. And she plied me with food, bags of apples, cheese, and tomatoes, clearly thought they didn't sell food where I was going. We agreed they'd sell my car for me and transfer the money to my account.

Gunnar dropped by and paid me in cash for the summer's work, there was no point in making things complicated by bringing the taxman into it, he said. *Right, no point,* I answered. Mother hugged me as hard as on the day I'd arrived, and I had to promise to call often, once a week, at least. And remember to send cards. Contact them as soon as there was anything. Whatever it was. Look after myself, was all they said, their constant refrain. And I promised.

Next morning, I am up early, a bright September sun over Jæren and an almost completely calm sea. Not a boat in view. I eat breakfast standing up, clear the remaining food into the trash and lock the door carefully behind me as I go. I wander up to the main road, and carrying my precious box of space books securely under one arm, I stand at the bus stop, smiling, waiting for the bus, I arrive in Sola and change to another bus that goes to the airport, check my luggage, go to the departure lounge and find the gate for the plane to Copenhagen from where I'll catch the 3:15 flight to Vágar. I am on my way to the Faroes. And I'll tell Havstein that I don't intend to leave again.

3

Departure terminal. Delays and cabin staff. I wandered aimlessly around Kastrup Airport and tried to kill time, without success. There was far too much time, I was surrounded by minutes. Father had been worried I'd miss the connection, so he'd arranged for there to be nearly four hours before my flight for the Faroes left Copenhagen. Forty-five minutes had gone. Time brought in reinforcements and boredom arrived with overwhelming firepower, a military parade through the terminal. I threw my hands in the air, but nobody took me to jail, so I wandered back into the electronics store I'd already visited twice, browsed through the same stuff again, electronic déja vu, the eternal junction plates, small handheld vacuum cleaners for the fastidious and portable PCs the size of a postage stamp, almost. But didn't want that. Didn't have enough money anyway. Instead I ended up with a Walkman and a self-help tape for only 149 kroner. A bargain. So what do we do now, little friend?

Have you ever asked yourself what the meaning of your life is? Have you wondered where you came from? What you should do? Have you ever felt desperate? Inadequate? Small? This cassette will help you find direction in your life. You too can go places. The world is yours. Begin by saying to your-self: Every day on the earth is a good day. Breathe in. Breathe out. Repeat.

I managed to listen to the cassette four times before the plane took off, and a couple of times more before we came down from the clouds and landed in the fog at Vágar. I knew the entire first side by heart. I breathed in. I breathed out. I repeated, and as we drove out of the underwater tunnel at Streymoy, I thought how every day above ground was a good day. A great tape in that way. So easy to remember. I sat glued to the bus window as we drove along the familiar road into Tórshavn, and I noticed how good I felt. Terribly good, and nothing could knock me off balance now. Rain on glass, windscreen wipers keeping time at the front, steering us through a contourless, green landscape, the few passengers that chatted quietly between themselves, mountains that said nothing.

I had butterflies in my stomach as I got off the bus on Tórshavn quay at half past four and the wind hit my face. It was raining horizontally, and I was drenched before I'd even left the harbor and reached the street, yet this was a kindly rain, a forgiving rain that offered promise and didn't bother me in the least. I lugged my bag and box toward City Burger, and as I walked along I thought the fog over Tórshavn looked like somebody had taken a gigantic roll of Scotch tape and taped everything up, sticking the sky to the land with clumsy precision. God's big vacation project, Year One, his proudest achievement. At City Burger I bought myself a Jolly Cola and Hawaii burger, it tasted like cardboard and plastic, as it should, and I think I was a happy person at that moment, as I stood at the bus stop in Niels Winthersgøta waiting for the bus to Gjógv, and I felt how good it was to be back, finally, because this was the Faroes and there was nowhere I'd rather be, here in Tórshavn, with its roads that stretched north and south, its mountains and gravel, its people, the boats on the fjords and lakes, and all that water that rained down on me and the people that lived here, in this country written so small, where the days were the same as elsewhere, some good, some impossible to get through, mostly tolerable, and I waited for the bus and thought how I should have come here years earlier, yet everything was a part of me already, the streets, the buildings, I could have walked with my eyes closed from the ferry terminal in Kakagøta up to Café Natúr, past the Hotel Hafnia and H.N. Jacobsen's bookshop, up to Havnar Bio to find out what was playing at the movie theater, or I could have wandered down to Frants Restorff's bakery at the crossroads of Sverrisgøta and Tórsgata, and farther on to the Steinnatún kiosk where we bought our late night takeout food when we were out by the harbor on weekends, I could have walked blindfolded from Tórshavn and northward over the mountains to Kollafjørður, swum over Slættafello and Reyðafelstindur, plotted my course to Funningur, Gjógv, and all the way home, I waited for the bus that would come soon and you should have taken a photo of me then, Kodak, processed it and sent it to someone.

But there were no flashing cameras.

Just rain.

And it didn't bother me.

I took the long way, the milk route, got off at the crossroads at Oyrarbakki, and waited over an hour outside the Shell station before the bus going farther turned up. We stood like abandoned children, we passengers, scraped the gravel with our heels and looked at our watches. Mine said half past seven. It had said that for over a year now, and I still hadn't managed to get myself a new one. But I had time to wait. And when the bus eventually arrived, we divided ourselves smoothly, disappearing our separate ways without a wave goodbye or an exchange of telephone numbers. I thought how Sofia had probably often stood here alone, waiting for some bus or other, whichever came first, and I could almost see traces of her on the ground. Should have been a plaque put up for her.

As we swung down towards Gjógv, I could barely sit still in my seat, I was the first and last but one to get off the bus, an old fisherman puttered off after me and I nodded to him politely despite not recognizing him, and then half-ran the last few hundred feet to the Factory as I prepared my opening sentence and pictured their surprised faces as I came in the living room, nearly a month before they expected me, and pronounced I wasn't leaving again. Not this guy, no. I'd decided to stay. For certain.

But the door was locked. And nobody came to open it when I rang the bell. There was no welcoming committee or standing ovation, no arms flung themselves around my neck and said they'd missed me. Nothing, null, nix. And for a moment the same feeling of panic came over me as I'd felt in Jæren. I stopped and tugged at the door handle, it didn't turn. It was as locked as could be. So I walked around the building, but all the windows were shut and there was nothing to be done but give up, wait for somebody to come back. I sat on my box of books at the front door, took out an extra sweater, a wool hat, put them on and put my bag on my lap, huddled up and made myself small to avoid the rain, though that was impossible. It was pelting down from all directions and seeping through all my clothes, until I was soaked to the skin, and I sat there freezing and feeling pathetic, I told myself that I should have phoned beforehand, warned them I was coming, as any normal person would do, instead I'd chosen to turn up like a jack-in-the-box. Problem was, nobody was opening the lid.

And I think I half dozed, I know I was as wet as it's possible to be when a car finally parked in front of the Factory and the car doors opened and they got out, the whole gang. At first they didn't see me, I blended in with the bad weather, and it wasn't until I got up that they stopped, stared at me, as though they didn't quite believe their eyes.

"Mattias?" Anna was the first to speak. She came closer. I just stood there.

"What are you doing here?" They all came up now, stood in a semi-circle and looked at me. I must have looked wet. A disheveled puffin confused about the seasons.

"I was bored," I answered. "So I came earlier than planned. Surprise!"

"How long have you been sitting here?" asked Havstein.

Hours must have passed. I was drenched.

"Not long," I said. "What's the time?"

It was a quarter to midnight. I'd been sitting there far too long, and everyone knew it.

"Where have you been?"

Carl looked at me.

"At the movies. We didn't know you were coming."

It was quiet for a couple of seconds before the meeting I'd pictured began to take form. And then came the hugs, then came the joy at my coming back early and the mood picked up, they all talked at once and asked if I'd swum all the way.

"But come on in and put some dry clothes on!" commanded Havstein, I followed him with the rest in tow, Carl took my bag and we went inside, I went straight to my room and tore off my wet clothes, I was freezing. The rain had soaked into my bag too, so I had to borrow clothes from Havstein, pants that were too short, a shirt that was too big, Charlie Chaplin upside down, and we laughed as I walked into the living room, Carl opened a bottle of wine and Anna stood by the stereo, put on some music, and I looked around. They were all here. Palli. Carl. Anna. Havstein. Although things didn't feel quite right. Find *one* mistake. Sofia was absent, and her absence was momentous and clear in all their faces now that I looked, suddenly I felt I'd been away for years, the emptiness was deafening, the sound of a thousand dogs that didn't bark and I saw how vital my return was, because the whole Factory had changed, turned around ninety degrees. The furniture, the people, everything was in the same place as before, and yet it didn't resemble the place I'd first come to at all. We somehow went on waiting for somebody to arrive, for somebody to suddenly open the door and say *hi, I'm back*. And behind all our laughter that night, baked into all our stories, in all the plans we laid and the ideas we had, lay the knowledge that we would have dropped everything we were doing and given everything we owned to have Sofia back. And if I'd possessed the power, I'd have turned the wind, rolled back the fog, called in the storms, changed the polarity of the world so that every compass was useless. But that isn't how it works. There's not a thing that can be done. The earth is not attached to anything and you can't move it an inch. So all you can do is wait, hope things will get easier, in some weeks or months or years, and one day they will, because they must. One day your shoulders will be a little less tense, your breathing a little calmer, one day your pulse will have settled and you'll no longer sit in your chair, staring apathetically and blindly before you, you'll start to walk again, step by step, out of the door, into the sun or rain, but you will need to go carefully, because the world will have shifted a little to the side since you were last out, and it will have done it in the opposite direction than the one you'd hoped. But you will learn to move again, inch by inch, and one day the traffic will flow almost as it should and you'll wait for the green man and walk with everybody else at the cross-walk, and have new things to protect, new people to care for, and summer will come, and winter, and time will fly and you'll try to keep track, it will freeze and thaw and old newspapers will pile up in the basement, you'll have to chuck them out in the end, fill the recycling bin in the street, and you'll stand there holding big plastic bags and realize that you don't know which you miss most, the people who've gone or the safety of life as it once was. Which is when you'll start smiling, carefully at first, because you'll see that the two things can no longer be separated, and even if there may not be connections between everything, there always are between the things that meant something, and you are still here.

Carl poured some wine. We drank. Havstein drank Jolly Cola and lifted his glass. Anna danced around to music I didn't recognize, and Palli asked how it had been in Stavanger, I told them I'd worked on a farm and seen Jørn again, it hadn't gone well, I said, but I'd expected that, it wasn't a surprise that it had gone that way. You lie in the bed you make.

"But we have to try not to lie in it too long," said Carl.

"True," answered Havstein.

"I don't intend to go back," I said.

Havstein's gaze met mine.

"What do you mean?"

"There's nothing left for me in Stavanger. So I'm going to stay with you. Indefinitely."

"Are you sure? I mean, are you moving here?" asked Carl.

"There's no better place, is there?"

"Maybe not."

Everybody stopped talking. The room went completely silent, apart from the music. Anna had sat back down in the sofa, next to Palli, she drank from her glass quietly, looking down, her gaze slightly averted.

"Is something wrong, or what?" I asked.

Havstein rubbed his face with his hand, crossed his arms, not a good sign.

"We were at a meeting in Tórshavn today," he said.

"And?"

"They're closing us down."

"What do you mean?"

"Cost cutting. They're closing the Factory down. Too few people live here. Or we're too far from Tórshavn. And then, on paper at least, the people that live here function too well to need support. It wasn't easy to tell what was most important, in their minds."

I felt the anxiety grip my throat and I felt nauseous, my breath quickened, I began to shiver again.

And it tumbled out of me:

"But what will happen to *us*, then?"

"Us? I don't know. Anna and Palli will probably get social security payments and apartments somewhere or other, further education, adult education. Carl will have to seek a residence permit or leave the country, and you'll probably lose your offer of treatment and have to get a new work permit. I'll help you with that. We'll find a solution, you'll see."

"And you?"

He shrugged his shoulders. It was raining.

"I'm not sure. I'll probably be relocated."

"When?"

"In seven months. The doors close on April 1, next year."

"Fuck . . ."

"Yes."

"So what should we do?"

"What do you mean?"

"I mean, we have to protest! Tell them this isn't fair. That they can't close us down. None of us has anywhere to go." I was the only one talking, the others were staring into the floor, they'd talked already.

"That boat's gone, Mattias. The decision's made. We have to find ourselves something else to do, that's just the way it is." And then he added: "You should have called before you came."

So the evening wasn't as it should be, it clamped up, wouldn't move. We opened more wine, started the wake early. I had to fight to keep panic at bay, all prospects were gone. After this there were only cliff edges to walk out from. Kjerag. Anna played old Charlie Parker records, and the mood improved a smidgen, we talked about things that were all right and went smoothly, we got drunk and danced in the living room, Anna put on another CD and turned up the volume, and I had to shout to be heard over the music that poured from the loud-speakers, I shouted *everything comes out right in the end*, and Anna turned the volume up more, and I shouted *and this will come out right, too,* and Anna turned the volume up to max, and I shouted *I'm so glad I found you guys,* but nobody heard and the Beach Boys won the day, somebody grabbed me and swung me around, I closed my eyes and danced blind, let myself go where my body wanted as the music wrapped itself like a Band-Aid over the room, soothing us, and I remember thinking, though I didn't shout it, *God only knows what I'd be without you*, and then the song finished and "I Know There's an

Answer" began, I lost hold and knocked over a lamp, stumbled toward the sofa, eyes closed, plunged over the back of it, landed with a crash behind it and when I opened my eyes, Havstein was standing over me grinning.

"Come on, we're going on a trip."

"Now?" I said and laughed. I was in no state for a trip. "Are you sure we shouldn't wait a bit? Until tomorrow morning or next week or some other time?"

"Nope, come on, you'll appreciate this."

"I'm not so sure."

"I am."

"Really?'

Havstein commanded us into our outdoor clothes and out of the Factory. He dragged us out to the car and arranged us like cheap ornaments in the seats. I rolled the window down and stuck my head out as he got the car moving and drove up the hill and out of Gjógv.

"Where . . . where are we going?" asked Anna, unable to stop giggling. "It's two-thirty in the morning," mumbled Palli, looking peeved. Carl was dozing in the front, his head lolling from side to side as we swung down toward Funningur.

"Wait, and you'll all see."

"I want to go home," Palli moaned. "Can't you just drive me home first? I'm not really up to excur . . . escurs . . . to trips right now."

"Fresh air's good for you, Palli. Non-prescription. Completely free of side effects."

Palli sniffed and grumbled to himself, stared out the window and Havstein looked at his watch.

"Damn," he said, "this'll be a near thing."

"What?" I ventured.

"Wait and see."

Havstein slammed down the accelerator and we bombed down the empty road toward Streymoy, then after crossing the bridge he wove in and out of the narrow backstreets, taking unfamiliar short cuts, I clung to the headrest in front of me, thinking how if we had an accident now there'd not be a single tooth left between us. But Havstein didn't crash. We sped through the landscape southward and drove up endless hills. I saw Skælingsfjall rising far ahead, and then I realized what he had planned for us.

"Are we going up there? Now?" Havstein drove into Skælingur and searched for a suitable place to park. "Yes, we're going up there. A great idea, don't you think?"

We did our best to keep up with Havstein as he walked briskly up the mountain slopes, a steep walk, tough going, but we did it, and for every inch we clambered up the view got better, the rain had stopped and the clouds from earlier were being blown away by the wind, it wasn't as cold as I'd feared either, one of the final nights of warmth, Indian summer on the Faroes, and I grabbed Carl who was lagging behind, dragged him after me by the arm and Anna hauled Palli along, the landscape opened up and below us all the islands came into view so we could see almost the whole country, and the sun had just started to rise, so we gathered our remaining strength, dragged ourselves up the path, shedding clothes as we went because it was so warm, tying jackets around our waists and taking turns to push each other on, Havstein shouted that it wasn't much farther and even Palli did his best now, had understood our aim, and this is among the things I remember best, the night we conquered Skælingsfjall in half the time it should have taken, that night we were spiders along the gentle slopes of the mountain and we reached the top almost at the moment the sun rose cautiously over the horizon far out into the Atlantic and spread across the landscape, washed over Tórshavn far below and the villages around it, and then eventually the mountainsides too, the whole country, and up toward us, we sat huddled together with a rock behind our backs and in the end sun in our faces, blinding us, and I remember how we laughed, how we screamed, up there on the mountain top, and I remember we screamed because it was so beautiful, because we'd managed to struggle all the way up here to see this, and this was the country we lived in, and it *was* a beautiful country, a place where people had been born, had died, but most of all we screamed because we knew that it would soon be over, in less than seven months we'd go our separate ways forever, and of course we could get together again, but it would never be the same, we'd never go back home together again, never wake up under the same roof in a closed down factory in Gjógv, where hardly anybody lived any longer, and those screams are what I remember, cries of joy and despair into emptiness, a despair about money controlled by idiotic politicians in ministerial positions given out like candy drops in a country in perpetual debt and companies that are closed down and people that are left to their fate without jobs without money without plans or prospects pushed aside forgotten hidden away sent packing on the wind and those who can't manage now must wait for better times and it isn't true there's always another bus, or train, or boat, that's just what people say to comfort those who miss the departure and have to go back to the start where nobody lives anymore and we were quiet after that and the sun lay gently on our faces making them soft and I don't know why, maybe it had to do with the sun rising over the mountain, or maybe it had to do with everything and nothing, but it was on that morning, up there on the mountain that I suddenly came upon the idea of what we should do, and I leaned toward Havstein and said: "Let's go to the Caribbean."

"We'll just move," I said. "Go away. We'll build a boat. A sailboat. And we'll leave."

He just laughed to begin with. Then he saw I meant it seriously and his smile vanished.

"It's not that easy."

"It's as easy as we make it."

"Can't we at least fly?"

"No."

It had to be a boat. And we had to build it. I don't know exactly why I insisted on that, but it felt important. Perhaps because I wanted us to do it ourselves. Prove we could create something with our own hands. One last push.

"But what will we do there, Mattias?"

"Same as we do here. Work."

"Doing what?"

"Anything."

The others joined in the conversation and I did my best to convince them that this wasn't just a good option, it was the only one we had. There was skepticism at first, but I painted them marvelous pictures, laid plans the size of football pitches and colored the continents and oceans between them with optimism's gigantic colored crayons.

"And it's not exactly like going to an unknown country. Havstein knows the Caribbean inside out. And we've all read the guide. A few times over. We know where we're going. It's just to cross the sea, and come ashore. There's no reason to stay."

Everybody nodded quietly around the semi-circle.

"Palli? You've always talked about building a boat, haven't you?"

"Not always. I—"

"And Havstein," I continued, "Havstein has waited for this for twenty years."

And we all knew, although nobody said it, that this wouldn't be just a move, but an evacuation. We'd need a good wind behind us.

And we'd need money.

That morning, as the rain started pouring again and we came down from the mountain and drove home to our beds, I felt lighter than ever before, I was sure we could do it, it seemed right, things seemed to make sense, and for once I'd solved a problem instead of letting myself be pushed over by it. We had a plan, a crazy plan, possibly, but a plan. It was time to put an end to the low level activity that had reigned in the Factory since Sofia's death, time to fill the empty space with work. We had things to do. Lots.

We all padded into the Factory and up to our bedrooms, but I didn't go to bed right away. I unpacked my wet luggage, put the driest garments in the wardrobe and hung the rest over the chairs and table. That was when I remembered them. My books! My box of space books was still standing outside, in the rain, I'd forgotten to bring it in when the others arrived. My heart thudded in my chest, I ran down the stairs, ran out, but as I lifted the damp box it fell apart, the sodden books fell out landing in the puddles outside the Factory. I went down on my knees and began picking them up feverishly, trying to dry them on my shirt sleeves, but the pages were stuck together and several books had come unglued already, they crumbled in my hands, ruined, wads of paper loosened from old, tatty covers and floated out over the ground beside me, nothing to save. I sat on my haunches, staring at what was left of the books I'd collected since I was ten, the official book about the moon landing from 1969, Buzz Aldrin's biography, books about the moon, about Mars, about outer space and the farthest flung corners where nobody would want to set foot, and an atlas of the stars, the cosmos, books on Jupiter and the Andromeda Galaxy, and comets and satellites and meteorites that might come crashing through the atmosphere to end the whole party at any moment. There was nothing I could do. Neither about the meteors nor the water. Carefully I gathered the remains of the books, the loose pages, the ruined box, and threw it all in the trash can outside the front door and went back in, padded quietly up to my room, lay under the heavy duvet, dreamed of nothing.

4

And then autumn came. The last on the Faroes. It was that autumn everybody got sicker, maybe it was something in the air, smog, I don't know, at any rate it wasn't fresh enough. And slowly but surely we started to lapse back into old habits, and into old files, into fresh delusions, Havstein restarted a program of modest medication for Anna and Palli, anti-psychotics as a food supplement. It was a good thing we were leaving.

We began building the boat too, and as the leaves fell from the non-existent trees, Carl told us how it was he'd set to sea in a yellow life-boat and almost got shipwrecked in Gjógv three weeks later. It was that autumn we saved every krone and lived on the cheap, when Palli's grandma died and Carl and I moved into her house in Tórsgøta, Tórshavn, when we filled in complicated travel claims for imaginary trips between Gjógv and Tórshavn, and we scanned with detectors for loopholes in the law, the rules and regulations and we wound the authorities that were closing us down around our little fingers, there was money to be had, and we extracted what we needed, not that any of us really understood how, it was that autumn we worked so hard we almost forgot we were sick, we were ants, entrepreneurs of the mental trade on never-ending shifts, no time to lose, no scope for changing our minds, to turn back and reconsider. The snowball I'd cautiously rolled down the mountain that morning several weeks ago had grown to gigantic proportions, as it rumbled on with enormous force, lives would be lost in trying to stop it now.

It was the boat or nothing.

Didn't we just see the world at an angle? Wasn't that what Havstein had said when I once asked him what was wrong with us? For people with a different view on reality there are liberties others never have. The privileges of the insane, because they know not what they do. We'd talked about it once. That we couldn't be blamed for our actions, our ideas, in the same way as others. That we were God's curious creatures. On a good day that's what I felt. And on the days we came up with the most idiotic proposals and plans, nobody could hold us responsible for it. Because, when you're told often enough that you have no grip on reality, that you mix your private fantasy world with the accepted world view, then you're forced to give all your ideas equal consideration. That's how it was possible to propose crossing the ocean in a homemade boat. I couldn't be held responsible for that. I was guilt free. You can't pass me off as insane. Or an idiot. You owe it to listen to me. Even you have trouble knowing whether it's me or my illness speaking. You take what you get. That's what we've done for years already. I reckon that's why no one automatically wrote the boat idea off as ridiculous from the outset. True, we went on deliberating for a couple of days, Havstein added and amended, guiding us discreetly away from our most extreme suggestions, like copying Thor Heyerdahl and sailing in a reed boat or building a submarine and traveling undetected, like Captain Nemo, surfacing at the coast of some island. We laid plans, sketched, and tapped our calculators red hot until we all agreed it was achievable within the deadline. And one day Havstein gathered us all solemnly round the kitchen table and said: *okay, hoist the topsail!*

From that day our speed increased with every orbit, we spun around our own axes and worked twice as hard as before, dug deeper and deeper into our pockets and put all we had on the table and I remember how Carl came in smiling one day, he'd been down to town and spoken to the bank, and as we sat there in the kitchen with the figures before us he put a piece of paper in front of me.

"For the boat," he said. "I've got some savings we could use. If you want."

I looked at the sheet. I could not believe what I saw.

Carl had exactly $142,000 to spare. It was just under half of what we needed.

Silence fell around the table.

"What is this?" I asked. "This is nearly a million kroner!"

"Where did you get that from?" Anna cut in, and pierced Carl with her eyes.

"I was a photographer. A few years back," he answered, and shrugged his shoulders.

Nobody said a word more. Carl passed the paper to Havstein. He took it, looked at it, put it down with a heavy sigh.

"That's a lot of money, Carl. It really is a lot of money."

"I know. I invested a bit too little in the last boat I used," he answered, adding a smile that fell short of the real thing. "I'd prefer to travel better this time."

"Are you sure about this, Carl?"

He nodded. "Yeah. Absolutely."

"Okay."

First there was just the silence. The internalized jubilation that spread vaguely through the body and settled itself carefully somewhere inside. Then the smiles came creeping, tears erupted. We smiled. Smiled as we never had before. We shouted and howled on top of each others' voices and we hung around Carl's neck, Santa Claus in mid-October. The boat was going to happen. You could be damned sure of it. We were ready for evacuation.

This is how we did it:

Carl's money got us the hull, and with help from a DIY boatmaker in Tórshavn we rented a mold and cast a forty-foot sailing boat, we worked in an enormous warehouse with the instruction manual in one hand, tools in the other, hefty disagreements flared up about how and what to do, yet we always agreed in the end, worked as one when push came to shove, decided on the sandwich method and greased the mold with release agent, greased and polished, applied thick gel coat, followed by layer upon layer of polyester and sealant and fiberglass, of fiberglass and sealant and polyester, and rolled and smoothed, and then repeated it all, ad infinitum, finished it all with insulating Divinycell and yet more layers of fiberglass and polyester and sealant, and then more fiberglass in the bottom of the boat for added strength, until fiberglass was all we could think about during the day, and we dreamed of polyester at night, and we turned the mold over, repeated every step, working quicker this time, we knew now that when the fiberglass was saturated its color shifted from white to transparent, we knew every air bubble had to be rolled out, knew that it had to be sixty-four degrees Fahrenheit in the room for things to set, we learned from our mistakes and sheer repetition as our money ran out and we had to get more careful, work more quickly, cut back on mistakes, topcoat, gel coat, freeboard, port and starboard, we didn't have the money to do the work twice, we reinforced the bottom, laid lead down by the keel, made calculations for the center of gravity without quite getting it right, paid some local sailors to have a look, but too late, they stood on the concrete floor of the warehouse and laughed, told us we'd be sailing with a slight list all the way, it would be a lopsided boat, but a boat all the same, we argued, and moved on to the deck, molded it, worrying whether things should be this way or that, fixed and riveted it to the hull, and watched our money vanish from our bank accounts and our doubt grow bigger by the day, with a faint unease that the boat would never float properly, that it might keel over and capsize in the waves, just like Alexander L. Kielland twenty years prior, but all we could do was hope for the best, decide that it *was* good enough, that it had to work.

Carl and I became weekly commuters, we spent our weekends with the others in a soundless Gjógv and the rest of the week down in Tór-shavn. I got back the job I'd had before summer and continued with the hopeless task of creating forests on the Faroes along with the ever-optimistic Herluf and Jógvan, and Carl got a job at the docks, loading and unloading the ships that came in. He soon got us a good deal on freight, and it wasn't long before everything we needed for the boat was transported from the mainland to the Faroes for a symbolic sum. I'd usually go home through town after work, walk down Eystari Ringvegur in the twilight, past the stadium with its training sessions and the whooshing sounds of the bowling alley opposite, down through Viðarlundin Park with its beautiful trees and art gallery and then up toward the SMS Shopping Center where I'd buy the bare essentials at Miklagarður, then I'd walk with my shopping bags into the town center, and I remember thinking there were more trees in town these days, seemed that way at least, I noticed gardens here and there with big trees, bushes on street corners, and I thought perhaps it was possible after all, if only they could spread, like a reverse desertification, these clusters of trees that everybody was so proud of that they marked them on the town map, if one could only get them to spread across the islands, if one only kept planting more, it might just work. But I was also aware that these trees only stayed alive because the houses shel-tered them from all sides, protected them from the saltwater carried on the wind each day in foul weather, and that in the long run you couldn't win. You could plant trees on every slope from island to island, but for each tree you planted the previous one would shrivel up and die, and when you'd finally finished, when you'd planted the last tree and looked back, there'd be just a handful of trees left standing, scattered thinly across the country. But there was no giving up. I went on with my work, planted seeds between the big trunks, and walked in circles to make the experience last, while my council wages dripped into Havstein's account, krone by krone.

And then I remember a Saturday afternoon, it's the end of October, Carl is sitting in Palli's grandma's sofa staring straight ahead, seeing nothing, and the telephone rings. Carl gets up carefully, goes out into the hall, to the telephone table, I hear him talking in a quiet voice, *Right,* he says *really, are you sure?* And then *okay.* Then he comes back in and says just one thing: *Pilot whales.*

I'm instantly out of my chair. I look at him, straight.
"Where?"
Carl blinks.
"Sandágerðisvík," he says.
I'm confused. I don't understand.
"Where's that?"
"Ten minutes from here. By foot."

And I remember we're running. Running as hard as we can along Niels Finsensgøta and out toward Sandágerði, running until we have the heavy taste of blood in our mouths and yet that's nothing compared to the blood that will already be flowing down there in the bay, we run as hard as we can, yelling at each other, but neither can hear the other, but that's unimportant, makes no odds and it's the sound of our shoes over the asphalt I remember, the people we pass on the road and the crowd assembled on the hills above the beach, Carl and I crash through almost tumbling over the edge, onto the beach, out into the water, where hundreds of pilot whales are killed by precise Faroe Islanders in minutes, hours before cell phones and landlines have been ringing around the villages, men have dropped what they were doing because of the rumor that there might be up to a thousand whales in the fjord, five schools, all that's needed is to decide how many schools to take and where they should be driven in, and people at work are given time off, allowed to drop their tasks and throw themselves into their cars with the radio on, down to the harbor, out to the fjord, the whales are coming in, the men have placed the boats in a semicircle around the small whales, sixty or seventy boats, maybe more, impossible to count, they coax the whales into shallower waters, some men leave their boats, jumping out into the icy sea and are met by others who wade out from the beach, equipment in hand, hooks tied to thick rope, they move in and grab the closest whales, drive their hooks down their breathing holes, it makes it quicker they say, and the blood flows, the blood drenches the beach and our shoes in red, an entire bay colored red, and hundreds of pilot whales are killed with practiced efficiency, a grotesque vision to the untutored eye, to me it all looks chaotic, unplanned, but Havstein has explained what happens and I try to concentrate on that, there's no danger, he's told us, they know what they're doing, it's been done for centuries, there are nearly a million pilot whales out there and they only take what they need, there are rules, systems, old equipment was shelved long ago, only the select few are permitted to participate in the kill itself, and it's over in seconds, think of them as big fish, he said, there's more blood, that's all, it's no worse, this isn't commercial fishing, this is food for survival, barely nothing is wasted, the children eat the dried meat as a treat and I hold onto that thought as I drag Carl with me through the crowded beach and we stand there bewildered for some minutes as the six- to nine-foot-long whales drift in toward the beach, tails thrashing in the water, knocking anyone over who tries to grab their back fins or anything else, hundreds of pounds of whale against these small human beings, and I stand watching the men out there in the ice-cold water, and wonder how they can stay out there so long without going completely stiff, without losing the feeling in their fingers before I see them thrust their fists down into the whales' guts after killing them, warming their hands in the heat of the animals and it strikes me how much quieter everything is than I'd expected, I'd imagined screaming, hollering, a din, but everything happens in silence, as though somebody had turned the sound off and was only showing the pictures, apart from the commands and advice yelled back and forth, and the kids stand along the shoreline, with their mothers, and they follow events, watching their fathers at work, and the situation is robed in a deep solemnity, nobody laughs, nobody cheers, and

I search for some dignity in all this, search for the respect and think I find it somewhere, but I'm uncertain, these are beautiful animals dying, maybe I'm just overwhelmed, and I see men in blue boilersuits noting down the names of everyone involved, who's doing what, and these notes will form the basis for how the meat is divided when the whales are eventually brought to the butchers, all according to rules that scarcely anybody remembers the origins of, those who spotted the schools will get a whole whale and then going down the list people will get so much for this work or that, those who went in the water, those who hauled the whales into land, Havstein has explained it all, but I remember only fragments, the whales are numbered and divided into skinns, the men meet and give their names and are allocated meat by the skinn, a unit I don't understand, and the meat is sliced up accordingly, an abundance, enough for everyone, and what is left will be sent to the hospitals and the needy, to stores where those who weren't present will be able to buy it, and I drag Carl with me down to the water's edge to get a better view and somebody yells at us, tells us to grab a wet rope lying on the beach, it stretches out into the water where a Faroe Islander has hooked a whale and we grab it hard with both hands, dig our feet firmly in the wet sand, and when the signal is given, we pull, there are eight of us and we pull all we can and the whale is hauled to land, then we move on to the next rope and pull again, one after the other the whales are brought in to land, and I'm not sure if I'm happy about it or not, but I do it, do what I'm asked because I'm a polite person, and one of the men dressed in blue walks over to us, takes our names, writes them in his book, and tells us to come to the butcher tomorrow, early, before seven, we're entitled, he says, to enough pilot whale to last us well into the New Year, bewildered, I only just manage to thank him before he slaps me on the back and walks off, I look over at Carl who's holding another rope, he's gone pale, and he looks at me, straight at me, and says:

"We've got to go now."

"What?"

"We've got to go. Now!"

It was dark when we got home, wet, frozen. We were subdued, changed into dry clothes and went out to the car. Carl sat behind the wheel and looked blankly out the windshield, I sat beside him, put the heating on.

"Are you all right?" I asked.

"The tunnel to Kollafjørður is closed," was all he said. "Road work until eleven. We'll have to take Oyggjarvegur."

"Over the mountain?"

"Yes."

The dark on the Faroes. Have I mentioned that? No? That nothing's darker? No streetlights once you're out of town. Hardly any traffic in the evening. When you turn off your headlights you can't even see your hand, even if you hold it close to your face, even if you can feel it against your skin. You see nothing. And nothing is darker than Oyggjarvegur on a Saturday night in October, rain, fog three feet thick, dew on the road, a half-hour's drive, steep drops and no guard rails, the middle of nowhere. That was the road we took. The very longest route.

We drove down the Norðari ring road and turned in toward Oyggjarvegur, Carl tailed a car going in the same direction, following its lights for some minutes before it picked up speed and vanished over the horizon in front of us. Carl said nothing, just brought his speed down, leaned across the wheel and stared out between the window wipers, scanning for asphalt twelve feet ahead. Before the early nineties when the tunnel between Kaldbaksbotnur and Kollafjørður was opened, Oyggjarvegur had been the only road into Tórshavn. These days people didn't use it much. Not at night, anyway. On a cloudless, postcard-perfect summer's day it was probably the finest route you could take, driving across wide plateaus on good asphalt roads, and farther in along winding stretches of road on the edges of slopes that overlooked Kollafjørður and Kaldbak, but in the autumn it was like driving blindfold in a trash bag. The headlamps hit small cats' eyes at the edge of the road, and the best you could do was aim to stay in the middle of the road, hope for no oncoming traffic.

We'd driven almost all the way down to the quarry when the rain got so heavy Carl had to pull to the side to wait for the worst of it to pass. He parked at the side of the road next to one of the big stone breakers and turned off the ignition, we sat in total darkness as enormous raindrops hammered on the roof, trying their best to come through the metal. I couldn't see him, and could barely hear him through the deafening rain, but I sensed it nonetheless. That there was something seriously wrong. That he was sitting there crying.

"Carl?" I asked, in his direction. "Are you okay?"

The rain just fell harder and harder.

It was raining cats and dogs.

"I can't take anymore," he said. "I just can't take it any longer."

And the sea goes on rising.

And everything will flood.

And before I could say more, he exploded in the dark, he screamed as loud as he could and I heard him beating the car roof with all his strength, his fists going through softness before they met metal that bent with the force, his feet thrashed the pedals wildly, I stretched my arms out and caught him for a moment, but he pushed me off and bellowed at me to fucking leave him alone, and I retreated to my side of the car, making myself small as he smashed into the wheel, into the dashboard, I heard the sound of the transparent plastic cover on the speedometer break and a second later everything fell silent, perfectly silent. That was when I grew seriously afraid. That was when panic really set in again, and in that moment I realized neither of us was in control, and we had no Havstein here to take care of us. Perhaps we'd never get in control, because we weren't right, had somehow fallen apart, and there was something wrong with Carl, but none of us knew what, even though we'd discussed it, Sofia, Anna, Palli, and I, countless times. We had so many theories, all more or less built on fantasy, symptoms we thought we'd observed. Havstein had eventually mentioned PTSD to us. Post traumatic stress disorder. That was just about all we knew. But we had no idea what the cause was, what we should do to hold him in check, what situations Carl should avoid or the consequences of his having a relapse. We weren't allowed to read books on psychiatry. That was the rule, and it was non-negotiable. So I sat there, waiting, even though I had no idea what I was waiting for. Maybe just better weather. And cautiously I lifted a hand and switched the roof light on. Carl looked straight at me, and in his eyes I saw pure, white fear, he was breathing quickly, mumbling things nobody could understand, not even with all the world's dictionaries.

"Carl?" I said, stretching a hand cautiously out to him.

"Don't fucking touch me!" he shouted.

"No, of course." I pulled my hand back quickly. Rolled the window down to let in some fresh air. Cold rain came in through the window, our breath turned to frosty clouds. So we sat there, in silence and darkness, until Carl was calmer and began to relax.

"I shouldn't have gone down to Sandágerðisvík today," he said finally. "I should have stayed at home."

I nodded.

I sat in silence.

For a long time.

Two cars passed us, their lights cut into the landscape, sliced into the cold, damp car before it returned to darkness.

So we sat there.

And then I decided.

It was now or never.

I took the chance and asked:

"Carl?"

"Yes?"

"How did you actually end up in that life boat?'

"You don't want to know."

"Would it help if you told someone?"

"No."

"I know almost nothing. What actually happened to you. I only want to help."

"There's nothing you can do."

"Come on—please."

"Do you really want to know?"

"Yes, I really do."

At first he looked at me as though he didn't understand what I was talking about. Then he turned to the back seat and grabbed a bottle of water, he took a sip and laid the bottle in his lap, looked at me again, a different look this time, lighter, unfocused, and then it began to roll, picture after picture, the entire story he'd never told any of us, not even Havstein perhaps.

"All right." Pause. "I'll ask you two questions, Mattias. And I know you'll answer *no* to both. Have you heard of Bill Haglund?"

"No."

"Have you heard of Pilica?"

I considered.

"No," I answered.

"That's what I thought."

"And?"

"Bill Haglund had the most onerous and difficult job you can imagine, and he had inadequate time and equipment to do it. Yet he managed to carry out his work, and managed it with pride and enormous skill. But I'll come to that later. I have to begin at the other end, or it won't make sense. I have to begin in Ohio. I come from Columbus, Ohio. I trained as a photographer, and worked for a handful of newspapers, big and small, in the US, before working for five years as a freelance photographer in Chechnya, Rwanda, and above all in Bosnia-Herzogovena. I took about twelve thousand photographs in that time. Only a tiny number were ever printed, few papers would take them. A lot of them were used instead as visual evidence in court and as documentation for the UN. Anyway, I won't go into all that. So I arrived in Bosnia-Herzogovena in the fall of 1992 as an official US photographer, and in 1993 I stayed at the Holiday Inn in Sarajevo, from September to February, most of the journalists did, they kept close together, practical reasons, exchanging information, because so much was happening at that time in Bosnia that one always felt one was in the wrong place at the wrong time, it seemed almost like part of their tactics, to create such mayhem that we ended up walking around in aimless circles missing it all. That was my impression at least, until I finally took the decision to leave Sarajevo, to give it up as my base, and so stop my day to day dependence on getting rides from the UN or Red Cross to the places I wanted to visit. So I went to Srebrenica, have you heard of it?"

"Vaguely."

"It was a Bosnian enclave, a Muslim city locked in and isolated on Serbian territory. I got there at the end of February, 1993, by which time there'd already been rumors for several weeks about what was happening there, and the rumors weren't good. Srebrenica was blanketed in deep snow, and they were short of absolutely everything, medicines, equipment, many houses were already destroyed, people were living on the streets in the snow. I remember a doctor I met from the World Health Organization estimating that between twenty and thirty people were dying every day and that thousands of women and children were in need of immediate evacuation. And in April, as repayment for empty promises, the Security Council declared Srebrenica, along with Tuzla, Gorazde, and Sarajevo, one of six so-called "Safe Areas." That was stupid too, of course. The UN dispatched a hundred and seventy Canadian soldiers without any mandate to shoot unless they were fired on directly, all they managed to do was prolong the time before the town went to hell some years later. I stayed in Srebrenica a few months before leaving Bosnia for long periods and going to Rwanda and Chechnya, Grozny, but I don't want to talk about that. You'll have to read about that yourself. If you want to. Anyway, the truth was I hadn't planned to return to Bosnia at all, I thought I had enough photographs nobody wanted, but then I got a call, from a BBC friend, he rang me one afternoon in March 1995, and read the orders Radovan Karadzic had made concerning Srebrenica's fate: *Create an intolerable situation of complete insecurity without any hope of survival or life in Srebrenica.* So here was the Serbian plan. The bombing started on the night of July 6, 1995. I'd been there for over a month, living in an abandoned house on the outskirts of town. The Canadian UN soldiers were replaced with Dutch soldiers, and Serbian tanks and artillery fired directly on the observation posts in the Potocari quarter and on the center of Srebrenica, the entire city. The noise, Mattias! The noise was the worst. Mortar grenades raining down on the city hitting people at random. Did you know they whine really loudly before hitting the ground? Well, they do. A hellish noise. And I saw so many dead. I ran down one street with a family, I don't know where we were running, I just followed them, I didn't hear the sound of shots, I just saw she was hit in the back of the head by two bullets that blew off her face, obliterated, in a split second, and then I stumbled and ended up lying next to her, her husband just went on running, the kids ahead of him, I tried to pull her out of the road, I don't know why, she was already dead, maybe I wanted to help, but they just shot her to bits in my arms, and I had to let go and run onward, run toward the UN base, in the middle of town, there must have been desperate people in the thousands there, the Dutch had no choice in the end but to cut holes in the defenses, let us into the camp."

"Did they get everybody in?"

"No. The pressure was too great, way too great. An endless stream, and I think in just a couple of days over twenty thousand people were gathered around the camp. Srebrenica was about to fall, and the Serbian infantry had advanced into the city. The Dutch pleaded with NATO for an air attack, but didn't get it, I don't know, maybe it was Clinton that refused, or Chirac maybe, or somebody else, I have no idea. And when the bombing was finally agreed on, it was too late, they barely hit anything, and it was after that the evacuation began. The Serbs intensified their attacks and forced the UN into an agreement they couldn't refuse, the Serbs sent in every bus they could find, the women and children were put on them, and any men between fifteen and seventy were separated off with the assistance of helpless UN personnel, according to General Mladic all Bosnian Muslim men were potential war criminals, so they needed to be interrogated before being released. They left backpacks, suitcases, identity papers in piles behind them, and the buses carrying the women streamed into Tuzla. But four thousand men from the Srebrenican enclave never arrived in Bratunac for the planned hearings. They'd gone. Disappeared into thin air. But nobody just disappears. The mass murder of men from the Srebrenican enclave began on July 13, and when it went quiet again six days later, over seven thousand Bosnian Muslims had apparently vanished off the face of the earth. It was 'evil written on the darkest pages of history,' as the International War Crimes Tribunal judge put it. And that was how I met William D. Haglund."

The rain had stopped.

A car drove up behind us, slowed down. I looked at Carl. He looked at me. The car braked, swung in front of us so its headlights went into our eyes, somebody got out, walked toward us. He shouted at us in Faroese, and I only half-understood him.

"Sorry, do you speak Danish?" I yelled back.

He walked close up to the car.

"Do you need help?"

We needed all the help we could get. But not the kind he could offer.

"No thanks, we're just resting for a bit," I answered, rather bewildered and uneasy. "We'll drive on soon." He smiled and stretched out a hand. We shook hands and nodded. Almost overwhelming.

"Great. I was just worried something might be wrong. Wanted to make sure nothing was up." He studied us for a moment, as though he couldn't quite believe what he was seeing. "Tourists?"

"Yes," I lied, pretending to be embarrassed.

"Take care then, when you drive on. This is a dangerous road, when it's as dark as this. You should take the other road back."

"Thanks," I said.

"No problem."

He walked back to his car, we heard him exchange words with his passenger, then laughter. He pointed at us, started the car and continued down the slope.

I rolled up the window feeling troubled.

"Maybe we ought to go home," I suggested. "Back to Havstein."

"Forgotten places, Mattias," Carl went on, not taking in what had just happened. "There are forgotten places, just as there are forgotten people. Barely anybody thinks about Srebrenica now, most people haven't ever heard of Gorazde, and few know what happened in Visegrád, on the bridge over the Drina. In these places you find the people that were forgotten before anyone noticed them. That's where you find those who never became famous, whom nobody heard from, or knew about, the people who stayed behind. This is the real no man's land. There are no past heroes here, no astronauts who have grown old and been forgotten, only people you never thought existed at the outset. And it was in this no man's land I met William D. Haglund, early in the summer of 1996. Bill was the forensic expert to the War Crimes Tribunal in Bosnia, and the man in charge of the excavation of mass graves in Cerska, as well as half a dozen other places. It was here that the men who disappeared from Srebenica resurfaced. He'd just come from the excavations in Rwanda when I met him, and I can tell you right now, Mattias, I've never met a finer man than Bill Haglund, and it upsets me to think he's remembered by so few people, that his honor was in tatters by the time he'd finished and traveled back to his wife and family in Seattle."

"What do you mean?"

"When I first met Bill, he was a person with humor, who could laugh at himself, a little eccentric perhaps, yet absolutely focused on his task. And while everybody else wore blue UN uniforms, Bill always made a point of working at the graves in a shirt and tie, and a distinctive broad-brimmed, brown hat. He had enormous respect for the people he dug up, often referred to the corpses as gentlemen. When the work with the graves in Bosnia began, he knew from the start that every minute had to be used to the maximum, because the Bosnian summer is short and it's only possible to dig from April until some way into October. He also had to be prepared for the corpses to be tangled up in deep graves, rather than lying in systematic rows under the surface, as they were in the old days. I remember how Bill stood for hours at the foot of the grave in the morning, just looking, as if he was trying to solve a jigsaw puzzle, trying to work out, for example, which arm belonged to which foot, one couldn't just wrench at an arm, the body belonging to it might lie much farther down and the arm would simply come loose if he pulled too hard."

"Was that awful, seeing all that?"

"It was appalling, Mattias. And the sound when they got them up. I'll never forget the sound, a huge damp sigh from the wet earth as it released the bodies. They found one hundred and fifty people in the grave at Cerska. But that wasn't the worst."

"No?"

"No. After Cerska we moved on to a grave near the football field in Nova Kasaba, and that was when I noticed Bill getting tired. He'd spent months just getting all the equipment in place before starting work. The War Crimes Tribunal in Bosnia who'd commissioned the excavation had forgotten to put money aside for the project, and the UN couldn't provide funding. There was so much equipment missing to begin with, a mortuary, a cold room, digging machines, X-ray machines, bags, shovels, they didn't even have cars to get around in. And there were ninety of them, pathologists, radiologists, archaeologists, and anthropologists, experts from all over the world. So they were forced to scrape together equipment from any source, outdated military stuff, friends and acquaintances, every contact they had, they even dug in their own pockets, until eventually the organization Bill represented, Physicians for Human Rights, came to the rescue and paid for the excavation, while they waited for more money from the US government. Meanwhile the Norsk Folkehjelp turned up and loaned Haglund a dog team to sniff out mines, to make the graves safe before they started digging. Most of the graves lay deep in Serbian territory, you see, and Haglund's team were terrified somebody might sabotage the excavations to cover the evidence, it would only have taken one grenade, Mattias. So Bill tried to convince NATO and the UN that they needed to guard the place at night, but they refused, they didn't want to get involved like that, they were only prepared to go as far as escorting the team in and out of the area and to watch over them while they worked. In the end, Bill and some of the others took turns sleeping by the mass graves, because that was the only way to get the NATO soldiers to stick around. I ended up doing it too, I figured it was easier, it meant I didn't have to go back and forth, so I slept out in the field alongside the pathologists and forensic experts, and what fabulous nights they were, you should have been there, I've never seen such clear starry nights, you totally forgot where you were once it was dark. All your concentration would be taken by the sound of the stream burbling past, the birds twittering in the big trees and the balmy air that surrounded you as you lay there dozing. But it wasn't doing Bill any good, not in the long run. He'd get up before anybody else, start work, and they'd work for twelve hours a day, first they'd prod the earth with long steel prongs to gauge its resistance, then they'd pull them up and sniff them, it's the only way. After a while, as the graves are located and opened, each body is examined, registered as evidence, measured and marked with a little red flag. There were so many flags after a while. Far too many flags. And Bill showed me stuff, how he could tell when people had had their hands tied behind their backs, had been murdered, and these men weren't soldiers, no way, I saw so much ordinary clothing, sneakers, Adidas, Levi's, and I watched all of this start to take its toll on Bill too. He grew edgier, he'd answer abruptly when people asked him things, he'd bark his orders, he became impatient and lost his sense of humor, with each body they pulled up, more just kept coming, it was endless. Bill had promised to oversee an excavation in Croatia too, so he began making the hundred and fifty mile journey back and forth regularly between the two sites, and then when the boss of the temporary mortuary had to travel back to the United States, Bill took that job on too, he slept in his car, traveling between three places, just pulled to the side of the road at night and slept for a few hours before driving on. He was supposed to have a week's vacation with his wife of twenty years, but he cut it down to three days, people said he'd started falling asleep in interviews, and every time I saw him the rings under his eyes had grown bigger, his mood was a bit worse, like the calendar was beating him up."

"Fuck."

"Things only got worse. That fall the rain came. We transferred to Pilica, where they thought there might be up to a thousand dead in the grave, it was probably the most important site for the War Crimes Tribunal. But it was a complete mess, Mattias, the rain turned the grave into a swimming pool, the water had to be pumped out every morning before they started. It was the ghastliest thing I've ever seen, I couldn't even photograph it. The water ruined everything, Christ, it was just an enormous pool of semi-decomposed people. Then one night, I'm sleeping outside with Bill, it's one of our last nights, and I wake up and hear a sort of noise through the rain, I get up and climb out of the tent, but it's so dark I can see barely three feet ahead, I find a flashlight and pistol next to Bill and take them out with me, and then I hear a dog barking, and, and, well, sometimes there'd be dogs coming at night, to the graves, and they, well, you can imagine, so I, I just wanted to get the dog away before it spoiled things for us, see, so I move to the grave, step by step, and it's raining so much I can barely see the ground ahead, even though I've got the flashlight, I go to the very edge of the grave, stand there shining the flashlight, but I can't see a thing and everything's quiet, it's as if, I don't know, but the damn dog's gone, it's damn well hiding or something, or it's run home again, and I'm about to turn back, but as I do the dog jumps at me from behind, so I panic and lose my foothold and my feet slip from under me, and I'm pulled backward and land on my face, in the grave—"

Carl stared straight ahead of him now, saying nothing. I stretched a hand out again to put it on his shoulder, but he shoved it off and I had to pull it back.

"Carl, maybe we should, we should just—"

"And I scream, I scream like never before, I yell for Bill and I have my eyes closed, because I can't bear to look around me, but I can feel where I am, and even though my eyes are shut I can see stuff, right, you wouldn't want to know what I see, and it's like being in quicksand, I start being dragged down, when I reach my hands out, my fingers glide through wet, rotten flesh and it's the worst stench imaginable, and I shout out for Bill, but it feels like a lifetime before he comes, in his underwear, and he grabs my arm, as hard as he can, pulls me up, and he's angry, livid, I try to tell him what happened, but he's just furious, and next morning I've had enough and leave, I go back to Sarajevo and check into a hotel, and I stand in the shower for days before it has any effect, then I sleep for a week before taking a flight to London. By which time I've decided I'll never take another photograph as long as I live."

Carl was quiet now. Completely quiet. He sat crying, his hands in front of his face and I couldn't help him, I could only wait for the worst to pass and then calmly ask him to swap seats with me, before I drove the rest of Oyggjarvegur and continued toward Kollafjørður, the long way home. We were already one and a half hours late as I parked outside the Factory at about nine, Havstein came out pointing at his watch and looking angry, I took a step out of the car and he stood in my path.

"What have you two been doing?" he asked. I looked at Carl who stood there helpless, eyes blank, seeing nothing.

"We broke down," I answered. "The car's not quite right. And we had to take the Oyggjarvegur too."

"Why?"

"Road work in the tunnel."

"And you broke down too?"

"Yes, but it went fine. We used the jumper cables and stopped another car."

Havstein looked at me skeptically. I didn't feel comfortable.

"There aren't jumper cables in the car."

"Damn. Well, that explains why it took so long!" I answered, trying to smile.

Havstein snorted, and changed the subject.

"Did you get to see the pilot whale slaughter today?"

I couldn't bear to start on that.

"No. Must have passed us by."

"Oh well. There's some hour-and-a-half-old dinner waiting for you. Come on." Havstein waved us in and I heard him saying something or other about trust between people, but couldn't hear what.

We had to eat alone that evening, the others had finished ages ago, but that suited us perfectly. It was hardly the night for big discussions, and when everybody went to bed relatively early, one by one, there were no protests from either me or Carl. We stayed up, sat on the sofas, and almost felt normal again.

"Do you feel better now?"

Carl nodded slowly. "Yes. Thank you. For saying nothing to Havstein, I mean." He shot a sudden, sharp glance in my direction. "And all this stuff I've told you today, you're not to tell a soul, understand? Not a soul."

I understood.

"But what have you told Havstein about all this?"

"Nothing. Or, rather, I just said I was in Bosnia for a year, with the KFOR. That nothing particular had happened, but that I have fragile nerves. And that I've got a wrecked marriage behind me."

"And do you?"

"Yeah. And I've got kids, too."

Then he continued his story from where he'd left off on Oyggjarvegur, though he was a good deal calmer now. He told me more about Bill Haglund, Bill had returned to his family in Seattle in October 1996, by which time he'd been involved in the excavation of 1,200 bodies in a year, he'd met the deadline the War Crimes Tribunal had given him, yet within a week of coming home, he was informed that he'd been suspended from his position and that his work in Bosnia was to be placed under the microscope. There had been complaints about his leadership style, about the absence of security around the graves, the mislabeling of body parts, etc. Of course Haglund felt angry, hurt, and dejected, after all, he'd achieved the impossible, five mass graves in three months, with inadequate help and equipment, what more could you ask! He was cleared eventually of all accusations and it was agreed that nobody could have done differently, but it must still have hurt. Then the story returned to Carl, he'd gone to London with no plans, really, just to be back in the civilized world, and it was there, in a hotel bar in Kensington, that he'd met Stina, an Icelandic actress with the National Theater in Reykjavík. She'd been in London filming for a week, a small role in a British film, and because of her, Carl stayed on in London for her three remaining weeks of filming, and on the day she was leaving, she asked, almost for fun, if he'd like to come to Iceland with her, and he said yes. He had nobody waiting for him, nobody demanding that he should be here or there, the money from the sale of photographs to the press and Bosnian War Crimes Tribunal had finally given him some solid capital to live on, and he thought it might do him good to get as far away from Bosnia and Rwanda as possible. Stina had a little apartment on the outskirts of Reykjavík and they squeezed themselves in there for some months, celebrated Christmas and New Year, met her family, and maybe it was because the apartment was so small that she got pregnant so fast, then they discovered it was twins, they sold her apartment in town and bought a family-friendly house in Akranes. Stine continued to commute into the city, and Carl stayed at home like a caretaker, he fixed and repaired, cleaned and kept order, and was happy with that, a calm, quiet time. They got married in Reykjavík that July, when she was six months pregnant, a big wedding and everything, and when the twins arrived in October there was a genuine *Love Boat* atmosphere at home. Carl stayed at home with the kids, and it was then he started sleeping badly. The nightmares came with increased frequency, and he suffered more and more from hallucinations. His head scrambled the experiences he'd had in Bosnia, Chechnya, and Rwanda and mixed them into a mass that made it increasingly difficult to concentrate. He developed an anxiety that something might happen to the children. When he played with them in the sandpit, he became convinced there were corpses buried under the sand, he saw sneakers poking up, the smell of rot filled his nostrils, and in the end the kids were banned from playing in the sandpit altogether. Meanwhile his headaches worsened, migraine-like, and he thought that the kids seemed restless in his presence, that he made them insecure. He didn't dare say anything to Stina, he'd only ever told her he was a photographer, not where he'd been and on the rare occasions she'd asked him, he'd told her about the United States, the years before he'd gone to Europe. Eventually she sensed it, that something was wrong, without knowing what, his behavior grew steadily stranger, until it couldn't go on any longer. She grew frightened of leaving him with the children, sent them to day care, but not even that helped. Carl became more and more depressed, stopped talking, slept nearly all day, and gradually the barrier between reality and dream began to erode. And it's around now that Carl gets out of bed, in the beginning of December, the store windows are decorated for Christmas in Reykjavík, and the lights are hanging over the street in Akranes. Carl eats his breakfast, puts on some warm clothes, goes out. He takes the bus into Reykjavík and then on to the airport in Keflavik. He puts himself on a flight going East to Ehilsstaðir and from there takes a bus to the harbor in Seyðisfjörður. He walks to and fro until it's dark, and then at night he sneaks on board one of the big boats. He carefully lowers an inflatable lifeboat onto the sea, and then lowers himself over the side of the ship after it. He tugs the straps, and the life boat blows up in seconds, cone-shaped, like a tent on the sea. He's not completely conscious of what he's doing, he's somewhere between dream and waking, but all he can think is that he has to get away, now, he has to get away from the kids before he destroys them, and he has to get away from the corpses that might surface in the sandpit at any time, unveiling him to Stina. Then he takes the oar and paddles out beyond the breakers, out into the open sea, and he paddles until he can't go on, until he collapses in the bottom of the boat, falls asleep, and for the first time in months he sleeps through an entire night, no nightmares, no harsh sounds waking him, no pounding headache. Next morning he wakes in a panic, his head is completely clear, and he sees he's in the middle of the Atlantic in a rubber dinghy. He can't breathe at first, can only feel the fear that's grabbed him, squeezing him tight. He grows terrified of falling into the sea and seals the rubber exit, and with it the window, sits there in those few square feet inside the cone-shaped rubber tent for several days as the waves drag the dinghy up and down. He has no idea where he is, or where he's going, but as the shock subsides and his reason returns, he concludes that he's likely to be carried by the Gulf Stream to Norway or England, he'll get there sooner or later as long as he can hold out. And the days pass, routines take over, he learns to know the dinghy, finds the little container with portions of drinking water in a side pocket, he has equipment for fishing, a flare, sunscreen, a navigational map. He manages to open the sluice in the bottom of the vessel so that the plastic keel fills with water to prevent it from turning over in the waves. He survives. The days pass. And for the first time since leaving Bosnia, he wishes he had a camera, so he could take pictures from the boat. But he hasn't, and after another week in heavy seas and after being blown backward more than forward, he starts running out of drinking water, he hasn't caught a fish for days, and there's something wrong with the boat, it's started leaning to one side in the last few days, maybe there's a leak somewhere, but he can't find it. So he closes all the openings again and waits, just waits, lying at an angle, for nearly two days, before he dares open up and look out again, and even though it's dark, he can see that the waves are breaking against land far ahead, he sees land, is convinced that it's Norway, and for the first time in weeks he takes out the oar, paddles frantically, because it is New Year's Eve and the boat is lying low in the water, it's leaking, it's clearly leaking, and Carl paddles as hard as he can, but he can't get beyond the breakers, the stream isn't bringing him closer to land, but farther away, and he thinks he sees people on the beach, maybe he's mistaken, but yes, there must be, and a moment later they send up a New Year's rocket, and Carl's pulse quickens, because there *are* people on the beach, and he fumbles about, finds the flare, sticks it out of the opening and sends it up, a red light above the ocean, and he knows they must have seen him, and he paddles against the stream trying to reach land, but it's not happening, he's not moving and the boat lies low in the water, it's going to sink, and he sees two people get into an old wooden boat, they're coming toward him, and he's so happy, he yells, but nobody hears him because of the wind and rain or because he's run out of strength, and he gathers some belongings and prepares to leave the boat, because a row-boat is coming, and the next thing he remembers he's sitting in the kitchen wishing us all a happy New Year.

That was what he told me. Nothing more. And we never talked about it again. He just repeated what he'd said earlier that night, that I had to promise not to say anything about what he'd told me. I promised solemnly. I promised even though I was burning to know why he'd lied to Havstein about what had happened, and wanted to ask about Sofia, and I would have had a hint of reproach in my voice I think, I wanted to know why he'd seemed so unaffected when she'd been ill and died, and whether it had anything to do with what he'd been through. But I didn't ask. I knew more than enough already.

----■----

November. With everything that month brought. Carl was clearer to me now, since he'd talked about what he'd gone through, he'd become three-dimensional somehow, and it was somehow reassuring to think he was sicker than me, it meant I could take care of him, or at least that's what I imagined, although I couldn't know if he went around the house in Tórsgøta thinking the same about me. We had an under-standing for one another, and each did our best to avoid knocking the other off balance. I never mentioned the whale slaughter to Carl again, I scanned the papers for war movies and shows that might not be good for him to watch, when there was construction in the street and the risk of pneumatic drills being used I'd warn him in advance, so he wouldn't be frightened by the noise and think it was something else. I let him sleep with the light on. I usually tried to make dinner for him, low fat foods that I imagined were good for him. And, for his part, Carl tried his best to ensure my life stayed on the rails. He let me play the Cardigans albums that I'd gotten from Sofia as often as I wanted, and Swedish pop filled our living room most afternoons until late into the evening, I sat glued to the speakers, searching her out in the sound, like a retired archaeologist, until the neighbors started complaining and Carl treated me to some earphones so I could have the volume as high as I liked without worrying about being in anyone's way. Carl was good at encouraging me, too, telling me I was doing important work at Hvitanesvegur and that the boat would be finished on time, there was no need to worry. And he reminded me to call Mother and Father once a week, every Thursday, at a quarter past seven Faroese time, to report that everything was fine, that I was alive. I said nothing about the boat.

Life in Tórshavn was different than life in Gjógv. It reminded me of Stavanger, as though the city had been washed in water that was too hot and shrunk it to a third of its size. Carl and I got better at going out in the evenings, after we'd finished working. Hung out a lot at Café Natúr, drank gallons of coffee or beer and got to know the staff, we went out bowling or to the movies in Tinghusvegur, saw whatever was on, regardless. We hung around Niels Finsensgøta, went up to the Manhattan occasionally when Carl wanted to hear live music, or took the car up to the drive-in Burger King near the SMS Shopping Center. We were never bored. Not really. And we talked, we talked and our conversations were like endless serials, starting in the morning and continuing when we came home from work, through the late afternoon and evening until we put them aside for the next morning and then picked up again. We discussed how things might turn out, ought to turn out, we talked about self-healing and the boat, what we should do, where we should go, I wondered if Carl was frightened of going out to sea again, but it didn't seem so, he didn't say anything about it and I didn't ask. It was too late to turn back. We'd be gone on the first of April, heading for Granada or Tobago, as we'd decided, collectively, and we were following Columbus's footsteps so we'd avoid leaving new ones of our own. We'd started getting the money in place, but time-wise we still weren't on track. It was just a matter of getting the boat on the water, of working on, everything works out in the end.

And then the snow came. Lots of snow, in just a couple of nights. The road to Gjógv was the first they closed, one chalk-white Saturday a fort-night before Christmas, and for three days we were marooned. We waded around outside the Factory, linked in a human chain, built snowmen and waited for better times, and when they finally cleared an opening, the mailman found his way through to us with a letter to me. The first I'd had. I took it into the kitchen, tore it open impatiently, wondering who on earth would have thought of writing to me, scanned the contents swiftly.

It was Sofus!

Sofus in Tórshavn had taken up a correspondence, written a six-page letter that the Norwegian post office had finally forwarded from Jæren, it took half the day to read, I curled up in the sofa reading about his life in Tórshavn, about school, about Óluva who still lived in Copen-hagen and to whom he hadn't talked for so long, but he wanted me to know that he'd met new people, he'd moved on, he wrote, and not long ago there'd been a whale slaughter just down from where they lived, and I thought, I was there too, I didn't see you, didn't even look out for you, why not? And then the thought hit me:

This demanded a surprise visit. Of course!

A pre-Christmas visit.

With glad tidings of comfort and joy.

I took Carl with me, we pushed the car uphill on snow that just kept coming, and set off from the top, the car gliding down to Tórshavn in an hour and a half. Sofus lived way down Landavegur, almost at the very end, but we found it on the first try, rang the bell and waited impatiently on the steps before the door was opened and Óli came into view.

"Mattias!" he exclaimed.

"Merry Christmas!"

"Isn't it a little early?" he leaned out and looked up, as if checking the date by the weather.

"Best to be on the safe side," I answered. "Christmas almost always comes before you expect it."

"True enough."

Óli-type sentiments again. Had the hang of it now.

"And this is Carl." Carl took Óli's hand. "Carl's from all over the place."

"Is he?" answered Óli. And then to Carl in Faroese: "Is that right?"

"Carl only speaks English. He's mainly from America."

Óli swapped language and greeted Carl again. Improved communication.

"You'd better come in, both of you. Selma hates drafts."

"Who doesn't," I said as we followed Óli into the hallway, into the living room, and I noticed that although this house was different they'd decorated it exactly like the one in Gjógv. Thought they must have taken Polaroids before they moved. It was like coming back home. We sat on the sofa as Óli called out for mother and son, there was a commotion upstairs and then they came down the stairs on the double and into the living room, Selma gave me a warm hug, greeted Carl, and disappeared into the kitchen to put the coffee on and then Sofus came running over to me.

"Mattias!"

"Hi."

Massive hug from Sofus too, not sure I'd expected that.

"I got a letter from you," I said.

"Me too . . . from you."

"I promised."

"So, Mattias," shouted Selma from the kitchen, "you've been to Norway?"

"Yes," I shouted back, "But just for a visit. There's no better place than this, you know."

She didn't answer, I wasn't sure she'd even heard.

"Why don't you come and visit more often?" Sofus wanted to know.

"Didn't think you needed me anymore, you're such a big boy now. Going to big school and stuff, with lots of friends, I'm sure. Have you got yourself a girlfriend?"

"Yuck! No way!"

"Oh come on, Sofus," said Óli. "That's not quite true."

"I don't have a girlfriend!"

"So what about Annika then?"

"Annika's just nice."

"Who's Annika?"

"A friend."

We pressed him a little, he rather liked it, I think, Annika was as good as a girlfriend anyway, in the universe of a twelve year old. Sofus explained how she was in the same grade, lived on Perskonugøta and was wonderful at kicking a football, better than him. She had very long hair, two brothers, an orange bicycle with a bell with three different rings, and she had tons of CDs. These were no trifles. I supplied the simultaneous interpretation for Carl and he nodded enthusiastically at everything.

"It sounds as though you're the luckiest guy in Tórshavn," said Carl. "To have a . . . friend like that."

I translated for Sofus.

"But she isn't a girlfriend."

"No, of course not," Carl and I answered in chorus, each in our own language, and I thought to myself, remember to be kind to her, Sofus, you must always remember to visit her as frequently as now, bother yourself with the life she's living ten years from now, you must never start to hide yourself away, because then people will disappear, you'll lose them, one by one, and they'll never come back.

Selma came in with the coffee. We drank coffee. Our cups were refilled. We drank more.

"So, Mattias, are you living in Gjógv permanently now? Sofus said you work planting trees. That's great. We need that."

"The Factory's being closed down."

"What?"

"There are too few mental cases on the Faroes, doesn't seem to be worth the effort. Not even half the effort. The state's decided to close the whole caboodle down."

"Oh, no."

"Oh, yes."

"They're depopulating Gjógv, bit by bit, I just don't understand it."

"We'd better start swimming, or we'll sink like a stone."

"I don't understand that, either."

"It's an old song," I said. "The times they are a-changin'."

"They are, it's true."

"Anyway it's probably worse for Havstein."

"What do you mean?" asked Selma.

"He's the one who set it all up, didn't he? He initiated it and built the Factory up from nothing, his father chipped in with the money, and Havstein put all his energy into getting the place to work, converting it, getting it shipshape. Imagine if everything you'd built up was taken away, it can't be easy."

"You shouldn't believe everything you hear, Mattias."

"What do you mean?'

"Just that things aren't always what they seem. Havstein has some problems," sighed Selma. "It's a long story."

"Really?"

Óli stared down into the floor, blankly, he didn't like this at all. Selma cleared her throat.

"There was a time when he ... well ... I think he drank too much. I've heard. A family weakness, it goes way back." A look of shame crossed her face. "He should tell you himself. I shouldn't talk about it."

"So it's not true, any of it, is that what you're saying? Wasn't it even his project? The Factory, him and his father's?"

"Mattias—" Selma went quiet, averted her gaze, apologized for having brought the subject up. Óli got on track again, distracted us, talked about other things, asked us what we'd do now, and the subject I most wanted to discuss vanished from view, they'd battened down the hatches, there was no more to be gotten from them, no use resisting.

So I reluctantly changed my focus, told Selma and Óli about our plans, how we'd decided not to be spread to the winds, and how we'd agreed to leave. I told them about the Caribbean, about the boat, the hull that was already molded down by the harbor, about the rigging that would arrive in February, and how we'd leave on the first of April. Assuming we had the boat ready, that we'd raised enough money and managed to finish it all. And nobody must know about it.

Sofus was sad and Selma put her arm around him.

"Are you going away again?"

"It looks like it, Sofus."

"How long will you be away?"

"A while. A pretty long time."

Óli looked over at me and Carl. I think he was sad, too. Almost.

"Do you need help?"

Which was how we got six more hands to help us with the boat. Selma sewed cushions and ordered furniture along with Anna, beds, sinks, tables, goodness knows what, everything we needed, they divided the responsibility over the phone, while Óli drew on acquaintances and services from far and wide. And he came down to the building shed almost every afternoon, with Sofus, and they made such a sweet pair, Óli with his big carpenter's belt round his waist and his worn out blue overalls, Sofus dressed identically, overalls with the legs generously cuffed and a miniature version of Óli's belt. Sofus sometimes brought Annika with him too, she'd sit on a beer crate and watch him work, and when he saw that she was watching him, he'd work even harder, really put his back into it, tightened the screws even more firmly. And every day the stiff skeleton in the warehouse down by the harbor looked more and more like a boat.

I didn't go back to Stavanger that Christmas. No point somehow. Havstein invited everybody's relatives to the Factory instead. But not my parents. I didn't tell them. And I still hadn't told them we were going to the Caribbean in three months, I didn't mean any harm by it, that was just how things were.

I'd gotten a book about Arctic gardening from Mother and Father, where or why they'd bought it, I don't know, but it was beautiful, even though I didn't exactly live in Greenland or Alaska. They also sent the usual supply of socks and chunky wool sweaters. Grandma had knitted a wool hat for me, but she'd gone senile since I'd last seen her, had lost the plot slightly, and the hat was bright pink, about a yard long and wide enough for me and Havstein to fit both our heads in. But it was warm, and that's always something.

One January evening I was walking along Sverrisgøta with Carl toward Manhattan when I heard somebody call my name, it wasn't a friendly voice, but it got me, by the throat.

"Mattias! Stop!"

I froze. Carl turned, looked at me, then laughed.

"What have you gotten yourself involved in?"

"Go ahead, I'll be with you in a moment."

"Who the hell do you think you are?" The voice drew nearer, but was no friendlier for that. I turned, Eyðis stood there before me, I hadn't seen her since the summer, the night at the cabin in the middle of nowhere, the night before I'd gone home.

"Oh, hi."

"Hi? Is that the best you can say? What the hell do you think you're doing?"

"Not a lot."

"You've got some nerve."

"I do? I'm sorry."

"*Sorry?* Haven't you ever learned it's rude to abandon girls in the morning? Or were you away from school the day they taught that?"

"I had a proper absence note. I was at a funeral."

"What are you talking about?"

"I was late, I had to catch a flight. There are hardly any flights from here to Norway."

"You could have told me."

"I'm sorry."

"I liked you, Mattias. A lot."

Her hair had gotten even shorter over the fall and winter. Only the merest rumor left. She still had her denim jacket and the same nose. I wondered if she'd gotten shorter or if I'd grown. I didn't ask.

"I wanted to get to know you, didn't you realize?"

I hadn't realized. But I think it made me happy to hear it. But I was getting cold. It was snowing and the snow was settling in a layer on my jacket. I wondered where the nearest St. Bernard dog might be, and who would dig us out in the spring if we stood here much longer.

So I said: "Come on," and I gave her a hug, a long hug, I held her close and I wondered whether to bend down and scoop up enough snow to make a snowball and throw it onto the roof or whether it was best not to. And just then I was kissed, firmly, precisely, I received forgiveness in Sverrisgøta and the snow stopped, the dogs went back to their baskets and we went up to the Manhattan and walked through the doors as the band started playing.

Eyðis became a permanent fixture with me and Carl and in Tórsgøta after that, she'd sleep up in my room several times a week or I'd go back to her new apartment in Varðagøta, and she'd come up to Gjógv for the weekends to Havstein's great joy, he was so proud of me, he said, so pleased I'd dared to attach myself to someone again, there were slaps on the back and the red carpet treatment, I explained our situation to Eyðis, that we weren't quite normal, she took it surprisingly well, didn't seem that surprised, and for a moment I was worried it had begun to show, that our faces were papered with the message that we weren't fit to be left to our own devices. And maybe it was true, maybe we were wrong to hope things would improve day by day, still, we had to get away as soon as possible.

I dreaded talking about the Caribbean with Eyðis, I'd told her the boat building was just a hobby to keep us occupied, and I'd totally gagged the others from mentioning anything about our real plans, for evacuation, which was a plain impossibility, since it was all we talked about when we were together, and making it taboo led to odd conversations filled with polite phrases about the weather and Faroese tradition and fishing and moving and Danish state support and the charms of puffins and Ólav's Festival and everything else we'd already discussed to death a year before, so I was relieved one evening when we'd gone to bed early and I saw that Eyðis had no intention of sleeping, that there were things she wanted to talk about.

"Why haven't you said anything? Why haven't any of you told me anything?"

I pretended not to understand.

"Told you what?"

"I know that the institution at Gjógv is being closed down in a couple of months, Mattias."

"How do you know that?"

"How do I know? Are you serious? Christ, it's common knowledge. Don't you read the papers?"

"No," I answered, as a shock went through me. I didn't read papers. Barely watched TV any more. Neither did Palli, Anna, or Carl. I knew

Havstein did, that he kept himself updated, but he never told us what they wrote.

"There's a big debate going on in the papers and on TV. There's a big protest about them closing you down. Didn't you know, really?"

"No."

"So what are you planning to do? When it's over?"

I didn't quite know how to answer, but she beat me to it.

"Please, don't just disappear this time, Mattias. Promise to tell me well in advance this time, okay?"

"I'm leaving on April 1," I said. "In two months' time."

"Where to?"

"Grenada. Or Tobago."

"Where are they?"

"The Caribbean. You have to take a boat. It's a long way." She looked confused and shrank into the bed, I had to hunt for her in the sheets before I found her again. Then I told her about the boat, how it was nearing completion down by the harbor and how we were planning to go off unobserved on the first day of April, before anybody discovered it.

"Jesus Christ," she said when I'd finished.

"Christ, indeed. But it's not his fault."

"Whose?"

"Jesus Christ's."

"You're pathetic!"

"I know."

She used four seconds to decide, before asking:

"Can I come?"

"Do you want to?" I asked, surprised.

"There's not much to do around here anymore. Besides, I reckon it would be good for the Faroes to get a break from me. Not to mention you."

"Me?"

"I think it would be good for you, too."

"A break?"

"No, if I came."

"You think so?"

"Everybody needs somebody to look after them."

"Even people who keep themselves to themselves?"

She nodded, her head tilted.

"What did I know, thinking myself able to go alone all the way?"

"Excuse me?"

"You should read Robert Creeley."

"Should I?"

"Mm." She smiled and pushed me under the duvet.

And then something happened, as things have a habit of, without your being able to say how or why, when you've completely lost perspective, when you thought you'd decided on something quite different, it hits you. I lay there, face pressed into the duvet and mattress as Eyðis sat yelping and laughing on top of me, and that was when it suddenly struck me there was nothing I wanted more than to take her with me, and the thought that I hadn't already asked her myself terrified me. Eyðis. She'd appeared from nowhere and I'd understood nothing. Hadn't even given it a thought. But she was here now. And this is the moment which I can point to and say, *here*, right here, in a bed, in a pink room in Tórshavn, spring 2001, I exploded, Mattias, head over heels in love for the first time in fifteen years.

"So can I come?" she asked.

"Yes, you can. But you have to prove you're crazy first. Otherwise you don't get a life jacket."

"I live alone in a cabin without electricity in the summer. Besides I've gone through a whole winter in Finland wearing only thin sneakers. And I'm the only girl on the Faroes with such short hair. Feel."

I felt her head with one hand, rubbing her scalp back and forth.

"No reasonable person would have such short hair in a place like this."

"No?"

"No, it's very cold when the wind blows."

"Yeah, you're right. That's insane."

Which is how Eyðis joined the team. She moved out of her apartment and in with me and Carl. Havstein, Anna, and Palli joined us a month later, in mid-February, to be nearer the boat and so as to be able to work down at the harbor every day. We'd begun clearing out the Factory, driving anything we'd decided to take aboard down to Tórshavn. Wasn't much, some books, clothes, boxes, stereo, CDs, and the like. Then one day Havstein asked me and Carl to come up to Gjógv with a van he'd rented. We drove up in the morning and then stood there, in Havstein's office and stared at the twelve massive filing cabinets.

"Are you serious?" asked Carl.

"Are you really going to take these with you?"

"That's right."

"Havstein," I said, "they weigh a ton. At least. We'll sink before we reach open sea."

"Well. They have to come."

Carl went optimistically toward one of the cabinets, tugged at it. It was heavy. Heavy as hell.

"No fucking way," I said. "It's impossible. Forget it."

"They're coming with me, or we're not going."

"They're too heavy."

"Maybe we can take the records out and leave the cabinets," ventured Carl.

"They'll still be too heavy." I knew I was right. "What do you want with them? Are you thinking of starting a practice out there? You could at least tell us why you want to take one and a half tons of extra weight on board, don't you think?"

"That's my business." Havstein stared at me. "I thought you knew that."

"Still—"

"So, what's it to be, boys?" said Carl.

He looked at me. I looked at him. We looked at Havstein.

"Come outside with me for a moment," I said. Havstein followed me into the hallway. "Listen, it's not just that they weigh a ton, think about their size, there won't even be space on board! What's so important about these papers? I'd like to know if I'm going to go down with them."

"They're not that heavy," Havstein objected. "I've calculated it in."

"Why can't you answer my question?"

"It's not anybody's business."

"Everything that goes on board is everybody's business!"

"We all have our reasons."

"Sure. And what are your reasons?"

"Let me ask you a question, Mattias. Why did you really become a gardener?"

"No, let me ask, why did you *really* become a psychiatrist, Havstein? Why can't you just tell it as it is?"

"What's that supposed to mean?"

"Was it because it's such a great career? So respectable? Didn't turn out that way, did it?"

"I don't know what you're talking about."

"What went wrong? Something went wrong, didn't it? Did things go wrong in Denmark? It all went to hell by FedEx, didn't it? Did you beat up your patients, steal their money, trick them into coming for appointments for years for no good reason? Did you break patient confidentiality? Or was it just that the times you were sober got shorter and shorter? Because that's what happened, isn't it? You started drinking, and once you'd started you didn't stop until the bottle was empty, but of course it was never empty, because there's always a store, isn't there, always a bar, always somewhere to go—"

"What are you talking about?"

"It wasn't actually your idea to turn the old factory into the Factory was it? Your father didn't throw the money in, did he? The idea came from somewhere else, directly from the state, you were put up here, out of sight, out of mind, in a place where you could do minimum harm, because you were already damaged goods before you moved back to the Faroes, they couldn't have you in town any longer, couldn't have you in the office down there with you being so unstable. But why didn't they just fire you? Why didn't they just leave you to it, instead of putting you up here with your own institution to run? Why was it so dangerous to let you go? Was it something you'd done? Something you said?"

"My grandfather—"

"Okay. So you stop drinking, you clean up your act and move here like a man in exile, and patients come, patients go, but nobody notices anything, nobody notices that you've lost control, that you run your practice and treatment by whim instead of by the textbook, before you finally stop treating anybody at all, for fear they might actually recover and leave you, because that's what it boils down to, isn't it? You're frightened of being alone. But nobody knows that, not the people who live here, not the people who finance your life, and most of all, not the people who pay for the archive that just grows and grows in volume, because they don't even know about it, do they, we're the only ones who know you have these files, and we don't even know anything really, because it's all so fucking secret, and that's probably best. Since it's illegal for you to keep them, isn't it, you could be thrown in fucking jail for it, you've got confidential papers there, papers that have nothing to do with any patients you may or may not have, papers you have no good medical reason to have, papers you've collected or stolen or bought from God knows where, for God knows what reason! Don't you understand, it's *you* that's lost control, Havstein, you put that control out to sea years ago." I spat the words out at him, filled with the disappointment that he'd lied to us, or worse, he hadn't even lied, he'd said nothing, all those little episodes that I'd thought he'd instigated because he had some insight, because they were part of a bigger plan, not just pure coincidence or impulse, and as I stood there, tears of rage rising, I thought how Sofia might have been alive if he hadn't kept her there, if he'd sent her back to Tórshavn or Copenhagen, although I also knew that wasn't really true, she'd wouldn't have survived there either, and this thought shut me up, I stood there glaring at him, right at him, impossible to second-guess what he'd say.

"Are you finished?"

"Yes."

"Good. Then we can be done with this lunacy."

"Only you can do that."

"Who have you been talking to?"

"You know I'm not going to tell you that."

Silence. Like after a bombing raid. My ears were whistling, I heard a discreet, embarrassed cough from Carl inside the office. Ignored it. I looked at Havstein. Waiting expectantly. The seconds passed.

"Okay. Grandfather was the reason for my becoming a psychiatrist," he began. "He owned several factories here and was a member of the Faroese Parliament too. And he had several fishing boats with over a hundred fishermen on his payroll. He was one of the wealthiest men in Tórshavn toward the end of the 1930s. He was well liked, a fair-minded man, generous to his employees, he helped them with money to buy houses, held big parties for their families several times a year. But when the war came, he went into a panic, like so many. The British occupied the Faroes to secure the North Atlantic shipping routes and to stop the islands from falling into German hands like Denmark, and he was genuinely frightened for his fishermen, for his boats, he started to refuse to let them out, terrified they'd be fired at and sunk, or that they'd run into submarines or mines or whatever else he imagined lurked under the waves, in Grandfather's opinion the best option was to stay on land, stay at home and not go out, and he didn't want the German patrol boats getting ideas either about Faroese vessels and the need to take these little islands. So they stayed on land, making an entire country invisible, and Grandfather held a powerful and protective economic hand over his employees. But the money couldn't last, not in the long run, he watched it dwindle, and it was then things went seriously downhill. That was when Grandfather had an idea."

Havstein accompanied his story with careful gestures, as though he was frightened big movements might bring him out of it, that he'd forget the order of things. I think I concentrated more on his hands than on what he was saying. I looked down the hallway, the door to Sofia's room, it was locked now. The key purposely broken in the lock. And Havstein went on.

"Grandfather got it into his head to invest in a railway instead, a railway was just what the country needed, according to him, it would make transportation easier, faster, it would turn the Faroe Islands into an industrial nation and replace the fishing industry. Imagine! A railway on the Faroes! A country of mountains and islands! With barely ten miles from North to South?"

This last statement hung in the air as a question, an invitation for me to comment on his grandfather's idiocy or lack of common sense. But I couldn't share Havstein's passion, I held my tongue and wondered when it would be suitable to interrupt him and his life story.

"To begin with, nobody believed him, they just let him talk. But when they realized he was serious, they got worried. But Grandfather plowed on, had plans drawn up for where the tracks should go, applied for patents and was refused but remained undeterred, compared various types of sleeper cars and so on, and in the fall of 1942, when the first railway workers came ashore at Tórshavn and unloaded vast amounts of equipment, when the first four hundred feet of railway were laid near Bláberg and Grandfather paraded up and down the town in a train driver's uniform, he was taken discreetly aside, they tried to talk sense into him, but it just made him furious, frustrated, there had to be a railway, surely everybody must understand that, but the problem was nobody did, and they took grandfather away, up to the hospital. And he wasn't allowed out again until he died, twelve years later, and during all that time he didn't once go beyond the exercise yard in the back. Grandfather became the most famous psychiatric patient on the Faroes, kids wanted to see him when they visited the hospital, they flocked under his window hoping to catch a glimpse of the madman, stories abounded, it was said he'd always been mad, that he'd never taken care of his factories, his boats, his fishermen, but that wasn't true, they'd meant everything to Grandfather, before he'd come up with the railway idea at least. But it was too late to do anything by then, he grew more and more crazy in the hospital and his treatment got more and more heavy-handed. In embarrassed silence he was eased out of his position in Parliament that had, during its wartime separation from Denmark, acquired new legislative powers and grown in self-importance. Grandfather lay strapped to his bed when the war was over, lay strapped down on the spring day of 1948 when the Faroes were granted self-governance and recognized as an autonomous province of Denmark, he lay strapped down until the day he died and nothing but rumors were left. Problem was, nothing hangs around longer than a rumor, and life only got harder for my grandmother afterward, she and the children kept as low a profile as possible, Father took a job on a fishing boat, kept himself to himself, settled in Tórshavn without too much fuss, as did his sisters, got themselves modest jobs in filleting factories and as seamstresses. Unfortunately the whole family was marked now, and when Father went into a depression as an adult, the family packed him quietly off to Switzerland, where he stayed for three months so nobody would know. But nothing remains secret for long, somebody always reveals the password at the most inconvenient time, so when I was born Argus's eye was upon me from the first, I was held under constant observation for fear I might have mental problems. But I didn't. I was as healthy as a horse. And when I told my parents I intended to study psychiatry, they almost fell over with delight. Father saw it as the chance to bring an end to the rumors that still dogged our family, I'd show them, take the bull by the horns, by that time he'd managed to get himself elected as a representative of the government through sheer perseverance and back door politics, and had eventually acquired a few friends there who had his best interests at heart."

I couldn't hold back anymore. I interrupted:

"I asked you about the archive, didn't I?"

Part of me was suddenly worried he might stop half way, offended. But he didn't. His gestures grew larger, he was determined to get to the end.

"No, you didn't just ask about the archive. You asked about everything, Mattias. But it's coming, it's coming. Be patient. It all hangs together. Anyway, I went to Copenhagen, studied psychiatry, got a job, and things went well, it was great. Father sent me tons of letters, asking me how things went, and my answers were always the same, *things are fine, going well,* and for ages things did go fine, in fact they went okay until one day in March 1979 when ▇▇▇▇▇ came into my office. That day my life changed. In just minutes my life, as I knew it, was over forever. And I knew it the moment it happened. I'd been on leave for a couple of days, a little break to regroup after getting news that one of my patients, with whom I'd become very involved, had taken her own life just days after I'd recommended she be discharged from the hospital, and I was sitting there in front of a pile of papers that had amassed while I'd been away, when he came in, unannounced. He didn't have an appointment that day. He was forty-eight hours early. But there he was. I'd been seeing ▇▇▇▇▇ on a weekly basis for a couple of months, he was suffering increasingly from insomnia and panic attacks. I'd explained in depth what I felt his problem was and I'd asked him to keep a diary of his episodes, their duration, the symptoms and their strength. He'd had some pills. I was convinced we were making progress. So there he sat, in my office, without any appointment. He didn't want to talk. He didn't want me to say anything. When I opened my mouth he held up his hand, asked me to be quiet. So we sat there. Ten minutes. Fifteen minutes. Twenty minutes. I looked at the clock, I had other patients waiting outside, a line growing, I imagined them sitting there restless, nervous in the imitation leather seats out in the corridor, beneath optimistic pictures of landscapes in soft colors, wondering why I didn't come to call them in. So in the end I gave up waiting for him to say anything, I got up slowly, went around the table and over to him, rested a hand on his shoulder, and that was when he did it, I didn't have a chance to react. He was too fast. ▇▇▇▇▇ stuck a hand inside his jacket and in the next second he'd pulled a revolver out, stuck the barrel in his mouth, and pulled the trigger, right there in the chair where he sat, in my office. And I know it's weird, but I don't even remember the shot making any noise. All I remember is the wet sound of his head as he tumbled out of the chair and hit the floor in front of me, he lay on the floor and I stood at his side for the few seconds it took for a nurse to come storming in, mouth open and hands limp at her side. That's how I remember it. Her hands hanging uselessly at her side. Then I walked calmly over to my desk, got my jacket, walked past her and through the waiting room without even looking at the other patients, without saying a word, I left the building, walked into town and then disappeared, for days. I didn't call in sick, I told nobody anything. I wandered calmly around Copenhagen for days, and in the evenings I sat in a restaurant or bar trying to work out why he'd done it, just at the moment of my touching him. I thought how he'd still have been alive if I hadn't stood up, if I'd just stayed in my chair, if I hadn't rested a hand on his shoulder. After nearly a week I turned up at work again, nobody asked where I'd been, nobody reprimanded me for walking out, they were empathy personified, when they talked to me they folded their hands and tilted their heads, spoke gentle words of caring. I continued having a few beers or drinks after work, in the hope that it would stop me from mulling over what had caused two of my patients to take their own lives in such a short space of time, when, to my eyes at least, they'd been on the road to recovery, but it was no use, and I grew frightened of going into work, frightened it might happen again. I demanded my patients take off their jackets before sitting down, paid more attention to what they were doing with their hands than what they said. In the end I grew so fearful that I'd take a good, stiff drink for courage before I even walked into my office in the morning and saw my first patient. And it's impossible to go on like that. In the long run. I took longer and longer periods of sick leave and stayed at home, behind closed doors, talking only to Maria, who I've already told you about. I was living with her at the time, she saw me getting worse, wanted me to see a psychiatrist myself, but I didn't want to, how would it look to Father, a psychiatrist seeking help from a psychiatrist, it would have destroyed him utterly, just when he'd thought the family name was being restored. Anyway, by December, I was exhausted, there wasn't a day my head felt clear, I waded about in a fog, even though I'd started working a little again, and it was on one of those days I stumbled into the bookstore where I bought *Fielding's Guide to the Caribbean*, and it was shortly after that when Maria left, it was in early January 1981 that I called Father to tell him I had problems. Father came as quickly as he could to Copenhagen, stayed with me for a few months while I pulled myself together, stuffed the corks back into their bottles. It was Father who wanted me to come back home, when I got better, back to the Faroes, and so that's what I did, I came back that summer, stayed in, mostly, took some auxiliary nights at the hospital until one day Father came home with an offer. The council had agreed to build two homes for psychiatric patients who were making the transition into ordinary life, or people so institutionalized that they'd never be able to live alone, would I like the job of leading the project? He thought it could be organized, that he could get the committee to agree, and surprisingly enough I had excellent references from Copenhagen. Father thought it would be good for me, to start small, taking it easy, working confidence up, in myself and my patients, I'm not quite sure which he was hinting at most. So I said yes. Took the job. And this is where the archives come in, the files. The idea came to me in 1983, I'd just finished a group session that morning when it dawned on me that there might be, hypothetically at least, connections we'd never made, a kind of psychiatric Rubik's cube waiting to be solved, and that if we solved it, found the combination, we might be in a position to take better care of people. To help them."

"What do you mean?"

"Okay. Listen. There are basically two kinds of psychiatric suffering."

"And they are?"

"The right and the wrong. Now don't interrupt me, please."

"Sorry."

"Anyway. I renewed contact with some old colleagues of mine at the hospital in Tórshavn that autumn, and rang some psychiatrists at the Rikshospitalet in Copenhagen, I explained what I wanted to do, talked them into it, bit by bit, until they eventually let themselves be persuaded and began the painstaking work of copying the long term psychiatric files from the hospital archives. We invested money and time on it, a pristine job, nobody would ever be able tell that the documents held down there in the cellar under tight security were copies, the handwriting, the notes were all replicated precisely, and the originals were sent up here, to me, put in the cabinets that were continually filling up and added to. A complete collection of psychiatric notes from Denmark and the Faroe Islands, 1900–2000, was there, you and Carl being the latest additions."

"So you'd collected them all?"

"Far from it." He smiled as he completed the next sentence, grandly and emphasizing each word, as though he'd finally fulfilled his life's work: "Only the right kind."

I didn't know what to say. So I said:

"So . . . did you discover anything?"

It was quiet for a moment, Havstein thought, for a long time, as though evaluating whether he should say more or whether he should just walk away. But then it came, a broad smile that I'll never forget, and he leaned carefully toward me, and whispered some words into my ear, things I understood, things I'd somehow known all along. I listened, with big ears that turned the world upside down, and when he was finished, I went back to Carl who was waiting impatiently in the office.

"We're taking the filing cabinets," I said.

"Are you sure?"

"Yes, I'm sure."

"If you really think it's best, then fine. Can I ask why?"

"This is strictly on a need to know basis."

"And I don't need to know, right?"

"Right."

The archives were stored in the warehouse down by the harbor with everything else we were taking, and I told nobody that in this colossal pile of papers one particular file was missing, a file that dealt with an anonymous patient with a passion for buses who had eventually written herself out for good. We used that last month to finish the work on the boat, most of the fittings that Anna, Palli, and Eyðis had dutifully ordered from Norway, and had adjusted and installed in the cabin, had to be taken down again to save weight, we removed everything superfluous to make space for the files, weighing and adding up the pounds until we were sure we'd float, we left only the toilet and galley. The filing cabinets were emptied and left on land, the papers packed in plastic and laid in the bottom as a sort of floor covering, we took one of the old sofas from the Factory and bolted it fast to the floor between piles of files, it looked absurd, but suited our needs, additionally we laid three thin mattresses on the journals to protect them from water and so that anybody that wasn't on duty up on deck had somewhere to sleep, and so we could sit in relative comfort when we all needed to be below deck at once. Originally we'd been disappointed that our money didn't stretch to equipping an entire engine room, but even this turned out for the best now, leaving the space available for water and food storage, and we got hold of a used outboard motor as a substitute from a guy in Klaksvík so we'd have motor power for when the wind dropped, and to get safely in and out of harbor. Adjustments and more layers of paint and coatings were done in shifts, we worked around the clock, I took the night shift with Carl, we'd given up our jobs, slept through the day, and at about ten in the evening we'd wander down to the harbor with Eyðis and relieve Havstein and Óli. But it was on the night we brought in outside help, and the hull was lifted from its crib and out of the warehouse, and the rig was mounted to the foot of the mast—it was on that night that it hit me how serious this was, that it sank in for me that we were about to leave the Faroes for good, and that there was no plan for our return. That was when I started sleeping badly again. I'd lie in bed, wide awake, then get up, sit in the living room downstairs, listen to the others snoring and turning in their sleep above. I got through the nights on auto-pilot, my brain unplugged, by day I struggled to get the enormous sails in place with all their weight and all their wires and ropes, a tangle, I got caught and lost my temper, I screamed and shouted and Carl came to my rescue, I gave up several times only to try again half an hour later, Eyðis did everything she could to make things better for me, but it was no good, it wasn't her fault, and gradually she kept her distance as we worked, I hardly saw her before we wandered back home at about six in the morning, and I didn't talk to her about it, I couldn't blame her or say it would pass soon, because I wasn't sure it would, I didn't understand it myself, I thought perhaps I was nervous we wouldn't be ready on time, so I started working a double shift, I went at ten in the evening and staggered home at two in the afternoon, creeping up to the bedroom to lie down. Havstein wore the same worried expression I remembered from nearly two years earlier when he talked to me, but he was tired too and didn't really know what to do, nobody ever said it directly, but he was the one with the overall responsibility for making sure everything was ready on time, and at the end of the day, it was his Caribbean we were going to, he'd get the blame if it didn't live up to our expectations and if life didn't improve, get easier.

It was one of the last days of March. I woke Eyðis up when I came home at around two, she rolled out of the duvet looking disheveled.

"We need to go to Saksun today," I said.

She yawned and looked at the clock.

"Have you just gotten home?"

I nodded.

"You must get some sleep, Mattias. You'll wear yourself out like this. You're wearing me out, you do realize that?"

"The boat will be ready soon. By tomorrow perhaps."

"What do we have to do in Saksun?"

"I want to deliver a present."

"Do you even know anybody there?"

"Kind of."

She sighed, rubbed her face, gave me a hug.

"Okay, Mattias, okay. Give me half an hour, and I'll come with you."

"I'll wait downstairs."

I closed the door behind me and met Havstein on the stairs on his way up to bed, utter jetlag in this house now.

"I've left the package on the telephone table. It's kind of you to do this, Mattias."

"Thanks."

I walked past him, put on my coat in the hallway, took the package and went to the car, waited for half an hour.

Thirty three minutes later Eyðis woke me up behind the wheel, she wanted to drive, fine by me, I walked around the car and got into the passenger seat, shut my eyes, the car started up and we swung out into the narrow streets and up toward Hoyvíksvegur, heading North.

I was woken up by the sun in my eyes halfway between Hvalvík and Saksun, Eyðis was driving at seventy miles per hour along this narrow road, no doubt bored.

"Good morning," she said.

"We're going fast enough, aren't we?" I mumbled, checking that my safety belt was fastened.

"So, when do you intend to tell me why it was so crucial for us to come out here today?"

"I'm delivering a book."

"A book?"

"Yes."

"I see."

I asked Eyðis to park in front of the small white church with grass growing on its roof. A day for romantic idylls. As it should be for one of our last days in the country. Like the last week of your summer vacation when you were a kid, you remember? The clarity of the air that week. How it was hardly ever cloudy. I took out the package and asked Eyðis to hold it as I opened the trunk and took out a shovel, opened the gate and walked into the graveyard behind the church, Eyðis following close behind.

"Are you going to dig some bodies up too now? Is that it?"

"No, I'm not going to dig anything up. I'm going to bury something."

We went up to the stone wall, and stood before Sofia's gravestone.

"I don't like this, Mattias. I don't like it at all."

"It'll be fine."

"Did you know her?"

"Yes, I knew her. But only a little, as it turned out."

Eyðis bent down and read the inscription.

"She wasn't old. What happened?"

"She was hit by a bus."

"I'm sorry, Mattias."

"Don't be. She was very fond of buses. It could have been worse."

I put the shovel in the ground, lifted the earth and left it to the side, and peered over my shoulder on the lookout for residents who might think I was desecrating graves or worse.

"Have you got the package?" I asked quickly.

Eyðis handed the parcel to me, and I lifted *Fielding's Guide to the Caribbean plus the Bahamas* out of its paper. It had been Havstein's idea to leave the book here, so we'd feel we were taking Sofia with us, in some way or other. I lay the beat-up book in the earth, with all its scribblings, its underlinings, all its additional sheets tucked inside and years of research still intact, I felt a little uneasy, even though deep down I thought it was good, that it drew a line under things, somehow. I returned the dirt to the earth, patted it carefully down with the back of the shovel.

"Is it kind of to give her a map of where we're going?"

"Havstein asked me to do it."

"Do you think she'll find the way? With the help of the book, I mean."

I smiled, though I'm not sure it had the intended effect.

"Maybe she'll take a wrong turn and end up in the Bahamas. She could be a bit scatterbrained." We laughed, a laughter that was out of place, that didn't contain what the advert promised.

We put the shovel in the car and wandered over the slopes towards Pollur, the little lake below. It was low tide and the lake was reduced to an enormous sandy beach, we walked over toward Vestmannhavn and I gave Eyðis the long version, about Fielding's Caribbean and about Sofia who I'd started to adore without really knowing it.

I sleep in the car on the way back too, only notice Eyðis patting me on the head as though I'm a little boy going home long past bedtime, and I don't remember getting back, I don't remember going in, or talking to anybody or doing anything at all, and when I wake up again it's the last night, Palli is standing in my doorway, almost jumping up and down with excitement, talking about the boat and Havstein, and Havstein has said that the boat's ready and that the boat is finished and that we must pack and that we're leaving early tomorrow morning and he says we've got to get up and that we're going to meet at Café Natúr in a couple of hours and that the boat is finished and *isn't it fantastic* and *we're going to the Caribbean* and they're about to launch her, Anna's tying a bottle of champagne to the rope that'll smash against the side of the boat and christen her in half an hour, and I have to get up and get dressed and come and then he's gone and I'm left standing alone in my bedroom and the floor is cold, I'm already packed, have been for days, it's the last evening of March and by this time tomorrow we'll be gone, we'll have evacuated this country.

So we christened the boat. We got her out to sea, and she floated. Then we moored her securely in the harbor and went to Café Natúr.

We were in good spirits, but I was so tired, had problems holding myself upright, and reality and fiction began slowly to slide into each other, turning into a mess, and the harder I tried to pull myself together, the further I floated out, and this is how I remember things, I'm sitting at one of the tables in the middle of the venue, it's Saturday and there's barely space to move, I clutch onto my beer and the mood's pretty good, it seems, spirits high, because in a few hours we'll board the boat, Eyðis wanders around the café saying goodbye to friends, she's told them we're going, has talked to her parents and everybody knows now that we're off, and Havstein, Anna, and Palli have told their families that they're leaving, I've lied and told everybody I've called home, but haven't, I can do it when I arrive, I think, just as good, I think, and in the confusion, hidden behind dozens of heads and backs, there's a band playing, and they're playing loud, it's barely possible to keep a conversation going, so we mainly smile at each other, that is, I think I'm smiling, but can't say for sure, it might be that my mouth's just open and I lift my glass, I drink, I think I'm drunk, I look around and see Carl light a cigarette and give me a thumbs up as our eyes meet, he arches one eyebrow and takes a deep drag on his cigarette, and I think how sitting there, right there, is one of the best friends you could have and I hope things will improve for him, and I look at Havstein who can't help me, but has nonetheless, I look at Anna who hasn't been herself since Sofia went, but who's worked day and night all these months so we could get away, she's ready to leave, and I look at Palli who already misses the Faroes, just as I do, he's gazing around the café, and I can see what he's up to, he's trying to take a snapshot of the whole room, this place, so he can remember every detail, like a mental snapshot, and I'd have done the same, but I ran out of film long ago, and the film got overexposed, the light got in and it all went white, and now I see myself getting up, I bang into the table and stand there swaying, prop myself up on Havstein's hands, he's saying something, but I can't hear what and I answer with a snort before I cast off my moorings and sail out into the café, point myself in the direction of where the crowd is thickest and disappear into it, hey presto, I'm gone, and I pop up on the other side and from here I can't see my friends, can't hear them, but I certainly know they're there, and I stand face to face with the vocalist of a band I don't recognize, stand right in front of one of the loudspeakers and can't even hear my own thoughts if I'm thinking at all and between two songs I lean over the vocalist, lose my footing, lunge toward him and land in front of the drums, there are shoes around me on all sides and the floor is dirty, sticky, the vocalist has dropped his microphone and it's just inches from me, so I grab hold of it and shout into it, can barely hear my voice as it reverberates through the room and for a moment I can hear my thoughts again, and then I close my eyes, and then I start to sing, sing whatever comes into my head, don't know where it comes from, at first it's just words, the band seems to be waiting, waiting for me to shove off or for me to hit a note, and the vocalist stares glumly at me, or maybe he's just confused, probably the latter, and I ask if he's going to drop the bomb or not, but he doesn't know himself, and I start for some reason on "Forever Young," the Alphaville song, don't know why, but I do, even though I don't want to live forever, in no way, I shout, *who wants to live forever*, and so I'm there, singing on my own, and remembering the words, I haven't heard this song for nearly twenty years and that's probably why I sing it rather than any other, and behind me, far behind me, I hear the band finding my key and following me, they know the song, I lie on the floor like a drunk teenager singing Alphaville songs and I don't want to stay forever young, but if I could stay here, on the Faroes, then I could, then I'd be forever young, stumbling between two stars in Smurfland where the rain just keeps hailing down and the mountains get greener by the day, meanwhile I pretend and am believed, they believe me, all of them, and bet their money on it, and now the whole café is silent, only the song can be heard, it rises from the floor, pushes its way past elbows and bodies and heads and beer glasses, my voice holds as never before and I notice the customers stop what they're doing, frozen to the spot, the bartender leaves the taps open and the beer runs over, down over the counter, onto the floor and it washes over me, I am under water or beer, not easy to tell, and somebody pulls at me, but I don't want to budge, don't want to move an inch, and the band stops playing, but I don't shift, I lie there, the vocalist tears the microphone from my hand and they start playing "My Favorite Game," but it's a bad choice, since I know my Cardigans, I know them to my fingertips and they don't know that, and I grab the vocalist's legs, pull as hard as I can so he falls, landing like a sack at my side and he's not angry anymore, just surprised, I yell at him, but I'm not certain what I say, he says something about karaoke though I realize it's not meant as an invitation when he shoves the microphone in my face, and I mumble the lyrics to "My Favorite Game" before I find my foothold, steady myself and belt the lyrics out, the band doing everything they can to keep up, I sing as hard as I can and the applause hits the roof, a roaring wall comes toward me and I can't even hear myself, but I know where I am, I know this song backward and forward, I sing louder and louder and I think of the book I buried with Sofia yesterday or one day recently and I should have buried her CDs too, but it's too late now, impossible, because we're leaving soon and we'll never be back and a part of me or all of me no longer wants to go and I think that the Faroes are the best thing that ever happened to me and I think of the beach in Gjógv, of the house in Tórsgøta and of the mountains, I mustn't forget the mountains and all the people I've met here that I didn't believe existed, I don't want to go, I'm a pilot whale caught in Hvalvík or Miðvagur out of season, I don't want to go now, I want to keep on driving my car along these roads, over the mountains through the darkness of the night, through the dense, low fog of the morning, I can almost speak the language now and I want to stay here with the people I've found, but this is not where the future is, because in a few hours I'll carry the final boxes on board, and I think to myself I'll never forget all this, never forget all of you even though we're already forgotten, and I motion to the band to take it one more time and they'll do anything I want now, and the vocalist has come to sit next to me on the floor and I take the verse one more time, draw on all I have and a bit more besides, this is the last time I'll sing and it's not over until the fat lady sings and she hasn't arrived yet at Café Natúr, and so I go on, and on, faster and faster, a tinkling of windowpanes and the glass shatters from the pressure, chairs crack under their own weight and I finish the song, let the guitarist play the theme one last time, but almost nobody is listening to him, because the applause has already exploded and I just have enough time to see Havstein standing on a table with Carl, they're not looking pleased, they're not laughing, have worried faces or at least it seems that way before I tumble out of the window, land on the asphalt below, and there's total silence.

– – – ∎ – – –

Headache. Like the fall of the Roman Empire. I lay out to dry on deck, gazing at a leaden sky. The boat was rocking on the water and Palli stood beside me on cautious sea legs, stacking crates of food that Anna was taking below decks, while Carl secured the lifeboat astern and Havstein talked on his cell phone, fast, excitedly, I only caught fragments, because of the birds, I think, making such a racket, no manners at all. Far above, the clouds made zigzags across the sky, braiding themselves into each other, and at the other end of the harbor lay the Smyril Lines Ferry, filling its car decks, allowing its passengers aboard. Perhaps it was sunny or raining, I'd given up guessing. Then a face leaned over me, blocking my view.

"Are you awake?" asked Eyðis. "We're ready in a minute."

"What happened?"

"You ruined everything for the band, Mattias. You lashed out. They had to throw you out. But we came and got you. I don't think you should go back there for a while. But you're a great singer. I never heard anything so beautiful."

I gave an answer, wasn't easy to hear what I said. I was given a kiss and nothing more was said.

"Here," she said, throwing a green poncho in my lap. "Havstein wants us all to be wearing these when we leave." Then she left and the gulls flew away. I lifted myself to a half-seated position, turned around to look for Havstein, but couldn't see him any more, must have gone below decks to organize something or other, which was when it suddenly occurred to me that none of this would have happened in the last year if I hadn't turned up on the Faroes that day. Gjógv wouldn't have been discovered, the authorities wouldn't have figured out that Havstein was taking in literally anyone just to fill the empty rooms in the Factory, or the empty space within himself, and so found a reason to close the whole shebang down, Carl would have perished at sea as he was destined, Sofia would have survived, she might even have gone to Copenhagen one day, Jørn wouldn't have lost a friend, I wouldn't have lost my footing so completely, we wouldn't have built the boat, Eyðis wouldn't have been dragged into all sorts of things I couldn't grasp the significance of, and we'd never have been seen, never discovered. It was as simple as that. So long as I was involved, it would go on like that. It wouldn't change.

There was nothing I could do about it.

I weighed my possibilities.

Weighed them this way and that, at lightning speed.

And then I watched it happen. I saw myself get up. Stand on deck. Take my rain jacket off.

I saw myself running.

I watched it in that moment, I ran, ran off the boat, down onto the quay, past Sofus who didn't understand what was happening, but who looked upset, I ran across the quay and I heard Havstein shouting and I heard Carl shouting and I heard Eyðis shouting, but I didn't hear a word, I just ran, ran faster than ever before, the Smyril Line ferry sounded its horn and the crew were about to cast off their moorings and I ran toward the ferry, I had no bags, I just ran as hard as I could without turning back, gaze fixed straight ahead, and I ran past the unloaded containers along the quay, ran through the parking lot, and with every step I took, I was more certain I knew what I was doing, and I was cutting it close, I raced up the passenger bridge, the steward had already gone, the doors were already closed and I banged on them hard, a face stared back at me uncomprehendingly from inside the porthole, opened the door carefully and I disappeared inside, past the face, and I came on deck as the ferry left the quay, started its motor and began stealing out of the harbor, pointed in the direction of the Shetlands and Bergen, and down there in the harbor our sailboat already looked tiny, but I could still distinguish them from each other: Havstein at the rudder, Carl in the bow, Eyðis, Palli, Anna, and they'd cast off their moorings too, were moving out of the harbor, I watched them raise their sail, catch the wind, pick up speed westward as I turned, went down to the bar, sat in a chair and waited for the band to start playing or for nothing in the world to happen.

But that wasn't what happened.
That wasn't what I did, of course.
Not this time.
For once I wasn't about to go off.
No way.
From now on I'd take responsibility for those around me.

I got to my feet, put my magnolia overalls on and zipped myself in, put the green poncho on so we looked completely alike, all of us, like sea grasses, appropriate, since when it came to sailing the seas we were all green, with no idea about sailing, apart from Carl, who again thought it best to find the Gulf Stream so we'd turn up where we wanted sooner or later, it was, in his opinion, no more complicated than that, though to be on the safe side he'd gotten us some good navigational maps, compasses, gyroscopes, VHF, GPS, and God knows what else, as well as a stack of manuals so we could read how to use all of these on the way, there'd be time enough for that, just us and the wind, an unbalanced relationship of dependency.

And then they came. Just minutes before we left, Sofus, Óli, and Selma. They came to check that everything was okay, and that we had everything we needed. And we did. Nothing was missing, everything was in place, and as Havstein and Palli cast off our moorings and let the boat slip past the enormous passenger ferry *Norröna* and through the harbor and as I clung to Eyðis at the back of the boat and waved, Óli and his family followed us out in their new wooden sailboat, until we were well past the breakers and had reached that line in the water where the waves grow higher and the open sea begins, then they turned, went back to the harbor with Sofus pounding on the ship's bell so it rang out over the whole town and for a moment, everybody stopped, dropped what they were doing and tried to locate the sound, turning their heads to work out where it came from, but that was only something I imagined, since in truth hardly anyone saw us leave and we disappeared as soundlessly, as undramatically as we had turned up, and a couple of hours later, when I'd crept over the deck, terrified, and helped Palli and Carl hoist the sails, the Faroe Islands were reduced to a parenthesis in the sea and we were gone.

LONG GONE BEFORE DAYLIGHT

The moon is moving away from the earth and there's nothing you can do about it. It is distancing itself soundlessly, four centimeters per year. It is said that the moon once orbited the earth at a distance of only forty thousand kilometers. Now it is an average of 384,000 kilometers from us. And the days are longer. It's true. The moon is responsible for the tides, and the friction of the tide holds the rotation of the earth back. By around 0.023 milliseconds a year. In billions of years the moon's orbit will almost be the same as the earth's, the days will be 11,000 hours long and it will look as though the moon is still in the sky over one part of the world, but much farther away, until one day it can no longer be seen. And we disappear like this too, I look at old photographs of myself that Mother took, but they aren't me, I have gone long ago. Cells have died and renewed themselves, hair has been cut, teeth have fallen out and been replaced with new ones. I am not the person you knew. I sleep eight hours each night. I blink 17,000 times. I live large parts of my life behind closed eyes.

People didn't arrive on the moon first. That's just something you believe. Sound arrived first, in January 1946, American defense set up a three kilowatt transmitter, sent radio signals up to the moon and took readings of the echoes. And ten years before Buzz Aldrin became a name fleetingly remembered, the Soviet Union's *Luna 2* landed beside the Mare Imbrium, close to the Archimedes crater. With nobody on board. The probe had two small balls containing the insignia of the Soviet military. The intention was to spread these across the moon's surface, leaving behind an indelible sign of life, of intelligence, of raw power, Lord knows. But all that was left behind was a little crater, almost impossible to spot amongst the others. *Luna 2* hit the moon's surface at ten thousand kilometers per hour. No brakes can cope with that. But it was, I think, an attempt at least, and it worked, in its way, and if nothing else it forced the USSR and the USA to abandon plans to send nuclear rockets to the moon's surface so the explosion could be watched from earth, indisputable proof of who'd got there first, in the days when that mattered.

But the moon is still hanging there. Only 380,000 km from here. Nobody goes there anymore, after the Apollo Program they forgot about the whole place. By the time the twelfth person returned to the Landing Module on December 19, 1972, people were already looking for new worlds, new planets, preparing to go to Mars.

The moon itself says nothing. It never asked to be visited anyway.

The moon holds its tongue.

- - - ■ - - -

I won't tell you much about Grenada. Just the most important things, things that come to me now, that haven't merged into other memories, as practically everything that happened to us in those years did, I lost track in the end, unable to point to any particular moment and say, *it happened then, that's when it happened,* the years knitted into one another and days, events or their absence grew indistinguishable. When I think of Grenada, I do so with a rare lightness. During those years as far as I remember the problems were never bigger than we could tackle, they didn't gather momentum, didn't assault us and dump us helpless on the ground.

It's said that when Christopher Columbus discovered Grenada on

August 15, 1498, he merely threw a disgruntled glance at it and named it *Conception* before sailing on, not even bothering to go ashore, in his eyes it was probably just another island in an endless string of islands that spread southward, a fistful of rocks in the Caribbean. A little island barely twenty-two miles long and eleven miles wide, at most, a quarter of the size of the Faroe Islands together, but with double the population. And like the Faroes, this is both a rainy and autonomous land under a protective hand, the Queen of England is Granada's monarch, I'm not sure if she's even been there, whether she ever sat hunched over a map looking for the minuscule island that barely anybody can place on a map let alone goes to, transported unknowingly there by some cruise ship, Norwegian owned perhaps, the Royal Caribbean Cruise Lines perhaps, swimming on the beautiful beaches by the Grand Anse or in St. George's, or embarking on a three or four hour hike in the jungle, at the foot of the mountains, the Grand Etang forest, then swiftly back to the boat, getting back on board and rushing to the cabin, washing off the dirt, changing into a smoking jacket before the anchor is raised, the ship sails on and dinner is served in the mirrored dining hall to the accompaniment of easily digested lobby music served up by the ship's pianist, Luther, who's from the Ukraine, not that anybody cares, but he has his paperwork in order, does as he's told, never goes ashore, stays on deck and stares at the wall, disinterested, like Columbus, until the passengers are back on board and the only trace they leave behind is the wake in the ocean.

It took us over three weeks to get here, and I was seasick and soaked every nautical mile, every inch of water we passed through, I hung hopeless, useless over the railings, lay clinging to the very deck, but we crossed the ocean in a homemade sailboat, and when, early one morning, we'd anchored in St. George's harbor, moored the boat and come in to land at the quay, sleep still in our eyes, as we set our first footprints in the sand, a new era began, and these were the loveliest times, years you'd want to frame and send to friends if you could, and it would be nine years, almost to the day, before we left the islands again, for good, before we left the country, before I, Eyðis, and our son Jákup boarded the last evening bus to the airport at Point Salines, fastened our seat belts, and listened attentively to the safety instructions. And minutes later the plane lifted over the islands, over the Caribbean and flew us to Venezuela, and further south to Rio, and from there to Amsterdam, Oslo and finally Stavanger, where we put down our luggage for good, and bought an apartment before the month was out, slid into the town again, slid into the rooms, into the bad weather and average days, as though I'd never been away.

But that wouldn't be for another nine years.

What did we do in the meantime?

What became of us?

We got better, grew healthier, became our real selves at last, so that we had to get to know each other all over again, Eyðis could take much of the credit for things going so well, she was the common sense one among us, kept things in order when we weren't in a state to make decisions ourselves, to find solutions to problems, however trivial, she kept things going until we were on our feet, men and women, until she could lean back knowing that she'd got us going, she could see it was good, and unless an opposite force came to influence us, we would carry on, moving forward seemingly forever, at least that's how it seemed, after a while, after those first two years, after we'd sold the boat, moved from the big apartment in St. George's and out into the countryside, to an old house in Grenville that we took over for next to nothing from neighbors who were happy it wouldn't stand empty, after we'd done several rounds with the authorities and got our work and residence papers sorted, Havstein's specialty, the iffy paperwork, after we'd joined forces with the surrounding farms and got our business properly under way, it all looked pretty good, we'd sit on the beach in the evening, just us or the neighbors too, fabulous Eyðis with her round belly and Carl who started taking pictures again, documenting the group as the time rolled and our beards grew, Happy Ville, and I couldn't stop looking at her, taking her in my arms, and we'd talk about the Faroes, an endless stream of evenings that overlapped to become one single night on the beach, we talked about Sofia, how she should have been here, how she'd have loved it, a better climate to look at the same things through. She could have taken buses to and fro, complained about the rain, who knows, and so we talked and the calendar ripped off its own pages, as we sat with our backs turned toward it.

Mother and Father visited us every other year, for two weeks, neither more nor less, Father suffered from nerves and exhaustion from the journey the first two times, but after a while it became part of his routine and in the last few years they got quite settled in, Father would take us out to his favorite restaurants in St. George's as though he lived there, greeting the proprietor, quite the worldly globetrotter. Otherwise we talked sporadically on the phone, wrote briefly, kept up correspondence and contact, sent me the Stavanger Aftenblad, a newspaper a month, I kept myself updated, was a good student and shared the news with my classmates, other than that we gathered around the Internet, studying the Faroe Islands on the webcam, following the seasons as they changed in Tórshavn, Klaksvík and Tvøroyri, watching the snow come and go, the New Year fireworks, and when people came into the picture we stared hard, trying to identify them, not that we ever managed, they looked like blurred figures on archival films, doing things we couldn't take part in, on the way to places we couldn't go.

Perhaps it was all that sun, twenty-eight degrees all year round, perhaps it was the four thousand overwhelming hectares of forest or perhaps it was something quite different, but I think Havstein became a happier person in Grenville. He no longer had responsibility for us, we all looked after one another in equal measure, and when the files that we'd carried with us along worn tracks and through dense forests were eventually ruined in the damp air, I think it may have come as a relief to him. The pages crumbled and disappeared without his ever throwing them away, it happened on its own, it was just to sit and wait, and I often think it had some meaning, although it probably didn't, but I often think things resolved themselves on their own, as most things do, if only one waits long enough, and finally he got rid of the last papers and filled his shelves with other possessions, CDs, books, healthy things that didn't demand attention or excessive care, and once the files were gone for good, we never said another word about them.

Jákup was born during our fifth year on Grenada, I sat in the backseat with Eyðis as we raced to the hospital in St. George's, Havstein clutching the wheel. I woke up on the floor of the delivery room just as Father had done, and I remember calling home just afterward, waking him up, in the middle of the night, I could picture him clearly before me, Father, in his underwear, in front of our old telephone table in Stavanger, waving Mother away as she tried to take the receiver from him, on a telephone line with a delay, we talked over each other, and I had the urge to call NASA and ask if anything was happening in space that morning, but I didn't, it wasn't so important any more, things were happening in Grenada and I was almost certain the world slowed down, in those first few hours, that it slowed down from its 1,000 kilometers an hour to give Jákup a gentle start on the earth.

And something happened that night, didn't it?
Yes, it did.
A lot happened.
I wanted the whole world to meet Jákup.
Wanted everyone to see him.
To see this fantastic person who had appeared here in Grenville, Grenada, the Caribbean.

The next morning I stood looking absentmindedly through some CDs in a little shop in St. George's, while Eyðis and Jákup slept in the hospital, I flicked through some panpipe and Rastafarian recordings, my mind only half present, when I suddenly came to a complete stop, I caught my breath, an avalanche went through me, took me thousands of miles East. I looked down at my hands, they were holding the last Cardigans album. *Long Gone Before Daylight*. I glanced around me, as though at any moment I expected somebody to leap out at me and reveal it was all a joke, I expected Sofia to pop out from behind the counter, to smile crookedly and begin to laugh at me as I stood there in the Caribbean, rooting in the Scandinavian pop. But nothing happened. The other customers had their noses in the old vinyls and cassettes, the shop owner was busy with his own thing. He barely looked at the cover before digging out the CD disinterestedly from a drawer in the back room. I didn't sleep that night. Instead, after going to the hospital to visit my family, I sat up with the head phones Carl had once given me, sat in the living room and listened to the album, over and over, read the liner notes meticulously, searching for us between the lines. Nina Persson had dyed her hair. It was black now. Just as nice. Sofia would have liked it, I thought; the hair, the music. She'd have papered the walls with the liner notes if she could. She'd have liked Eyðis a lot, she'd have lifted Jákup up, danced in the big living room and sung that she loved us, all of us, for what it was worth, we'd have sat up in her room, our ears on stalks, that expression of hers that demanded we listen properly, catch every nuance, every little vibration that oozed from the speakers.

Grenada. Nine years. For the first two years we got by doing small jobs, in restaurants, in shops, Palli and Anna worked on board a cruise ship, in the bar, were away for weeks at a time. The rest of us killed time after work, wandered about St. George's, took long walks, went down to the beach, swam, spent time together. Eyðis tried to learn the local patois, she never quite succeeded, but it was entertaining to listen to, both for us and the local farmers, rasta-Faroese-gobbledigook, interwoven island languages, we joked about her taking a patent out, Faroese-Patois, publishing a text book, a totally new and unusable

Esperanto. Later, when we moved to Grenville on the east coast and we left the little colony of American and European expats, we set ourselves up in cocoa, joined a cooperative with our neighbors, production wasn't massive, but big enough, we delivered regularly to the capital, were paid in cash, and drove back home while our cocoa was loaded onto boats for transport to other islands, Trinidad, Tobago or further, to Grenada's other export destinations; Britain, Germany, Holland. For a while we'd considered sheep as a source of income, there were great opportunities in that, no doubt. But it was voted down. Our expertise lay with wooden sheep, and besides we'd seen enough sheep for a lifetime.

So we became cocoa farmers, eyes turned skyward, on the look out for tropical hurricanes that could wreck everything for us at any moment, but never came, not to any severe degree, and I remember the walks we used to take, when we didn't feel like sitting on the beach anymore, we walked in the humid forests, in among the teak and mahogany trees, and I finally felt like a kind of Columbus, or a Robinson Crusoe, discovering new paths, new places, and we climbed up to the Grand Etang Lake, in the middle of a volcanic crater, sat with our feet in the warm water, taking the view in just as we had on that morning on Skælingsfjall long ago, and talked about our plans for the future, alternative ways of organizing things that might make our work easier, production more effective.

And then I remember the day we decided to go home.

Mother had been ill for some time, and Father wanted us to be around for the time she had left. A few days later we sat in the living room with her, synchronized swimming on the TV, and I remember they looked like flowers, opening like the petals of a flower, in new and even more complicated formations than in Mother's time, even synchronized swimming had moved on, leaving her behind, and finally one night she died, undramatically, after four days in the central hospital, Father was the only one with her, we'd been to visit earlier in the day, bringing sweets, the obligatory sweets, the medicinal chocolate, but we'd been the ones to eat it, she didn't want any, hadn't eaten for days.

So we stayed on in Stavanger. Eyðis had put the idea out to me and the others a few days before we were due to leave, that it might be time, she thought, to move back, but not to the Faroes, at least not yet. She wanted to live in Stavanger, she'd probably never seen herself growing old on Grenada. And me? Well. I'd been away a long time. We asked Jákup too, worried he might say no, his friends were on this side of the world after all, but it went fine, surprisingly well, Jákup was ready for anything, even though he felt the cold, even though he always shivered in the damp and the rain. I took him round Stavanger with me, showed him Byhaugskogen, Stokkvannet, and the two of us went for walks, from Kampen, past the villas on Eiganes, through Færøygata, down toward the theater, and from there up to Våland where Jørn had once lived.

Havstein, Anna, Palli, and Carl decided to stay. We did discuss the possibility of everyone traveling to Stavanger in those final days, but it was unrealistic from the outset. Havstein couldn't start all over again, and there was the weather too. The warm climate. The possessions they'd accumulated, everything they'd built up over the years. The secure income, for life. I couldn't argue with that. Although I had a childish hope they'd throw it all in and come with us, at the last minute. But they didn't. So only the three of us went, and when we left the island, a sort of subconscious disappointment hung in the others, as though we'd left them in the lurch, as though it was a mean thing to do, all things considered. Perhaps it was this, and the huge distance that caused our phone calls over the sea to grow ever shorter, and more infrequent, until they dried up altogether some years later.

We made it a tradition to go to the Faeroes every summer, Eyðis, Jákup, and I, visiting Eyðis's parents, as well as Óli, Selma, and Sofus. Little Sofus was twenty-five now and lived in Dr. Jacobsensgøta, a fisherman, he'd got married, but not to Óluva, she'd never moved back, stayed in Denmark, and not to Annika either, Sofus found himself another wife from town, married after four months, and we always had to visit them during the first few days of our arrival in the country to eat skerpi, either that or pilot whale, because Sofus would be the first in the water when the whales entered the fjord, he'd wade about for hours, knife at the ready, working, while his wife stood on the beach watching, there seemed to be a favorable wind in his life, and somewhere inside me I hope that in some strange way it might have something to do with our meeting, to do with our driving his radio-controlled car through the streets of Gjógv, with our building construction sets, our talking. But for all I know it had nothing at all to do with that.

On a couple of occasions Father came with us, and every time I was there, every time I came to Tórshavn and walked through those old streets on my arrival, I'd always think I saw Havstein and the others, as though I believed they'd suddenly moved back and were ready to continue where we'd left off. But they were always people who just looked similar. And we'd drive out to Saksun, I'd take a small pair of shears, clip the grass around Sofia's grave neatly, and the gardener in me would surface and I could be there for ages, on my knees, as I worked my way across the flower bed, planting new flowers, turning the earth so the soil could breathe properly. And then there was Gjógv, I'd always go back, the Factory had been dismantled and gutted, cement bags piled outside, no idea what they were planning to do. Otherwise Gjógv had woken up from its torpor, every house was inhabited again, there were even people at the beach on fine summer days, and the houses were freshly decorated, lawns maintained, Gjógv had regained its color, grew stronger and stronger with each year, they didn't give up here, and the same went for a number of villages in the country, they grew, slowly but surely, things were looking up, and on our last visit, as we passed the old shop that had been closed so long, for so many years, I saw that it had reopened, I went in, bought an ice cream, took it down to the beach and sat on the grass. Just sat there and stared, and that was when I caught sight of it, a decaying rowboat farther down on the beach. I wandered a few yards down to it, and there it was, Óli's little boat, the one we'd fetched Carl in one New Year's night. One of the seats was broken, I thought how it might have happened as we rowed back in again, perhaps I'd grabbed it too hard, I'd been so terrified that night, or so happy, who could tell.

Eyðis and Jákup had been up on the grass-covered slopes, clinging to the wire fence at the edge of the cliff, watching the puffins as they flew around randomly, and stretched their wings or busied themselves with essential tasks. They walked down toward me and the boat, I gave Eyðis a hug, I put my arms around them, and shut my eyes to the tourists who were pouring off the bus to stand in front of the natural harbor with cameras and sun hats, and I thought how I should have had a camera now, taken one last picture of us standing here. And after I'd had the picture developed, I'd have pointed to it and said:
This is Mother.
This is Father.
This is us.
This is our Family.
Kodak moment.
The final one.

— — — ■ — — —

April. I'm forty-nine. And this is our apartment. We live in Stavanger, on the first floor. If I stand close to the window, lean to the left a little,

I can see most of the town center. Heavy clouds hang over Saturday's Stavanger. It's been raining for weeks. You don't know me, haven't any idea who I am. I am nobody in particular. But, I do also exist, I also subscribe to a newspaper, I also cut that little square of grass each week during the summer, clean my car with the correct equipment and remove mildew from my garden furniture with American products I've ordered from the TV shop. I go to the cinema, drink beer from a glass and never from the bottle, watch TV from 16.30 to 17.25, and own the *Dr. Phil Home* collection on DVD. I get up in the mornings, get dressed, go to work at eight. You don't need to know where. I'm the best at what I do. On occasion I still sleep badly, some nights I don't go to bed at all, just rise from my desk and get straight into the shower when the time approaches seven, other nights I go to bed early, set the old metronome by my bed and sleep to its evenly paced, slow clinking after an hour. I vote. I submit my tax forms on time, the figures correctly entered. I sit in the 43rd car you pass on the highway on your way to work.

I stand in the kitchen, pouring coffee from the pot into the thermos and from the thermos into a cup. Four CDs stand on my window ledge, leaning to the side and collecting dust in unchanging formation: *First Band on the Moon. Life. Gran Turismo. Long Gone Before Daylight.* I look at the clock. It's still early. It's only five o'clock on the East Coast of the United States, Buzz Aldrin is sleeping in Florida and dreaming of space, or maybe he's dead, and Jørn is sleeping in a hotel room in Ohio, or he's up with his child, he's given a concert and can't go to bed. It's been three weeks since they left, another five-month tour, off to Europe next, then Japan, Australia, as they play themselves into the pages of history. I keep their concert schedule on my fridge, follow their travels, strike through the venues with a pen as they cross the continents, put a cross for each town they play in.

I saw Jørn a lot in the months before he left, a couple of times a week at least. We went down to the shore one afternoon, before the snow had melted, walked down to the smooth rocks where we'd sat so often twenty-five years ago, that we'd visited almost daily in the summer and autumn of 1986. We stopped going shortly after I got together with Helle, not quite sure why, whether he'd felt like a spare part when there were three of us, or whether it was Helle who'd made the place her own. It may have been both. But we went down there again some weeks ago, Jørn and I, sat on our jackets on the large boulders, looking across Gandsfjørðen toward the Dale psychiatric hospital on the other side, where nearly all the lights were out, despite its still being early afternoon. It had been an asylum seekers' reception center since then, Jørn thought, perhaps it still was. And that was when he told me more about his brother, and I couldn't understand why I hadn't heard about it before, why nobody had told me, not a word. He'd disappeared too, in the spring of 2001, Jørn's brother had just vanished one day, his parents came in from work, his room had been tidied, his bedclothes folded. A search had been launched, international inquiries made, but nobody had seen him, all trace stopped some hundred yards from the house, from there everything was open, everything was possible, everything was inexplicable. And then there was Roar, Jørn talked about Roar too, apparently he worked for a company making a new kind of airbag, he'd started there the year after I left and Jørn had basically lost contact with him after that, read about him in the papers mainly, there'd been quite an uproar, the equipment had proved useless, life threatening, Jørn saw him now and again, in a store, in a restaurant, and I said that's the way things go, and I asked if he'd seen Helle at all, over the years, and yes, he had, and she had two kids.

"Good looking?"

"Her kids?"

"Yes."

"No."

I said nothing about the fact I'd seen her myself, only four days earlier, in town. I'd seen her children, beautiful children, I'd walked toward her and thought of saying hello. But changed my mind at the last moment, it had been such a long time, there was no longer any point, and I pulled my hat farther down over my forehead, stared into the ground, and when I looked up again, I realized she wouldn't have recognized me anyway, I look very different than I did then. And the last I saw of her she crossed the road some way in front of me and disappeared into a shop with the children.

April. Summer should be here any moment, this is just a test.
I look at the time.
Now?
Perhaps.
Why not?
Then I go out into the hallway, past the door into Jákup's room. He's twelve now and still has a few teddies on the bed, by the end of the year they'll be hidden away, replaced with more grown-up things. His walls are already covered with pictures and drawings, magazine clippings, posters for bands and films I don't recognize, apart from a big Perkleiva poster Jørn gave him and that makes his friends green with envy. I put my sneakers on and walk down the stairs, walk out of the front door and to our mailbox, the daily routine, a part of me always looks forward to getting the mail.
I open the lid and look inside.
And there's a letter.
Get hardly any letters these days.
Just junk mail.
A special offer on white goods this week.
Last week it was two packs of mince for the price of one.
Coupons for the latest instant soup.
Vacuum cleaners. Electric drills. Summer clothes. Imported cars. Houses for sale.
But today there's mail.

I fish out the letter, take it in with me, walk through our apartment building and into the shared garden courtyard at the back, the weather's getting warmer, I've noticed it in the last few days, something has begun to happen, the air has grown softer, rounder at the edges. I've finally changed out of my winter shoes, put on my blue sneakers. I stand out in the garden, with its flowers carefully planted out and growing side by side in their beds, in their boxes, and I look at the envelope, *Air Mail. Caribbean.* A Grenada stamp, I open the envelope and pull the letter out, the very first I've received, hold a protective hand over it to stop the rain from making the writing smudge on the page as I read, and this, this very moment can be seen, seen from the moon, from outer space, wherever one might please, a planet can be seen rotating apparently effortlessly on its own axis, dragging clouds and rain with it as it revolves, and below them sea and land, swaths of land that at first glance appear uninhabited, but which are overpopulated in reality, and drawing closer, huge buildings can be seen, cities, then smaller things, vehicles, houses, before it becomes apparent that wars are taking place over vast areas of this planet, while in other places people are busy with their lives and daily tasks, people are quarreling, hugging each other, leaving each other, and then as one draws even closer to the surface, no more than a hundred meters away, an almost insignificant person will come into view who fears being seen, he stands stooped over the tulips with a letter in his hand, in the middle of the garden, his feet planted on the ground, and he is getting a suntan from reading, it has been raining here for several weeks, Sellafield radiation clouds have hung heavily over the town where he lives, but they're finally breaking up, he reads through the pages intently before he puts the letter back in its envelope, folds it, tucks it in his back pocket and goes back in, up the stairs to his apartment, through the front door, and as he closes his door, he is forgotten already, and that's all right, because he's just like you, he also washes his clothes without phosphates or fabric softener, he also watches the Eurovision song contest and follows the voting through the night, and he also looks out for cheap flights in the autumn. He is one of the forty-five percent in this week's market research who agree or do not agree on an issue you'd never have believed anybody would research. He votes. He submits his tax forms on time, the figures correctly entered. He sits in the 37th car you pass on the motorway on your way home from work.

And now, all he wants is for you to leave him in peace.

But pull away a few kilometers and wait, you will also see that each night this planet is covered with people lying on their backs in the grass and staring out into space, thinking there must be a system, this gigantic desolation cannot be meaningless, all these planets, galaxies, moons, stars, satellites, meteorites, and comets can't have been placed here accidentally, can't be rotating around each other just aimlessly, there must be a purpose, loneliness can't be the only thing projected onto the skies, it's impossible, unthinkable. So they point out the constellations for each other, wait for shooting stars, close their eyes before they pray and mumble wishes for things that never tumble from the sky, and they don't say it, but they hope that there's someone out there with competence steering the ship, someone in charge, looking after them as things gently and quietly go to hell or to heaven, at home or at work, in apartments or houses, that there's an explanation as to why friends simply vanished or why the telephone stopped ringing after they told colleagues they were ill, and yet they know it isn't true, there is nobody steering, it's only an old habit that makes them clutch at the grass while the planet spins at hundreds of kilometers an hour, and perhaps they know that if God *did* ever consider looking for them, the earth was the last place he'd look, he'd have lost interest before he even came close. But in the meantime, as they wait for everything and nothing, they make do with what they have, make their packed lunches, get in their cars, including each Tuesday that comes their way, they drive around alone, at random, or visiting friends, family, while they continue to launch probes on never-ending trajectories, outward, looking for water on Mars or the moons of Jupiter in the hope it might prove something, give them a sure sign that there is someone out there in command, someone who can tell them that they are visible, that they do their best, that their lives are true and meaningful, that they are not alone.

ABOUT THE AUTHOR

JOHAN HARSTAD, winner of the 2008 Brage Award (previously won by Per Petterson), is a Norwegian author, playwright, graphic designer, drummer, and international sensation, with books published in eleven countries. His first novel, *Buzz Aldrin, What Happened to You in All the Confusion?*, was in 2009 made into a Norwegian TV series starring *The Wire*'s Chad Coleman. Harstad lives in Oslo.

ABOUT THE TRANSLATOR

DEBORAH DAWKIN graduated from Drama Centre London in 1983 and worked in the theater for many years in Norway and the United Kingdom. She has worked as a full-time literary translator since 2004 and has had a long relationship with Johan Harstad's work.